James Philip

Love is Strange

TIMELINE 10/27/62 – BOOK TWO

Copyright © James P. Coldham writing as James Philip, 2014.
All rights reserved.

Cover concept by James Philip
Graphic Design by Beastleigh Web Design

The Timeline 10/27/62 Series

Main Series

Book 1: Operation Anadyr
Book 2: Love is Strange
Book 3: The Pillars of Hercules
Book 4: Red Dawn
Book 5: The Burning Time
Book 6: Tales of Brave Ulysses
Book 7: A Line in the Sand
Book 8: The Mountains of the Moon
Book 9: All Along the Watchtower
Book 10: Crow on the Cradle
Book 11: 1966 & All That
Book 12: Only in America
Book 13: Warsaw Concerto
Book 14: Eight Miles High

Coming in 2020

Book 15: Won't Get Fooled Again
Book 16: Armadas

Standalone Timeline 10/27/62 Novel

Football in The Ruins – The World Cup of 1966

Timeline 10/27/62 Stories

The House on Haight Street

USA Series

Book 1: Aftermath
Book 2: California Dreaming
Book 3: The Great Society
Book 4: Ask Not of Your Country
Book 5: The American Dream

Australia Series

Book 1: Cricket on the Beach
Book 2: Operation Manna

Check out the latest news about the Timeline 10/27/62 Saga at
www.thetimelinesaga.com

and

The details of all my other books at
www.jamesphilip.co.uk

Chapter 1

17:31 Hours Zulu
Friday 22nd November 1963
HMS Talavera, Fareham Creek, Portsmouth

"My fellow Americans," the familiar voice began. It was a relaxed, purposeful voice. It was a voice that reached out into homes and resonated about hearths. It was a voice that spoke to the hopes and fears of all generations. It was a voice that divided and yet retained the power to beguile, momentarily, even *his* most virulent detractors. It was also the most familiar voice in the world; the voice of the man who honestly believed that *he*, truly and rightfully spoke for the world. What was left of it. "My fellow Americans," the voice said again, "and to this great nation's friends, wherever they may be, near and far," the voice was stilled for an instant, for dramatic effect, "may God be with you in this time of trial."

Lieutenant Peter Christopher waved for the steward to bring him another beer. It was warm, stuffy, and a little humid in the wardroom of HMS Talavera with the ship closed up at ABC Condition One. There was an east wind again tonight and nobody knew how *hot* the rain beating on the upper decks of the destroyer might be. They would take the normal readings in the morning if the storm had blown over in the night, otherwise, they were stuck between decks trusting the fans and the filters kept out the worst of the muck for another day. Peter suspected the now very occasional ABC lock downs were simply to keep the crews of the ships stuck in harbour on their toes. Every report he had read on background radiation levels showed a continuing fall towards background readings between two and three times higher than before the war. Levels were lower in some places, higher in others but there had been no reported cases of suspected radiation sickness in the Fleet for several months.

The wardroom stank of damp serge, recycled air and stale cigarette smoke. The smoking lamp had been out for the last two hours and the enforced abstinence was not improving anybody's spirits.

"We have lived through the fire," the hated voice declaimed. There was a persistent, low-level background buzz over the ship's public address system. Nobody knew if it was radiation degrading the circuitry or just a bad component somewhere in the system. They could not do anything about the radiation levels, and spare parts were worth their weight in gold even if you could get your hands on them. "We have emerged from the valley of the shadow of death..."

The bloody man sounded more like a whiskey preacher every day!

"Already we are rebuilding our cities in memory of our immortal dead. Already our factories are running again at full capacity. Already our brave soldiers and sailors and airmen are carrying aid and succour to our loyal allies." The pitch of the voice fell and became almost musical as if he was reading a Shakespearean sonnet. "I know there are people in this great American continent who say that 'we have problems of our own'. They say 'we are as yet too damaged to be able to spare our scarce food, our scarce fuels, our precious manufactured goods, and that we should not risk our irreplaceable soldiers and sailors and airmen in harm's way'. And I hear you. I hear you all. But I say to you that we cannot stand by and do nothing because that is not the American way. Would you stand by idly while your neighbour's house burned to the ground? Would you do nothing to prevent his child starving to death? Would you have your local sheriff do nothing while outlaws loot and rape at will? I tell you that it is our Christian duty to carry American values, American good sense, and American charity into the lands of our so sorely injured friends and allies."

And presumably, further fire and pestilence into the lands of our foes?

Peter Christopher knew he was not alone in thinking that; not content with obliterating most of the old world the new Romans seemed hell bent on remaking the new one in their own smug, self-satisfied image. He flicked a glance across the wardroom table at the Executive Officer's stony face. Lieutenant-Commander Hugo Montgommery was seething in silence.

The wardroom steward delivered Peter Christopher's beer and he signed the chit. He had stopped listening to *that* preaching, hypnotic voice. The capacity to tune out the background noise was a thing they had all learned quite early. Instead of listening, he viewed the pinched, grim expression of the stranger in their midst.

He guessed that Captain Walter Brenckmann, USN (Reserve) was squirming inside. He had been a Boston lawyer, a 'corporate litigator' – whatever that was – the day the world went mad. Subsequently he had been swept back into the Navy and posted to the very edge of the still civilised, habitable world. Or so it must seem to an educated, liberal minded man who thought the military was finished with him after Korea. Brenckmann was CINCLANT's personal representative on the staff of the Admiral Commanding the Channel Fleet. He had arrived two months ago and seemed to have spent most of the time since getting to know people. It was well known that C-in-C Fleet did not have much time for the USN, so the poor fellow had been shuffled from pillar to post, shunned by the Admiral's staff. Brenckmann had visited Talavera several times. He got on well with the Captain and following the old man's example, the wardroom had extended an open invitation to the greying, rather forlorn lost soul. The fallout alert had trapped the American during one of his frequent visits.

"Today, I speak to you from Houston," the whiskey preacher preached, evidently with a tear in his eye, "from the great wounded state of Texas..."

There was a break while his audience – or perhaps, his technicians – filled the airways with rapturous applause.

"I speak to you today from the great wounded state of Texas. Yesterday, I walked down streets seared by the terrible flame of a war that this nation neither sought nor would have fought but for the monstrous actions of our enemies. Let it never be forgotten that this great, peace loving American nation desiring only to co-exist in peace with its neighbours and the peoples of the world was attacked not once, but twice. First at sea, then, without warning on land. Our ships going about their lawful business in international waters were the victims of a cowardly, dishonourable act of unprovoked aggression. Hours later the illegal, barbaric, puppet regime in Havana - almost certainly at the prompting of the Kremlin – launched a pre-meditated, cold-blooded, dastardly first strike at cities in the continental United States. Two unprovoked attacks. Two attacks without warning. What great nation in the history of the world has ever turned its cheek once, let alone twice before accepting that war cannot be averted. Even then we stayed out hand. Knowing that we faced unimaginable risks we stayed our hand several more hours. Hoping, praying that our enemies would repent, recant their evil ways and step back from the brink." The preacher's voice was slowly rising towards an inevitable crescendo. "We asked only that they stand down their offensive weapons. We asked only that they agree, in principle, to withdraw all their forces from Cuba." The voice was pleading, demanding. It was not the voice of one of God's lesser children, but of a man who sat at *His* right hand. "We only asked that they return to the status quo before the revolution in that sad island. That they hand over Castro and his henchmen. Hand him over to us so that he might face justice for his heinous *war* crimes against the American people..."

The applause overwhelmed the microphones.

Thirty seconds ticked by.

"What did our enemies do?" The voice asked, sadly, as if he was both disappointed and a little bemused. "What did they do? I'll tell you what they did, my fellow Americans! They readied their engines of war! They scrambled their bombers! They moved their missiles onto their launching pads! And they said *nothing* to us! *Nothing*, my friends!"

Peter Christopher was intimately familiar with the narrative.

We had no choice. It was us or them. What were we supposed to do? And anyway, the bastards attacked us first! For all he knew, it was true. Every word of it. Except, if it was all true why were the Americans constantly protesting their innocence? What were they so guilty about?

"They said *nothing* to us and ordered their nuclear forces to attack the United States of America and its European allies on the evening of Saturday 27th October 1962. I prayed that night. For our souls, for all of our souls. I prayed for the souls of friends and foes alike for we are all alike in God's sight. And then I knew what I must do. My fellow Americans, that was the darkest night of my life because I knew that for all our sakes, I could do no other than to uncover the sword of everything that was right and just in the world in *your* defence. In *your* defence and in the defence of the free world. In defence of the inalienable values passed down to us by our founding fathers..."

Lieutenant-Commander Hugo Montgommery cleared his throat.

"Steward, would you turn that *noise* off please," he glanced around the wardroom. He paused briefly to check that he was speaking for all the officers present. He was.

The silence that ensued was blessed.

"My apologies, Captain Brenckmann," HMS Talavera's executive officer shrugged to the American visitor. "We've been through a lot in the last year," he opened his hands, palms outward, "but one draws the line at some things."

The American shrugged, smiled wanly.

"That's okay. Next time I plan to vote Republican."

Chapter 2

Friday 22nd November 1963
Glebe Cottage, Government Buildings, Cheltenham

Tom Harding-Grayson nursed the last few drops of Brandy in his glass and decided not to meet the eye of his guest. Patricia, his wife, whom he had remarried within days of discovering she had survived the war, had excused herself and gone back to reading her book in the kitchen. Like so many people, when she read it was invariably something insubstantial, romantic or comedic, or from some distant past of which none of them retained any memory. The contemporary world was a grim enough place without reliving the grimness through somebody else's eyes. The kitchen had another advantage. With the kitchen door firmly shut she could hardly hear that hated voice bleating from the small transistor radio in the parlour.

"...they said *nothing* to us and ordered their nuclear forces to attack the United States of America and its European allies on the evening of Saturday 27th October 1962. I prayed that night. For our souls, for all of our souls. I prayed for the souls of friends and foes alike for we are all alike in God's sight. And then I knew what I must do. My fellow Americans, that was the darkest night of my life because I knew that for all our sakes, I could do no other than to uncover the sword of everything that was right and just in the world in *your* defence. In *your* defence and in the defence of the free world. In defence of the inalienable values passed down to us by our founding fathers..."

Henry Tomlinson, the Head of the reconstituted Home Civil Service and by the pleasure of Her Majesty Queen Elizabeth II, Permanent Secretary to the Cabinet of the United Kingdom Interim Emergency Administration, groaned and shook his head.

Tom Harding-Grayson glanced at his old friend and raised his glass to his lips. If he did not know how badly he needed to keep his wits about himself he would have loved to have got drunk. Patricia had left him the first time around because he drank too much. His colleagues, even Henry, had wearied of his intemperance. What was the use of having a first-class mind if it was soaked in alcohol most of the time? In the old days he would retort to the rhetorically posed question by countering; what was the point of having a Double First brain in an environment populated with inbred, incompetent nincompoops of the kind he worked with in Government. Yes, he had gone to the same school as most of Harold 'Supermac' MacMillan's cronies – Eton – and to Cambridge with some of the dunces, too. He had played cricket and rugby with several of the idiots in his younger days. They had not seemed such a bad lot during the Second World War and several of the ones who were not bright enough to park themselves behind a desk in MI5 or in some home ministry hundreds of miles from the front, had got themselves shot or blown up. Darwinism at its most piquant, dullards putting their heads above the parapet at exactly the wrong moment. Unfortunately, a lot of them had survived and because of their unimaginative politics, the immobility of their shared world view, their entrenched prejudices, and their devotion to maintaining the status quo and because most of them seemed to be related by birth or marriage to the Prime Minister, Harold MacMillan, they had ended up running the country. In the late 1950s Tom Harding-Grayson's brilliant career had stalled and finally crunched into the buffers well short of the lofty station which everybody had once believed was his inevitable destination. He had told the useless beggars – *Supermac's* inner circle - that if they kept on down the road they were on with the Americans it was likely to end badly.

Unfortunately, he had been proved right and being right gave him cold comfort. The Americans had turned up three years late for the First World War, they would not have turned up for the Second at all unless the Japanese had attacked Pearl Harbour, and Hitler had – presumably because he was insane – declared war on them. Even then they had only prioritised the European war because they had worked out that defeating Hitler was the most efficacious way to extract treasure from the, by then, bankrupt British Empire. Of course, his was a thesis which had never gone down well in Whitehall. Post war governments were too much in hoc to the Yanks, so seduced by the notion of the non-existent 'special relationship' that they failed to notice that they had become meek, well-schooled tame clients feeding off scraps from the tables of the new Romans. Unfortunately, having made his views abundantly clear throughout Whitehall Tom Harding-Grayson's brilliant career had stalled and eventually nose-dived into the ground. His had not been a soft landing. Losing Patricia had been the low point and it was a crying shame it had taken a nuclear war to reunite them.

John Fitzgerald Kennedy, 35th President of the United States of America had one of those strikingly mellifluous voices that seized a man's attention. It was probably because one tended to listen to, and actually *hear* what he said that one either loved or hated the man.

Tom Harding-Grayson was not so much interested in what the

duplicitous little demigod had to say, as to why he had gone to Texas and to William Marsh Rice University – generally known as 'Rice' or 'Rice University' - in the relatively undamaged part of Houston, Texas, to say it. The airburst that obliterated Galveston had wreaked havoc in the southern suburbs of the city but this was not one of those obsessively hand-wringing speeches Kennedy usually delivered when he visited 'a desecrated city', or rather, 'ruins that are the monuments to the memory of our sacred fallen'. This was a speech in which the familiar hand-wringing and the tortuous self-justification seemed to be laying a platform, a foundation upon which to lay a different, possibly new message. Tom Harding-Grayson should know because he had spent half his life putting words into his masters' mouths; it was so much safer than letting the fools think for themselves, especially when the fools were *Supermac's* friends and relations.

"Didn't the blighter make that 'Moon Speech' at Rice University last year? A month or so before the cataclysm?" Tom Harding-Grayson asked, rhetorically.

Henry Tomlinson nodded. If Tom Grayson, his oldest surviving friend had been top man at the Foreign Office in the years before the October War things might have been different. But he had not been and now the old friends were living with the consequences.

"About a month before the balloon went up, wasn't it? *'We choose to go to the Moon in this decade and do the other things, not because they are easy, but because they are hard...'*

"Yes," Tom Harding-Grayson mused aloud, wishing he had written that line himself. Rice University was not overlarge but it was very picky about who it let in. It was a private, research driven institution with well-established – some believed incestuous - links with the American aerospace industry and to the Pentagon. Kennedy had made the 'Moon Speech' at Rice because he knew it would go down well on that particular campus situated in what was otherwise generally hostile political territory. Now he had gone back to Houston and returned to drink at the same well. Why on earth would the little monster do a thing like that?

A sardonic smile began to form on Tom Harding-Grayson's lips.

"What's so funny all of a sudden?" Henry Tomlinson inquired.

The Permanent Secretary to Her Majesty's Foreign Office put down his glass. He did not begrudge his old friend his unlikely rise to the top of what survived of the Home Civil Service. Henry Tomlinson was admirably suited to corralling the rag tag chaos of competing vested interests within the United Kingdom Interim Emergency Administration and more important, he got on famously with the Prime

Minister whom Tom Grayson had always, on a personal level, never been friendly. Moreover, the Chiefs of Staff of the three armed services trusted Henry and the trust of such men was not to be underestimated in these times, when even small disagreements in the Government over ways and means were horribly likely to result in coups and putsches. All things considered Henry Tomlinson was the safe pair of hands the country needed in this strange tormented era into which they had been consigned by the paranoia and the unbridled folly of their so-called *friends* in the lost colonies.

"They plan to wash their hands of us," Tom Harding-Grayson said ruminatively. "All of us."

"...a little over a month before the war," the President of the United States of America proclaimed, the pitch of his voice dropping momentarily to a sonorously, magisterial baritone, "I committed this great country to the goal of putting a man – an American – on the Moon and returning him safely to Earth by the end of this decade..."

Henry Tomlinson almost choked on his brandy.

"As I told Congress in 1961, I believe that no single space project in this period will be more impressive to Mankind or more important for the long-range exploration of space; and none will be so difficult or expensive to accomplish. I say to you, my fellow Americans, that having passed through the valley of the shadow of death we owe it to the rest of Mankind to think the unthinkable and to fulfil our manifest destiny!"

There was absolute silence. A mutter of applause, then a mounting crescendo. Followed by foot stamping and screaming.

"To those who say..." The clamour drowned out the President's massively amplified voice. He tried again after ten seconds. "To those who say that the great work of putting an American on the Moon is a sideshow, ephemeral to the business of reconstruction. To those who say that a Moon Program will take scarce funds away from rebuilding our broken cities. To those who say that it is our Christian duty to offer succour to our enemies before we invest in our own national destiny..."

There was a rising chant in the background.

"To the Moon! To the Moon! All the way to the Moon and back!"

"Let me speak to the naysayers thus," Kennedy declaimed, his voice quivering with emotion and presumably, with floods of crocodile tears in his eyes. "America cannot put right every wrong in this world, nor should America feel honour bound to attempt to so do. America was attacked. American was terribly wounded. Do the naysayers honestly believe that America should forever accept the burden of the aggressor's guilt upon itself? I tell you now that I will *never* apologise to the American people for doing my duty. I will *never* apologise for standing up to evil. I will *never* apologise for having met force with force even though I will carry the memory of our brave fallen with me to my grave. What, I ask you, my fellow Americans, what shall our legacy to our children and our grandchildren be? Will that legacy be a world in ruins or a world in which Mankind looks to the stars? Shall we forever turn our faces back to the past, down into the darkness of the valley of death, or shall we lift our eyes upwards to look upon the sunlit uplands of hope and infinite new possibilities?"

"To the Moon! To the Moon! All the way to the Moon and back!

Chapter 3

Saturday 23rd November 1963
Captain's Cabin, HMS Talavera

"Take a pew, Peter," Commander David Penberthy directed, not looking up from his narrow desk beneath the compartment's single porthole. "I'll be with you in a moment."

Peter Christopher sat in the one available hard chair at the bow end of the Captain's table, fingering his cap, trying not to stare at the Old Man while he finished studying the open file before him.

The cabin was like its owner.

Everything had its place and everything was in that place.

There were few adornments, just framed photographs: of a passing out class at Dartmouth in the 1930s, the fast minelayer HMS Manxman anchored in the Grand Harbour at Malta, a battered, weather beaten Flower class corvette, a slim woman in front of a sailing boat, his dead wife.

The noise of the engine room blowers was a mere whisper, the distant turning of machinery, generators so far away as to be no more than a barely perceptible tremor transmitted via the stiff steel fabric of the destroyer.

Talavera was still closed up at ABC Condition One and would remain so for another few hours even though the radiation monitors on deck stubbornly continued to indicate *'normal'* radiation levels.

Or rather, new post-war *'normal'* levels of contamination.

The Jeremiads had predicted ten or twenty or even fifty times higher long-term increase in background radiation. Most of the science, so far, was showing increases in the range of two to three times higher than pre-war.

It was cold comfort.

The most pernicious fission products contributing to the raised background levels; Strontium-90, Iodine-131 and 133, had half-lives measured in tens of years.

Mankind was embarking on a huge and potentially disastrous millennia long physiological experiment in living with what previously had been regarded as high *short-term* dosages of radiation, exposure to which would have permanently disqualified *any* worker in the nuclear industry from *ever* working with radioactive substances again.

Peter's visceral terror of the unseen poison in the air, the sea and on any firm ground he was ever likely to step upon had slowly subsided over the months but the idea of living in a world that was forever irredeemably *blighted* never really went away.

It helped that he had spent most of the last year overseeing the overhaul and trialling of Talavera's radar and electronics suite.

He and *his* people – many of whom he had come to regard as brothers and close personal friends as much as men he commanded – had buried themselves in their work with a one-eyed determination that sometimes, enabled them to forget the tragedy of their old world.

Of course, there had been those who could not come to terms with the new reality.

One by one they had been sent ashore; one in ten of the destroyer's crew had been lost thus.

When a man lost hope, surrendered to despair there was no saving him. Several men had committed suicide in the days after the cataclysm. Two had simply disappeared over the side of the ship and others occasionally, since...

Peter shut his eyes for a moment, decided not to remember those awful days just after the war.

The thing was to forget one's life before the cataclysm; to live as if one's life had begun on Day Zero.

The old world was gone forever and no amount of grieving was going to bring it back.

The important thing was to honour the countless dead by one's deeds in whatever time one had left.

And to never, ever give in.

The worst of the easterly gale had blown over although the rain still fell in vicious, squally bursts across Fareham Creek.

Last winter had been the worst in living memory; this winter was threatening to be as bad. One storm after another thrashed up the English Channel, the first snow had fallen a foot deep across the South Downs last week and the rain which lashed against the destroyer's upper works, was laced with ice and overnight had begun to freeze on rails and exposed metal decks.

Peter had heard the phrase 'nuclear winter' a lot in the last year.

So much dust and debris had been blasted into the atmosphere that the Sun's rays never touched the ground in some northern latitudes.

Although he was not among their number it was hardly surprising that so many men had turned to religion for solace.

HMS Talavera's commanding officer pushed away his papers and turned to give the younger man his undivided attention.

There was a paternal gravitas and a steadiness about the Old Man that always infused renewed strength into the men around him.

"How is your young lady in Malta, Peter?"

The question took the younger man unawares.

"Er. Bearing up, sir." Peter regretted the evasive, stock answer the instant it escaped his lips. "Marija is the sort of person who always puts the brightest possible face on things. Her last letter was dated about five weeks ago and some blighter of a local censor had inked out whole sentences."

He choked down the anger bubbling to the surface. His face felt hot and he knew his eyes were probably burning with that anger.

"Sorry, sir. It's just..."

His Captain nodded, tight-lipped.

Commander David Penberthy had aged ten years in the last thirteen months. There were prominent grey streaks in his previously youthfully dark hair and his eyes, once unburdened by the responsibilities of command were often tired. The one man on board who could never allow himself to betray the fact that he was as sick at heart as his men was the Captain.

Now he hesitated, guilty for not having spoken privately to Peter Christopher in the days since his request for a transfer to the Mediterranean Fleet had been summarily rejected by some faceless staffer at Channel Fleet HQ.

"Having your transfer papers returned must have been a hard knock?" He asked.

The question might have been phrased rhetorically but it grasped the bull by the horns.

"Not for Talavera, obviously," Penberthy went on. "God knows where I'd find another hot shot EWO like you, Peter."

Talavera's commanding officer had reluctantly counter-signed his Electronic Warfare Officer's request for a transfer to Mediterranean Fleet in the knowledge that he was bound to lose an acknowledged *expert* – who was the envy of most other Captains in the Channel Fleet – sooner rather than later.

Brilliant young officers like Peter Christopher were in painfully short supply. Despite the hard-won lessons of the 1945 war the Royal Navy had clung to its traditions too long, undervaluing and failing to invest in the specialists and technicians it needed to fight modern wars.

Men like Peter Christopher, perhaps the only man on board Talavera who actually understood how *all* her advanced electronic systems worked, owned the future of naval warfare.

The young EWO had virtually rebuilt the ship's EMP – electromagnetic pulse – damaged radar and electronics suite after the October

War and had spent most of the last six months in constant transit around the fleet advising, training and in overseeing repairs, and the installation and testing of new equipment.

"That's good of you to say so, sir," the younger man said more stiffly than he meant.

The older man nodded, said nothing for several seconds.

"When you put in your papers, I promised that I wouldn't do anything to delay or block them."

He sighed.

"Fair's fair, and all that even though, frankly, I can't afford to lose you. I'm sorry your papers have been returned this time, but I'm not going to pretend I'm sorry that you won't be leaving us just yet. Don't worry. I'm not going to give you a pep talk, Peter."

He grimaced, seizing eye contact with his EWO and holding it.

"A pep talk is the last thing you need to hear from me or anybody else and that's not why I asked you to come to my cabin. When this current storm front moves over we'll be going alongside to fill our bunkers and provision the ship for thirty days at sea."

Peter Christopher sat up and took notice.

"While we're alongside we'll be taking on board a draft of around thirty odds and sods to make up our numbers. Fleet HQ hasn't given me much information about the new men. They're mostly general service lower rates it seems. We'll sort the wheat from the chaff once we've got them assigned to their divisions. That will be your job."

"My job, sir?"

"The priority is to identify anybody with useful technical skills. The rest can fill the holes in our sea duty men rosters but I don't want men with any kind of background in electronic or mechanical engineering wasted on general duties regardless of their official rate or trade."

Peter thought about this.

"Won't I be stepping on the Exec's toes, sir?"

The Captain chuckled and shook his head. "It was his idea. You can do the vetting and hand him the list when you're finished. I'm planning to send the Executive Officer and the Master at Arms ashore with scavenging teams as soon as we come alongside."

Peter digested this news and detected belatedly that there was more to come.

"When we sail Talavera will be officially designated a *Leader*. In the old days a full captain would have come aboard with two dozen staffers, tactical and comms supernumeraries. That won't be happening with us. However, to reflect the new responsibilities

Talavera's wardroom will, of necessity, be assuming in a couple of days, I find myself being advanced one ring, and Mr Montgommery and *you*, will both be advanced half a ring. The Executive Officer will effectively become my flag captain for 9th Destroyer Squadron. Before you ask, I have no idea when 9th Destroyer Squadron will be formed or what other ships will be assigned to it. Things seem to be happened in an unholy rush and I'm sure we'll find out why soon enough. You will become the Squadron EWO responsible for the tactical co-ordination of all units in close company with Talavera. Basically, that's the role you've been filling here in Fareham Creek for the last months now and the C-in-C has instructed me to tell you that quote 'the promotion is well deserved'. The promotion will be substantive and take immediate effect."

He glanced at his watch. "In slightly less than forty hours. I've already briefed the Executive Officer and the Chief. I will be addressing the crew as soon as we are at sea. You can put the new ring on your sleeve at any time after that, Lieutenant-Commander Christopher."

The younger man stared dazedly into space for several seconds as David Penberthy stood to shake his hand. It still did not really sink in until he was stumbling back towards his own cabin.

He had just gone from a relatively green watch keeper to third in command of one of the Navy's most modern ships and the Electronic Warfare Leader of a whole – albeit as yet unformed - Destroyer Squadron!

His cabin was designed to bunk two officers but he had always had it to himself; the man who had been posted to join Talavera last autumn having disappeared in the cataclysm.

A Lieutenant-Commander!

Did that warrant a single cabin? He tried to sit still at the tiny corner desk. He could not stay still. He got to his feet, paced two steps to the bulkhead, and back again. He wished he could go topsides, take a turn around the upper decks, uncoil a little of his roiling internal angst.

He felt a little guilty to be so elated, so excited. He was still here in Fareham Creek and Marija was still in Malta over fifteen hundred miles away, enduring whatever she was enduring, *alone...*

Except she was not alone, she had her family, her friends, people who depended upon her and mercifully she still lived in a place virtually untouched by last October's madness.

Chapter 4

Saturday 23rd November 1963
Gzira Waterfront opposite the entrance to Mediterranean Fleet Headquarters, Manoel Island, Malta

The banner was threadbare in several places. Every morning as the sun rose and people began to set off to work a group of women gathered opposite the gates on the Gzira side of the heavily guarded bridge onto Manoel Island.

The protesters were women of all ages; since the summer they had stopped bringing their children because sometimes the British half-heartedly tried to clear the pavements on which they set up their makeshift daily camp beneath the awnings stretched out from the houses of supporters.

A large number of women came every day, to show solidarity, perhaps only for a few minutes or an hour or two.

Mostly, the women organised themselves to ensure that there would be at least a dozen of them outside the gates, holding their banner, from dawn to dusk every day. There was never any shortage of volunteers.

The women came from all over the Maltese Archipelago.

Some had travelled from Xlendi, Victoria, Xaghra and Sannat on Gozo, carried across the stormy strait disregarding bans on travel to the main island by sympathetic fishermen. Like the women from Mellieha, Rabat, Mdina, Mosta, Birzebbuga, Marsaxlokk and Marsaskala they had been put up in Sliema, Valletta, Floriana, Kalkara, Msida, Senglea and Cospicua by their sisters.

The Gozo women, perhaps because they were farthest from home and separated from the free members of their families for weeks on end, tended to be the most implacable of the protesters but all the women shared the same fears and the same outrage. The big grey warships riding on their anchors in Sliema Creek to the left of the bridge, and clustered about the slab-sided depot ship HMS Maidstone in Lazaretto Creek to the right, acted like silent, ever present goads to the women.

In their eyes burned a sense of betrayal and it was this more than anything that lingered in the memories of every man who stood on the bridge – rifle in his hands – confronting the women of Malta.

Was this what gallant little Malta, the famous George Cross Island, had suffered for two decades ago?

Was this the reward of the Maltese people for standing by the

British in their darkest hour?

Was it for this that the three cities of Cospicua, Vittoriosa, and Senglea had become in 1941 and 1942 the most heavily bombed cities in the world?

Why was the oppressor's jackboot on the necks of the Maltese?

Such was the message in the eyes of the women of Malta that day and every day on the Gzira waterfront opposite the bridge to Manoel Island which accommodated the Headquarters of the British Mediterranean Fleet and the Military Administration of the Maltese Archipelago.

The soldiers manning the gates were newly arrived on the island. This the women could tell because these men had not yet acquired the leathery tan of men long exposed to the sun.

It was obvious that to these men the cool of the breezy November day still seemed to them like a balmy spring day at home before the cataclysm struck. There was uncertainty and curiosity in their eyes and as the women had discovered in their dealings with the majority of the British rankers with whom they had ever come into contact, guarded but entirely genuine sympathy.

An hour ago, an officer had ordered the soldiers to sling their black L1A1 Self-Loading Rifles over their shoulders before he walked across to the women.

'My men mean you no harm, ladies,' the young, fresh-faced subaltern had declared in a voice that was slightly tremulous. 'You have a perfect right to peaceful demonstration on public property. My men will not take any action against you unless or until you trespass on military property.'

Marija Calleja had introduced herself to the boy.

'Second Lieutenant Jackson at your service, Miss Calleja,' he had smiled before he remembered he was supposed to be the enemy. 'I'm delighted to make your acquaintance. I've heard so much about you...'

Marija's stern expression had cut him off in mid-sentence.

'Yes, well,' the young man blustered, embarrassed by her cool, mildly vexed scrutiny. 'We don't want any trouble today.'

Marija had collected her thoughts, aware – as she was always aware in these situations – that the women behind her were hanging on her every word.

She did not know if she liked that, or the way they others increasingly looked to her to say, and to think, the thoughts that were on their own tongues.

'Before the October War,' she explained evenly to Second Lieutenant Jackson, 'my brother played football for the Dockyard team against the Navy, and the Army, and the Royal Air Force's teams at the Empire Stadium,' she glanced momentarily over her right shoulder in the direction of the ugly, oval arena hidden by the buildings a short walk away.

The local stadium was modelled, albeit on a less grand scale, on the much grander Empire Stadium that until a little less than thirteen months ago had stood at Wembley in North London.

'Now you,' *the British*, 'use it as a clearing house for my brothers and my sisters who dare to speak out against the tyranny of your *occupation*.'

'Miss Calleja, I...'

Marija pointed beyond his shoulder at the tops of the tents peeking above the razor wire around the old parade ground on Manoel Island.

'My brother was beaten up by *British* thugs before he was *detained* at Her Majesty's pleasure without trial over there!'

She had not raised her voice above a low monotone but Second Lieutenant Jackson felt as if he was being subjected to a coruscating dressing down.

The young man's cheeks flushed with anger.

'I really must...'

Marija put her right hand on his left elbow in a gesture of sad friendship.

She had no personal grudge against this young man who was simply obeying his orders. He had had no personal part in her brother's savage beating or the decision to detain him. She could see from the expression in his grey blue eyes that the fresh-faced subaltern was very new to Malta and that he did not begin to understand the damage the actions of his superiors had already wrought.

'I know it is not your fault, Lieutenant Jackson,' she assured him. 'I know that you were not one of those *animals* who put my brother into the hospital on HMS Maidstone. But while my brother and so many others like him remain unjustly in *British* prisons,' she half-smiled, 'please do not imagine that you and I can be guided by the angels of our better nature.'

The subaltern swallowed hard.

He nodded curtly, spun on heel.

The gaze of the women fell on his retreating back like a sudden squall of storm wind hastening his passage back to his men.

Marija Calleja placed her left hand on the corner of the ten-foot-long banner, and clasped it to her breast.

It was odd how heavy such a relatively flimsy, insubstantial thing as thirty square feet of sewn together bed sheets became when one had been holding it up for over half-an-hour.

Even when one had been holding it up with the assistance of several other women.

Her throat was dry and her voice had grown hoarse from chanting.

Judging by the comings and goings of staff cars and the number of launches plying the waters of Sliema Creek the British were having some kind of conference at HMS Phoenicia, the ancient fort at the far end of Manoel Island overlooking Marsamxett across the water from the massive ramparts of Valletta. Was that why the young officer had been sent across the road to request some kind of truce?

The British were very odd.

They had a capacity to be ruthless that shocked their friends and foes alike; yet sometimes they were almost childishly trusting and optimistic.

Second Lieutenant Jackson seemed to think that the anguish of the women of Malta might be assuaged by old-fashioned reasonableness and civility.

She ought not to be surprised anymore; time and again in her dealings with relatively senior British officers she had discovered there was a fundamental disconnect between what she said to them and what they actually thought she had said. Often, they would look at her with the bewilderment of a worried parent listening to the meaningless prattling of a small child.

As if the occupation and all its evils were in some way her fault!

It was one of those overcast autumnal days when the wind blew down Marsamxett Harbour and Sliema Creek from the south east until ranks of two-foot-high swells drove against the sea walls slowly rocking the big ships in the anchorage.

All the women wore several layers of clothing, although their lower legs and sandaled feet were exposed to the chill of the wind. There was rain in the air and lonely flecks of moisture touched faces and blinked eyes.

Before the war the waterfront – to the British 'The Strand' and in her native tongue the 'Trix lx Xatt' - would have been filled with traffic and with passers-by at this hour approaching noon. However, petrol was virtually unobtainable for civilian use and even if people had had the money in their pockets to spend – which few had - there was hardly anything to buy in the shops and the waterfront was sparsely populated.

The decline in living standards and the emptying of the shops had been a gradual process. When there had been runs on vital supplies – sugar, salt and flour – the British had re-imposed a version of the 1945 rationing system. Nobody was actually starving. Not yet but most Maltese who were not in the direct service of the British were hungry all the time. Many of the mothers who protested outside the gated bridge to Manoel Island were thin from feeding their children with their own rations.

"I should get into the queue," Marija announced apologetically.

She always felt guilty leaving the others because so few of her sisters had visiting rights. Many of her friends did not even know where their loved ones – mostly, but not exclusively men - were being held let alone possessed the precious *authorities* required to visit them, wherever they might be imprisoned.

The first round ups had been just before Christmas last year and at least half Marija's sisters outside the gates had not seen their loved ones since then.

At first Marija had tried taking in photographs of the missing, and lists of names into the Manoel Island Detention Camp; the guards had stopped that after a month.

Today she had cigarettes, a couple of packs of playing cards, two pads of writing paper and some pencils, and several photographs of children of the men she had identified on previous visits in her brother's old canvas knapsack.

He had carried it with him everywhere he went; and now she did likewise.

"They take ages processing us but they always make us leave on time even if we've only been inside for a few minutes."

Another woman took her corner of the banner.

Others murmured comforting words.

There were the normal hugs, kisses, and a few tears.

She was their leader – even if she had never claimed or sought that leadership - and they never knew if the British would allow her return to them again later that afternoon, or ever, for that was what the British occupation of Malta had come to.

At a little before mid-day Marija carefully made her way across the road and took her place at the end of the queue of a score of men and women.

The others chided her for her insistence on standing all day, every day that she was in the front line of the Manoel Island picket. She would retort, good-naturedly that she was only on the 'front line' two or three days a week – the rest of the time she lived at the St Catherine's Hospital for Women in Mdina where she worked – while they were there all the time.

Besides, she had no intention of displaying the tiniest chink of weakness in front of their oppressors.

Nevertheless, when she crossed the road, she limped a little and as she stood in the queue she ached from head to toe. Her remade broken childhood body was not fashioned to stand or to and walk long distances, or in any way countenance standing up for hours on end. She felt a little light headed from hunger, swayed; but would not allow herself to lean against the low stone parapet of the sea wall curving onto the bridge.

From long habit she let her mind wander into daydreams that helped her to neglect the aching of her reconstructed bones. Near the bridge the harbour narrowed to the breadth of a brick arch supporting the road from Gzira onto the island at its closest point to land where Sliema and Lazaretto Creeks merged. Flotsam and stains of oil coloured the relatively tranquil surface of the water, cigarette filters and fragments of cork drifted with a faded red buoy from a lost fishing net, all washing against the sea wall.

As she always did when her spirit was being tested Marija thought about Peter Christopher.

Lately, his letters arrived more regularly, albeit a month delayed. She remembered receiving the first letter after the war in April, the tingling breathless excitement reading the big military postmark – 2 Feb 63 – and recognising the unmistakable flowing handwriting on the envelope addressed to *Miss M.E. Calleja, 59 Triq St Julian, Sliema, Island of Malta*.

Of course, by then she had moved out of the family home into the tiny second floor room at the St Catherine's Hospital for Women in Mdina.

She had received the letter nearly seven weeks after it was posted.

The relief, the flood of bright, joyous hope had reduced her to a fit of uncontrollable sobbing.

Margo Seiffert, the Director of the Hospital and her long-time mentor and friend, had believed she must have received bad news and that she was having some kind of hysterical attack until she explained, and had tearfully shown her the letter.

Or rather, both letters; the one Peter had written as the fury of the nightmare seemed to be coming to an end, and the letter he had penned a week later after HMS Talavera had returned to port. It was the conclusion of the first letter, the words that had emerged from the disaster like a shining beacon of hope lighting the way out of the darkness that she had committed to memory, and carried in her heart ever since.

'*...it seems to me that no matter how bad things are we cannot* *afford to give in. If we despair then we are lost. While we survive, while Talavera and my crewmates survive, we owe it to ourselves to be worthy of surviving. Everything has changed but some things remain the same. You have always been and will always remain my best friend in the world and the one person I trust above all others. As I write I am looking at your picture. While I look at your face, I can still believe that there is hope. If we both live please wait for me because I am on my way to you.'*

Marija blinked.

Somebody was talking to her.

"Miss Calleja?"

The tall, weather beaten man in his thirties in the crisp uniform of a staff sergeant of the Royal Military Police inquired solicitously, his expression a little anxious.

His grey eyes were studying her face.

"Forgive me, I was miles away," she shrugged, registering the man's concern and knowing it was more than just professional.

If Staff Sergeant Jim Siddall had been the man who had led the squad that arrested her little brother Joe on that December morning last year, he had also been the man who had kept her informed of his whereabouts and his wellbeing ever since.

The Redcap had had no part in Joe's subsequent interrogation, or the beatings he had endured at the hands of the Empire Stadium interrogators. On the one occasion Marija had questioned him about that episode Staff Sergeant Siddall had become evasively monosyllabic. He had been ashamed, and from that moment she ceased to treat him as her enemy.

Another time she had asked him to carry messages between her and her brother and on behalf of the relatives of other detainees but he had refused. That would have been crossing an unwritten line and she had not asked him to cross that line a second time.

So far as she knew he told her no lies.

Nor had he ever asked or expected anything remotely improper of her.

"I've been ordered to escort you to the Administration Office at HMS Phoenicia, Miss Calleja."

Marija did not think this was good news.

"I do not wish to miss my visiting hour with my brother, Staff Sergeant Siddall."

"I'm sorry," the man apologised, his gaze sliding across the road to the group of women holding the banner with its quietly excoriating condemnation of everything that the uniform he wore and of which until the last year he had been immensely proud to have worn all his adult life, represented to the protesters. "I can't do anything about that. Look, I want to avoid a scene..."

"There will be no scene," Marija sighed.

It was a guiding principle of the protest that she and her sisters continued to treat individual British soldiers, sailors and airmen with personal respect and civility. The men responsible for the crimes against the Maltese people were not the ones who manned the gates and barricades, or even those who carried out most of the arrests, spot searches, document checks or faced down the rioters in Senglea and Valletta with tear gas and rifle butts.

One look into the eyes of a good man like Jim Siddall was enough to know that many among the hated British were disgusted by what was being done in their name.

"I will come quietly."

"It isn't like that," the man protested, softly. "You're not being arrested, or anything."

Marija straightened to her full height, attempting not to wince at the pain in her hips. The man was a full head taller and she raised her face to give him an oddly maternal quizzical appraisal.

"No? We both know that is not true," she shrugged. "The reason I am here, that I and my sisters are here every day is because we are already under arrest, Staff Sergeant. All of us, every day." A quirk of her lips impersonated a smile. "Malta is our prison and you – *the British* – are our jailers."

Jim Siddall's jaw worked; no sound emerged from his lips.

He shook his head.

"I've got a car waiting the other side of the gate. It is a bit of a climb up to the fort..."

"I am quite capable of walking," Marija protested.

Her protestation was somewhat undermined the next moment when her left foot twisted in a pothole. She had been on her feet for several hours and she was stiff, clumsy. She would have fallen but for the soldier's gentle, supporting hand.

"I know you are more than *capable* of doing anything that you set your mind to, Miss Calleja," Jim Siddall grinned. "But I organised the car, anyway."

Several women had crossed the road, scowling protectively.

"I'm fine," Marija assured them, waving them back. "Somebody wants to talk to me in the fort. That's all. Staff Sergeant Siddall has kindly 'organised' a car. I don't even have to walk up the hill."

The soldier stood back, not wanting to make eye contact or

confront the other women. He watched them retreat, felt their eyes burning into him.

"We should go," Marija declared. "They will only worry if we delay."

The man nodded.

He took one last look back at the ten feet long banner.

IS THIS HOW YOU TREAT YOUR FRIENDS?

Chapter 5

Saturday 23rd November 1963
Tent 17, Manoel Island Detention Camp

Joseph Calleja was lying on his cot in the twelve-man tent when the big Redcap appeared at the open flap. Most guards only moved around the camp in pairs, wielding night sticks; the newcomer was, as ever, unarmed, remaining as much a loner now as he'd been before the war. Tent 17 was half-empty since the latest relocations. All six remaining occupants had returned to it in case they were called to the visiting rooms, although only Joe actually expected a visit today. He had no idea what the time was and with a sinking feeling suspected that visiting hour was already long over. When a guard entered the tent, everybody stood to attention or the whole tent suffered the consequences. That was the rule. The six men in the tent began to sulkily roll to their feet.

"Stand easy!" The tall newcomer growled. He pointed at Joe, indicated for him to follow him out of the tent.

"Whatever you say, Tommy," the unshaven young man with the mop of rebellious brown-black hair acknowledged. He had always known the British were bastards. Before the war they were on their best behaviour – by their standards – after the war they had taken off the kid gloves. They had been on his case in the old days ever since he became an apprentice electrician at the Senglea Dockyard at the age of sixteen. But for his father's protection and his big sister's positively saintly notoriety, he would have been locked up years ago. The British would probably have thrown away the key, in fact.

"Get your skates on, Calleja!" The soldier barked.

Despite his mile-wide streak of obstinacy – the one he had been born with and had been working on ever since – Joseph Mario Calleja quickened his step as he passed the other man and emerged into the blustery, cold grey afternoon.

"Walk with me," Staff Sergeant Jim Siddall demanded.

"You have seen my sister?"

"Yes, she's..." The big man hesitated. "She's fine. Still ruling the roost down at the gates when she's not in Mdina." As soon as they were out of earshot of the tent the big man's voice lowered and his tone became awkwardly friendly, almost confidential. "Marija is well, I think. Although all the standing around at the gates isn't good for her. Not that she'd admit it."

Joe had begun to wonder why the soldier never asked him *any* questions about his alleged, or real, links with the communists, the Maltese Labour Party, the inner circles of the Dockyard unions, or about any of his supposedly *subversive* activities or alleged partners in crime.

"You know you're wasting your time with my sister, Tommy?" He put to the older man as they walked towards the perimeter fence on the Lazaretto Creek side of the island. The superstructure of HMS Maidstone, the big depot ship, dominated the view towards across Lazaretto Creek towards Msida above the barbed wire topped fence lines. The ground beneath the two men's feet was hard packed mud. No blade of grass remained from the base playing field this space had once been in kinder, different times. "She's got that Admiral's son she's never met in her head *all* the time."

"I know," Jim Siddall chuckled. "But that's not why I keep an eye on you, Joe."

"Then why, Tommy?"

"That's complicated."

In the beginning Joe had been painfully conflicted to be seen talking to the big man. He had no intention of collaborating with the *enemy*. But then he discovered somebody had spread a rumour that the scary Staff Sergeant with the hard eyes who never, ever lost his temper, was sweet on Marija. Any man who was sweet on the heroin of Vittoriosa-Birgu could not be all bad and the communal, herd consensus had concluded that Joe had no choice but to humour the Tommy. It was only later that Joe discovered that it had been Jim Siddall who had stopped the security goons at the Empire Stadium beating him to death that awful cold day in January. He was unconscious by then but the others said the big man had turned up with a squad of Redcaps - bayonets fixed to their SLRs - and started 'kicking the crap' out of the bastards running the place. *They* also said that other men had been beaten to death in the rooms beneath the stands at the Empire Stadium. Joe did not know what to believe. All he knew was that it had been a bad place to be and the man who was in charge *was not* British. That had confused them all. Why would a Yank be in charge of the archipelago's main clearing house for alleged subversives, terrorists and fifth columnists? He had asked the big man once; he had chuckled sourly and said nothing.

"Marija is at the fort," the older man explained.

"She's been arrested?"

Jim Siddall thought about this for several moments as if the question had been gnawing at his guts.

"No. I don't think so."

Both men had automatically half-turned to look up towards the bastions of the citadel which housed the Headquarters of the Mediterranean Fleet, the Military Administration of Malta Command, and the offices of the Internal Security Department. The civil administration of the Maltese Archipelago was still based in Valletta and nobody really knew whether the real power lay with the men in the suits or the uniforms. That, Joe Calleja, mused idly, was another oddity of the *British* way of conducting business. There was a Lieutenant Governor in Valletta, and an Admiral in Fort Phoenicia but who was actually in charge? The Royal Air Force had command bunkers and sprawling barracks at Luqa, the biggest airbase on the main island while the Army had commandeered Fort St Angelo at the seaward end of the Valletta peninsula, and the old World War II war rooms beside and beneath the saluting gallery which overlooked the Grand Harbour. It was not clear if, or how often the three services communicated with each other. Traditionally, it seemed, the Commander-in-Chief of the Mediterranean Fleet – since he arrived on the island in February to replace his assassinated predecessor, Vice-Admiral Sir Michael Staveley-Pope - was, de facto, the man who actually ran the show in Malta, which probably explained why those ISD (Internal Security Division) bastards operated out of HMS Phoenicia.

"The fort was called HMS Talbot during the last German war," Jim Siddall said for no apparent reason. Unlike ninety-nine percent of his fellow servicemen on Malta the big man had been required to attend an intensive two-week *pre-embarkation familiarization* course. Since – at the time - he was to be attached to the small pre-war Counter-Intelligence Division of the Royal Military Police in Malta, it had been deemed desirable for him to be educated in the ways, and the history of the Maltese. He was not convinced the course had helped him understand the Maltese, or anything in particular, any better than he had before but he had arrived in the archipelago equipped with a positive mine of useless information.

"Why *Talbot?*" Joseph Calleja asked.

"The Navy had to call it something, I suppose."

Manoel Island had originally been called *l'Isola del Vescovo* or, in Maltese, *il-Gżira tal-Isqof* which translated roughly as 'the Bishop's Island'. And so it had remained until post medieval times when in 1643 Jean Paul Lascaris, Grandmaster of the Knights of Malta, had built a quarantine hospital – a *lazaretto* - on the island, in response to the periodic waves of plague and cholera brought to Malta by visiting ships. The island had not obtained its modern name until the 18th century, renamed in honour of António Manoel de Vilhena, a Portuguese Grandmaster of the Knights of Malta under whose leadership the original Fort Manoel was built in 1726. At the time the fort was a marvel of 18th century military engineering. Although some uncertainty existed as to the guiding hand behind the original plans for the structure, the general consensus was that the grand plan was the work of one Louis d'Augbigne Tigné, somewhat modified by his friend Charles François de Mondion. The latter was actually buried in a crypt beneath the fort. Somewhat mishandled by the Luftwaffe in the early 1940s Manoel Fort – currently HMS Phoenicia – retained its impressive internal quadrangle parade ground and arcade. The baroque chapel of St. Anthony of Padua within the fort's walls had been almost totally destroyed by bombing in March 1942 but had subsequently been rebuilt as the base chapel, albeit not quite in the magnificent style of its pre-German war pomp.

Yes, useless information...

"What is Marija doing at the fort if she hasn't been arrested?"

The question brought Jim Siddall down to earth with a jarring bump.

"I don't know," he admitted.

"You're ISD, you know everything."

They'd reached the end of the avenue between the tents, turned, and begun to retrace their steps. There were around three hundred men in the camp, few were outside their tents. Idleness was the predominant camp regime. There were no activities, just endless days waiting around when nothing happened. Once a month the British moved detainees in, or out, occasionally a man was taken away for interrogation. Nobody got knocked about. After the 'incidents' at the Empire Stadium the British Military Administration had posted a general order to the effect that *'the physical abuse of prisoners or any other person in custody is absolutely forbidden other than in cases of self-defence'*. The order, posted on the gates to the camp and pinned inside every tent went on to specify that *'violence occasioned in self-defence must at all times be reasonable and proportionate to the degree of force encountered'*. Joe had not met any other detainee who had been interrogated by a Yank since awakening in hospital in January. The British interrogators sometimes yelled and screamed but not often. They might manhandle anybody stupid enough to be awkward; taking no pleasure in it. The worst of it for the detainees was the boredom and not knowing what was going on outside, and in having no direct contact apart from infrequent, rarely scheduled visits. There were no letters, in or out of the camp. No access to lawyers, no appeal. Once you were in the system you were trapped. If the British had been nasty about it the whole thing would have been intolerably cruel. As it was, life in the camp was just unimaginably tedious, wearying, dispiriting, depressing and dreary. It was as if the British did not really have their heart in their work. Joe Calleja knew Staff Sergeant Siddall did not have his heart in it. He might be sweet on his sister, he might not. Either way, like most of his compatriots he did not need an excuse to behave like a human being.

"I'm not ISD," Jim Siddall growled, irritably.

"Oh, I..."

"I'm a Redcap," the soldier declared as if he was clinging to the idea like a sailor holding onto a broken spar in a shipwreck.

"You were on my case before the war?" Joe Calleja reminded him, expecting to be ignored.

"That was different. That was just routine *police* work. You worked in the dockyards. You had access to secret equipment. You had associates who were known communists. You turned up at all the wrong demonstrations. Oh, and there was that funny stuff you were involved in with the Union. So, we kept an eye on you. But that was all." Jim Siddall waved at their surroundings. "This?" He asked, speaking to thin air. "This is just *wrong*."

The younger man blinked in astonishment.

"But I never said that," the big man added ruefully.

"I had nothing to do with the troubles after the war," Joe said before he could stop himself. He could not help himself compounding his admission. "None of my people had anything to do with the killings or the sabotage."

The big man already knew that.

Within hours of the October War while the firestorms still raged in the devastated cities of Northern Europe and the Soviet Union, sleeper agents had emerged from their long slumber. In Italy and across the Mediterranean and in the surviving cities of the old country there had been a wave of assassinations and bombings. Leading politicians, businessmen and churchmen had been gunned down. Power stations, oil refineries and railways had been sabotaged. Here on Malta the C-in-C Mediterranean Fleet and his wife had been murdered outside their official residence. Other senior officers had been butchered in broad daylight. The American Consul had been burned alive in a petrol bomb attack on his car. Aircraft had been blown up on the tarmac at Luqa. A cruiser, HMS Lion, had had her decks raked with sub-machine gun fire as she left Marsamxett Harbour one morning. There had been random bombings in Valletta and on the Sliema waterfront targeted at bars and restaurants frequented by British officers and other ranks. The wave of attacks had only stopped with the massive roundups of last December and January. Joe Calleja remembered those times with terror and confusion.

"Marija is okay?" He checked. He might not be very happy being locked up in this hole but he could live with it so long as he knew his family was all right. Especially, Marija.

"She's a little thinner, I think. Standing in the road holding up that bloody banner for hours on end can't be very good for her," the soldier replied, glumly. "But she's okay."

"Most times you tell me very little when we have these little chats?"

"I tell you about your family. That they're okay."

"I mean apart from that?"

"I'm in the Army. I don't pick and choose which orders I obey, Joe. Nobody's ordered me *not* to tell you that your family is okay." Jim Siddall checked his wristwatch. "If you were a *real* communist agent provocateur, you'd know that, Joe."

The younger man bristled then realised he was being teased.

"I am a communist," he hissed.

"Maybe." Jim Siddall shrugged as if it did not matter. "I have to go."

Joseph Calleja watched the tall man stride away.

Then he began to worry about Marija.

Chapter 6

Saturday 23rd November 1963
HMS Phoenicia, Manoel Island

"Can I offer you a cup of tea, Miss Calleja?"

Marija looked at the sinewy man of about her own height – five feet and five or six inches - in the immaculate dark blue uniform of a commander in the Royal Navy, with politely quizzical brown eyes. She guessed the officer sitting on the other side of the polished mahogany desk was in his late thirties or early forties. His severely cropped dark hair failed to conceal the tracks of two separate scalp injuries. One was just inside the hairline above his left eye, two inches long and jagged. The other was above his left ear, a straight forty-five-degree slash with ugly suture marks. Shrapnel injuries, she assumed. She had grown up in a war-scarred generation and this man's scars bore no comparison with her own, mercifully hidden wounds. He was returning her gaze with eyes that betrayed absolutely nothing of his real thoughts.

The man had introduced himself as William McNeil. And added: 'I'm attached to the Staff of the C-in-C Middle East in Alexandria. I'm on my way back to the United Kingdom and I've been asked to review a number of outstanding files here, on Malta, and other places. *En route*, as it were.'

The man wore an expensive-looking watch on his left wrist. Marija guessed it was an aviator's chronometer similar to those she seen RAF pilots at Luqa and Hal Far wearing. It distracted her eye. Seeing this Commander McNeil glanced down at the timepiece, half-smiling.

"A gift from my brother," he explained. "He was a fighter pilot."

He had a clipped, pitch perfect accent that was in some small way a caricature of an actor in some old British World War II movie. It rather reminded Marija of Alec Guinness in *The Malta Story* and she had tried not to smile. Marija's father liked to remind his children that 'if something seems to be too good to be true, it probably is', and for some reason that she could not put her finger on, the scarred, cool-eyed man studying her from across the other side of his borrowed desk, seemed if not 'too good to be true' then somehow, *too...English*. Another film she had seen as a teenager was *In Which We Serve* and Commander William McNeil sounded exactly like Noel Coward. Nobody she had ever met had ever sounded *exactly* like Noel Coward.

"I thought I was under arrest Commander McNeil?" Marija replied, finding no difficulty sounding a little vexed. She sat on the edge of the hard chair a sour faced Wren had pulled up for her while she was waiting. She sat very still, careful to maintain an appearance of seraphic calm that suggested complete indifference to her current situation. "Now you are asking me if I would like a cup of tea? Forgive me, I am a simple Catholic girl and I am confused?"

"A simple Catholic girl? That I doubt, Miss Calleja." The man half-smiled as he spoke but his eyes were not laughing.

"Am I not under arrest?"

"No. Should you be under arrest?"

Acknowledging that the question was rhetorical Marija did not dignify it with an answer. She folded her hands in her lap, waited for her interrogator to continue. She had known that sooner or later the British would pull her in, attempt to persuade and if persuasion failed, attempt to frighten and intimidate her into acquiescence. Her fortnightly column in the *Times of Malta* – no more than two hundred and fifty politely, moderately scolding words – was a thorn in the ISD's side that they could not risk removing without abandoning the fiction that they were not behaving like Fascists. Miraculously, the *Times of Malta* remained sacrosanct; the one public organ of information untouched by martial law because the British knew that without at least one trustworthy means of speaking to every Maltese, the archipelago would eventually become ungovernable.

Commander McNeil grunted and opened the well-thumbed Manila file on his blotter. The file was an inch thick and several pages were partly torn. It was a file that had been in transit and had passed through many hands.

"Your brother doesn't seem to care what happens to the rest of his family."

Marija recognised this for a statement and replied accordingly.

"Joseph answers to his own conscience," she said evenly, "as do we all."

"Really?" The man didn't look up. "I'm told young Joseph has been a constant trial to your father. Your father holds a very responsible position. Deputy Dockyard Superintendent. You and he must have had *words* many times about Joseph?"

Marija understood what was going on.

"My father and I have never had *words*, Commander. About Joe, or on any other subject." Sitting still on the hard chair was beginning to hurt. Her old injuries and their lasting effects caught up with her when she was tired, unable to move freely, or stretch. However, if a little pain was the cost of her apparent serenity then it was worth it. She had no intention of showing weakness in front of *this* man. "My father is a good and an honourable man."

"I'm sure he is."

Marija ignored the sneering undertone. Instead, she began to look around the office. There were pictures of cruisers and destroyers on the wall. ISD operated out of huts erected outside the walls of Fort Manoel, not inside citadel. Yet Jim Siddall had driven straight past those ramshackle post-war buildings into the fortress. He had jumped out, held the door for her. He had offered her his arm in support like a perfect gentleman; she had declined it. The photographs of the room's normal occupant's family were placed face down to one side of the blotter in their gilded frames. Had they survived the cataclysm of the October War? So many of the sailors, soldiers and airmen on the island had lost people they loved. A little voice in her head reminded her that even in these strange times she remained one of the lucky ones. She had lost nobody and by the grace of God, Peter had survived.

"I came here today to visit my brother," she reminded Commander McNeil. Nothing irritated the British so much as to be accused of *rudeness*.

"Yes. I'm sorry. That cannot be helped."

"I'm sorry," she queried, resorting to her most quizzical expression. "It was my understanding that *you* were the masters on this island?"

The man scowled before he remembered that scowling at *this* particular young woman was not in his script. He closed the open file, sat back in his chair, took a deep breath.

"I was at the Embassy in Ankara when the curtain went up last year," he sighed. His left hand went up to his head. "Every window in the city blew out in the first strike. I was lucky. I just got cut up a bit." He fixed Marija in a cold, sterile stare. "My wife and my two young sons lived in a place called Chatham. That was supposed to be a temporary thing. They were going to come out to join me for the rest of my tour just before Christmas last year. Unfortunately, Chatham doesn't exist anymore. Neither do any illusions I might once have entertained that any of us are the masters of *anything*."

Marija glanced at the gilded frames face down on the table.

"I am sorry. If anything happened to my family, I don't know how I would carry on, Commander."

"Day by day, Miss Calleja." The man appeared to come to a decision. "Perhaps, we might walk together? If you are able, that is. I know this has probably already been a long day for you. I don't think you've been up here before and the view across to Valletta is quite stunning."

The mid-afternoon sun was breaking fitfully through threatening, fast scudding clouds as Commander McNeil followed his guest out onto the old parade ground. Several Land Rovers, a couple of Jeeps and half-a-dozen big Bedford trucks were parked, seemingly at random, in the surprisingly large open space within the bastion walls.

Marija paused at the edge of the pavement surrounding the parade ground before stepping, very cautiously the six inches down to the ground. She was stiff and sore from sitting uncomfortably, unmoving on the chair. She swayed, steadied, regained her balance and realised that McNeil had been waiting anxiously, coiled like a spring to catch her if she fell.

"It has been a long day," she conceded, waving away his concerns.

They began to walk, unhurriedly between the parked vehicles.

"In case you were wondering I am not attached to the Internal Security Division," Commander McNeil announced. "Or at least, not in any meaningful way. It is simply that by operating under the general umbrella of ISD fewer questions are asked, that sort of thing."

"If you are not with Internal Security who are you with, Commander?"

"That I am not at liberty to divulge, Miss Calleja."

"What are we doing here?"

"Ah, now that's a good question."

They walked on until they came to the southern wall. McNeil led Marija through two doors and a cool, vaulted tunnel to the outside of the ramparts. They emerged onto a platform above terraces of white stone steps that led all the way down to a vacant granite quay. Across the grey blue waters of Marsamxett Anchorage the great walls of Valletta reared up, filling the horizon like the side of a valley. On the other side of the harbour Marija watched a car driving slowly along the long curve of the Great Siege Road. Looking down Marsamxett towards Floriana she saw an old destroyer tied up alongside the refuelling jetty. She squinted hard but could not make out the ship's pennant number.

"We can speak privately, now," the man assured her. There were large, finished stones awaiting their turn to be rebuilt back into the walls of Fort Manoel as part of the slow, ongoing restoration of the ancient fabric of the citadel. The fortress had fallen into general disrepair before the siege of 1940 to 1942 during which the bombing had made things ten times worse. All restoration work had ceased in October last year. "Let's sit down," McNeil suggested. "If it starts raining, we can shelter in the tunnel."

Marija sank gratefully onto the nearest stone.

"Things here on Malta," McNeil began, "are nowhere near as bad as they are elsewhere in the Mediterranean. Obviously, things were chaotic here just after the war. We'd assumed that Soviet war plans included disruptive fifth column operations, assassinations of prominent civil and military figures, sabotage and so forth, but we'd never imagined those activities would be so," he shrugged, "*extreme.* Or that they'd continue for so long after major hostilities had ceased."

Marija listened. The leadership of the Maltese Nationalist Party had been targeted by a series of cold-blooded murders and bombings. A score of senior British officers had been assassinated within hours of the outbreak of war. The Commander-in-Chief of the Mediterranean Fleet and his wife had been gunned down outside their official residence. The offices of the archipelago's civil administration had been virtually demolished by a massive bomb in a lorry driven into the square next to it. Afterwards, the British claimed that the mass detentions, the street searches, the random arrests were in response to the anarchy of those weeks.

"The situation on Cyprus bordered on an all-out civil war for a while. At Gibraltar the Spanish are threatening to invade to quote 'restore peace'. Meanwhile, the Egyptians have shut the Suez Canal. If Malta wasn't the key to what remains of my Government's last hope of retaining a voice in the rebuilding of the old world, I suspect we'd have pulled out long ago. Pulled out and left the island to the tender mercies of its neighbours. That might yet happen, of course."

Marija did not know why she was being told this so she asked what seemed to her to be a very, very obvious question.

"Do you have the authority to have Joseph released, Commander?"

"No. He's safer where he is for the moment, anyway. Who knows what mischief he'd get up to if we let him out or who he'd associate with?"

"Joe's no fifth columnist!"

"He's a communist sympathiser. A union agitator. A troublemaker. What's the difference?"

"All the difference in the world!"

"On that we shall have to agree to disagree, Miss Calleja."

Marija wanted to slap the man's face.

"This is all a game to you people." This accusation drew no response. "Why did you prevent me visiting my brother?" She knew the answer. Whatever he said there could only be the one answer. He had done it to make a point. He had stopped her visiting Joe because he could and because he had known it would hurt her.

"For which I apologise," Commander McNeil drawled. "I'm sure Staff Sergeant Siddall will arrange a new visiting pass within the next few days. I'm a busy man. I have several people to meet on Malta and I have a seat booked on a flight to England in thirty-six hours' time."

Marija decided this was a little too mysterious for her taste.

McNeil pulled out a pack of cigarettes. American Lucky Strikes. He offered her the pack.

"I don't smoke," she frowned, disapprovingly. "Which I'm sure you already know."

"But you always bring Joseph cigarettes?"

Marija's frown deepened and the Englishman shrugged. He lit up, inhaled long and deep, unhurriedly, before exhaling raggedly. He almost coughed.

"I can't kick the habit. I cough like a coal miner in the morning. Probably all the dust I swallowed when I was buried under the Embassy in Ankara last year." He grinned rather grimly. He took another drag of his cigarette. "The thing is that my principals want to know who they can talk to when the time comes to mend the fences ISD and idiots like them have broken in the last year."

"You are speaking in riddles."

"Yes, force of habit, sorry. I'm not a real commander. I've never even been in the Navy. I'd get sea sick on the Sliema to Valletta ferry, probably." McNeil screwed up his face, relaxed. "I'm in the Intelligence game. I'm not a spy, or anything that glamorous. You'd think the war changed everything but actually, in my bailiwick, nothing much really changed at all. The thing is to know who your friends are. The people whom one can trust. I was sent here to find people my principals can trust. People with whom they can do business."

"And you think I'm one of those people?" Marija did not know whether to be flattered or appalled.

"You are a minor a saint among your own people..."

Marija blushed and the displeasure flashing in her hazel eyes momentarily distracted the man.

"You are, whether you like it or not," he carried on, quickly. "You're the little girl who rose from her sickbed, endured the unendurable, became a nurse and in the last year a midwife. And now you are a leader of the dispossessed. After today you will also enjoy the additional cachet of having been arrested and interrogated by the brutal agents of perfidious Albion."

Marija suppressed a childish urge to stick out her tongue at the Englishman. She avoided the man's gaze, elected to watch a passing whaler from one of the destroyers in Sliema Creek progressing sedately down Marsamxett.

Peter! He was going to talk to her about Peter!

Renewing eye contact she did not trouble to veil her suspicion.

"Having identified you as a potential *friend*," the man confessed, "it behoves us to strengthen your influence amongst your own people whenever the opportunity arises."

"Is Sergeant Siddall one of *you*?"

"One of us? That's an interesting question. Honestly, I don't know. I strongly suspect that his own people tolerate him because they believe he spies on you rather more than he actually does. If, that is, he spies on you at all. Like your esteem in the eyes of your *friends*, his contact with me will raise him in the esteem of *his* people. It will put him beyond suspicion. Those who will have been whispering about where Jim Siddall's loyalties really lie will be looking a little bit sheepish this afternoon. As for the good sergeant, well, he'll be a much happier man now that I've rescinded the order requiring him and his *friends* to read your – albeit censored - correspondence with Peter Christopher."

Marija's jaw hung slack for a second.

"You were..."

"Your letters to Peter and his to you were being steamed open, read, copied and resealed prior to onward transmission. I gather a number of letters, which you presumably assumed had been lost in the post, were detained indefinitely by ISD on 'security grounds'. This will not happen in future. I informed the local ISD Sector Chief that your mail is being analysed in England and that the people back home don't want his 'grubby fingerprints' all over the *evidence*. The file I had on the desk in the office back there is ISD's 'correspondence digest' on you two young lovebirds."

"We are not lovebirds!" Marija protested without real passion. "We have always been friends. That is all!"

"Have it your own way. I plan to take the file with me back to England. If it was within my gift, I'd extract the letters that didn't get through to you. Unfortunately, I can't do that. Sorry. Peter being related to who he is related to means that my hands are tied."

Marija got to her feet very stiffly, crossed her arms across her breasts. "What do you want?"

"I want you to know that my principals and I have a vested interest in the wellbeing of your brother, your family, and you."

At the same time McNeil's *principals* would not hesitate to use their letters to blackmail Peter's father.

Marija was silent.

Chapter 7

Monday 25th November, 1963
Government House, Cheltenham, Gloucestershire

"The Americans want to know why we haven't issued an official response to Kennedy's *Moon Speech*, Prime Minister?" Sir Henry Tomlinson spoke with a brisk patrician confidence that many of his previous political masters had found more than a little disconcerting over the years.

"Cakes and circuses," the imposing, impatient man in the armchair by the window guffawed.

He had been listening to Elgar when Permanent Secretary to the Cabinet and the Head of the Home Civil Service, had knocked on his door to deliver his daily ten o'clock briefing.

"When the Foreign Secretary has calmed down, I'm sure he'll want to draft something emollient."

Alexander Frederick Douglas-Home, Earl of Home, since July 1960, Her Majesty's Secretary of State for Foreign Affairs, was one of the few Tory grandees from Harold MacMillan's cabinet to have survived the cataclysm, and the only one to still be in his old post.

"I took the liberty of discussing matters with Tom Harding-Grayson, Prime Minister," Henry Tomlinson replied.

"Oh?"

The Prime Minister reluctantly dragged his gaze away from the grey circle of the Chiltern Hills beyond the Race Course. Cheltenham Race Course was rapidly disappearing under the concrete runways of the new airfield.

He had never been a man of the turf – notwithstanding that he had spent many happy days at the races with his hero and throughout the 1950s his political mentor, Sir Winston Churchill in happier times - but he regretted having to sweep away so much sporting history and tradition. Thankfully, most of the building work was out of sight of the ever-spreading and proliferating compounds of the relocated heart of Government. The view from his first-floor office window was the reason he'd chosen it from all the other available rooms in the sprawling old mansion. In his darkest moments he found a kind of solace staring out over that unburned, un-blasted vista of an England that by and large no longer existed.

Sir Thomas Harding-Grayson was the man who ran the Foreign Office apparatus and pulled Alec Douglas-Home's strings.

Poor Alec, he had never come to terms with what had happened, he would always live in the past. By rights the leadership of the Party and the Government ought to have been his last year but he had been too broken, too distraught.

Notwithstanding, the Prime Minister needed men like Alec, good men who could hold the Party in line behind him even if what they had once called 'foreign policy' was a luxury they could not afford in this mutilated brave new world.

The Foreign Secretary had backed Kennedy's stance before the crisis despite having received advice from the Government's law officers that the American blockade of Cuba was illegal under international law. An innately calm, rational man who had been perhaps the only immovable, unbreakable pillar of the MacMillan Cabinet, the Foreign Secretary increasingly retreated to his estates in Scotland.

"What does Tom think, Henry?"

The Prime Minister asked.

"He thinks if the Yanks want to throw untold treasure into putting a man on the Moon, we should let them get on with it, Prime Minister."

"He does?"

Henry Tomlinson was fifty-five years old. Harrow and Cambridge – Trinity College – educated he had spent Hitler's war in MI5, and risen to be the acting number two at the Cabinet Office on the eve of the Cuban disaster. He and his family had been at their cottage in the Brecon Beacons when three-quarters of the government and the senior Home Civil Service had been wiped out. Of the survivors, he was head and shoulders *primus inter pares*, first among equals. He had become the natural leader of the administrative side of the Provisional Government – shortly thereafter renamed the *United Kingdom Interim Emergency Administration (UKIEA)* - in exactly the same way the Prime Minister had known himself to be, false modesty apart, the natural leader of his surviving political contemporaries.

"This wouldn't be another one of Tom's *cynical* outbursts?"

"Perhaps. But closely argued, as always."

"Test it on me, Henry," the Prime Minister invited.

"For all their promises of beneficence," the head of the Civil Service drawled, "we all know the Americans aren't about to foot the bill for paying for one hundredth of the cost or rebuilding one great European city. Let alone the reconstruction of any small part of any European *competitor* industry. What little *charity* we can expect from our wartime *Ally* will be in the form of parsimonious food handouts and miscellaneous uncoordinated donations, scraps from the table of the victors, basically. Even if JFK was some kind of latter-day Father Christmas, which he isn't, he wouldn't have a snowflake's chance in

Hell of getting a major foreign aid program through Congress. Tom Grayson says the prevailing mood in Washington is that if we'd *flushed* our V-Bombers and Thor's sooner Buffalo, Baltimore, Boston, Chicago and Seattle wouldn't have got hit at all. The Americans are *not* our friends, Prime Minister."

The Right Honourable Edward Richard George Heath, Prime Minister of the United Kingdom Interim Emergency Administration was as silent and unmoving as a block of granite for a long time.

Sir Henry Tomlinson waited in silence.

Presently, the man in the chair by the window stirred.

"Does Tom think Kennedy will win if he runs for a second term next year?"

"Tom says he'll run," the other man said. "As to whether he'll win?"

"If he runs, he'll win," the Prime Minister decided. "He'll blame us for everything if he has to. But he'll win, Henry."

The Cabinet Secretary said nothing.

"*They* blow up the world and then they talk about putting a man on the Moon," Edward Heath shook his head. For a moment his profile was silhouetted against the light, his overly prominent straight nose jutting towards the Chiltern Hills. Then he returned his full attention to Henry Tomlinson. "They've stolen too much from us already. No more. No more."

"Is that wise, Prime Minister?"

"Somebody has to demonstrate to them the limits of their power."

"But even so…"

"I did not accept the heavy burden of the premiership from Her Majesty to see my country – what remains of it – subsumed into some latter day new Roman Empire. There will be no Pax Americana while I am Prime Minister. Not here, in these islands, or in *any* of those territories and dominions for which we remain responsible."

Unlike the majority of the Prime Minister's closest political allies Henry Tomlinson had seen this moment coming.

Edward Heath was not really a political politician - if that was not an oxymoron, he did not know what was - he was a far too moral man and, in many ways, a stranger in his own Party.

"I'll meet with the War Cabinet and the Chiefs of Staff on Wednesday. I will put my case before my colleagues," Edward Heath pursed his lips, collected his thoughts, "at the next scheduled meeting of the full Cabinet on Thursday next week. And then we shall proceed."

Henry Tomlinson weighed the moment carefully.

"You have my complete support, Prime Minister."

"You may well be joining me in exile then, Henry!"

The Cabinet Secretary raised an eyebrow.

As had been foreseen in the spring food and fuel stocks were running low; without guaranteed deliveries of American grain and Middle Eastern oil people would starve and freeze in England in the coming months. American grain had been slow arriving, and thus far had arrived in pitifully small parcels. Since the US Congress had stopped all oil exportation from the Americas, oil now had to come all the way around Africa and pass through the Atlantic – the playground of the United States Navy – to reach the United Kingdom. The great American consumer and the voracious maw of its continental industry came first, second and last in Washington.

Viewed from across the Atlantic the White House complacently assumed it was only a matter of time before Edward Heath got used to the idea he was supposed to be acting like an obedient little client.

This hardly seemed like a propitious moment to be tweaking the tiger's tail.

"We've been loyal and obedient allies thus far, Prime Minister," he observed. "Precious little good has it done us."

Edward Heath nodded.

"*Operation Manna* proceeds as before?"

"Yes, Prime Minister. The Americans shadow and occasionally pester our ships but otherwise, all proceeds as planned."

Edward Heath turned away from his most trusted advisor and gazed out across Cheltenham Race Course to where an airstrip long enough to safely operate long-range bombers and transports had been scoured from the landscape. As he watched, a Comet jetliner swooped in to land.

"Why have *they* made no attempt to inhibit Operation Manna?" He asked softly.

Henry Tomlinson could not answer the question.

"Tom Grayson says it is because they don't believe the evidence of their eyes," he offered apologetically. "He thinks they've taken their eye of the ball because we've failed to concentrate our 'naval assets' to protect the five main convoys. Besides, they've mothballed so many of their ships since the war they're not presently really in a position to do much more than 'demonstrate' in the North Atlantic."

The Prime Minister guffawed at this.

He had never liked the notion of dispersing the Royal Navy's 'assets' although he had understood the case for 'committing to holding what we have and supporting our surviving friends'. Moreover, there was the small matter of the crippled industrial infrastructure of the British Isles, the total loss of Chatham Dockyard and the post-war reduction in the capacity of every other naval facility in home waters. The Navy's thin grey wall of fighting ships needed dockyards and dry docks to keep them at sea and if those docks were at Gibraltar, Malta, Sydney, Auckland and Simons Town in the Cape then that was where a proportion of the Fleet would have to be stationed.

If he had learned anything in the last year it was that the sustenance of the Home Islands was not a thing he trusted to anybody else's good will. The Admirals were right, no matter how he hated splitting up much of the fleet into penny packets, the trade routes with the Commonwealth had to be policed.

Operation Manna.

But for Operation Manna his Party, the Armed Services, and *the people* would have had every right to have demanded his head by now.

For the last year he had been presiding over an ongoing domestic humanitarian and governmental crisis that beggared his imagination.

He felt physically sick when he was so foolish as to contemplate the enormity of the disaster that had befallen not just his country, but much of what he had loved of the old world.

He had fought off the old guard in his own Party – who for reasons best known to themselves – had tried hard to reduce the scale and scope of Operation Manna.

He had been ridiculed by idiots seduced by Washington's promises of succour in the immediate aftermath of the October War.

Men whom he had regarded as close personal friends and unshakable political confederates had conspired and plotted to undermine him, openly questioning his claim to the premiership when – with the assistance of his former political enemies – he had gambled everything on the success of the most ambitious and wide-reaching incarnation of Operation Manna.

Now, for the first time in the last year he saw a glimmer of hope at the end of the tunnel.

Against all the odds the worst deprivations and ravages of mass starvation and disease might, conceivably, be kept at bay this winter, albeit only until the spring.

His detractors would never forgive him but then if the last year had taught Edward Heath anything, it was that everything he had once thought he understood, loved and respected about Parliamentary democracy was in this harsh new age a meaningless bagatelle.

The man who headed Her Majesty's United Kingdom Interim Emergency Administration was slowly coming to terms with the new realities. He had never been anything other than a man of deeply held political and religious beliefs; and like any man whose beliefs have been torn apart and remade by tragedies beyond normal human comprehension he had emerged from his test of fire tempered in ways few who knew him well from before the cataclysm could begin to understand.

The Prime Minister viewed Sir Henry Tomlinson with hard, inscrutable eyes for some moments.

"It is not enough just to survive," he sighed, betraying for a moment the bone deep weariness in his soul, "not enough."

The other man nodded but said nothing.

"You and I will hang together if I fail," Edward Heath remarked, a hint of mischief quirking his lips for the most fleeting of moments.

When at around eleven o'clock Henry Tomlinson strolled distractedly – his mind still preoccupied with his conversation with Edward Heath - into his office two doors down the first-floor landing from the Prime Minister's room the Angry Widow was waiting for him.

Until the dreadful, chaotic weeks in the immediate aftermath of the cataclysm the Cabinet Secretary had never met or exchanged words with the attractive, meticulously turned out thirty-eight year old mother of twins who had, by sheer force of personality – and no little intellectual acuity – contrived to turn the Ministry of Supply into a going concern in recent months. Much as he enjoyed their encounters, he, like others, was sometimes left a little drained and rather breathless by their conclusion.

"Airey tells me you boys are up to something?" The Minister of Supply half-asked, half-demanded before Henry Tomlinson had time to get both feet inside his office.

'Airey', was Airey Neave, the forty-seven-year-old war hero who had escaped from Colditz and had assumed the duties of the Angry Widow's chief of staff, protective uncle and smiling assassin. He had won a Military Cross for getting out of Colditz, and added a Distinguished Service Order by 1945. Airey Neave was the man who'd read the indictments to the leading Nazis on trial at Nuremburg.

Neave was a rare thing, a surviving national treasure.

"Does he indeed? I haven't seen the old rascal for the last few days?" Henry Tomlinson countered amiably.

He stepped around the low coffee table on which a tray with a silver tea service had mysteriously appeared during his interview with the Prime Minister.

"Bottlenecks at the West Country depots," his visitor explained. "I was tempted to knock heads together but Airey convinced me that things hadn't reached that stage yet. Do you know that the reason we had to cut the petrol ration last month because those fools at Transport don't understand that they actually have to distribute fuel not just burn it!"

Henry Tomlinson was fully aware of the inadequacies – incompetence and negligence, if one was being honest - of several of her ministerial colleagues.

However, it would have been crass to detail them now.

At least until he discovered to what he owed the pleasure of the lady's visit.

"I thought you'd be in longer with the PM," Margaret Hilda Thatcher observed, settling in one of the two chairs next to the coffee table. She began to busy herself with the tea service. "Shall I be mother?"

The Cabinet Secretary had meetings scheduled, a thousand and one things which required his imprimatur but knew when he met his match. He might be able to urbanely fob off most ministers and their underlings; the Angry Widow was different.

He sat opposite the woman, watched as she poured tea into two cups.

"No milk today, I'm afraid," she apologised, sparkling a smile at the man.

People got carried away with Margaret Thatcher's head girl bossiness, her simmering impatience with process and her persistent questions.

The dazzling smile complicated the picture, if only because it tended to mask the steel behind her blue grey eyes. It was the furnace-tempered steel in the woman that had seized Henry Tomlinson's attention the first time he met her.

"Dairy production is a matter for the Ministry of Agriculture," he chuckled emolliently.

"Quite."

"Darjeeling?" The Cabinet Secretary sighed, sipping his lukewarm brew.

"Airey brought back a couple of small tins from one of his forays last month," his visitor explained with a short flashing smile.

Henry Tomlinson sipped anew.

"It is the small things that one misses, don't you think, Margaret?" He prompted, filling the space she had left him with a moment of self-reflection he would have shared with very few of her ministerial colleagues. Perhaps, that was because he was *not* on first names – or remotely familiar – terms with *any* of *her* senior colleagues. He still did not know how they'd arrived at being on 'Margaret' and 'Henry' terms.

Margaret Thatcher gazed into her tea.

"Yes. But we must always look to the future, Henry."

"Always," he agreed. "Forgive me. I lost my wife many years before the war. Your loss is much more," he hesitated, "immediate. Forgive my thoughtlessness."

The woman waved this aside.

"One in three of our people are gone and the bloody Americans want to stand on the Moon!"

"Funny old world," the Cabinet Secretary grimaced.

"So, what *are* you boys up to?"

"I'm not with you, Margaret?"

"My people have been warned to expect ships from the first convoys from the Southern Hemisphere to dock in the next ten days. Southampton, Weymouth, Plymouth, Bristol, Belfast, Cardiff and Swansea have all been warned. Is it true that Dublin has been warned to receive ships, too?"

Henry Tomlinson nodded.

The Government of the Republic of Ireland, Eire, was not and had never been a friend of the old country but the Prime Minister had been wise to make the gesture of sending several food ships to Dublin. If only to remind the Irish that Great Britain – for all that it was bloodied and mauled – remained a going concern.

"We've been living off scraps for the last year," Margaret Thatcher went on. "We've virtually exhausted our strategic stockpiles; we're living from hand to mouth. I hardly dared to hope Operation Manna would come to fruition. Now we're on the verge of getting through the winter without widespread starvation. My goodness, if we'd relied on the promises of our so-called former *Allies* our people would have starved this winter."

Her voice was quietly, melodically persuasive.

"So, I ask again, what are you boys ups to? And I don't mean trying to bribe the Irish Government to stop its proxies fomenting civil disorder in Ulster!"

"What does Airey think we're up to, Margaret?"

"Airey says next year is election year in the United States." The woman paused to quirk a brief frown at the older man, whom in many ways reminded her of her late husband, and continued: "Until this time next year Kennedy, or whoever wins next November doesn't give a fig about us."

"Airey may be right."

"Presumably, the Prime Minister discussed these and other matter with Her Majesty at Balmoral two weeks ago?"

"I couldn't possibly speculate on the subject of the Sovereign's conversations with her first minister, Margaret."

Henry Tomlinson's visitor put down her cup and saucer and wagged a finger at him. Her peers invariably interpreted this gesture as rudeness and impatience, assuming that they were being taken to task by the 'upstart young thing in a skirt' in their midst.

However, the Cabinet Secretary understood that when Margaret Thatcher bearded him in his own lair she was in earnest and it was in his best interests to listen very closely to what she had to say.

"The Prime Minister is on very thin ice on this one," she informed him.

"Oh, how so?"

"You and I know what probably happened to those American destroyers in the Gulf of Mexico last year, Henry," Margaret Thatcher reminded the Cabinet Secretary, sternly. "We know that the US Navy was acting illegally in international waters. We know that what happened was *their* fault. We know that *they* launched a massive first strike against the Soviets and their Warsaw Pact Allies *without* informing, let alone consulting, *us*. We didn't even know they'd pulled the trigger until their people in East Anglia attempted to order RAF personnel to participate in the launch of dual key Thor missiles from *our* bases in England, Henry. It was a miracle the entire V-Bomber force didn't get wiped out on the ground. As for what happened to our friends in Europe! Goodness, has anybody even attempted to estimate the death toll in Germany and France and Belgium and Holland?"

Henry Tomlinson shook his head.

He said nothing.

"The point is," his visitor declared, sadly, "that *we* know, *we in Government*, what happened but most of *our own* people don't. Most of the people *out there*," her left arm swept towards the tall windows and the grey countryside beyond, "think that we were the victims of a vile Soviet sneak attack and that our gallant *Allies* across the Atlantic did their very best to save us. Which, of course, is exactly the substance of the barefaced lie that the Kennedy administration has been peddling for the last year."

She vented a contemptuous snort.

"In those brief interludes when they're not indulging in posthumous existential public hand-wringing!"

"And now," the man breathed, his tone less than sanguine, "they want to conquer the Moon."

"Exactly! How long do you think it'll take them to blow it up?"

"I think we'll leave that one for our children to worry about, Margaret."

He gathered his courage and looked into her eyes.

And asked *the* question.

The *only* question that mattered: "You'd support a *radical* change of policy, I take it?"

"Yes," she replied without hesitation. "Emphatically, yes. But we must take *our* people with us."

Henry Tomlinson allowed himself time to digest the implications of this caveat before he asked a second, even more important question.

"Would you'd be happy for me to communicate the essence of our tete-a-tete to the Prime Minister, Margaret?"

"Henry," the Angry Widow smiled that smile that came out of nowhere to charm the hardest-hearted of men. "Far be it for me to dictate to the Cabinet Secretary what he may, or may not, communicate to his political master."

Chapter 8

Monday 25th November, 1963
HMS Ark Royal, 193 miles WSW of Ushant

Vice-Admiral Julian Wemyss Christopher placed the dark-visored grey blue flying helmet on the Chart Room table and looked around at his assembled Flag Staff.

None of them had known each other very well when he assumed command of the British Pacific Fleet at Hong Kong last year. In the intervening fourteen months they had made good – with a vengeance - that particular deficiency.

The Fleet Commander implicitly trusted the professional excellence, loyalty and common purpose of *all* the men gathered around him. If the Chart Room table had been circular rather than rectangular a less pragmatic and hard-headed man than Julian Christopher, might have let his thoughts roam into the mists of former eras and contemplated myths and legends which had no part in this savage new epoch. However, he was not Arthur and the men around the Chart Room table were not mythic knights; but they were the steely core of the finest fighting fleet in the World.

The deck under their feet whispered as an aircraft was catapulted into the sky. The carrier was charging into twelve-foot swells, periodically thumping into bigger waves at twenty-seven knots as she launched and recovered her fighters.

"Any developments?" Julian Christopher asked.

The clumsy flying suit accentuated his tall, angular frame. His grey hair was swept back, his dark eyes questing. His voice was quiet and calm, deadly in its precision. He glanced up at the radar repeater on the aft bulkhead.

Ark Royal and her screening destroyers had moved out ahead of the merchant ships.

HMS Belfast and her frigates had fallen in astern of the convoy.

Other escorts flirted with the big ships on either wing of the fleet.

"We think we've got another Yank SSN on our starboard bow, sir. Lowestoft and Rhyl are trying to herd her to the east. We have at least three major surface units to our west, holding steady at about ninety miles on a bearing of approximately two-seven-five true."

"Very good."

The Admiral studied the plot.

Very little that had happened in the last year had challenged his long-standing suspicion and disdain for America and all things

American.

The imbeciles had been buzzing his ships and making mock torpedo runs against his screening anti-submarine frigates for the last eight days. The American's *games* had begun forty-eight hours after the new nuclear-powered leviathan-sized super carrier USS Enterprise had replaced the USS Midway as flagship of what the Admiralty called the 'US Navy's Western Approaches Squadron'.

This 'Squadron' in question – officially designated *CINCLANT Task Force 27* - had been on station, off and on, for the last three months, a formidable battle group comprising at any one time at least one big fleet carrier and up to twenty other smaller warships and support vessels screened by two, sometimes as many as three nuclear attack submarines.

Soon after the October War the US Navy had withdrawn the majority of its major surface units to port and subsequently mothballed over fifty percent of its major surface units. This meant that at any one time a significantly high percentage of the USN's combat ready assets had been *wasted* in maintaining a presence in the eastern waters of the North Atlantic.

Maintaining such a presence was *wasteful* in terms of the wear and tear on ships and their crews – for every ship on station another would be undergoing repair and replenishment, or training and unavailable for deployment elsewhere – and served no strategic or tactical purpose other than to antagonise America's former European allies. Given the drastically reduced size of the US surface fleet it spoke volumes for the muddled geo-political thinking of the Kennedy White House; and worryingly, suggested an abysmal appreciation of the likely reaction of those *former* allies.

Now the idiots were playing *war games*!

Vice-Admiral Julian Christopher did not like leaving his people at a time like this but the needs of the Service came before the needs of any of its servants.

Besides, in Rear Admiral Sam Gresham, flying his Rear-Admiral's flag on HMS Belfast, he could not have wished for a better deputy.

He scanned the faces around him.

"Fleet Standing Order Number Seven remains in force until further notice," he declared with sombre vehemence.

FSO7 specified that if the shadowing USN forces interfered with or in any way impeded the progress of the Fleet or approached within gunnery range of any of the merchant ships, his captains were authorised to use force. Moreover, the level of force that they were authorised to employ was wholly at their discretion short of deploying nuclear weapons.

In a few minutes time he would surrender the nuclear prerogative – *Arc Light* - to Sam Gresham.

He made eye contact with his Flag Captain.

Frank Maltravers had taken command of the Ark when she was docked in Sydney. He had been an unknown quantity to Julian Christopher but since proved himself to be a rock of a man. A former Fleet Air Arm pilot he had been kicking his heels as Naval Attaché in Australia. Like Rear-Admiral Sam Gresham, the Ark's Captain, and Rear Admiral Nigel Grenville, currently commanding the Hermes Battle Group off Cape Trafalgar, he had enthusiastically signed up to turn the peace time Pacific Fleet into the efficient, war fighting machine they had all known it was going to have to become.

It helped that they had been away from home when disaster struck. Or at least, it helped in the sense that they had been able to view events in Europe and America with more distant, if only partially dispassionate eyes unscarred by the nuclear torch. As soon as the scale of the cataclysm became apparent, they had understood that an ally whose actions had led to the indiscriminate mass destruction of both friends and foes alike, was no friend at all. From that conclusion what flowed next was self-evident; a friend so lacking in scruples, and apparently bereft of moral conscience would – sooner or later - as likely consume its friends as its foes unless one stood up to it.

"Look after my Flagship while I'm away, Frank."

"I'll do my best not to run her aground in your absence, sir," the huge, bearded commanding officer of the Ark Royal chuckled.

Julian Christopher half-smiled.

"Until we meet again, gentlemen," he saluted, and the room returned his salute. "Good hunting!"

Emerging onto the windswept flight deck of the carrier the deck crew ushered Christopher to the awaiting 893 Squadron Sea Vixens.

He clambered, lithely for his advancing years, up the ladder and eased himself into the navigator's empty seat of the leading fighter. Willing hands strapped him in, adjusted the connection to his helmet, and checked his oxygen mask was correctly in place and working. There was a light tap on his helmet, a burst of static over the intercom.

"Ready to go, sir?" The pilot inquired.

Julian Christopher hit the mask switch. "Yes, carry on."

There was another light tap on his helmet, he looked up and gave the yellow jacketed crewman a thumbs up signal. The long, polished Perspex cockpit swung down over him and locked into place.

The Sea Vixen was moving, its folded wings swinging down to the horizontal. The locking mechanisms clicked through the whole airframe, or so it seemed. The fighter jerked as the starboard catapult head dragged it forward. The twenty-ton interceptor rocked on its landing gear, reverberating with the idling fury of is twin Rolls-Royce Avon Mk 208 turbojets. Glancing across to his left Christopher could just make out the twin-boom tail of his fighter's wingman dragging onto the port catapult.

Suddenly the Avons cycled up, roaring. The nose of the fighter crouched down like a sprinter setting in his blocks before a sprint.

Christopher took a deep breath.

The next second he was pressed back into his seat as if a giant's foot was resting on his chest. He glimpsed the grey deck race past, and then there were only the storm-tossed waters of the Bay of Biscay under the wings and the Sea Vixen was climbing steeply like a bat out of Hell. He tried to look over his shoulder to find Ark Royal, all he saw was an empty ocean.

"Pilot to passenger, are you comfortable, sir?"

"Yes, thank you."

"We're heading up to angels three-five for a look around before we turn for our destination, sir. Out."

Christopher sat back to enjoy the flight.

He had sat in the observer's seat of a Swordfish once; that was over twenty years ago, in the Mediterranean. The *Stringbag* had rolled and tottered down the deck of the old Illustrious so slowly that he had been convinced the aircraft would fall straight over the bow into the sea. But after a while it had unhurriedly floated into the air and very slowly, surely drawn ahead of the carrier. They had arrived at Malta after dark in the middle of an air raid, landed by the glow of the distant searchlights and the flash of bombs in the night. Compared to a Swordfish a de Havilland Sea Vixen was like something out of a Buck Rogers or a Flash Gordon cartoon. Twenty years ago, he had thought trundling off the Illustrious at sixty miles an hour was the height of scientific military technology and now here he was riding six miles high in a chariot of the gods.

He had wondered how he would feel about going home. The country he left fifteen months ago to assume command of the British Pacific Fleet at Hong Kong no longer existed. The war had come and gone so fast that few of his ships had even had time to raise steam, let alone contemplate joining the fight. In the days after the war he had organised his ships into three battle groups based around his carriers; Ark Royal, Hermes and Ocean and sailed north into the Sea of Japan where the US 7th Fleet was known to be assisting the civilian authorities deal with the refugees from the strikes on the Sapporo and Sendai areas. The Hermes Battle Group had proceeded as far north as the Inland Sea before the Americans made it abundantly – and rather crassly - clear they did not want the Royal Navy trespassing in *its waters*. When the 7th Fleet had refused an offer to co-ordinate fleet supply train activities, Christopher, in the absence of orders from Fleet Command in the United Kingdom had reluctantly ordered his ships to sail for Australia.

It was in Australia that Julian Christopher had learned the true dimensions of the cataclysm wrought across huge swaths of the Northern Hemisphere, and first realised that potentially his ships were all that stood between his country and despair. He had drawn up the first planning draft of what later became Operation Manna in Sydney on Christmas Eve last year. By then it was obvious that Britain's closest military ally regarded the Pacific as an American ocean. Moreover, by then for unspecified reasons of 'continental security' the Panama Canal had been unilaterally closed to all 'armed vessels' other than US Navy warships. The world was in shock, the nuclear genie was out of the bottle and the accepted rules of the game of international realpolitik no longer applied. In the United Kingdom nobody had the time or the inclination to think beyond the immediate challenge of surviving the brutal winter clamping down over Northern Europe as if it was the frigid harbinger of a new ice age.

The long range strategic maritime trade routes of the world had been fractured and the European wealth that had created and sustained those now fractured trade routes was lost. Worse, the old balance of power had been eliminated. Everywhere insurgency and civil war threatened. India and Pakistan's border wars had reignited, parts of South East Asia were on fire, in South America Chile and the Argentine teetered on the edge of war. The story was the same from Africa to the Middle East to the Manchurian hinterland. The old world order was broken and nobody knew how much more blood would be spilled before order was restored. Or, indeed if *order* might ever be restored.

Operation Manna would not have been possible without the wholehearted backing of the Australian and New Zealand governments, neither of whom wanted to find themselves friendless upon the southern extremities of the new American maritime dominion.

To Julian Christopher the geopolitical nightmare in which the old country – what was left of it – found itself was simply expressed; until such time as the Royal Navy retained mastery of the Mediterranean and reopened its trade routes to what had been the Empire, and was now more or less 'the Commonwealth', its survival depended almost entirely on reopening and sustaining its trans Australasian and South Atlantic sinews of commerce. In the long term a failure to re-establish the mastery of the Mediterranean or to re-establish both two key oceanic supply lines would, literally, be the death of *his* country.

The immediate priority was to ensure that in the United Kingdom as many people as possible survived this coming winter. Afterwards, he would turn his mind to the Mediterranean hoping in the meantime that no new calamity befell British arms in those most problematic of waters.

He squinted at the new blips on the radar screen by his right hand.

"Passenger to Pilot. What am I seeing on my screen?"

"That will be the Enterprise Battle Group's CAP, sir. Coming up to investigate us, sir. ETA within visual range in about three minutes."

"Thank you. Out."

The USN had pulled out of Holy Loch immediately after the cataclysm and probably regretted it ever since. The latest intelligence was that CINCLANT was looking for forward bases in Ireland or the French Biscay ports. Officially, the Irish government had not made up its mind yet. The French, to their credit, had warned that any American vessel approaching their shores would be fired upon. No formal request for the re-establishment of base facilities had been placed before the United Kingdom Interim Emergency Administration headed by Prime Minister Edward Heath. In the present climate the existence of a powerful US Navy battle group in the Western Approaches, almost but not quite barring the path of the first Operation Manna convoy was an incredibly clumsy, ill-considered provocation. A crass reminder to its old 'special ally' that it was Washington that was calling the shots.

Hubris was the downfall of every great empire.

Hubris was what blinded great men to reality.

The aircraft and the nuclear attack submarines of the Enterprise Battle Group were playing *war games* but the British Pacific Fleet was not *playing games* with anyone. It was odd that having *committed* the unthinkable – unleashing thermonuclear Hell across the northern hemisphere – the Americans seemed incapable of actually *thinking* the unthinkable. That his former allies complacently assumed that the survivors would meekly go back to 'business as normal' in the aftermath seemed, to Julian Christopher, so surreal that it defied belief. Likewise, he could hardly imagine how perturbed the US Navy would be to discover that the primary objective of the *Atlantic War Plan* developed by Christopher's staff – and currently before the Prime

Minister - assumed that the 'forwardly deployed battle group' of CINCLANT Command would be the first target of the United Kingdom Defence Forces in any future war. Although the Enterprise Battle Group was, on paper, more than a match for the leading squadrons of Christopher's fragmented Pacific Fleet, he had never been a man who placed much faith in 'paper facts'.

Christopher had been a student of American tactical and strategic naval doctrine for two decades. The USN had ended the 1945 war with more ships than it had men to man them and successive US administrations had opted to save money by putting new technology into old hulls instead of building new ships from the keel up. The Americans had, quite reasonably, decided that its preponderance of naval air power and its overwhelming superiority in nuclear submarines spelled 'victory' in any conceivable future conflict. However, this was a policy designed for the world in which it had been made; not the new post October War world. In the old world the US Navy had enjoyed a massive technological and firepower advantage over any likely foe and the next most capable navy on Earth, the Royal Navy, was on its side. While the US Navy remained – on paper – invincible, other than in its undersea fleet its margin of superiority over the Royal Navy had been hugely reduced in the last year. Moreover, the Atlantic War Plan did not envisage a confrontation with the USN anywhere other than in British waters beneath an umbrella of land-based RAF aircraft.

Put bluntly, any plan which proposed engaging the USN in deep water beyond the effective reach of one's own air cover amounted to a suicide note. This was why if it came to it the Atlantic War Plan foresaw drawing a single battle group – like that based around the USS Enterprise – relatively close to shore and hitting it with everything including the kitchen sink short of nuclear weapons. While the Enterprise Battle group operated so close to the British Isles it remained inherently vulnerable to a land-based air attack supported by as many as a dozen modern advanced non-nuclear-powered submarines based at Plymouth.

The new Oberon and Porpoise class diesel-electric submarines were *not* the equal of nuclear-powered hunter killer boats that could sail submerged around the globe; but they were fast, agile and quiet and they could operate submerged for very long periods. These boats were so highly prized within the Navy that ever since the cataclysm they had been held back, their crews drilled to the highest possible pitch of efficiency and combat readiness; the nation's last resort, its undersea fleet in being. If the United States Navy had had any real appreciation of the capability of these 'diesel-electric boats' the Enterprise Battle Group would have never come within a thousand miles of the Western Approaches. A dozen Oberons and Porpoises operating together would be a submarine wolf pack from Hell!

"Pilot to passenger. We have company on our starboard side, sir. Two F4s coming in to eyeball us."

"I see them." The McDonnell Douglas Phantoms were big elegant, business-like beasts. Two great white sharks of the sky in close formation, rising to meet the two Sea Vixens.

"These chaps are just trying to be friendly, sir." The Pilot said quickly. "They've switched off their radars and they're broadcasting old-fashioned NATO IFF codes like they're going out of fashion."

"What's our combat status?"

"Hot and ready, sir."

"Very good."

The leading Phantom drifted in until it was level with Julian Christopher's Sea Vixen, and little more than thirty yards away, wingtip to wingtip. The pilot raised his left hand, waved. Appeared to salute. Before he could stop himself, Julian Christopher had returned the gesture. The Phantoms flew in company for about thirty seconds, waggled their wings and broke away in a long, slow, shallow turn to the south west. There had been talk of buying Phantoms for the Navy's proposed new fleet carriers but somehow, Christopher didn't think that was going to happen now.

"Passenger to Pilot. They don't think we pose any danger to them, do they? Over."

"No, sir," the man in the front seat confessed cheerfully. "They can see us coming before we know they're there and they can fly twice as fast as us. Oh, they've got two or three times our combat endurance, too. And much better missiles, probably, we think. Over."

"So, we can't fight them?" Julian Christopher asked, brazenly ignoring intercom protocol in the way that only Fleet Commanders could ignore it.

"I wouldn't say that, sir. Just not at long range. Now, if we can get into a dogfight, that's a different game! Any time you give us the go ahead, sir! Over."

"Thank you. I didn't doubt it for a minute. Out."

Chapter 9

Tuesday 26th November 1963
Situation Room, Government House, Cheltenham

Sir Henry Tomlinson stepped ahead of the Prime Minister to open the door. He let his political master precede him into the Situation Room and followed him inside, pausing to shut the door behind him.

Government House had been the country pile of a now dead newspaper mogul whose papers had consistently demanded a 'harder line against the Soviet juggernaut'.

He at least had had his last – dying as it turned out - wish come true.

The building was a sprawling, neo-classical abomination of a mock-Tudor mansion that had sat in several hundred acres of sculpted Gloucestershire landscape framed by the Chiltern Hills on the flood plain of the River Chelt, from which the nearest town, Cheltenham some four miles away had taken its name.

The Ministry of Supply had requisitioned the estate and its attached farms in January. Urgent work had been necessary to secure the immediate perimeter but Grenville House – the previous owner had thought of himself as every inch a new Elizabethan – had become the de facto seat of the United Kingdom Interim Emergency Administration on 1st March 1963.

Excluding the areas of the country too devastated to have yet been surveyed, the UKIEA's writ ran in all the surviving major centres of population and in perhaps eighty to ninety percent of the countryside. Some regions were effectively still under martial law, mostly parts of Ulster and the borderlands with the wasteland of the Greater London area, the South East, East Anglia and Merseyside. Elsewhere, some measure of civil order had been restored. In the territory controlled by the UKIEA strict rationing was in force and had thus far kept the general population as fed and as healthy as possible in the post-war circumstances. It was a sad truth that medical services, especially the efficacy of disease control measures and the re-establishment of basic public sanitation, had been greatly facilitated by the unavoidable 'die off' during last winter and the early spring of the most seriously injured, the old, the very youngest, and practically everybody who had had serious pre-existing health problems before the cataclysm.

Nobody in Edward Heath's administration walked through the doors of Government House with anything other than a very, very heavy heart. They were living through terrible times and they owed it to the survivors, and to the memory of the dead millions to do their best for their country.

There was a loud scraping of chairs on the polished oaken floor.

"Good morning," the Prime Minister boomed in the voice he once customarily reserved for those days when he stood at the helm of his racing yacht at Cowes, or for when he was conducting a choir or an orchestra.

Since last year he had had no opportunity to indulge either of his life's passions - music or yachting - outside of politics. Heavy sat the cloak of leadership but cometh the hour, cometh the man. It did not matter that but for the random, wholesale murder of the twenty or more men ahead of him in the succession to the leadership of the Conservative and Unionist Party, that he would never have risen to lead his people in such a time of trial. He had learned as a young man that life was what one made of it and fate was a cruel mistress; having joined the Army as a private soldier in 1940, and risen to Lieutenant-Colonel by its end.

In the intervening five years he had led men in battle, witnessed the true cost of war in the trail of shattered bodies, hopes and lives it left in its wake.

The experience had steeled him for the challenges that lay ahead. Last November in the week after Lucifer's hammer had fallen the survivors had demanded a figurehead around whom they might cluster about for safety, and he had been it. He had seized the moment with both hands.

Henry Tomlinson followed the Prime Minister down the side of the long, rectangular table in the middle of what had once been the Machiavellian newspaper robber baron's banqueting hall. The Prime Minister took the middle chair on the long side of the table with the imposing brick hearth at his back and waved for his colleagues to sit down. The Cabinet Secretary drew up a chair to his master's right hand, opened his big notebook and looked up, his eye roving around the faces of the members of Edward Heath's War Cabinet. The three service chiefs sat directly across the table from the Prime Minister, while the political members of the group flanked him.

Tom Harding-Grayson had diplomatically withdrawn to the left-hand end of the Cabinet Table, where he too, like Henry Tomlinson, had opened a large, well-thumbed hardback notebook.

"Thank you all for attending this meeting at such short notice," Edward Heath said, bringing the conference to order.

He turned to his right, looking beyond his Cabinet Secretary to where Alexander Frederick Douglas-Home, Earl of Home had settled in a cloud of regal dignity. His would be a calm, detached voice of reason no matter how sorely today's discussion tested his personal equilibrium. Douglas-Home had been the only other viable candidate for Prime Minister in the week after the cataclysm fell. He had been too slow recovering from the shock of the catastrophe – in fact he had never really recovered – and Edward Heath had snatched up the reins of power.

"Particularly you, Alec," a respectful nod to the elder statesman, "and to you, Jim," he added, looking to his left where a brooding man shrugged acknowledgement, "as you both had the farthest to travel."

"I serve at your pleasure, Prime Minister," the other man replied, a flicker of mischief in his eyes for they both knew he had initially owed his elevated place in this august company only to the absolute necessity of maintaining the fiction of political unity to the outside world.

Edward Heath guffawed.

He still had not decided if he actually liked the Right Honourable Leonard James Callaghan, the fifty-one-year-old Member of Parliament for the constituency of Cardiff South East, but he respected him more with every week that passed.

He had offered the rump of the Labour Party – Her Majesty's Loyal Opposition – the Ministry of Defence to reassure those who tacitly assumed he planned to be a war monger bent on revenge. He had subsequently also asked Jim Callaghan to speak for Wales in Cabinet because he had come to trust his feel for the mood of *his* people.

The Prime Minister directed his gaze towards the only woman in the room.

"I asked Margaret to join us because, frankly, everything we do, and everything we are going to talk about today revolves around supply, and Margaret is achieving the impossible at the moment."

"You are too kind, Prime Minister," the Angry Widow protested, leaning forward in her chair to flash her increasingly famous smile at her leader. "One is simply doing the best one can in a *difficult* situation."

Edward Heath guffawed, again.

He was distracted momentarily by the oddity of Margaret Hilda Thatcher electing to seat herself to Jim Callaghan's left, rather than to Alec Douglas-Home's right.

Most curious...

Jim Callaghan cleared his throat.

"Prime Minister," he began, lugubriously, "the Chiefs of Staff," a look at the three men in uniform across the table, "take the view that given that the first item on the agenda is Operation Manna that, with your permission Vice-Admiral Christopher should join us directly."

Edward Heath sobered.

He had taken it as read that the recently returned Commander of the British Pacific Fleet would attend the War Cabinet and could not for the life of him comprehend why the man was not already in the room.

Despite his own extensive military experience, he sometimes found the workings of the minds of senior officers baffling.

He masked his irritation.

"I agree. Would you ask him to join us please?"

The stocky, pugnacious man sitting at Alec Douglas-Home's right elbow grunted his impatience. Iain Norman Macleod, the Chairman of the Conservative and Unionist Party and Minister without Portfolio in the United Kingdom Interim Emergency Administration stirred impatiently. Edward Heath could never tell whether his colleague's restlessness was from the pain of an old war wound, or the tedious first outward manifestation of some new intellectual or doctrinal outpouring.

"Yes, Iain?" He inquired, urbanely.

"Does Supply get a vote in our deliberations today, Prime Minister?"

Edward Heath understood that Macleod's question was political, not tactical. Did the Angry Widow's inclusion at the top table infer that a permanent promotion was in the offing? Or was it merely an opportunistic manoeuvre to keep her in line?

"The War Cabinet's role is to inform my future submissions to the full Cabinet, Iain. Margaret will have her right to vote at that forum. As will *all* our colleagues at the *next* scheduled meeting of the full Cabinet."

Edward Heath's patience was forced.

It was almost as if until that moment he had not really accepted the enormity of the actions he had been contemplating the last few weeks. Today marked a jumping off point on a road upon which if he hesitated, or took a single ill-considered step all would be lost. He was a man used to keeping his own counsel, a very private man for somebody who had adopted a career in politics, and his sense of personal honour and duty was momentarily suffocating as the silence around him deepened when Vice-Admiral Julian Wemyss Christopher was ushered into the Situation Room.

The newcomer was immaculate in his freshly pressed uniform, his left breast laden with medal and campaign ribbons. He came to attention, removed his heavily gold braided cap and looked to the Prime Minister.

"C-in-C Pacific Fleet reporting as ordered. Sir!"

Edward Heath appraised Julian Christopher.

There was a teak hardness in the tall, lean frame of the veteran of the Malta Convoys, the Battle of the Atlantic and the Korean War. His hair was completely silvery grey, his face deeply tanned, lined. The eyes were like blue diamonds, unforgiving. Everybody told him that this man was the best fighting Admiral in the Royal Navy and that the men of the Pacific Fleet were devoted to him. The man had made such an impression on the Americans that they had asked – well, demanded actually - his removal from his command.

They did not like his 'attitude'.

The Prime Minister had had Alec Douglas Home stall, asked him to try to convey to their *Allies* that the removal of a British commander at sea simply was not done and that matters would be best resolved on Admiral Christopher's return to the United Kingdom.

The Americans tended to believe what they wanted to believe and this had kept them happy thus far.

The Prime Minister rose from his seat, smiling broadly.

"Welcome home, Admiral Christopher." He indicated the vacant chair next to the First Sea Lord. "We won't stand on ceremony this morning. Take a pew, we're all eager to hear the latest news of Operation Manna."

"Elements of the Ark Royal Battle Group will escort the first Operation Manna convoy into *British* waters within the next forty-eight hours, sir," Vice-Admiral Julian Wemyss Christopher reported to the Prime Minister. "Once the first *parcels* have been delivered to UK ports the Ark Royal Battle Group will replenish and return to meet the second convoy. At that time the returning ships of the Pacific Fleet most in need of repair and dockyard time will be replaced with fresh units from Channel Command. This pre-planned redeployment received the green light seventy-two hours ago. Likewise, fixed wing land-based air assets have stepped up patrol activity over the Western Approaches and Biscay. All available submarines, excluding HMS Dreadnought have been stationed so as to screen the western flank of the Hermes Battle Group which is currently moving into position one hundred miles west of the second convoy. HMS Dreadnought has been tasked to shadow the Enterprise Battle Group for several days."

Edward Heath listened impassively.

He had never believed that leaving the fate of the British people in the hands of the Kennedy Administration was commensurate with either common sense, or, even had he taken the Americans at their word, in any way prudent.

He would *never* take *anything* on trust from *any* American President after the events of the 27th, 28th and 29th October 1962.

That spring he had faced a very simple dilemma.

If he did nothing then the British people would starve and freeze to death in their untold millions in the coming winter.

If he placed his trust in the men who had wrecked half the northern hemisphere, aid and succour *might* be forthcoming and the worst of the travail in the coming winter *might* be significantly ameliorated, *or not,* depending upon how things panned out in Washington.

Or he could gamble *everything* on one last, literally do or die, appeal to the Old Country's real friends and allies in those numerous former dominions where it was not yet *de rigor* to spit on the Union Jack.

He had not hesitated; and chosen the latter do or die option.

It was both the honourable and the pragmatic thing to do.

Had his senior colleagues in Government or in the military rejected his wish he would have resigned and probably had a short, final conversation with his old service revolver.

Then as now there would have been no shortage of former friends and political confederates who would gladly have handed him the ammunition.

Edward Heath completely understood that Operation Manna would have remained no more than a gesture, one last grand hurrah of the lost Empire but for the grey-haired hawk browed, patrician Vice-Admiral sitting across the table from him.

The task had been ludicrously ambitious, almost vainglorious, but Julian Christopher had turned an optimistic, vague aspiration into a monumental endeavour utilising every man, ship and aircraft at his command. He had excluded the United States Navy from huge tracts of the Pacific that it tacitly assumed were *American Seas,* collected every British and Dominion registered vessel on those seas, scoured the whole Southern Ocean for merchantmen.

Once the word had gone out ships began appearing off Australian and New Zealand ports until harbours were jammed with shipping.

Then Christopher had flown to Hong Kong, Singapore, to India and the Persian Gulf. First priority had been tankers, then refrigeration ships, grain carriers. Later, general purpose cargo vessels and liners.

The United Kingdom had gold, and a plethora of overseas assets to trade abroad in those countries that had not already appropriated them or illicitly transferred them into the grasping hands of their American proxies.

But mostly, what the United Kingdom still had was people, skills, real military clout east of Suez, and a determination to guarantee the continuation of trade in the Indian Ocean and the South Pacific and Atlantic.

The Americans had stood back and watched, not really understanding what was going on, misinterpreting consolidation for hoarding and retrenchment, a sure sign that the Commonwealth was putting a wall about itself. Finally, when the true purpose and magnitude of Operation Manna belatedly became apparent, they simply did not believe their eyes.

"There have been no *incidents*?"

Margaret Thatcher's demanding soprano sang out from diagonally opposite the stern-faced admiral.

"No, Ma'am," Christopher informed her. "None worthy of the mention."

"You intrigue me, Admiral," the Angry Widow smiled a smile to melt the heart of an ogre.

Julian Christopher was no ogre except to his US Navy counterparts.

"Oh, the Yanks buzz our pickets from time to time," he conceded with a throwing away gesture of his right hand. "They like to let us know they're around. My own flight from the Ark Royal was intercepted by two Phantoms off the Enterprise. Just a social call."

"A social call?"

If Julian Christopher noticed, or cared, that several of the men in the room were quickly wearying of what they interpreted as the Minister of Supply's attempt to hijack the briefing, he betrayed no hint of it. To the contrary, his entire attention was now focused on the woman whom he had never met until he walked into the room a few minutes ago.

"We try to make sure we don't come upon each other unawares, Ma'am," he half-smiled like a wolf licking its lips before the hunt. "We advertise our presence to each other in essentially benign ways. We switch off our targeting radars, for example. We broadcast our IFF – indication friend or foe – as *loudly* as possible. We don't creep up on each other. Not ever. In military terms we tend to approach each other with our rifles slung over our shoulders and with open hands. By the same token my Fleet operates under well-publicised rules of engagement."

"Fascinating. Tell me more, Admiral?"

Iain Macleod groaned out aloud.

Alec Douglas-Home chuckled, breaking from his perennial grim-faced brooding.

Tom Harding-Grayson exchanged thoughtful looks with Henry Tomlinson.

The three Chiefs of Staff sat like poker-faced brass monkeys while the Minister of Defence, James Callaghan, softly drummed the fingers of his left hand on the table.

The Prime Minister seemed lost in his thoughts.

"The Yanks know that my Captains are authorised to use force if their ships are threatened, or any vessel under their protection is threatened by *any* action by *any* third party. The USN is also aware that my Captains are authorised to take pre-emptive *action* if they believe that *any* third party is preparing to take *any* action which may endanger *any* vessel of aircraft in the Fleet."

Iain Macleod cleared his throat.

"That sounds like an invitation for somebody to start another bloody shooting war?"

Julian Christopher broke eye contact with Margaret Thatcher with what might, in other circumstances, have been reluctance and mild irritation.

He set his sights on the Chairman of the Conservative and Unionist Party of the United Kingdom and Northern Ireland.

"With respect, sir," he observed coolly, "we are still in the shooting war that commenced in October 1962. It's just that a lot of people who ought to know better don't recognise the fact."

The remark whipped across the table like the crack of a rifle.

The scowling Minister without Portfolio winced, recoiled and opened his mouth to deliver an outraged rebuttal that died on his lips as he met the unyielding stone-cold eyes of his assailant.

"The Americans are *not* our friends, sir," Julian Christopher said in a voice that had the calculating, razor-sharp edge of a scalpel. "They like to tell themselves that they are but they're no more our friends than the Romans were two thousand years ago, or the Normans were nine hundred years ago. History is written by the victors, sir. If we are not very, very careful, we here in these islands will be remembered as a footnote in the history of the glorious Pax Americana."

"That would never do!" Declared Margaret Thatcher with a clipped soprano vehemence that briefly fixed the attention of the room upon her.

She seemed to be sitting a little apart from all the others. Her hands were clasped before her on the table, and she sat unmoving with not so much as a single hair out of place. Her blue jacket and cream blouse were bright, new in ways that the dowdiness of her male colleagues and the careworn uniforms of the military men emphasised. She was at once the youngest person in the room – she and nine years younger than the Prime Minister – and indisputably the most vibrant, determined, and confident of them all.

Edward Heath had recognised the magnetism.

He had known Margaret Thatcher for many years. They had never been close and would never be friends but in these strange times unlikely alliances formed. He had been unsympathetic to her attempts to find a safe constituency during his time as Chief Whip. Frankly, he found her pushy and irritating, exactly the sort of rolling stone the Party did not need post-Suez.

Nevertheless, whenever he managed to set aside the woman's stridency and her potential for spreading chaos in the soporific ranks of the Parliamentary Party, she had stood out like a sore thumb on the grey, complacent back benches.

He had been Chief Whip for four years before being appointed as Minister for Labour in October 1959, and then Lord Privy Seal the following year. The Chief Whip's job in Harold MacMillan's Government was not one of bullying the rank and file into line; it was to know the mind of the Party and to *know* everything about its disparate constituent parts.

So even when he had been cold-shouldering Margaret Thatcher's best endeavours to find a safe seat in the House of Commons, he had been careful to learn everything he could learn about the woman.

By the time she won the Finchley seat in 1959 a few days short of her thirty-fourth birthday she was already a trained chemist and a qualified barrister. At some stage she had found time to marry a millionaire businessman and to give birth to twins, all the while doggedly trying to get into Parliament.

And now she was the undoubted rising star – the only one, there were no others – of his ramshackle, hard-pressed and most likely, within weeks or at most months, doomed administration.

"Exactly," he rumbled, deliberately breaking the strangle hold the Angry Widow and the Fighting Admiral had begun to exert on *his* War Cabinet. "That would never do!"

Margaret Thatcher nodded her satisfied concurrence and after bathing Vice-Admiral Julian Wemyss Christopher in the warmth of one last dazzling smile, she graciously surrendered the floor.

The Prime Minister nodded.

"Is it your view," he posed to the three Chiefs of Staff sitting opposite him, "that Operation Manna has reached a point where we can confidently expect it to proceed to a successful conclusion, gentlemen?"

Admiral Sir John David Luce, First Sea Lord and Chief of the Naval Staff, cleared his throat and looked Edward Heath in the eye.

"Yes, sir," he said. He was not a man to whom prevarication came naturally. He had been pencilled in for the role he currently held before his predecessor and his handful of superiors in the Senior Service had been blown away in the cataclysm.

When the Prime Minister raised an eyebrow, Sir David Luce – who spoke for his Army and Air Force colleagues as Chief of the Defence Staff - quirked a fleeting smile and elaborated.

"The Americans knew what we were up to months ago but I don't think they believed what they were seeing. Besides, they were so preoccupied with what they perceived as Julian's, forgive me, Vice-Admiral Christopher's, high-handedness and lack of co-operation with the United States Navy in the Pacific and the Indian Oceans, that at one stage they weakened their forces in the North Atlantic by sending a second carrier battle group to the Pacific. That ill-advised strategic rebalancing and the fact they've put so many units into mothballs – to take advantage of some kind of bizarre 'peace dividend', it seems - implies that, even if they ever seriously considered it, they are in no position to interdict Operation Manna. Short of war, that is, sir."

"Yes, well," interjected Air Marshall Sir Samuel Charles Elworthy, Chief of the Air Staff, "if we'd co-ordinated Operation Manna with the US Navy we'd probably have had a lot less bother assembling the necessary merchant shipping." He held up a hand, partly in apology. "Not my place to meddle, I know, David. It just seems to me that we've burned an awful lot of bridges with the Americans over this thing."

The First Sea Lord nodded thoughtfully.

Edward Heath waited and then when the Chiefs of Staff remained silent, he stepped back into the fray.

"I would go to war tomorrow if the choice was between going to war and watching *our* people to starve this winter."

The Chief of the Air Staff gave the Prime Minister a hard look.

"As would I, sir," he retorted with immense dignity.

"We are all patriots around this table," Edward Heath said brusquely. "We all serve at Her Majesty's pleasure. We are all the custodians of the world's oldest surviving democracy. Among ourselves," he let the thought hang, suspended in the ether, "we have a duty to speak freely, one to another, for the good of our country. What happened in October last year would not have happened, could not have happened, if honest men," he glanced to Margaret Thatcher, pursed his lips in self-deprecation, "and women, had tried harder to understand each other better. We shall not repeat that mistake. Around this table we *shall* speak our minds. One's personal views may not carry the day, but those views will always be listened to and respected by *me while I hold the Premiership*." He nodded to the Chief of the Air Staff.

"Thank you, sir."

The Prime Minister turned to Margaret Thatcher.

"How do things look from Supply, Margaret?"

"Things are in hand, Prime Minister."

She motioned to General Sir Richard Amyatt Hull, who had been Chief of the Imperial General Staff at the time of the cataclysm but since been re-designated Chief of Staff of the Army, a title that more accurately described his remit.

"As we speak General Hull's boys are moving into place to secure vital transportation and dock hubs. I have issued General Hull with authority under the War Emergency Act to use whatever force is required to secure and safeguard supplies at docks and in transit. The main strategic depots are already secured and fully ready to receive replenishment."

Edward Heath sighed.

In the mayhem after the October War – he hated people referring to the abomination as 'the cataclysm' – Soviet agents had murdered at will, attempted to disrupt surviving communications, bombed refineries and set fire to irreplaceable fuel stocks. Inevitably, many of those responsible for these outrages would resurface again in the coming weeks.

The evil of war was without end.

"Looters will be shot on sight," General Sir Richard Amyatt Hull said with a transparently heavy heart.

Such policies went against the grain, no matter what the situation.

"*Anybody* who interferes with the free movement of strategic supplies will be detained by the Internal Security Division."

His lips twisted in distaste at the mention of the loathed appendage to *his* Army.

"I admit that there has been some disquiet in the Service but the British Army will do its duty, sir."

"These are harsh times," the Prime Minister agreed.

Chapter 10

Wednesday 27th November 1963
HMS Talavera, Portland Harbour

The Royal Fleet Auxiliary Sycamore had come alongside shortly after dawn. Despite her fresh coat of grey paint and a superficial attempt to chip off the worst rust patches on her superstructure, the RFA Sycamore still looked exactly what she was: a thirty-year-old collier long overdue for the scrap yard. In fact, she had actually been recovered from a scrap yard; and hastily crewed by merchant seaman who had found themselves, overnight, in the Royal Navy.

Peter Christopher joined Commander Hugo Montgommery, the destroyer's executive officer at the bridge rail to observe the activity on the gun deck immediately below. Big wooden pallets were swinging down into Sycamore's after hold and coming up loaded with crates containing four unfused reloads for Talavera's 4.5-inch Mark III main battery. As each crate was manhandled to the deck the eighty plus pound, four feet long 'fixed' rounds were fed down scuttles to the magazines below the water line. It was hard, warm work on a frigid November morning when the rain drizzled constantly and now and then, squalled hard from the south west.

The Executive Officer kept glancing at the Sycamore as if he was afraid her rust would somehow infect his ship. High above their heads the four-ton double bedstead of the Type 965 airborne early warning radar turned. Talavera had been swinging around her anchors in harbour for nearly three months and the Captain wanted everybody on the ball. Forget about peacetime sea keeping duties. They had four hours to ammunition the ship and they had already used up two of them. Hugo Montgommery had sent work parties over to the Sycamore to speed the process.

Many of the draft who had come on board yesterday in Portsmouth were standing around idly because there had been no time to do more than allot them to their new messes before Talavera sailed. First, they were scheduled to sail on Friday morning, then on Tuesday afternoon, suddenly the order had come to complete bunkering and to rendezvous with RFA Sycamore at Portland. The Captain was still being coy about Talavera's mission once it cleared Portland.

"Guns says our rusty friend," Hugo Montgommery scowled at the ancient merchantman's rusty flanks constantly threatening to rub up against his ship's immaculate plates, "only brought us three Sea Cat reloads?"

"Still in the factory shipping boxes, sir."

Peter Christopher had been astonished to discover there were *any* Sea Cat reloads. The rule of thumb was that the more complex the weapon system, the more dire the ongoing re-supply situation was likely to be after the year-old catastrophic dislocation of the entire British industrial base. New production missiles and torpedoes, any kind of sophisticated modern electronics spares were like gold dust whereas World War II technology like reloads for the main battery, or shells for the 20-millimetre Oerlikon cannons and ammunition for small arms were plentiful. Oddly, Sycamore had also brought out more Squid rounds for the stern mounted mortar than the destroyer had magazine and ready locker space to accommodate.

"Sorry, Peter," the Executive Officer growled, turning away from the rail. "What was it you were saying about the new draft?"

"We sailed before we got their papers, sir."

Hugo Montgommery swore. Fifty percent of his attention was still riveted on the ship alongside grinding against the destroyer's rubber, cork and hemp fenders.

"The Chief and the Paymaster are trying to sort out the ship's records, but..." Peter shrugged. "Most of them are so green or so stupid they didn't even demand movement papers before they shipped out of the depot. The only proof we've got that any of them are who they say they are is their dog tags and several of them have lost those."

Hugo Montgommery swung around, momentarily forgetting the slow gyrations of the two ships' hulls in the chop behind the Portland breakwaters.

"They sent us fucking deserters and defaulters?"

The younger man had not planned to put it quite that bluntly but he nodded, nonetheless.

"I'd say that what we've got is a draft straight out of the defaulters' barracks at Lee-on-Solent, sir."

"Marvellous! And now the useless beggars are standing on *my* deck picking their fucking noses!" The older man shook his head like a terrier emerging from a rabbit sett. "Does the Captain know yet?"

"Er, I thought you'd like to break the news to him, sir."

Hugo Montgommery cursed again.

"You have the watch, Peter," he decided, straightening to his full height and checking his cap was square on his cropped head.

"I have the watch, sir."

Peter Christopher watched the Executive Officer stalk off the bridge in high dudgeon. He gazed down at the laboured activity on the fo'c'sle, then he did a quick methodical turn around the open bridge, taking a long hard look aft to identify who was on deck and what was going on, and checking critically for any indication anything was amiss. Then he repeated the scrutiny forward. Both twin 4.5-inch turrets were traversed to starboard to give maximum access to the shell scuttles. There were bodies everywhere, unloading the pallets swinging between the ships, passing shells along sweating human chains. He identified the cap of his friend Lieutenant Miles Weiss, the Gunnery Officer.

He cupped his hands to his mouth.

"Guns!" He shouted. "Guns!"

Miles Weiss's pale face turned up to look at the bridge twenty feet away. He waved acknowledgement.

"There are too many wires and ropes lying about forward of A turret!" Peter shouted. "And tell off any loafers to report to the Master at Arms for employment!"

"Aye, aye, sir," the other man yelled, waved and started bellowing orders. From where he was standing behind B turret his field of vision was limited, and sensibly, his attention was directed at the handling of the reloads coming across the destroyer's deck rather than forward of A turret.

Peter stepped across to the nearest bridge intercom.

He opened the panel, snatched up the handset.

"Master at Arms to the bridge. Master at Arms to the bridge."

The broadcast would inform the Captain that he and the Executive Officer were already rounding up the newcomers by the time Hugo Montgommery told him the bad news. The Old Man did not expect his officers to sit on their hands when there was work to be done.

Further inside the anchorage a tanker down on her marks wallowed around her cables. A wisp of smoke rose from her single stack. Beyond her the long, low black shape of an 'O' Class diesel-electric submarine was creeping stealthily to sea. In the greyness of the morning the lights of Weymouth twinkled through the drizzle. They said the lights were coming back on in a lot of towns but it could never be as it was before; the fires of Hell had swept the old world away. In mute testimony to the new reality Talavera was replenishing her magazines in a home port with the watch closed up at Air Defence Stations. What kind of peace was that?

The Master at Arms, a small veteran Chief Petty Officer with a broken nose and a ruddy, scarred complexion trotted up the steps to the bridge and reported while Peter was half-submerged in his dark foreboding. Legend had it that CPO 'Spider' McCann had once been the Mediterranean Fleet's featherweight or bantamweight boxing champion.

The Bridge intercom buzzed angrily for his attention.

It was the Executive officer.

"Muster the new draft on the stern, if you please, Mr Christopher," Hugo Montgommery commanded with what seemed like entirely genuine amusement.

"Aye, aye, sir." Peter turned to the Master at Arms whose much abused face had remained unmoving during the short exchange between the two officers. "Let's see if we can do this without delaying the replenishment evolution, if you please, Mister McCann."

Talavera's senior non-commissioned officer – technically junior to the greenest sub-lieutenant straight out of Dartmouth – had served with both the Captain and Hugo Montgommery before and enjoyed both men's unqualified respect and trust. When Peter had reported on board the ship in that now long ago age of reason before the world went mad a bare seventeen months ago, the Executive Officer had told him that 'there were only four people in Chatham who have the right to give *the Master* a direct order; CPO McCann's wife, God, the Captain and on a very, very good day, *me.*' Hugo Montgommery had also told Peter that Spider McCann was the first man in Christendom he wanted by his shoulder in a tight corner.

There was a loud metallic clunking thud on the deck behind B turret.

Instinctively Peter rushed to the side of the bridge, arriving just in time to see a mishandled 4.5 inch reload rolling towards the port rails pursued by two burly gunners' mates. It seemed as if the shell was going to win the race, drop into the cold grey waters of Portland Harbour until, when it seemed impossible to intercept the missile, one gunner's mate fell on it as if he was tackling a fleet-footed left wing at Twickenham. Instantly, his companion fell on top of him and the wayward reload, instantly arresting both man and shell's seemingly irresistible slow-motion slide over the side.

Lieutenant Miles Weiss rushed to the heap of men and the now – thankfully – captured round. Peter could tell it was an HE, or 'common' reload. He allowed himself the comfort of a long, deep breath. Unfused or not, dropping a shell on a steel deck was never going to be an evolution that recommended itself to him as light entertainment. The Gunnery Officer, a keen, boisterous man, enthusiastically slapped both gunners' mates on the back.

"Guns! Peter called when the big men had hauled themselves, and their prize off the deck. "What's the score so far?"

"We've loaded forty star shell and four hundred HE so far, sir!"

The other man yelled. "There's another fifty or so HE to come over then we'll start on the SAP. The chaps are getting handier now that we've got a good rhythm going!"

"Carry on!"

Talavera's forward magazines had been designed to carry three hundred rounds per barrel. Minor modifications to bulkheads, mainly to strengthen and stiffen the forward third of the ship during her recent rebuild had reduced that capacity to between two hundred and sixty and two hundred and seventy rounds per barrel. Talavera had been ordered to load forty star shell, four hundred and sixty high explosive, and five hundred semi-armour piercing rounds, over forty tons of ordinance in approximately four hours. Given *six to eight* that would not have presented an insuperable problem alongside an ammunition wharf in port but across the decks of two gently rolling ships, the one – RFA Sycamore – with slightly a higher freeboard, it was a real struggle. It was only now as Miles Weiss's men got their second wind that the operation was finally gathering momentum.

There were ninety minutes to go before Talavera cast off from the mooring buoys and went to sea.

Over five hundred rounds still to come aboard.

It would be a close-run thing.

Peter Christopher made his way down to the enclosed conning bridge. He studied the Type 965 repeater. *Long range traffic only.* Satisfied, he rang through to the CIC.

"Bridge here. Anything on the board?"

"No, sir. We're picking up a lot of chatter from the Yanks. A lot of it is in the clear. All nearby friendly units are observing radio blackout as per Fleet standing orders."

"Very good."

Peter had learned very early in his career that while some officers could be effective watch keepers while preserving a demeanour of glacial, calm inactivity, that he could not. He simply was not built that way.

He needed to keep moving, thinking, talking, checking and re-checking *everything*.

He did not trust himself to assume *anything*.

When he was officer of the watch the ship and everybody on board depended on him being on his toes at all times.

He rang down to the control station in the forward engine room.

"Bridge here. Put the Chief on the line, please."

He waited.

"I'm still waiting for a bunker check report," he said tersely, continuing without waiting for a reply. "How long before we can light off number two boiler?"

The second of Talavera's Admiralty 3-Drum Boilers would be *'lit off'* in the next ten minutes and a 'bunker report' would be delivered to the bridge as soon as the rating with the report chit in his hand could reach the bridge.

"Very good, Chief."

Talavera had taken on six hundred and thirty-eight tons of heavy bunker oil at Portsmouth, about eighty-five percent of her maximum load. Earlier that autumn the ship had grounded briefly on two occasions while anchored in Fareham Creek during low tides and there was a small possibility, she might have sprung a seam in her double keel, or suffered some other minor underwater damage. Bunker fuel leakage, contamination or excessive seawater ingress into the bilges might signify unseen damage.

So far so good.

The short run to Portland to seaward of the Isle of White from Portsmouth had not thrown up any significant mechanical defects and the hull seemed, on first inspection, as tight as a drum but it did not pay to take anything for granted.

A breathless, sweating junior Engine Room Artificer skidded to a halt before the officer of the watch, who took the clipboard clutched in the man's right hand and studied the single sheet – which was only lightly smeared with light lubricating oil – intently for some moments.

The bunkers were 81% full and sea water contamination was negligible. There were eight inches of water in the Boiler Room bilge. The Engine Room bilge was dry. The bunkers were cleaned with sea water, there was always trace contamination.

Moreover, there was always water in the Boiler Room bilge. The environment of the Boiler Room spaces generated heat, humidity and condensation by the bucket load and there was invariably a steam leak somewhere in the system. Eight inches of water seemed a lot but it equated to less than thirty minutes a day of pumping out.

The absence of significant heavy bunker oil contamination and the fact that the Engine Room bilge was dry after the run from Portsmouth tended to indicate that Talavera had come to no harm touching bottom in the muddy waters of Fareham Creek at the end of September.

"Carry on," Peter Christopher nodded to the panting artificer who fled back down towards the cauldron of the Boiler Rooms. Peter did not watch him depart. He stepped over to the nearest communications handset. "Bridge for the Captain."

"Captain here," rang out David Penberthy's unusually terse voice.

"Officer of the Watch, sir," Peter retorted mechanically. "I thought you'd like to know the latest bunker report gives the ship a clean bill of health, sir."

"That's good news. How much gas have we got left in the tank after last night?"

Once out in the Channel Talavera had worked up to twenty-nine knots. Her stern had dug deep into the black water and her bow had cleaved a great furrow in the cold dark waves.

"Eighty-one percent, sir."

"Perhaps we weren't quite down to the sludge in the bottom of the bilges like the Chief was afraid?" The Captain of HMS Talavera chortled as he and the younger man did the mental arithmetic and approximately reconciled the Engineering Department's original bunker capacity estimate with the amount of fuel the destroyer had burned in the high speed overnight steaming trials. They must have had at least thirty to forty tons more bunker oil on board than the Chief had estimated seventy-two hours ago.

The Chief – Lieutenant-Commander Neil Fisk was relatively new to Talavera, having come aboard only two months ago – as the Engineering Officer was always referred to, was a quietly spoken man of very few words who was never happier than when he had his arms up to the elbows in grime and his head stuck inside a grubby manual or peering into a gearbox or boiler.

Nobody talked about his predecessor; John Cook. John had been a decent man profoundly happy in his marriage and devoted to his three young children. He had never come to terms with things after he finally accepted that the road where they lived just outside Chatham no longer existed. In retrospect it was inevitable that he would commit suicide as so many others had done before him. The only oddity about the event was the manner in which he had done the deed; wrapping himself in a loop of anchor chain as he stepped off the stern. Divers had found his body buried chest deep in the mud of the Creek within a few feet of where he went into the water, his arms waving slowly in the ebbing tide.

More than once Peter had caught sight of Spider McCann, the Master of Arms, standing at the stern deck house rail beneath the quadruple Sea Cat mount gazing thoughtfully down into the green grey waters. He and the Engineering Officer had not been close friends, service relationships and the protocols governing the conduct of commissioned and even the most senior non-commissioned officers did not allow for such things but the two men had shared a mutual respect. They were both men of Kent, both were from families deeply rooted in the Naval society and traditions of the Medway towns, and both had been widowed by the 1.17 megaton ground burst that instantaneously erased hundreds of years of history and the nation's oldest naval community.

John Cook had been the last of Talavera's five suicides.

Another seventeen men on board her that dreadful night thirteen months ago had deserted, although eight had subsequently re-joined the ship of their own volition. Men who deserted and returned voluntarily were always accepted back into a ship with a clean slate. The Admiralty had attempted to crack down in the first weeks after the war; but most Captains were only too eager to welcome back a man, any man, who came to his senses and asked to be readmitted to the brotherhood of his old crew. Such were the realities of the new age in which every ship was a repository of untold grief, loss and incendiary outrage.

Anger was too small and too frail a word to describe how Peter Christopher's generation felt about what had happened to the old world. His generation had never seen the face of their enemies. His father's generation had fought Hitler, that generation had known their enemy. Not so their sons and daughters. The Soviet Union had always been an amorphous thing forever beyond and below the horizon, too far distant and in many ways incomprehensible to the generations brought up in the diminishing austerity and gathering optimism of the post-1945 western world. Every last scintilla of the future of which Peter Christopher's generation had dreamed had been shredded, blasted and incinerated not by *the Soviets* but by *Uncle Sam*. That the moribund, complacent hide-bound, inbred incompetents who had overseen the terminal decline of the British Empire were partly to blame for the catastrophe was a self-evident truth. But Harold MacMillan and his cronies had not actually *caused* the cataclysm, that had been an act of malignant hubris far beyond the limited imagination of Supermac's feeble-minded crowd...

"Sir?"

The voice of the yeoman standing by his shoulder snapped Peter out of the brooding introspection which had fallen upon him without warning. He had not heard the other man come on the bridge.

"Yes, what is it?" He asked, removing his cap and running a distracted hand through his tousled hair. 'I need a haircut,' he told himself.

"RFA Sycamore reports she's dragging her stern anchor, sir."

Chapter 11

Wednesday 27th November 1963
Government House, Cheltenham

"It was so good of you to make time in your busy schedule to fit me in," Margaret Thatcher declared as if she was reciting from articles carved into tablets of stone.

Her whole being communicated how extremely pleased and flattered she was to be spared a few minutes of the great man's time.

The tall patrician man with the handsome weather-bronzed features and the bearing of a man who had commanded others in battle more times than he could casually recall took the Minister of Supply's cool white manicured hand in his own large, calloused grasp. His grip was gently firm and when the woman closed her other hand over it, he half-smiled, and imperceptibly, bowed his acknowledgement.

Since their first encounter Vice-Admiral Sir Julian Wemyss Christopher had spoken to his colleagues and made certain, very discreet, enquires about the background, character and qualities of the thirty-eight year woman – the sole representative of her gender in the first rank of Edward Heath's United Kingdom Interim Emergency Administration – who seemed to have an uncanny knack of either enchanting or completely alienating everybody who came into contact with her. Everything he had learned in the last few days had heightened his curiosity so when the 'Angry Widow' had invited him to join her 'for tea' that afternoon he had dropped what he was doing without a moment's hesitation.

"I confess," he assured his host, "that your invitation provided me with the perfect excuse to escape, albeit briefly I fear, the interminable merry go round of meetings that have become the bane of my life ever since I landed on home soil. I can honestly say that never was an invitation to tea more gratefully received and subsequently more instantaneously accepted than your kind invitation, Madam."

Margaret Thatcher had never been above flirting to advance, or to ease her way in politics but she never, ever let it distract her from the main thing. If there was quiet amusement in her blue eyes that afternoon it was tempered with a steely appreciation of the manner of man whom she had invited into her inner sanctum. Into her home, what little there was of it to call home in this bleak old house outside Cheltenham.

The man was taking in his surroundings. He noted the children's toys, old battered wooden things tidied away in a wicker box. Two threadbare armchairs and between them in front of a low brick hearth in which a few coals glowed apologetically, a tray bearing a silver tea service. He had heard that some prominent members of the UKIEA were beginning to cultivate more modest lifestyles, at least for public consumption. He doubted the Angry Widow had time for that kind of nonsense. No patience for artifice. There were several small photographs in metal frames on the narrow mantelpiece above the hearth. The bespectacled older man who looked like a banker or an accountant must be the dead husband?

Margaret Thatcher's gaze followed her visitor's eyes.

"Denis was my rock, Admiral Christopher," she said quietly, with deathly purpose. "My rock. I will never forgive *those people* for taking him from me. *Never!* Not if I live to be a hundred-and-one!"

The man decided that the precise identity of *'those people'* was a thing best explored another time.

"It must be difficult carrying the burdens that you carry," he suggested emolliently, "and to care for your children? You have twins, I believe?"

"Indeed," the Angry Widow replied. "Mark and Carol. I see little of them during the day, and when I have to travel, I must leave them entirely in the custody of a nanny. But my sacrifices are immaterial in comparison to that of so many others. Please, do sit down. This is the one room in this *place* where I try to avoid standing on ceremony."

"Avoiding standing on ceremony isn't as easy as most people imagine," her guest sympathised. He was appraising his host as he spoke, trying to explore beyond the immaculately presented, not one single hair out of place, utterly self-sufficient, controlling persona that she projected with apparently effortless grace and assurance. There was something almost *regal* about the woman.

"How do you manage it, Admiral?"

Julian Christopher did not make the mistake that so many of Margaret Thatcher's detractors made. The huskiness in the woman's voice was not a tease, it was a subtle test. Anybody who took this woman at face value, or who mistook her femininity for vulnerability was a fool.

"I don't as a rule," he said truthfully. "I am closer to some of my senior subordinates than others but when all is said and done, I remind myself that I'm the man who might, at the drop of hat, have to send each and every one of them to their deaths."

The woman nodded and continued to weigh his answer as she poured two cups of tea.

"I am reliably informed that you detest milk in your tea, Admiral," she checked, passing him his cup and saucer.

"I compliment you on the efficacy of your intelligence network, Madam."

"Airey has spies everywhere," the Angry Widow smiled.

"Ah, the remarkable Mr Neave," Julian Christopher grinned. "He and I have met, of course. It was at an investiture at Buckingham Palace just after the war. I should imagine he's a good man to have at one's side at times like this?"

"Airey and some of my colleagues in Government don't get on very well."

"I'd heard that. But then one hears a lot of things. Several of your colleagues don't approve of me either." He continued his slow appraisal of the room, little more than ten feet by twelve. Closed doors led off to each side and an overly high, broad window given the other proportions of the room, occupied at least half the wall space opposite the entrance to the corridor at his back. This must once have been quarters for servants. He sipped his tea, a Ceylonese blend of leaves, he guessed.

"Several of my *colleagues* still secretly believe that the world will someday be remade in the image of its former self," Margaret Thatcher remarked ruefully. "Even if that was possible, I am not convinced that would be a very good idea. Some of us came into politics to change the world rather than to preserve the status quo."

There was something disarmingly wifely, straightforward and utterly transparent in the woman's earnest expression that almost but not quite beguiled the fighting Admiral.

"Was the old world really so bad?" He asked.

"No," she shot back immediately, "but it was far from perfect and it was nothing like the picture postcard rural idyll that so many of my colleagues now mourn. Britain was a nation in systemic decline, Admiral Christopher. In a few years West Germany would again have been the pre-eminent European economic powerhouse, what was left of the Empire would have been gone and who knows what would have happened to our old traditional trading relations around the world with the rise of Japan and Hong Kong as efficient low-cost exponents of mass production. In the years before the October War Britain enjoyed a golden age because, America apart, every single one of our global economic competitors was still recovering from the ravages of the Second World War. But for the war of last October all those old competitors, and many new ones, all equipped with modern post-1945 industries would have swept our old-fashioned manufacturers from the world stage. Every one of our major industries; steel, shipbuilding, textiles, coal, electronics and pharmaceuticals would have been in rapid and probably terminal structural decline by the end of this decade." Margaret Thatcher realised she was hectoring her guest. "Forgive me," she smiled transient self-deprecation, "my *colleagues* refer to me as the 'Angry Widow' for good reason."

Julian Christopher's whole attention had been galvanised by this strangely normal and yet, utterly *different* woman. She reminded him small ways of his late wife, Joan; except that Joan had never had *this* woman's inner steel and slow burning *rage*.

"Madam," he murmured, leaning slightly towards her in conspiratorial confidence, "any one among us who is not *angry* about what has happened ought not to be in a position of power."

Margaret Thatcher did not reply for a long time. She put down her cup and saucer on the tray on the table between her and her visitor and rested her hands, clasped in her lap as she held long, curious eye contact with the man.

"I don't know what happened to my husband," she said, her voice neutral. "The children and I were staying with friends in Herefordshire. It was half-term. Denis had promised to get away from work for a few days. My constituency, Finchley, no longer exists. One of the bombs that destroyed London exploded three thousand feet above the High Street, they say. I'm told that nationally the death toll from the attack, starvation, disease and the cold of last winter may be as high as thirteen million. I think I have a right to be *angry*. The only thing I don't understand and I don't think I shall ever understand, is why so few of my colleagues aren't *angry*."

Julian Christopher had been back in England long enough to fully ingest the mood of the Chiefs of Staff and of the caucus of key senior civil servants who were actually running the country. There was a dangerous undercurrent of frustration – verging on contempt – directed at many of the leading members of the United Kingdom Interim Emergency Administration. The UKIEA was top-heavy with politicians who seemed more preoccupied with preserving their 'status' and fighting their 'corners' than in actually governing the sorely wounded nation. Moreover, it seemed that several of senior the members of the UKIEA operated much in the fashion of absentee landlords sending their placemen – other than Margaret Thatcher there were no women in the higher echelons of government – to Cheltenham to represent their feudal interests. Julian Christopher's impression was that the political classes were standing back from the fray – which was as disgraceful as it was inexcusable in such times of dire extremity – waiting to see what happened next. Presumably, they were positioning themselves to pick up the pieces if, probably when, Edward Heath's administration fell flat on its face.

Julian Christopher was a man who had never had much time for politics of the non-service variety or for politicians in general; privately, he was of the opinion that the situation called for putting a few of the more useless articles up against a wall and shooting them. Realistically, he could not think of any other way to encourage the others to start doing the right thing.

"Are you *angry*, Admiral Christopher?" Margaret Thatcher asked before the older man realised, he had briefly lost himself in his thoughts.

He blinked at the woman.

He saw the prim, attractive housewife, noted the handbag on the floor by her chair, and for some seconds he was unable to reconcile *that* Margaret Thatcher with the one who had just asked him the most subversive question he had ever been asked *in his whole life.*

She knew!

His eyes must have betrayed him because Margaret Thatcher nodded, wordlessly.

Julian Christopher raised his tea cup to his lips, sipped thoughtfully and placed the cup and saucer back on the tray on the table separating him from the remarkable woman who had so effortlessly shattered the steely carapace of defences he had spent a lifetime perfecting.

Nobody was planning a coup.

Not as such.

A coup d'état was not really a practical proposition.

The Army, the Navy and the RAF would have had to have formed a common view, set up several staff committees to thrash out the details of a proper *coup d'état*, and even in these dreadful times the Generals, Admirals and Air Marshalls were not ever going to sanction anything that crass. In the Army one could never get any two regimental staffs to agree about anything, likewise in the Navy submariners and destroyer men were different animals, and in the RAF bomber and fighter men fiercely defended their respective bailiwicks. No, it was more informal than that and provoked rather than plotted, by the strategy paper he had submitted to the Admiralty on the subject of *'Medium-term Operational Contingencies subsequent to the conclusion of Operation Manna'*. It seemed his old friend David Luce, the First Sea Lord had circulated the document – intended at that stage only as a general briefing document to feed into the ongoing strategy review post-October 1962 - to the other Chiefs of Staff and that eventually, it had found itself in the Prime Minister's in tray where it had sat, festering for some weeks and months until...what? Now that was a question! Suddenly, everything had changed, he had been summoned home ahead of his Fleet and plunged into the melee of what passed for politics in Cheltenham.

"Do you know what the Prime Minister is planning?" Margaret Thatcher inquired.

Julian Christopher shook his head.

"It is my understanding that he has not confided his specific intentions to the Chiefs of Staff."

"You surprise me?"

The man grudged a half-smile.

"The Chiefs of Staff will stand behind the Prime Minister whatever *lawful* steps he mandates under the War Emergency Powers Act." Those powers were of a summary and somewhat draconian nature.

Margaret Thatcher was genuinely surprised.

"The Chiefs of Staff have given the PM a blank cheque?"

"That is my understanding, Madam."

"Goodness me..." Her amazement was short-lived. "Isn't it odd how at times like this that one finds oneself recollecting all those occasions on which one has tweaked the tail of the man in whose hands one's life now rests?"

"It is a funny old world," the man agreed.

"Isn't it just." There was no fear or doubt in Margaret Thatcher's face. If anything, her jaw was jutting defiance.

Chapter 12

Wednesday 27th November 1963
Portland Bill, overlooking Portland Harbour

Captain Walter Brenckmann USN (Reserve) let the old Zeiss binoculars hang on the strap from his neck and straightened his cap on his head. His companion, a crew cut twenty-five-year-old Marine Lieutenant from Dearborn, Ohio on looked on at the activity in the anchorage below. On the other side of the car the two officers' guardian angels, Marines carrying M16 rifles and holstered 1911 pattern Colts under their coats paced uncomfortably on the exposed hillside as full daylight threatened to break through the angry, scudding overcast that seemed so low that they could almost reach up and touch it.

"What do you see, Lieutenant Devowski?" Asked the older man.

"A lot of activity, sir."

"And?" Walter Brenckmann pressed his new aide. Karl Devowski came with his new post as Acting Naval Attaché to the Embassy of the United States of America to the Court of Balmoral.

"And what, sir? I'm sorry, I don't understand." The Marine put down his glasses and stood to attention as he addressed his superior.

Walter meant to tell the kid to stop doing that; but had not got around to it yet.

He waved airily at the great sweeping panorama of the finest natural harbour in Northern Europe that the brightening of the day was gradually revealing below them as they watched.

"In 1914 the British assembled their entire Fleet in this anchorage; three dozen dreadnoughts and battlecruisers, fifty cruisers, and literally hundreds of destroyers and smaller warships. Column upon column of grey ships. I believe it was Winston Churchill who coined the phrase 'castles of steel' to describe the lines of battleships. In 1914 the British were the pre-eminent naval power in the world but *that* war wasn't eventually won by seagoing 'castles of steel'."

"No, sir," the Marine Lieutenant re-joined tersely. "It was won by Pershing's doe boys smashing the German Army in the forests of the Argonne, sir!"

Walter Brenckmann stifled a sigh of resignation.

Kids today were so well educated that they knew absolutely *nothing*!

"Actually, in the autumn of 1918," he corrected the kid, "while Pershing's green Army was hopelessly bogged down in the Argonne, the French were pinning the Germans in front of them while the British defeated, in detail, what remained of the fighting strength of the enemy to such good effect that they broke through the supposedly impregnable Hindenburg Line and in so doing, forced the German surrender."

"But we..."

"We came three years late to that war in the same way we came two years late to the next world war twenty-four years later. The Brits forgave us that. The Brits have forgiven us a lot over the years. They won't ever forgive us for what happened last year."

"Even if that's true, sir," the younger man observed, primly respectful, "I don't see that it is going to be a problem."

The Acting American Naval Attaché waved again at the vista before the two men.

"What do you see, Lieutenant?" He asked again with a fatherly patience.

"I see a lot of water and not many ships, sir."

"Ah, but what are those *ships* doing?"

Lieutenant Karl Devowski raised his glasses to his eyes.

Two older 'C' Class destroyers were oiling, one to each side, of a rust-streaked tanker in the middle of the anchorage. Inshore of them one of the rebuilt air defence Battle class destroyers was cross-decking ammunition from what looked like a requisitioned tramp steamer of pre-WWII vintage. Even from the best part of a mile away he could tell the ammunition ship was having trouble holding station. The anchorage was so large it seemed to have its own special sea conditions. Protected from the south west gale by the bulk of Portland Bill and the long ribbon of Chesil Beach which linked the island to the coastal town of Weymouth, the wind swirled across the bay stirring a low, eddying swell within the eastern breakwaters that enclosed the seaward side of the anchorage. The Battle class destroyer with her high lattice masts was rolling slowly and the ammunition ship's stern kept sliding northward. At one point the two ships had broken apart and come together again. Periodically, the destroyer churned her port screw to press closer to the merchantman.

"From her pennant number the destroyer is HMS Talavera," Walter Brenckmann explained. "She was running radar trials out of Chatham the day the war happened. A lot of her people had families in the Medway Basin. Obviously, they don't have any more. But that's not the thing."

"I still don't understand, sir?"

"How would you feel about cross decking ammunition on a day like this in peacetime, Lieutenant?"

"The Brits are crazy, sir. Everybody knows that."

"What Executive Officer in peacetime would allow his paintwork to bump and grind up and down the side of a rusty old scow like that?"

The Marine did not respond and the older man realised the young man was beginning to suspect he was being mocked.

"You're new over here, son," he said lowly in his best courtroom fatherly manner. "I spent three years on a tin can in the Atlantic fighting side by side with the Brits and yes, they can be a little crazy. But what's going on down there ain't crazy. All you've got to do it look at it from their point of view. That destroyer cross-decking ammunition is doing it down there for a reason. Everywhere up and down this coast British ships are filling their tanks and taking on bullets wherever and however they can in a God-awful hurry," he hesitated, wondering if he was being melodramatic. No, he was not being melodramatic, he decided. "They're not doing it because they like doing it either. They're doing it because they believe they must do it. They're sending everything they've got that will float to sea. Any day now the first of their big rescue convoys is arriving and they're telling us, *us*, Lieutenant, that if we mess with them, we're going to be in a world of pain."

The younger man frowned as he digested this.

"Why would *we* mess with their goddam convoys, sir?" The very notion of it seemed utterly preposterous to him.

"How would you feel if your best buddy burned down your house and killed your mother and father just to save his daughter's Wendy House from burning down?" He picked up his Zeiss binoculars and focused on the human chain manhandling 4.5-inch fixed shells into HMS Talavera's forward magazines. He tracked aft. A long wooden crate was swinging above the quadruple air to air missile launcher on the stern house. The flyboys did not rate Sea Cat as any kind of threat but if it ever came to a fight, they would not be dodging single shots, the Brits did not fight that way.

"That wasn't the way it was, sir," the younger man objected, becoming ever more respectful. He had already worked out that his new chief was not one of those old Navy arseholes who regarded Marines as knuckleheaded semi-evolved punch bags. Brenckmann reminded him of Mister Santos, the history teacher at his High School back home who coached the ball team. Mister Santos was grey haired, round-faced and wise-eyed and he had recognised in the angry, tearaway kid that everybody else had already written off something that the tearaway kid had never recognised in himself. Karl Devowski would never have got to go to college, or got to go to the US Marine

Corps Officer Candidate School at Quantico if it had not been for Mister Santos. Captain Brenckmann had the same calm, unflappable reasonableness about him and it underlay every word he said. "Was it?"

"It probably doesn't matter back home, Lieutenant," the older man conceded, "but that's exactly the way the Brits see it, and that's the thing that matters."

"Sir!" Called one of the M16-totting Marine bodyguards. "I think we've got a problem!"

If Walter Brenckmann had learned one thing above all others in his years in the US Navy it was that when a Marine admitted 'we've got a problem' he was unlikely to be joshing.

He turned to face the grim-faced youngster.

"We got people coming up the hill, sir."

Brenckmann nodded. "Shoulder your weapons. Nobody fires a round unless I tell you to!" He was already walking around the staff car, a big Plymouth shipped in from the States and instantly recognisable as being 'not of these islands'.

There were three vehicles coming up the hill: a small black police car, a camouflaged Land Rover and some kind of old, flat-sided civilian truck with a canvass enclosed cargo deck.

"What do you think, sir?" Karl Devowski asked unbuttoning his uniform coat to give him easy access to his holstered Colt.

"I think we show these guys our ID papers and make nice."

"What if they don't want to play nice, sir?"

Spits of rain carried on the wind as two uniformed police offices, both armed with ancient Webley pistols holstered but on lanyards around their necks, clambered out of the small black Austin police car. Men in brown Army uniforms tipped out of truck and formed into a short line. The soldiers looked like members of the new Home Defence Volunteer Militia. They were carrying Second World War vintage Lee Enfield rifles. Their officer, a tall, hatchet faced man of late middle years stalked stiffly towards the Americans flanked by the two policemen.

"Who the blazes are you fellows?" He demanded irritably.

Walter Brenckmann came to attention and Karl Devowski did likewise. Both men saluted crisply.

"Brenckmann," he intoned. "Captain, United States Navy. I am the Naval Attaché to the US Embassy to the United Kingdom Interim Emergency Administration, sir."

The officer scowling at him wore the insignia of a major.

"And this," Walter Brenckmann continued levelly, "is my aide-de-camp, Lieutenant Devowski, United States Marine Corps."

The militia officer eyed the two Marine bodyguards, each with their M16s slung over their broad shoulders. Belatedly, he returned the salutes of the two Americans.

"Cummings," he growled. "Second South Dorset Regiment, First Battalion Queen's Own Volunteer s. Were you aware that Weymouth, Chesil Beach and Portland are currently designated as restricted military areas?"

Walter Brenckmann affected wounded bewilderment, falling back onto a well-rehearsed court room expression.

"Restricted military areas? I'm sorry I don't understand the problem, Major Cummings?"

The other man was grinding his teeth.

"No, people like you never do," he muttered. He took a deep breath. "You and your men are under arrest for trespassing in a restricted area. Put down your weapons."

Nobody moved.

"Major, is this really necessary?"

Both policemen at the British officer's shoulder were fingering their pistols. A rifle bolt clicked loudly, then another and another from the ragged line of brown uniformed militiamen standing in front of the truck.

"Stand easy!" Walter Brenckmann called, exclusively for the ears of the two Marines with the M16s. He reached slowly into his coat and pulled out his ID card. "Major Cummings. I am obliged to show you my accreditation…"

Once disarmed the four Americans were instructed to get into the Plymouth and to follow the police car further up onto Portland Bill with the Land Rover and the civilian truck full of 'volunteers' bringing up the rear. The road terminated inside the quadrangle of an old white stone fort. Walter Brenckmann found himself separated from his men and marched to a holding cell two levels down in the bowels of the fortress. His captors did not bother to close the door but two regular Army soldiers equipped with L1A1 SLRs as opposed to the antiquated Lee Enfields of the militia volunteers stood guard in the corridor. After about an hour a subaltern stuck his head around the door and asked him if he was 'comfortable'.

"I can't recommend the coffee, sir," the young man, barely more than a boy apologised, "but the tea is usually drinkable at this time of day."

A few minutes later the US Naval Attaché to the UKIEA was nursing a chipped mug of bitter black tea in his hands while he contemplated the absurdity of the world in which he now lived.

Other than Major Cummings initial *terseness* Brenckmann and his men had been treated with respect and courtesy. There had been no real personal animosity, no unpleasantness and despite the fact he was not exactly free to leave on his own cognisance, the British seemed a little sheepish about putting him to such *inconvenience.*

"Sorry to keep you and your chaps hanging around, sir," announced a woman's voice – sing song and cheerful – to break into Brenckmann's thoughts as he stared into his tea.

A brunette in a WREN's uniform stood framed in the door.

"I'm not quite sure why they asked me to explain things," the girl, who couldn't have been more than eighteen or nineteen, went on, "but the Garrison has asked the Navy to send up somebody down to verify that you are who you claim to be, sir. I think the Navy are a little busy at the moment so there might be a delay. We're terribly sorry about that..."

"Busy?" Walter Brenckmann inquired wryly.

"Operation Manna," the kid replied, bewildered that he had to ask such a silly question. "I think everybody's convinced you fellows will try to interfere in some way!"

The American would have cracked up laughing at the young woman's sudden horror when she realised that she had inadvertently betrayed a huge national secret to a potential *enemy.* Except, it was not remotely funny. In fact, it was proof positive that everything he had been telling his superiors for the last few months was true. The Brits had worked themselves up into a frenzy and if CINCLANT made a single wrong move the Navy was going to find itself in a shooting war that it was not remotely expecting, ready or prepared to fight.

Chapter 13

Saturday 30th November 1963
HMS Talavera, 104 Miles SW of Ushant

The manoeuvring bell clanged.

Green grey water came over the bow as the destroyer pitched into the teeth of the gale, the whole ship shuddered and seemed to pause before she surged forward again, steadying onto the new heading.

Lieutenant-Commander Peter Christopher had seized the arms of his chair in the amidships CIC upon hearing the warning bell. Now he relaxed.

Talavera had been taking a battering in the cross seas for over an hour as she manoeuvred onto the flank of the Ark Royal Battle Group.

The weather had been uniformly foul ever since Talavera had steamed out of Portland Harbour into the teeth of a Force 7 Channel blow that had rapidly become a full gale. Meeting up with the frigates Rhyl, Lowestoft, Plymouth, the brand new first in class, Leander, she had exercised with the other ships for eighteen hours testing communications, conducting offset live fire trials and generating as much radio 'noise' as they could without making it obvious that they were attempting to impersonate a much larger flotilla than they actually were. Then the four ships had split up, Leander slowly heading back to Devonport to carry on making good the mechanical faults and deficiencies resulting from her rushed commissioning, Rhyl, Lowestoft and Plymouth to sweep for submarine contacts in the northern Bay of Biscay, and Talavera to relieve her sister ship Corunna. Corunna had suffered damage to her mid-ships and after deckhouses in recent heavy weather, and this combined with being too long out of dockyard hands had reduced her maximum speed to around twenty-six knots and severely curtailed her efficacy in her primary air defence role. Talavera and her older sister had crossed within a few hundred yards of each other, each ship flashing salutes and good wishes to each other as they rose and fell, one out of sight of the other, in the long Atlantic swells as the latest storm front passed over the Western Approaches.

Peter Christopher had tried to gauge the weather damage to Corunna's upper works from his position wedged against Talavera's bridge rail.

Leading Seaman Jack Griffin had tried to do the same from several feet higher up the destroyer's forward lattice mast and got knocked black and blue for his trouble.

It seemed two big waves had washed away many of Corunna's life rafts and her whaler, and although most of the external aerial wiring had survived intact water had got into her CIC and the adjacent radar and generator rooms.

Peter had always suspected the construction of the new deckhouses was too flimsy to withstand rough weather overlong but that was a trade-off to be expected when grafting a surfeit of modern technology onto a 1940s hull. Short of offloading the 4.5-inch forward battery there was no way to remove sufficient top weight to facilitate the construction of more substantial deckhouses so high above the waterline. Every ship that had ever gone down a slipway was a compromise between speed, capacity, structural robustness and seaworthiness. Talavera's deck houses were stiffer, much more heavily caulked constructions than those of her earlier sisters and he had personally supervised the re-welding of countless less than immaculately executed major welds while she was still in dockyard hands before the war. Perhaps, Talavera's deck houses would be drier than those of her sisters but only time would tell.

Talavera had the distinction of being the last of her class commissioned into the Royal Navy. Laid down late in the Second World War on 29th August 1944 at the yard of Messrs John Brown and Co on Clydebank, she had not been launched until 27th August 1945 and then only to clear the slip and in expectation of immediate scrapping.

The majority of unfinished War Emergency Program ships like Talavera were summarily disposed of in the years that followed, but Talavera, after lying half-built for four years, was taken in hand and eventually commissioned into the Royal Navy on 12th November 1950.

In an act that was typical of Admiralty bureaucratic muddle she was promptly been mothballed after a single, eighteen-month commission in home waters, and but for the decision to convert six aging battle class destroyers into so-called Fast Air Detection Escorts, she would probably have gone to the breakers by now.

For all that Talavera had been laid down over eighteen years ago she was a relatively *young* ship. Or as the Captain had once called her: 'An old sports car with hardly any miles on the clock!' Moreover, her youthful vigour had been massively enhanced by the radical nature of her conversion.

Of the original ship only the hull, engines, funnel, forward superstructure and her main armament remained. A huge new lattice foremast had sprouted immediately abaft the bridge - the base of this great structure straddling the entire forty feet beam of the ship –

topped with a four-ton Type 965 AKE-2 double bedstead aerial. A Type 293Q fire control array was mounted on a platform beneath the huge bedsteads. Aft of the single broad, raked funnel all torpedo tubes and light AA armament had been discarded and a big, blocky deckhouse containing generators and radar rooms had been welded to the main deck. Between this new superstructure and the old aft deckhouse, a new relatively slender lattice mainmast carried a Type 277Q height finder dish and several Electronic Warfare Support Measures (ESM) and Direction Finding (DF) aerials. The existing after deckhouse had been extended and strengthened to mount a quadruple GWS 21 Sea Cat Surface-to-Air-Missile (SAM) system, while on the cramped quarterdeck the ship retained its original Squid Anti-Submarine (A/S) mortar.

Peter had assumed this latter was an oversight since given the new profile of the ship with its towering radar masts and a superstructure that sprouted with fifteen to twenty-foot-long whip aerials, the Squid could never be safely fired over Talavera's bow.

Moreover, the destroyer's sonar suite was the one element of her electronic armoury that was distinctly *not* state of the art.

As for the GWS 21 Sea Cat SAM system he was unconvinced.

If the ship was under air attack she would be manoeuvring like a scalded cat and there was no way his radars could generate viable target locks on close range very fast-moving aircraft in that scenario.

These uncertainties aside – Talavera's primary role was neither anti-submarine work, nor tackling fast jets at close range – Peter was much more optimistic convinced that the ship was equal to her primary role.

Before the war the Navy had planned to build a new generation of big carriers and the converted *Battles*; Agincourt, Aisne, Barrosa, Corunna, Oudenarde and Talavera were going to be the state-of-the-art fast radar pickets around which the escort screens for the big ships of the near future would be built.

He doubted if there would be any new big carriers now. There were plans afoot to complete hulls of smaller warships already under construction but the order for the first of the new carriers had not progressed beyond the drawing board before the October War.

He watched the Type 965 repeater returns - for much of the last hour a useless blur - slowly resolve into a coherent picture of the airspace in a vast radius around the destroyer.

He re-checked the plot.

Ark Royal was twenty-two miles almost due east, her return sometimes merging with that of one or other of her two close escorts.

The Ark Royal's combat air patrol was in a thirty-mile-wide holding pattern at twenty-eight thousand feet approximately thirty-five miles north-west of Talavera. Invisible somewhere to the south a second radar picket, Talavera's sister HMS Aisne was quartering the seas astern of the carrier. The Aisne herself was below the horizon; only the signatures of her radars were visible. Like Talavera, she was broadcasting her presence fifty to a hundred miles distant depending on the vagaries of the ever-changing atmospheric conditions.

A buzzer sounded.

"Ark Royal's birds have turned onto a reciprocal with Talavera, sir."

"Very good. Paint them with everything we've got!"

Peter Christopher allowed himself a half-smile.

The veteran pilots of the carrier's Sea Vixens were running in to test the green newcomers who had thus far sat out Operation Manna in the comfort and security of their home port. They probably suspected the latest addition to the Battle Group was a barely seaworthy rust bucket crewed by conscripted land lubbers. They might be partially correct in the latter suspicion. Talavera's EWO chuckled to himself at the memory of the Captain's short, pointed *little talk* with the members of the latest draft at Portland, while the rest of the deck division continued cross decking eighty-seven pound four-foot-long fixed rounds for the ship's 4.5-inch Mark III main battery. The defaulters 'odds and sods' draft had come on board at Portsmouth just before Talavera put to sea and none of them had had a chance to get their sea legs yet.

It had begun to rain as the new men shivered on the stern, packed together around the tarpaulin shrouded Squid anti-submarine mortar, and crushed between the stern chains and jackstay rigging. The ship's White Ensign had banged and crackled as brutal gusts of wind broke it out.

'To a man you are a disgrace to the Navy,' Captain David Penberthy had bellowed into the megaphone. He had positioned himself on the aft deckhouse in front of the quadruple Sea Cat launcher. Spider McCann, the Master at Arms was at his shoulder, glaring malevolently at the upturned faces of the men on the stern. Two of McCann's stone-faced Master's Mates had corralled the new men in the open, where the rain swept hardest. 'The only reason any of you are still on board *my* ship is because Queen's Regs explicitly forbid me to throw you all over the side. However, Queen's Regs give *me*, as *your* Captain virtually free licence to make each of your lives a living Hell and if any one of you gives me *any* cause to so do, I bloody well will!'

Peter had heard every word – as clear as a bell – from his watch keeping post on the bridge over two hundred feet forward, from where he had been observing the desperate race to get the last few 4.5-inch SAP rounds aboard. The ship had been quivering softly, grey smoke whipping away from her single stack as Number Two boiler came on line. The wind carried away the roar of the engine room blowers while, oddly, leaving the megaphone-enhanced words of the Captain audible in virtually every corner of the ship.

'Coming aboard Talavera does not mean that *any* of you start with a clean slate. You will make a full report of the circumstances of your service in the six months prior to joining the ship to the Master at Arms. Failure to so do will incur brig time, loss of pay and seniority. Do not think for a single minute that because Talavera is short-handed any of you are indispensable, or that this fact will in any way mitigate any infraction, however minor you may commit on *my* ship. Right now, you are a collection of useless, untrustworthy *garbage*. It is up to you to convince me that you have a right to remain with the fine men whom I have had the privilege to command this last year.'

The old man had wound up his welcome speech with a terse warning to the effect that if any of the new men found themselves before a Captain's Table they would be very 'sorry'.

The entire draft had been assigned to the Master at Arms' Deck Division. Overnight the Talavera had acquired a twenty-eight-man cleaning, painting, rust scraping, head cleansing detail while CPO McCann oversaw the methodical sifting of the bad from the incorrigible.

The destroyer shuddered through each monstrous storm swell.

"We have bogeys at two-nine-one, angels three-seven!"

"Range five-seven miles, sir!"

"Label them Bogey A and B and vector the CAP onto them, please."

Behind him a talker raised the Sea Vixens.

The two 893 Squadron interceptors changed course.

Peter snatched up his intercom.

"CIC to Captain."

"What is it, Peter?" Captain David Penberthy asked, as if they were exchanging small talk at a cocktail party.

"Two bogeys on the plot, sir. I've vectored Ark Royal's CAP onto them on my own authority, sir."

"Very good. I'll attend CIC shortly. Carry on."

The CIC speaker called out.

"Ark Royal is talking to the CAP, sir."

"Put it on broadcast, please."

The carrier's air controller was confirming Alert Status Two was in effect. *Intercept with weapons hot but do not engage unless actively targeted or attacked.* The bogeys were American aircraft. They knew the rules.

"We're painting two more bogeys at two-nine-seven, angels one-zero!"

"Range four-three miles. Plot confirms CBC." *Constant Bearing and Course.* A collision course in layman's language. "Confirm reciprocal with Talavera, sir!"

The new bogeys were automatically labelled C and D.

Peter forced himself to think.

But only for a split second.

At that height and range the bogeys must have approached at sea level, only betraying their presence when they climbed – or in the jargon 'looked up' - to fix Talavera's location.

"Closing speed?"

"Five hundred plus knots, sir."

Weapons status: Peter ran the check in his head.

The Sea Cat launcher was battened down, inoperable in the storm. It would take several minutes to unlock and to warm up.

The main battery was unmanned.

Nobody had been allowed topside for several hours because of the wild seas so the two single 20-mm cannon were under protective tarpaulins like the nearby quadruple Sea Cat launcher on the aft deck house.

He did not hesitate.

"Sound Air Defence Stations Condition One and paint the new bogeys with the Sea Cat system as soon as they come within range."

He heard the clanging of the alarms.

He did not have anything to shoot at the incoming bogeys but he would worry about that later.

"All hands to Air Defence Stations Condition One!"

Peter watched the plot, the bogeys racing ever closer.

Men would be running onto the storm swept decks, into the empty main battery turrets forward, rumbling out of bunks all over the ship.

"CIC to bridge. I recommend we make revs for twenty-eight knots."

Hugo Montgommery came over the circuit.

"Very good, Peter." Off intercom he shouted the command to increase speed. Then: "My God, this is like the good old days! Keep up the good work, old man!"

Captain David Penberthy staggered into the CIC as the destroyer's twin screws began to bite deeper, faster into the angry North Atlantic seas.

"Captain in the CIC!"

"Stay in your chairs!" Talavera's captain grinned at his young EWO.

Peter stared so hard at the plot he could almost see through it to the other side. If this was a real attack, they were going to be treading water or dead in next to no time. If it was some twisted American practical joke it was in extremely bad taste. If Talavera had been at ADSC One ten minutes ago she would be opening fire with everything she had some time in the next thirty seconds.

The old man patted his shoulder.

"Right full rudder! The ship will come right to two-seven-zero!"

The order was repeated and the ship lurched up the side of, crested and fell away down the reverse of a swell, rolling with a slow, sickening corkscrewing motion until after an age, she finally settled on her new course.

Peter realised he and the Captain were both watching the readiness board above the plot like two hungry tom cats peering down a mouse hole.

The B turret indicator bulb turned amber, then green.

"Inform Mr Weiss that the main battery may engage the enemy as soon as he has a firing solution," Captain David Penberthy ordered, tersely.

Chapter 14

Sunday 30th November, 1963
Government House, Cheltenham

"One of our ships actually opened fire on two United States Navy aircraft!" Iain Macleod raged. "It actually opened fire without giving any kind of warning, dammit!"

Jim Callaghan closed the report on his desk, rose to his feet and walked to the window. His first-floor office had once been a library and many of the shelves around the walls were empty which he thought was sad. He did not respond to the angry complaint, having learned that there were times when trying to reason with Iain Macleod was like pouring petrol on an open fire.

"That madman Christopher will drag us all into a shooting war!"

The Minister of Defence turned and viewed the two men who had stormed uninvited into his office like they owned it. That was a Tory trait, another thing he had long suspected but not known for a fact until he started working beside his lifelong political adversaries.

George Edward Peter Thorneycroft, his deputy, was by nature a rather more sanguine man than Iain Macleod. Less brilliant, also but then he had other strengths which Iain Macleod would not recognise if they punched him in the face. More important, Peter Thorneycroft was actually on speaking terms with the Angry Widow.

"What's your take on this, Peter?" Jim Callaghan asked, folding his arms and resting his back on the high window sill. He asked the question with a thoughtful directness.

"The First Sea Lord says HMS Talavera was new on station and the Americans should have known better. Six proximity fused high explosive shells were fired at two fast moving A4 Skyhawk attack aircraft launched by the USS Enterprise. Neither aircraft identified themselves before undertaking a 'practice attack run' on the Talavera. Apparently, this sort of thing happens now and again. "The US Navy regards this sort of thing as some kind of demonstration of military 'virility'. It goes without saying that our people don't indulge in that sort of nonsense. The United States Navy is fully cognisant of our rules of engagement."

"How so?" Iain Macleod demanded petulantly.

"We regularly broadcast them in plain English. Every day, in fact."

"Perhaps, we ought to alter the 'rules of engagement'?"

Jim Callaghan sniffed. "No. We're not going to do that, Iain."

The shorter, stockier Chairman of the Conservative and Unionist

Party scowled at the taller man.

"Why not?"

"Because it is always a mistake to show weakness in the face of a bully."

"Somebody should talk to Admiral Christopher!"

"No, that's not a very good idea," Peter Thorneycroft decided.

"I'll bloody well talk to him!"

Jim Callaghan resumed his seat behind his desk. The trouble with the Tories was that they did not know if they were coming or they were going. It had not mattered so much in normal, peaceful times of comparative plenty but in the current circumstances it was a disgrace. Tories like Iain Macleod were in quasi-denial, others deluded themselves the Americans had been dealing with their allies in good faith all along, while others like Peter Thorneycroft and Ted Heath were fighting a never-ending rear-guard action to preserve a sense of reality. It was not until recently that he realised, with something of a shock, that of all the Tories the only one who seemed to share more or less his own appreciation of the new realities of the world was the Angry Widow. Politically, ideologically they remained a million miles apart. That was to be expected, nevertheless, he and she shared a common view of what the future held for their country if things carried on the way they had been going in the last year.

"No, you won't, Iain," Jim Callaghan said coolly. "If you interfere again in operational matters, I will order your arrest..."

"Don't be bloody ridiculous!"

"The Treachery Act applies to you in exactly the same way it applies to any other citizen. As does the War Emergency Act upon which the Government to which we both belong owes its authority."

"Steady on, Jim," Peter Thorneycroft murmured.

"No, I won't 'steady on'," the Minister of Defence retorted, trying not to lose his temper. "Sooner or later even you idiots will have to recognise that *everything* has changed. You two, me, all of us here in this *Government* building are having to sanction things that would have been abhorrent to us thirteen months ago; things for which future generations will rightly condemn us and yet *you* people are still playing politics. This isn't a bloody game, gentlemen. Playing politics is a luxury we don't have. If you want to carry on playing funny buggers and scoring personal points don't come to me wasting *my* time. Frankly, if it was up to me," he looked grimly at Iain Macleod, "I'd kick a few of you and your friends out of this compound. I doubt very much if you'd last very long out there in the real world that *my* constituents back in Cardiff have to live in."

The Chairman of the Conservative and Unionist Party looked at the Acting Leader of the Labour Party with open-eyed astonishment.

"We're all in this together, Jim."

"Some of us more than others, it would seem."

"How dare you question my loyalty!"

The Minister of Defence closed his eyes. If the Tories kept their word - which he did not think they would unless Edward Heath, against the odds was still Prime Minister in the spring - there would be an election in the New Year. Dates in May had been mentioned. The survivors had a right to be heard, to pass judgement on the ones *they* blamed for the cataclysm. Already, people like the two men in his office this morning were talking about delaying the election. They wanted to wait until things were 'on a more even keel', or for some mythical future date when 'everybody had had an opportunity to draw breath'. They both claimed it would be 'unfair to stage elections as early as next year because *their* – Conservative - constituencies had been in the parts of the country hardest hit by the war'. Neither of them were overly receptive or in any way sympathetic to the concept that elections were for the living, not the dead, and that if their argument for delay rested solely on the premise that proportionately more of their natural supporters were dead than survivors who were likely to vote for Her Majesty's Loyal Opposition, then by what conceivable right did they think they had any reason to continue to rule over the majority that remained alive?

The phone on the big desk rang twice.

"I have an appointment with the First Sea Lord, gentlemen."

"I want to be present," Iain Macleod declared heatedly.

Jim Callaghan picked up his desk phone.

"Would you ask the First Sea Lord to take a seat please." He replaced the receiver and gave the Chairman of the Conservative and Unionist Party a ruminative look. "Our business is concluded, Iain. I wish to have a private confidential conversation with my senior naval advisor. I'm sure Peter," he flicked a glance at the imperturbable Peter Thorneycroft, "will let you know if anything relevant to your portfolio is mentioned."

Iain Macleod frowned at his party colleague who shrugged imperceptibly as if to say 'the blaggard is within his rights'. Without another word or a backward glance, he stomped out of the office and slammed the big, heavy oaken door at his back.

Jim Callaghan watched him depart.

"The time will come, Peter," he observed, lowly, "when that man becomes a liability to your camp. At that time, I will remember whom among your number called him friend."

Peter Thorneycroft half-smiled.

"That almost sounds like a threat, Minister?"

"No, not a threat," Jim Callaghan assured him, "a prediction." He picked up his desk phone. "Please ask Admiral Luce to come in now."

Admiral Sir David Luce looked like he had not slept for forty-eight hours. The former submariner who had participated in the bloody fiasco of the Dieppe Raid in 1942, been a senior member of the staff that planned and executed the Normandy Landings in June 1944, commanded a cruiser during the Korean conflict, the Director of the Royal Naval Staff College and later Naval Aide de Camp to the Queen was a lean, forthright yet invariably charming man to whom an understanding of the nuances of the political niceties associated with High Command had always come easily. However, today he looked older than his fifty-six years.

The Minister of Defence shook the newcomer's hand, as did Peter Thorneycroft. The First Sea Lord placed his heavily braided cap on the corner of Jim Callaghan's desk and the three men took chairs within the pool of weak wintery daylight that fell into the office through the high leaded windows.

"Presumably Mr Macleod thinks he smells a rat, Minister?" The weary Admiral sighed.

"The Chairman of my Party always thinks he's detected the scent of a Rattus rattus," Peter Thorneycroft remarked, attempting to lighten the mood in the room. "That is his job after all."

"I don't like this infernal intrigue," the First Sea Lord retorted mildly.

"What about the other Service Chiefs, David?" Jim Callaghan inquired softly. He had come to personally like and admire the professional head of the Royal Navy and to rely on his advice in a way he could never bring himself to trust that of the two other Service Chiefs.

"None of us care for this manner of conducting business, Jim," David Luce confessed as he ran a hand over his thinning dark hair. "Charles is very," he hesitated, "uncomfortable with the whole thing."

Air Marshall Sir Samuel Charles Elworthy, the New Zealand born Chief of the Air Staff was threatening to become loose cannon. Distrustful of the growing Anglo-American rift he had argued that the surviving V-Bomber Force – around fifty operational aircraft – ought to be reintegrated back into a new trans-Atlantic military alliance as the first step in rebuilding old friendships. The Prime Minister had vetoed the suggestion after the briefest of very brief discussions and the Chief of the Air Staff had not been the same since.

"Should I speak to him personally?" Jim Callaghan asked.

"No, that won't be necessary. In any event Richard understands that we can't go on this way."

The opinion of Sir Richard Amyatt Hull, Chief of the General Staff of the Army was, in the final analysis the one that carried most sway. He spoke for the Army and without the Army civil order and the semblance of a common Governmental writ across most of the country would cease to exist in the blink of an eye.

"Charles, Richard and I are all agreed, Jim," David Luce went on. "Assuming, that is, that Her Majesty does not see fit to intervene. Regardless of the provisions of the War Emergency Act I owe my personal allegiance to Her Majesty, as do my fellow Service Chiefs."

"As do we all," Jim Callaghan said with the resignation of a man who knows that all the balls were now in the air and only the great juggler himself, God, had any idea how or where they might fall.

Edward Heath had flown to Scotland that morning, ostensibly for the Prime Minister's routine monthly audience with the Queen. Her Majesty had been closeted away at Balmoral since the summer where she could be protected by the Black Watch. There had been two attempts on her life in the chaos following the October War and only outrageous good fortune had saved her from serious injury on both occasions. *She*, of course, resented what she described as 'a suffocating blanket' of security and having to live in what was in effect, an armed camp.

This month there was absolutely nothing 'routine' about the Prime Minister's visit to Scotland. 'Routinely' the Premier flew north with a junior principal grade secretary from the Cabinet Secretariat a small team of bodyguards and several boxes of official papers to peruse. This time he had flown to RAF Dyce near Aberdeen with the Foreign Secretary, Alec Douglas Home and his Permanent Secretary, Tom Harding-Grayson, Vice-Admiral Julian Christopher, and the Angry Widow.

Alec Douglas Home's absence from Cheltenham could be easily explained away. The Foreign Secretary was a notorious absentee landlord from his Department and everybody knew Tom Harding-Grayson was the éminence grise behind that particular throne. The latter's absence was much more likely to attract attention which was why his wife, Patricia, had also flown to Scotland. If necessary, a rumour would be circulated to the effect that the pressure had got to *poor old Tom*, he was drinking again and he had gone off complex with his wife to *dry out* for a few days. Nobody would believe it but it was the best anybody could think of at such short notice. It had been announced – with no little fanfare – that Julian Christopher's presence at Balmoral had been specifically requested by the Duke of Edinburgh, himself a former Naval Officer. The Admiral had been a protégé of Prince Philip's uncle, the late Lord Mountbatten, and he wanted to hear all about the exploits of the British Pacific Fleet straight from the horse's mouth. It had been hoped that this news would distract overly inquisitive eyes off the ball and that nobody would notice that Margaret Thatcher had disappeared from Cheltenham at the same time as the others.

Oh, what a wicked web we weave...

It was hardly surprising that the Service Chiefs were getting nervous.

"My fellow chiefs have asked me to ask you," the First Sea Lord explained, at pains not to seem to be interrogating his political master, whom he liked and respected as a man and whom he trusted to keep a confidence, "why *that* woman is on the plane to Scotland?"

"I've given that question a great deal of thought, David," Jim Callaghan said with a sardonic twitch of his pale lips.

"Um," the professional head of the Royal Navy grunted. "The woman has undoubted organisational and analytical skills and she has a knack of getting things done but her and her *friends*, especially Airey Neave, have a particular talent for putting people's backs up. Frankly, I was under the impression she and the Prime Minister were..."

"Chalk and cheese?" Peter Thorneycroft suggested dryly.

"Yes, exactly."

Chapter 15

Monday 2nd December 1963
HMS Dreadnought, 207 miles SSW of Queensferry

Commander Simon Collingwood released the twist grip handles of the attack periscope as the gun metal tube slid smoothly into its well in the middle of the control room of the Royal Navy's first, and in the foreseeable future, only nuclear-powered attack submarine.

"Take us down to three hundred feet," he ordered quietly. He glanced up at the chronometer above the helmsman position in the forward bulkhead. "We will hold on zero-three-zero degrees for five minutes and then turn right onto one-two-zero degrees. Five minutes on my mark...now!"

The order was repeated back to him.

The diving officer was calling depths.

"One-zero-zero...One-one-five..."

Collingwood stretched his aching neck. The attack periscope had developed a fault so he had spent most of the last quarter of an hour on his hands and knees desperately trying to show no more than six to twelve inches of the scope above the water. Dreadnought was running silent, or rather, as silently as any four-thousand-ton man-made denizen of the deep could possibly run. Her Westinghouse propulsion plant was every bit as noisy as that powering the first classes of US Navy nuclear attack boats and Dreadnought had not – as odd as it might seem – actually been built to be a state-of-the-art operational warship. She was a work in progress - albeit a remarkably accomplished work in progress – primarily intended to be the foundation or test bed upon which the Royal Navy would subsequently develop its own unique design and tactical doctrines basically, learning as it went along independently of the USN. She was no less deadly than her US Navy counterparts but pound for pound, she was inherently 'noisier'.

"One-four-five feet...One-six-zero..."

The deck beneath Simon Collingwood's feet was inclined down by the bow by six degrees according the inclinometer above the planes man's head. The submarine was flying slowly down into the cold black depths of the North Atlantic.

Simon Collingwood had been stalking the Enterprise Battle Group for six days and until yesterday evening their quarry had been blissfully unaware of Dreadnought's presence – quite literally – in their midst. Now it was time to skulk away and live to fight another day because Commander Simon Collingwood was one of a growing number of Royal Navy officers who realised that one day, it was inevitable that there would be another war. But hopefully, not today. His orders had been to shadow the Enterprise Battle Group, collect combat intelligence and withdraw to a 'safe range' if discovered. He did not think the Americans had him in their sights right here and now but by the way they had suddenly begun to zigzag and the way the close escorts were clinging close to the flanks of the huge nuclear-powered carrier, something had panicked the Yanks. He was amazed how long it had taken 'the opposition' to catch the scent of the rat in *their* water; although not, in truth, very surprised.

The seventh HMS Dreadnought, pennant number S101, had been built by Vickers Armstrong at Barrow-in-Furness in Lancashire, launched by Her Majesty Queen Elizabeth II on Trafalgar Day 1960, and after much sweat, toil and terrifying trial and error commissioned into the Royal Navy in May that year. She was powered by a fifth generation Westinghouse S5W reactor that was in many respects identical to that fitted in the American Skipjack class hunter killer boats. In fact, handled adroitly, Dreadnought could be made to sound and manoeuvre *exactly* like an American boat.

The possibilities of this characteristic had first lodged in Simon Collingwood's mind over three years ago when he was posted to Groton, Connecticut, to train alongside his US Navy 'allies' ahead of joining the Design Project Team at Barrow-in-Furness, and later becoming the Naval Construction Liaison Officer (Engineering and Electrical Systems) as Dreadnought was slowly transformed from a lifeless half-completed hulk to a living, breathing deadly, mind-bogglingly complex fighting machine.

The Royal Navy had begun investigating the possibilities of seaborne nuclear propulsion plants in 1946. The work had never had a very high priority and during the Korean War, in 1952, all research was suspended. It had not been until in 1955, when the US Navy commissioned the *USS Nautilus* that the Royal Navy, until then the acknowledged masters of anti-submarine warfare had awakened to the fact that *everything* had changed. In exercises with the new American vessel it was horrifyingly obvious that the tactics and the technology that had won the Battle of the Atlantic simply did not work against the new undersea threat. Faced with attempting to join the nuclear submarine building *game* from what was essentially a standing start, in the mid-1950s there seemed no prospect of a British version of the *Nautilus* joining the Fleet for at least a decade at the earliest, or perhaps not even before the end of the 1960s. It was a depressing scenario for the Royal Navy and for the politicians who had let it happen by starving the original reactor research project of funds and, compounded their error, by stopping it dead in its tracks at the very moment the Americans were racing ahead.

Simon Collingwood felt the bow down angle of the boat alter.

The diving officer went on calling depths.

"Two-six-five feet..."

The Captain of HMS Dreadnought planned to run across the stern of the Enterprise Battle Group to test if the hunters had had more than a fleeting inkling of his boat's proximity to their massive charge. Two days ago, the big carrier had slowed to sixteen knots to save her smaller consorts a battering in the vile weather topside. Collingwood had taken the opportunity to steam up the carrier's wake and to sit – for the best part of seven hours – two hundred feet under her keel. When the weather had moderated the Enterprise had worked back up to twenty-eight knots and resumed flying operations. In a real shooting war he might have tried to hold station; he had opted for prudence and let the *target* steam off into the distance before running fast and deep to the east to get ahead of his quarry, then lain silent until the whole Battle Group obligingly sailed right over the top of him. It was the kind of sport a true submariner lived and died for, the most exhilarating, draining, marvellous, frightening, addictive thing he had ever done in his whole life!

"Two-eight-zero...Come up ten degrees on the planes..."

"Water temperature?" Simon Collingwood asked quietly in the sepulchral stillness of the control room.

"Consistent gradient, sir."

The Captain of HMS Dreadnought suppressed a scowl. He had hoped for a thermocline – a thin layer of water significantly warmer or colder than it ought, statistically to be given its depth in the water column, which would act as a partial barrier to sonar detection – somewhere between two hundred and fifty to three hundred feet down. Never mind, one rarely got what one deserved in this life.

"Level the boat. We'll check fore and aft trim then we'll go down to four hundred feet."

"Level the boat, aye, sir. Check trim, aye, sir."

"CVN Six-five is altering to starboard," reported Dreadnought's Executive Officer, Lieutenant-Commander Max Forton, without looking up from the CIC plot. The thirty-four-year-old career submariner had come aboard the boat three weeks after the October War. By then it had been confirmed that the boat's original captain and several other officers – detached to Southampton for training on the specially constructed Dreadnought simulator – had been 'taking in a show in London' and 'doing the town' when the balloon went up. "If we turn onto one-two-five pretty much about now she'll steam right over us again, sir."

Simon Collingwood smiled what he hoped was not an overtly predatory smile. He raised a hand to rub his stubbly chin. As many as possible of the boat's inessential functions had been turned off to quieten her operations. One such *inessential function* was pumping hot water for washing and shaving.

"Helm. Make your course one-two-five degrees if you please."

"The boat is trimmed fore and aft, sir," called the diving officer lowly. "Ready to dive to four hundred feet."

"Belay that. Hold at three hundred."

"Hold at three hundred feet, aye, sir."

"Range to CVN Six-five?" CVN65 was the US Navy's nomenclature for its first, eighty thousand ton thousand feet long nuclear-powered super carrier, the USS Enterprise. It was probably no accident that the Americans had deployed their biggest, most powerful and certainly most intimidating asset in waters adjacent to the European continental shelf prior to the arrival of the first of the Operation Manna convoys.

"Five thousand yards on the port bow, sir."

"Constant speed?"

"Negative, sir. It looks like she's working up to launch or recover aircraft. She's making twenty-three knots... Correction, twenty-four..."

Max Forton sidled over to join his Captain.

"She's obviously upset to see us go, sir," he observed wryly. The younger man was built like a whippet. Dreadnought's men knew him as an angry perfectionist with a wit that could sometimes be brutally sardonic, who knew every inch of the boat like he knew the back of his hand. Submariners did not mind if their officers were martinets so long as they were very, very good at their jobs. Besides, if Dreadnought's Executive Officer was a holy terror, they knew their Captain was probably one of the calmest heads in the Navy.

"We'll run a stern attack simulation once she's gone past us, Mr Forton," Simon Collingwood decided, mirroring his second in command's roguish smirk. "How many times have we sunk the *Big E* now?"

"About a dozen and counting, sir!"

There was a whispered murmur of chortling and gently gloating amusement in the control room.

"Everybody on their toes if you please," the Captain of HMS

Dreadnought declared quietly. With eighty thousand tons of aircraft carrier rushing towards the boat this would be a bad time for somebody to make a mistake. While the forefront of his mind ran methodically through the tactical complexities of the current situation and planned the simulated attack Dreadnought would carry out from astern of the carrier in about ten minutes time, he reflected on the delicious irony of his command's very existence.

HMS Dreadnought as a project would have been impossible without the active assistance of, and the subsequent massive transfer of the US Navy's most secret and most advanced technology. Dreadnought incorporated all the lessons learned in the design, construction and operation of the USS Nautilus, enabling the Royal Navy to bypass at least five and probably as many as ten years development time in joining the nuclear-powered submarine club. That this had been possible was down to two remarkable men, and a little-known clause in the 1958 US-UK Mutual Defence Agreement.

The first remarkable man was Admiral the Earl of Mountbatten, the First Sea Lord from 1955 to 1959. The second was Admiral Sir Wilfred Woods, Flag Officer Submarines in the mid-1950s and between 1958 and 1960 Deputy Supreme Allied Commander Atlantic based in Norfolk, Virginia. Mountbatten was the political powerhouse with a trans-Atlantic contact book unrivalled in history, Woods the professional and technical master submariner who had spent every minute of his time in America making friends.

Initially, the two men had planned to build a new generation of all-British nuclear boats. Given that the Americans had shut Britain out of the nuclear weapons loop at the end of the Second World War, this seemed a realistic basis on which to proceed. As late as 1956 Rear Admiral Hyman Rickover, the high priest and implacable guardian of the US naval nuclear power programme had vetoed Mountbatten's request to visit the USS Nautilus. In retrospect this marked the high-water mark of US-British non co-operation in the field because later that year Rickover came to the United Kingdom with an offer to supply third generation S3W reactor technology – then being deployed in the American Skate class nuclear powered attack boats - to the Royal Navy. Behind the scene Mountbatten had been hard at work, capitalising on his old friendship with Arleigh Burke, the US Navy's Chief of Operations. Eventually, Rickover was persuaded – presumably reluctantly – to agree to the transfer of the latest reactor technology under the terms of the 1958 US-UK Mutual Defence Agreement.

Dreadnought was built around an American power plant; a British hull populated with British combat systems heavily influenced by virtually unrestricted access to the Electric Boat Company's yard at Groton where vessels of the Skipjack class were currently under construction. Dreadnought was preparing for reactor initiation and her first 'in dock' dive trial at the time of the October War.

"CVN Six-five is making two-six knots..."

"She's altering course to port..."

Simon Collingwood glanced at his Executive Officer who shrugged and returned to his CIC plot.

"Helm. Steady as you go." He called across the control room. "Where's the nearest escort, Number One?"

"Two thousand yards off the *Big E's* starboard bow, sir!"

The carrier's change of course would put Dreadnought between her and the screening destroyer.

"Belay simulated attack evolution," he decided, thinking and speaking aloud. "All stop. Diving," he added, "hold us at this level if you can please. Rig the boat for absolute silence."

Absolute silence was a nice idea but wholly impractical, impossible to achieve on Dreadnought. Collingwood had studied the blueprints for the next class of Royal Navy hunter killers and they would – if they were ever built – incorporate all manner of new innovations to dampen sound outputs. Everything from massively cushioned power plants to several inches of rubber coating covering every inch of the pressure hull. No matter, Dreadnought would run as silently as possible.

The Americans had transferred so much technology and divulged so much classified information that even while the construction of the Dreadnought commenced on 12th June 1959, Rolls-Royce, the United Kingdom Atomic Energy Authority and the Admiralty Research Station at Dounreay had begun work on a wholly British nuclear propulsion suite. The first of a new class of nuclear-powered attack boats, HMS Valiant, had been ordered in August 1960 and laid down in a dock at Barrow-in-Furness adjacent to the already well-progressed Dreadnought in January 1962. Valiant's construction had not been well-advanced by the night of the October War and as far as Collingwood knew her partially formed skeleton had remained untouched since that day.

"Oops, that's torn it!" Max Forton groaned irritably.

The squealing, gravelly electronic rasp of a single long targeting sonar ping seemed to reverberate around and through the Dreadnought's pressure hull.

"Send S-One-Zero-One by target pings," Collingwood ordered. There was another submarine out there, probably beyond the Enterprise. He asked himself if he ought to have gone silent as soon as the carrier altered course. Perhaps. He had been playing hide and seek with the Yanks for a week and this was the first time they had got the drop on him. There was no shame in it. He listened to the sonar man sending HMS Dreadnought's pennant number in staccato pings of electrical energy.

There was a spine-chilling pause while the control room held its collective breath after the signal had finished.

"I have low speed cavitations bearing zero-zero-eight, sir."

"Range?"

There was a moment's hesitation.

"Between three and four thousand yards, sir. I think he must have been deep and periodically coming up for a look around."

That made perfect sense if there was more than one American SSN attached to the Enterprise battle Group.

New sonar pings began to scratch at the hull and the nerve endings of the men in the control rooms. The message seemed to go on forever. The Captain of HMS Dreadnought did not need to wait for a report.

SSN 589 TO S101 STOP IF EVER IN NORFOLK MEET ME AT VINCENTS BAR CAPTAIN STOP WE OUGHT TO COMPARE NOTES STOP GOOD HUNTING SIR STOP

Simon Collingwood drew breath again.

Okay, it transpired that the Captain of the Skipjack class attack submarine USS Scorpion did not want to trade torpedo salvoes today.

I can play nicely, too.

"Send," he ordered, his heart beat slowing: "THANKS FOR THE DANCE STOP I HOPE WE NEVER HAVE TO DO THIS FOR REAL STOP GOD BE WITH YOU SIR MESSAGE ENDS…"

Chapter 16

Monday 2nd December 1963
St Catherine's Hospital for Women, Mdina, Malta

Marija Calleja returned to her sparsely furnished, whitewashed second floor room – more of a nun's cell - overlooking the shaded, garden courtyard of the inner hospital as the dusk was fast falling over the hilltop city at the heart of the island. The quiet daytime coolness of the room had turned to a chill as the night settled, so she drew her shawl tighter around her shoulders as she sat stiffly on the bed and with hands that trembled still even after all these years, she steeled herself to open Peter's latest letter.

By the grace of God, it had been a good day.

Two baby girls born without apparent defects.

Both mothers were weary but overjoyed; and a little drunk with relief.

In the first days after the war they had braced themselves for horrors to come. Mercifully, such horrors had been rare. There had been more miscarriages, a few damaged babies. Perhaps, one-third more cases than in the two years before the cataclysm. Doctor Margo Seiffert, Marija's mentor and friend since her earliest adolescence, had produced statistics measuring the pre and post-natal 'conclusions' before and after the war. She wanted to correlate her clinical records against the daily radiation counts she knew the British authorities monitored at twelve separate sites on the Maltese Archipelago. The Surgeon General's Office of the British Military Administration of the Maltese Archipelago had ignored her requests. They had not even acknowledged receipt of those requests, this despite the fact St Catherine's Hospital had submitted all its live and stillbirth statistical returns to the SGO, as required by the BMA of the MA. The proliferations of official acronyms was one of the numerous small, maddeningly petty daily vexations of living under martial law.

Margo had a theory that the small increase in miscarriages and of births of babies with congenital or other problems – and it was only a very small increase from pre-war – might simply be a consequence of the poor diets common on Malta in the last year due to rationing and mothers tending to forego scarce food to feed their existing children. Because there had been no 'fallout bloom' over the islands the background level of radiation was possibly only marginally elevated since the war and, and Margo's thinking was that the true consequences of this apparently small increase in 'background radiation' might take many years to show through in the statistics.

Marija was not convinced she understood everything Margo had tried to explain to her. Her theory about the last year's miscarriages and 'defects' was based on her experience in Japan immediately after the Second World War when the Japanese were starving and their medical services in the big cities had virtually broken down.

Marija turned her thoughts from the events of the day to the here and now.

Peter's letter was post marked 29 OCT 63. It had been franked by BFPO GOS; if it had been posted in Gosport, it told her that Peter's ship was still based at Portsmouth. Or that it had been at Portsmouth around the end of last month. Many of his letters had reached her so badly mutilated by the censor that she had no idea where he was or had been for months. She took a deep breath. She had been promised the censorship would cease and what she held in her shaking fingers was an apparently undoctored envelope holding out the tantalising promise of a similarly unmolested letter within.

She broke into the envelope.

27th October 1963
HMS Talavera, Fareham Creek

Dear Marija,
This is our seventh week swinging around our anchors on our latest sojourn at Portsmouth and I think it is fair to say that we are getting royally cheesed off with the prolonged inactivity. I noticed that your last two letters (of 9th and 17th September) were more than usually 'censored' and had ISD stamps on every page. I hope this doesn't reflect on the Med Fleet's treatment of Joe, or suggest that you and your family are being overly put upon by the so-called security services.

Marija turned the three sheets of closely written script on the thin sheets she had retrieved from the envelope and gasped with pleasure. There was not so much as a comma deleted, inked out, smudged or otherwise physically removed from Peter's letter.

Things back in the old country improve a little, notwithstanding the rationing situation, which is now beginning to oppress the Fleet shore establishments.
People are quite horrified when I complain about your letters being mucked about so clumsily. It seems to me that if the rationale for holding onto bits of the Empire (or 'Commonwealth' as the politicos say

these days) is to maintain the British way of life then exactly the same standards of justice, freedom of speech and association and so forth ought to apply in those 'dominions' or 'protectorates' as apply at home. We're either all in this together or we're not, etcetera!

Marija's equilibrium was slowly returning. She forced herself to breathe deep and long in a useless attempt to still her rushing thoughts before she read on. Peter's letters tended to dance about all over the place which made it even harder to follow his thoughts when a letter was heavily censored. Often, she spent literally hours piecing together what he had been trying to say to her. A serious remark was followed by a quip, or an anecdote about the antics of a man in his division, or insights into the realities of life in the 'old country', a complaint about this or that naval idiosyncrasy, or a sardonic observation about his illustrious father's latest 'newspaper adventure'. It was pure bliss to be able to read Peter's *actual words*. The letters they had been exchanging for half a lifetime had become a long, unbroken conversation; a voyage into the unknown that over the years had become an exploration into the mind and the thoughts of one into the other.

She read and reread the letter until there was a gentle knock at her door.

It was Margo Seiffert who grinned wanly and dragged into the room. The older woman planted herself on the bed beside her younger friend. Marija held up the thin sheets covered in script, her mouth involuntarily quirking into a laughing, girlish smile.

"You have a visitor, my dear."

Marija knew who would be downstairs, cap in hand, pacing the small ground floor reception area. She said nothing, simply nodded.

"How is *your* young man?"

"Tied up safe and sound in Fareham Creek, that's the upper, inland part of Portsmouth Harbour," Marija sighed. "He's put in a second transfer request to be assigned to the Mediterranean Fleet and this time his Captain has allowed it to go forward."

Margo Seiffert patted the younger woman's left hand.

"You mustn't go getting your hopes up."

"No, I won't."

"Things will work out okay. Sometimes, you just have to have a little faith."

Marija strangled a giggle. The story of how Margo, then a Surgeon Commander in the United States Navy, had met the love of her life read like a latter-day fairy tale. On a liaison visit, a 'god-awful courtesy call' ashore at Valletta, Margo complained, she had found herself saluting and shaking hands with a 'short, balding man with big ears and the *kindest*, most *intelligent* green eyes' and her life had changed. 'You're never too old for love at first sight' she told Marija when they had gone together to the chapel in Kalkara within a stone's throw of the Bighi Royal Naval Hospital, to bid their private last farewells to the man who had – in different ways – saved both their lives. Surgeon Captain Reginald Stanley Stephens (Retired) had had a heart attack a week before and he had never recovered consciousness. The two women had kept a vigil at his bedside, knowing that the end was near. He died peacefully in his sleep with Margo holding his hand. The terrible sadness of his loss had hung over the women for days and then weeks. But then something strange had happened. They still regularly placed flowers on the grave, they still got tearful, the dreadful aching emptiness remained; but the hurt became bearable and their friendship, always close, sisterly, became almost like that of a mother and daughter. For Marija the death of her real-life saviour was like a delayed rite of passage into true adulthood; for Margo was like a licence to pick up the torch that had fallen from her dead lover's hands and to renew the battle. Together, they had moved on.

Staff Sergeant Jim Siddall straightened and smiled a tight-lipped smile as Marija slowly negotiated the last few steps and emerged into the waiting room of the St Catherine's Hospital for Women. His uniform was freshly pressed, creases razor-edged and his cap with its distinctive badge and red band was under his arm. He was unarmed.

Together the man and the woman walked out onto the cobbles of the plaza in front of the Cathedral, which loomed darkly in the east in the falling murk of the late evening. The twin city of Mdina-Rabat was unnaturally quiet behind its ancient ramparts, subdued as if the spirit of its people had been temporarily crushed.

"I received the first uncensored letter from England," Marija said dully in the night as they walked away from the Hospital. "Should I thank you, Sergeant Siddall?"

"No. I never had anything to do with that side of things."

"But you are here now?"

"Yes, I am," the man chuckled ruefully. "As my old Mum used to say, it's a funny old world, isn't it?"

Marija drew her shawl close around her shoulders.

"Two babies were born today. Both were pink and plump and...perfect."

"That's good news."

"Why did you come here?"

"There's talk *we* may be pulling out of the Med."

"The British? Leaving?"

"Yes," the big man muttered hoarsely. "Back home people are likely to starve this winter and they say *we* can't afford to hang on to what's left of the Empire. If it comes to it, we'll pull out quickly. Not quite overnight, but it won't be pretty. I've been assigned to a special unit to organise the rescue of families and individuals particularly associated or linked to the Military Administration. People who'd be liable to be labelled collaborators, or worse. Your father is the Deputy Manager of the docks at Senglea so he's an obvious candidate for reprisals after we've gone..."

"I will stay whatever happens," Marija snapped, feeling her face flush with anger.

"All Hell will break loose after *we've* gone. The Communists and Nationalists will be at each other's throats," the man protested with resignation. "You have no idea, Marija!"

"Enlighten me?"

"There is a fascist regime in Italy. In Sicily, sixty miles away there is a civil war going on. Along the North African coast south of Malta there's another war, more tribal than civil by all accounts, going on for the control of the oil fields they discovered a few years back. In Tunisia and Algeria there appears to be some kind of Holy war, a *jihad*, whatever that is in progress. There's bloodletting and chaos all around the Mediterranean. The Mediterranean used to be a British and American lake with the French and the Italians in the background. Now that the Americans have withdrawn their Sixth Fleet to home waters the Spanish, Italians, Greeks, Turks, Egyptians and Israelis are all flexing their muscles. The latest news is that Turkey and Greece will be shooting at each other soon. God knows what the crowd in power in Rome are up to. As for the Spanish!" Jim Siddall realised her was beginning to rant. "If the Mediterranean Fleet pulls out of Malta somebody else will move in. The one thing you can be absolutely sure of is that whoever moves in – and somebody will - *will* be ten times worse than *us*."

The *Times of Malta* occasionally carried foreign news implying discontent and lawlessness in the outside world; rarely dealing in specifics. People in the street gossiped about pirates at large in the eastern seas and it was known that British destroyers constantly patrolled the narrow seas between Sicily and Cap Bon. In the summer several of the long empty gun emplacements guarding Kalkara, Valletta and Sliema had been refitted with long-barrelled 3.7-inch guns. However, since there had been no attack on either Malta or on Gozo, and there had been no reports of piracy or any other incidents in the waters immediately around the archipelago most people had treated the reports of the spreading anarchy elsewhere with a pinch of salt. Life on the islands was difficult enough. The rationing and the myriad of stupid little restrictions imposed under martial law tended to distract most people from any lengthy consideration of the woes of others in lands beyond the horizon.

"We will defend ourselves if we have to," Marija declared with more confidence than she actually felt.

"With what? If we go, we'll leave nothing. In fact, we'll blow up, burn or scuttle anything we can't take with us."

Marija's angry eyes burned in the gloom.

"Anybody who remains on Malta with any kind of link with *us* will be branded a collaborator," Jim Siddall continued remorselessly.

"I think you are exaggerating..."

"Marija," the man groaned, "why do you think *we,* the British, have been acting like such complete bastards the last year? For our own amusement? One in three of my countrymen and women are dead and the rest are living on the edge of survival. Out here in 'the colonies' we're clinging on by our finger tips. The Yanks only pulled out of the Mediterranean was because they didn't want to leave one of their hands in the meat-grinder a moment longer than they absolutely had to!"

The woman folded her arms across her breasts as if she was cold.

The big military policeman was not afraid for himself; he was only afraid for her.

Chapter 17

Tuesday 3rd December 1963
The Embassy of the United States of America to the Court of Balmoral, UKIEA Compound Number 2, Cheltenham

Loudon Baines Westheimer II viewed the cool-eyed grey-haired naval officer standing before him with his cap under his arm holding a loosely approximate stance of attention with suspicion.

His aides said the man had gone native and in hindsight he ought to have objected more strongly when the Navy nominated him to replace Rear Admiral Armstrong, his predecessor when he was invalided back to the States. Apart from any other consideration the Brits would be insulted when they discovered the new US Naval Attaché was only a four-ring reservist.

He *had* objected to that.

Washington had informed him that since the 'Brits weren't talking to any of our military people about anything important these days' it hardly made any difference. And besides, Walter Brenckmann was already 'in country'. Apparently one of Brenckmann's oldest buddies was close to the Director at Langley. Not that it would do any good.

The CIA talked to American diplomats even less than the Brits.

"What do you think of Cheltenham, Captain Brenckmann?" The United States Ambassador to the United Kingdom of Great Britain and Northern Ireland asked, lighting another Luck Strike.

"At least it is safe to walk the streets at night hereabouts, sir," the naval officer replied with the clipped, New England accent that set many Texans, like Loudon Baines Westheimer II's teeth on edge.

He did not get on with any of Kennedy's people; he had backed his friend Lyndon *Baines* Johnson for the presidential nomination. LBJ and he shared a couple of common ancestors – two or three generations ago - and they had always been natural co-conspirators in the internecine southern machinations of the Democratic Party. LBJ was nowhere near as one-eyed as JFK about the new world order, thank God!

John Fitzgerald Kennedy and that meddling, womanising, preaching little brother of his might think that sooner or later, what little remained of Christendom was going to come to its senses and give him a huge fucking medal for what he did last year, but LBJ did not believe it for a minute and neither did Loudon Baines Westheimer II.

"Inside the compound maybe," the Ambassador grunted.

This was his second interview with the new Naval Attaché since his arrival in Cheltenham four days ago. The first interview had been to grill Brenckmann about how he managed to get himself locked up by the Brits in some old fort on Portland Bill. The local militia had accused him of spying and Westheimer had not got to the bottom of exactly what Brenckmann thought he was going to achieve 'spying' on a more or less empty anchorage.

'Gathering military intelligence is as much about establishing how a thing is being conducted as it is about what is actually happening,' the grey-haired naval officer had informed him.

'And what did you learn?'

'Very little, sir. However, I was able to gain further corroboration of what I already knew.'

'Which would be?'

'That the Brits are operating on a war footing at a unit tactical level, sir.'

'Like we aren't?"

'No, sir. We aren't. We won the war. The Brits didn't.'

Loudon Baines Westheimer II had given up debating what he considered to be ephemeral philosophical issues with Brenckmann at that juncture.

He had met a lot of Navy types like the Attaché.

At sea they were gung ho patriots, on land they had too much time to think and like too many people who had too much spare time on their hands they turned into air-headed crypto-liberals of the worst kind; the sort JFK had bussed into the White House before he learned the lesson of his folly. The Ambassador forced himself to focus on the present.

"What are you hearing about the incident with the two Skyhawks off the Enterprise?"

"Our guys behaved like absolute beginners, sir."

"Is that what you've told the Brits?"

"No, sir."

"Operation fucking Manna!"

"Sir?" Walter Brenckmann inquired solicitously.

"One minute the Brits are whining about the non-delivery of 'emergency supplies', whatever that means, the next they're running these huge fucking convoys past one of our carrier battle groups! Why the fuck would they think we'd empty our grain silos for them when we've known all along that they'd already secured their own source of supply?"

Walter Brenckmann wondered if the Ambassador really wanted to know. Westheimer was from a family of robber baron ranchers and oil

Page | 117

men. He had found his niche with the Democrats more because of his social and financial interests than out of any political or ideological sympathies with the Party. A big, broad man who dwarfed many of those with whom he met in his official duties in Cheltenham he felt imprisoned within the secure Government compound which had become his whole world. If ever he ventured out into the real world beyond it was always with a dozen heavily armed bodyguards. Westheimer was completely the wrong man for the job but Kennedy's people had had to pay off a lot of highly energized detractors after the October War and given that most of the plumb diplomatic assignments had been erased from the map, they had struggled to find a posting with a profile high enough to impress a man with the Ambassador's extremely high opinion of his own importance.

The man had been too stupid to turn down the appointment.

"It is because *they* don't trust us, sir."

"What choice have they got?"

Walter groaned inwardly. He said nothing.

"Well?"

Demanded the big man chain smoking from the comfort of the imported leather chair behind the broad uncluttered desk.

"I apologise, sir. I thought your question was rhetorical."

Loudon Baines Westheimer II almost bit off the filter of his Lucky Strike. "What choice have the Brits got?" He asked again.

The naval officer thought about this for another moment.

"Forgive me, sir. I don't think we've got off on a very good footing. Consequently, I have no feel for whether you actually want me to answer a question," he shrugged, "like that frankly, or to be *diplomatic*."

The Ambassador stubbed out his cigarette and reached for another. "Don't give me that Harvard crap, Brenckmann."

"Yale, sir. I took my law degree at Yale."

"Whatever. You fucking Ivy League guys are all the same. I never went to any of those fancy colleges and I did all right!"

"Yes, sir," Walter Brenckmann agreed.

The Ambassador's father had been one of the richest men in Texas, of course. Red neck Democrats like the Ambassador brought out the worst in him and he knew it.

"Premier Heath's administration took the view that no American government would ever, under *any* circumstances, empty its grain silos to help *anybody*. No matter what assurances they'd received from State Department."

"The President gave Premier Heath his word."

JFK's *word* did not count for much these days.

"The Brits only proceeded with Operation Manna after it became apparent that significant supplies of grain and fuel would *not* be shipped to the United Kingdom from American ports in time to make any difference."

Loudon Baines Westheimer II spread his arms.

"You know they wanted everything *gratis* covered by some kind of new Marshall Plan?"

"That was hardly unreasonable, sir."

"Try running that by the American people during the mid-term elections, son!"

The big man rocked back in his chair which creaked in protest.

"More Americans died in the war than in all the wars in our entire fucking history up until last October! We have our own problems back home! Don't these idiots over here get that?"

"Sir," the naval officer said evenly, suppressing a groan of despair, "I don't think the Brits are idiots but you need to know, and I think that Washington needs to know that they're done fighting *our* wars."

The Ambassador did not immediately get his head around the magnitude of what his underling had just told him. Knowing this, Walter Brenckmann attempted to paint his boss a picture.

"The Brits asked us for help to care for their sick and injured, to feed their children, to stave off tens of thousands, perhaps, millions of deaths in the coming winter and *we* played politics and tried to put a price on our *charity*. We attempted to *game* their national catastrophe for our own geo-political advantage. Consequently, if they didn't blame us for the war before they do now. Because of the short-sighted, frankly imbecilic thinking and actions of *our* Government, the United States of America's oldest and most loyal ally is half-way to regarding *us* as its worst enemy."

Loudon Baines Westheimer II was no deep-thinking internationalist, nor was he any kind of historian with any meaningful understanding of the course of either European or World history beyond the cursory State Department briefings he had had to sit through – reluctantly and with bad grace - before he got on the plane for England. He had not been sent to this cold, miserable archipelago off the ravaged coast of Northern Europe to make or to propose policy, he was a time serving mouthpiece.

In a few more months they recall him, he would go back to running the family business in Texas proudly proclaiming that he had done his duty by God and his Country.

"What are you saying, Brenckmann?"

"After 1945 Europe rose again from the ashes. It will be harder this time but Europe will rise again. However, this time there will be a difference. A year ago, the Europeans got dragged into *our* war with the Soviets. *Our* war, not *theirs*. *Our* war fought because we believed that *our* national strategic interests had been compromised. Now that *we* intend to wash our hands of the consequences of *our* war, it is hardly surprising that our allies – those few who survive – feel *betrayed*. We have two choices, Ambassador," Walter Brenckmann explained, knowing he was probably wasting his breath, "we can seek, belatedly, to make appropriate reparations for our folly, or we can continue down the road we have walked thus far. The former offers some small prospect of rapprochement. The latter will, sooner or later bring us into conflict with not just our old allies but the whole world." He shrugged. "We dragged our friends into a fight that wasn't theirs. They got the crap kicked out of them. Then we crapped on them again." His stare bored into the face of the American Ambassador. "How would you feel if you were the Brits, sir?"

"Whose fucking side are you on, Captain?"

"This country, England, is about the same size as New York State back home. *England* was hit by over twenty one-megaton plus strikes. New York State got hit by one. One third of all the people living in *England* before the war are dead now, One-third of the survivors, eight or nine million people, are living in damaged housing with barely enough to eat. Medical services and transportation are operating at about fifty percent of pre-war levels. Thousands of people are dying of diarrhoea and the cold every day. Most of the old folk have already died. *We* did this to them. How dare you sit there and ask me whose side I am on, sir!"

"You're sounding like a fucking Commie to me!"

That was when Walter Brenckmann realised that being a patriot meant more than wearing the uniform. Patriotism meant nothing if a man did not have the moral courage to stand up to people like Loudon Baines Westheimer II and what he represented.

"Just before I left my office," Walter Brenckmann went on, his expression forming into an agate hard severity, "I received a summary report of a SITREP from the *Task Force 27*."

"That's the Enterprise's Battle group, isn't it?"

"Yes, sir."

"Jeez, that must be one Helluva ship!"

"That's as may be, sir. It now seems clear that the Brits could have sunk the *Big E* any time they wanted in the last week. The Enterprise and most of her escorts too, I suspect."

Loudon Baines Westheimer II was terminally bewildered.

"It seems," the naval officer explained patiently, "that the British nuclear submarine Dreadnought was able to stalk *TF27* undetected for several days. When she was finally discovered by one of our SSNs, the Scorpion, she was within two thousand yards of the Enterprise and clearly manoeuvring to conduct a simulated attack from directly astern of the *Big E*. Initial tactical analysis of sonar plots recorded in recent days indicate that – employing tactics presumably learned from us at Groton – Dreadnought had been 'in company' with *TF27* for as many as seven days."

Loudon Baines Westheimer II's jaw hung slack for a moment.

"What the fuck happened when Scorpion went up against the Brit sub?"

"Scorpion's captain did the only thing he could do, sir," Walter Brenckmann assured him. "Assuming that HMS Dreadnought already had a firing solution on her attack board in respect of his command, the *Big E* and both destroyers in the carrier's flank screen he was extremely careful not to make any sudden movements, sir."

"What the fuck does that mean in English?"

"He signalled HMS Dreadnought in such a way as to communicate to the British captain that he had no hostile intentions towards his ship."

Loudon Baines Westheimer II lost his temper.

"How the fuck do you do that?"

Walter Brenckmann did not bat an eyelid.

"With the highest possible level of professional competence, sir."

"Why the fuck didn't he shoot at the Limey?"

"Probably because had he survived making a mistake like that – not that he would have - he'd have been court-martialled and drummed out of the service, sir."

Loudon Baines Westheimer II didn't even think of attempting to moderate his increasingly vile, inflamed uncouth bad humour.

"Don't try to be fucking clever with me!"

"Scorpion's CO was operating under rules of engagement that specifically forbade him to fire on a British warship unless fired upon first. Those standing orders were amended by the Defence Department prior to the Enterprise's departure from Norfolk to replace the USS Midway on station off Ireland. The relevant amendments removed the right of individual captains to vary or to re-interpret the strict letter of the rules of engagement. Under any circumstances."

"Scorpion's captain should be dismissed the service!"

"If you start cashiering men because they've obeyed their orders 'to the letter'," Walter Brenckmann pointed out, "that's hardly conducive to the maintenance of good discipline in the Service in the future, sir."

Loudon Baines Westheimer II glowered at his subordinate in fulminating silence so Walter Brenckmann carried on.

"It was my understanding that it was the policy of the Government and both Houses of Representatives that the United States of America should adopt a passive stance in Europe and the Middle East – essentially disengagement – while, simultaneously building its influence in the Americas, North, Central, and South, as well as across the Caribbean? This latter object was only to be supported by military force as a last resort? Sinking a British submarine in international waters seems to me no more consistent with the stated policy of my Government than those idiots on the *Big E* flying simulated bombing runs on one of HMS Ark Royal's air defence pickets, sir. Respectfully," he said with self-evident disrespect, "it seems to me that there appears to be something of a disconnect between the White House, the Defence Department and the Navy at present. *Respectfully*, sir, in my capacity as your senior naval advisor in the British Isles, I recommend that you communicate, in the strongest possible language to the State Department that if somebody over there in Washington wants to have a shooting war on his hands, he's doing a swell job."

"The Brits don't want a war..."

"I spent two hours the other morning standing on a windy hillside watching British sailors cross-decking eighty- or ninety-pound fixed rounds off an ammunition ship in Portland Harbour. They were working as if their lives depended on it, sir. I was arrested because I saw what they were doing and I was detained just long enough not to witness the departure of the destroyer which had been filling her magazines – which I believe to have been HMS Talavera – or the departure of any of the other vessels oiling and preparing for sea that morning. I don't personally believe the Brits want to get into a shooting war with us. However, if it comes to it, they will be ready."

Loudon Baines Westheimer II finally got a grip of his emotions long enough to realise he was being told something important that, moreover, ought to be scaring the shit out of him.

"I can't tell Washington that, Brenckmann!"

"They'll be starting to work it out for themselves about now, Ambassador. If you tell it to them straight that'll be to your credit." Sometimes you had to tell your boss things that ought to be patently obvious to him just to be able to look oneself in the mirror in the morning. "Whereas, if there is an unfortunate incident in the Atlantic, they'll start asking themselves why that Westheimer guy didn't hit the alarm button."

Loudon Baines Westheimer II lit another cigarette.

"You think you're some kind of smart arse, don't you, Walter?"

The two-war veteran in uniform viewed the sleek, self-satisfied civilian oaf who had been appointed to go abroad and lie for his country in the land of a spurned and lately, unjustly maligned and meanly treated true friend.

A little humility was too much to expect from a man like Loudon Baines Westheimer II.

Likewise, any sense of some higher purpose, or any sign, however flimsy, of some real insight or understanding of the new post-holocaust world that the expenditure of a significant proportion of America's nuclear arsenal had created.

It was not that Loudon Baines Westheimer II did not understand what his country had done; it was that he did not care and worse, he regarded *not caring* as a badge of honour that he wore with red-necked pride.

"No, Ambassador," he said, dropping all pretence of respectful deference. "I'm just a lawyer who inadvertently ended up in the Navy. Unlike you I've served my country in two wars. While you were smoking cigars and joshing with all the other fat, rich old boys on your ranch in Texas, I was on the bridge of a destroyer escort on the North Atlantic, or conning a fleet destroyer off the beachhead at Pusan. Back then I was fighting people whom I honestly believed to be my country's enemies. Thirteen months ago, we had no truer friends in Christendom than the Brits; if we're not very, very careful we will turn them into our worst enemies. And I do mean our *worst* enemies because unlike the Soviets or the Chinese or the maniacs in North Korea, the Brits understand us. They understand our every idiosyncrasy, our every weakness, and most dangerous of all, they understand exactly how we fight our wars."

Walter Brenckmann waited to be dismissed. When it did not happen, he dropped into the nearest chair, a Queen Ann style piece of furniture that was completely out of place in the tacky, tasteless leather-bound world of Loudon Baines Westheimer II.

The Ambassador's glare morphed into something contemplative.

"LBJ told Kennedy's people it was too early to cut back on the military," he said suddenly. "But nobody in Washington listens to the Vice-President. I swear to God I sometimes think the people around JFK have got chicken shit for brains, Captain."

Chapter 18

Tuesday 3rd December 1963
Balmoral Castle, Ballater, Aberdeenshire

If Vice-Admiral Julian Christopher had not previously been introduced to Queen Elizabeth II he would have been surprised and possibly dismayed to discover how small, fragile and slender were the shoulders upon which the weight of the world currently rested.

The attractive thirty-seven-year-old mother of three and the one last unimpeachable symbol of national unity shook the hand of the man who had been her late Uncle, Lord Louis Mountbatten's most remarkable protégé.

She met his concerned look with a wan smile.

"Please don't fuss, Julian," she commanded softly.

"I wouldn't dream of it, ma'am," the tall naval officer acknowledged with a tightness in his throat and a bothersome mistiness in his eyes.

He had never expected to meet the extraordinary young woman again.

He forced himself to stand to attention, bowed his head and moved on to have his hand shaken heartily by Prince Philip, the Duke of Edinburgh, who had once, briefly, served under him during his career in the Royal Navy.

"Ah, our modern-day Nelson returns at last!"

The younger man beamed broadly at his old Captain.

"Rather more Blackbeard, or perhaps, Long John Silver to my detractors, sir," the Admiral chuckled.

"I can't wait to hear about your latest adventures!"

The Duke of Edinburgh was of a similar stature to the older man, leanly made and roguishly handsome.

Born Prince Philip of Greece he was five years older than his wife whom he first met just before the Second World War when she was thirteen and he an eighteen-year-old very junior naval officer.

He was the son of a disinherited, impoverished European dynasty and she the heir apparent to Europe's most ancient and prestigious royal house.

"Wherever poor old Uncle Louis is now he must be jumping up and down in his grave cheering you on!"

"That's good of you to say so, sir."

At the Prime Minister's bidding the presentation line had formed in an oddly eccentric order.

He had led the line but thereafter precedence of rank and

hierarchy had been deliberately jumbled.

After Edward Heath came Patricia and Tom Harding-Grayson, Margaret Thatcher, Alec Douglas Home and lastly, Julian Christopher.

"I hear you had a dreadful flight up from Gloucestershire, Admiral?"

It had taken the pilot four attempts to land the RAF Comet 4 at Dyce between flurrying snow and low, dangerous clouds.

Julian Christopher had been seated across the aisle from Margaret Thatcher, who had carried on reading papers from her ministerial red box throughout the nerve-jangling drama as if utterly convinced that nothing on earth could harm so much as a hair on her perfectly coiffured head.

They had travelled slightly apart from the Prime Minister, the Foreign Secretary and Tom Harding-Grayson who spent most of the three-hour flight – normal flight time between Cheltenham and Dyce was a less over two hours but today the weather had made a mockery of the *normal* schedule – in low-voiced confidential conversation.

The Admiral had chatted for a while with Patricia Harding-Grayson, a charming greying woman who had made a name for herself in the late 1940s and early 1950s writing whodunits for adults in the style of a literary Agatha Christie. Needless to say, she had been less successful than Miss Christie in what had been for her, a diverting hobby rather than a career.

She was a lady who journeyed widely in Europe and America and had once been married to an Italian count.

"Having been recently launched off the bow of the Ark Royal in a Sea Vixen," Julian Christopher had quipped, "in a force eight gale, today's adventure was grist to the mill, sir."

It had not been lost on Julian Christopher that of all the members of the presentation line the most nervous had been the Angry Widow.

She had been preoccupied with checking her makeup in her compact mirror, visibly unsettled just before she was introduced to the Queen.

It was as if she had thought through every other aspect of this peculiar expedition to Royal Deeside but for the mechanics of actually *meeting* the Monarch.

Which was profoundly logical in a funny sort of way.

How does one prepare oneself for such a unique encounter?

Margaret Thatcher had been a little disconcerted when the Queen sympathised with her – one mother to another - for her having to leave her twins in Cheltenham for to make the journey to Balmoral.

The Prime Minister's party had not arrived at the heavily guarded royal estate until late the previous evening. There was no ceremony and the visitors had found themselves ushered directly to the 'guest wing' of the castle.

The Queen had already retired to bed and it had been a long, wearying day for the travellers.

Standing in the presentation line that morning Julian Christopher was struck by the oddness of the event, the unlikely niceties meticulously conforming to the vestiges of a court life that was already a thing of the past.

This was his eighth visit to Balmoral; his first for several years.

Previously, he had attended in the capacity of Admiral of the Fleet, Lord Mountbatten of Burma's senior aide-de-camp. Apart from the barbed wire all around the estate and the machine gun positions he had observed at the main gate, when he had opened his curtains that morning to be greeted with a wholly familiar, albeit faded green vista out of his first-floor bedroom windows.

At breakfast; toast, thin marmalade and muddy tea, he had watched two armoured cars – machine gun armed Daimler Ferrets - draw up outside the main house and the Black Watch guard change.

Most of the soldiers carried Sten Guns and side arms, a few hefted long-barrelled Browning fifty calibre sniping pieces.

After the presentations had concluded the Queen ushered her Prime Minister to a private room while her husband jovially herded the rest of the party into a reception room commanding a view of the breath-taking country to the south and west of the castle.

Julian Christopher found himself standing next to Margaret Thatcher, a little outside the circle of the conversation of Sir Alec Douglas Home, Tom Harding-Grayson and the Duke of Edinburgh. Patricia Harding-Grayson had returned to her room, her duty as a supernumerary having now been performed and satisfactorily concluded.

"Of course," Margaret Thatcher remarked, "Balmoral is not really a 'castle'."

The man was so taken aback that his companion was making 'small talk' that he was momentarily lost for a suitable reply.

"But I'm sure you are much more familiar with the history and the traditions of this place that I," the woman went on. "I didn't realise it was so far from the nearest town, I confess."

The Prime Minister's party had been flown from RAF Dyce to the Balmoral estate on two Wessex helicopters, both flying low and at breakneck speeds at little more than tree top height all the way.

"The estate itself goes back hundreds of years," he replied, finding his tongue. "I seem to recollect somebody telling me it comprises some fifty thousand acres, give or take."

"Fascinating," the Angry Widow said in such a way that the man was convinced she meant it.

"Lord Mountbatten was a bit of a fiend for the fact and figures."

"You and he were very close, I understand?"

Julian Christopher hesitated.

Louis Mountbatten was a hard man to be *close* to.

Like most great men he had had a marvellously keen eye for the main chance and known exactly when to withdraw his patronage from an underling who had in some way – often imagined rather than in reality - let him down or failed to come up to his unrealistically high expectations.

Mountbatten had never forgotten how badly the British establishment had treated his father.

Prince Louis Alexander of Battenberg had been driven out of the Admiralty in October 1914 on account of his German birth despite a lifetime's exemplary and unstinting loyal service to the Royal Navy and the British Empire.

When eventually, in 1954, his son Louis – the Battenbergs changed their name to Mountbatten during the Great War- became First Sea Lord it was as if somehow, the wrongs of the past had been acknowledged and their poison finally neutralised.

The injustice done to his father all those years ago had driven Louis Mountbatten all his life.

The man whom the Royal Household called 'Uncle Louis' was in fact Prince Philip's *grand-uncle*, since the Duke of Edinburgh was a grandson of his father, Prince Louis of Battenberg.

Mountbatten had appointed himself his *grand-nephew's* mentor and since the Queen's accession to the throne in 1952, become an integral part of the Royal Family.

The old man had been a friend of Edward VIII when he had been the darling of the nation as the gallant, fast living oddly human – if mostly in his fallibilities - Prince of Wales who had seemed somehow in touch with the ordinary man and woman during the dreadful years of the Depression.

He had been no such thing of course, and when he had to decide between his duty to the Empire and his own personal peccadilloes, the latter had prevailed and he had abdicated the throne, causing an irreparable breach between the two men. Thereafter, Louis Mountbatten had made it his personal business to ensure that the carefree, devil may care young naval officer – the then Prince Philip of

Greece – never made the same mistake…

"Admiral?"

Julian Christopher realised he had become trapped in his thoughts.

"Forgive me," he quirked a grimace of a smile. "I was thinking of Lord Mountbatten. Like everybody else, I try to pretend that what happened last year was just a bad dream. But when one remembers an old friend, or a family member who is no longer with us…"

"We all carry on as best we can," Margaret Thatcher agreed. "The only thing that we must *never* do is forget."

"Quite," Julian Christopher nodded. "We were talking about Balmoral," he recapped, thinking aloud as he re-ordered his scattered thoughts.

Although it was not impossible to achieve high command in the Royal Navy without being a social animal as accomplished with a cocktail stick as with a cutlass, it was unlikely that a wallflower unable to make polite conversation would ever again reach the pinnacle of the Service.

Over the years he had learned to tolerate fools in high places and become a tolerable party animal.

He had carefully honed his small talk, collected a library of anecdotes and quips for all occasions.

People often asked him about Balmoral and despite his reservations on this occasion and in front of *this* woman, he dutifully trotted out his pre-prepared party piece.

"Balmoral 'Castle'," he declaimed wryly, "in which we are now standing, is less a castle than a very large estate house designed by the renowned Aberdonian architect William Smith for Queen Victoria. I say 'designed by' advisedly. I believe the poor man was distracted to the point of despair by Prince Albert's modifications to 'his design' for the house. The house wasn't completed until 1856. Here it remains; a prime example of a style known as Scots Baronial; a style of architecture with origins in the sixteenth century, combining elements of medieval castles and tower houses with features reminiscent of a French Renaissance châteaux. I've always felt Balmoral was never one thing or the other, a peculiar mixture of only vaguely compatible parts. Scots Baronial was pioneered by such Scottish cultural luminaries as Sir Walter Scott and flourished in the nineteenth century during something of a Gothic Revival that was mercifully snuffed out by the First World War…"

Margaret Thatcher had inclined her head a little towards him and was listening with rapt attentiveness.

"Do go on, Admiral," she demanded. "I had no idea you were such mine of information?"

Some people have a born gift for irony and some do not.

The Angry Widow was one of the latter.

Her eyes told him she was a little amused; her voice conveyed not one scintilla of humour.

Julian Christopher determined to plough on regardless; that was what Admirals throughout history tended to do when they could not immediately think of a better alternative: "The nearest villages are Crathie and Ballater, between six and seven miles away. The estate goes all the way to Loch Muick to the south-east. Queen Victoria built a Royal Bothy - a hunting lodge - on the shores of the Loch. The view across the Loch was one which Lord Mountbatten never tired of, I recall. Before the war the Balmoral Estate employed well over a hundred people. Even in Queen Victoria's time it was a working estate. There were, probably still are I should imagine, grouse moors, large forestry plantations, several farms, herds of cattle, deer and ponies. Did you know there's a distillery on the estate?"

"Is that so?"

"Have you ever come across *Royal Lochnagar Single Malt* whiskey?"

"I can't say I have. My late husband was fond of a tipple."

"I can recommend a tipple of *Royal Lochnagar*," Julian Christopher continued as if he had not noted the flicker of pain in her voice. "I think there are around a hundred and fifty separate properties on the estate. Several of them are big country houses like Birkhall and Craigowen Lodge. The Royal Family would have used them for putting up guests before the war. I suspect that for reasons of security they are rarely used for that purpose these days."

"I really didn't realise you were so well connected with *these* people, Admiral?"

"I have been fortunate to have visited many places and met many interesting people in my travels, ma'am."

The woman stared out of the window and the playful, guardedly flirting tone of the conversation became quietly serious.

"Is Her Majesty really safe here?"

"As safe as she'll ever be," he replied. "But no. I don't think anywhere is safe. Not anymore."

The Duke of Edinburgh's small conversational circle had moved away as if to give the man and woman a little privacy.

Margaret Thatcher glanced at the men locked in earnest conversation across the other side of the room for a moment.

"Will there be a coup d'état?" She asked in a whisper.

Julian Christopher contemplated the question.

"The Chiefs of Staff have given me to understand that they stand four square behind the legitimate political leadership of the United Kingdom, ma'am."

"That, Admiral," she retorted acidly, "was not what I asked you."

"Forgive me I thought that was exactly what you asked me."

The Angry Widow was silent.

"The Japanese have a saying, ma'am," the man said after the quietness had begun to drag towards a full minute. "Which I believe seems to become more apposite with every passing day."

He hesitated.

"Death is lighter than a feather but duty is like the weight of a mountain."

"I repeat," Margaret Thatcher hissed, "is there to be a coup d'état?"

"No," the man sighed. "What would that achieve?"

"I don't know! That's why I'm asking! Please don't treat me like an idiot, Admiral Christopher!"

"Then please do me the courtesy of refraining from asking me questions you know I cannot in all honour answer, ma'am."

The Angry Widow's blue eyes were fixed on his face from the instant he half-turned to look at her.

There was diamond hardness in those eyes and an unlikely yearning to be understood that intimidated and yet excited the man.

For all that there was a quarter of a century between them in age he recognised the glistening light of battle in those beguiling blue eyes. He and the Angry Widow shared the souls of warriors of old.

"I," she swallowed, the words catching in her throat unspoken, "I apologise. You will no doubt have been forewarned that my impatience, and my *anger*, sometimes gets the better of me."

Julian Christopher understood that this was the one and only time they could allow themselves to differ over a matter of principle.

They were each in their own ways too stiff to bend in a storm without breaking.

"All will become apparent soon enough," he promised her, gruffly. "Then perhaps we should agree to begin again with a clean slate."

"I hope that will be possible, Admiral."

The man and the woman were too preoccupied with each other to react intuitively to the sudden commotion outside the building.

It was only when an air raid siren began to wind up into an ear-splitting frenzied ululating banshee howl barely twenty yards away that they blinked out of their brief trance.

There was a rushing of heavily booted tramping feet accompanied by the unmistakable clinking and banging of webbing weighted with ammunition and equipment.

"GET TO A SHELTER!"

Julian Christopher did not move.

He knew there was no time to get to *the shelter* even if he had known where it was because he had seen the two specs coming in low across the forest in the south.

Two Hawker Hunters – two beautifully honed fighting machines with fuel tanks or more likely iron free fall general purpose bombs hanging from hard points under their wings – rocketing in, closing the range at nine miles a minute.

Nine miles a minute, eight hundred feet a second.

There was no time to run, no time to think, to doubt, or to hesitate.

Both Ferret armoured cars opened fire with their 7.62-millimetre belt-fed machine guns at exactly the moment that Julian Christopher – rediscovering the hard tackling full-back he was in those years when he had played rugby for the Navy at Twickenham – hurled himself at Margaret Thatcher.

The woman did not have time to cry out before every last breath of air in her lungs was smashed from her flying body as the man dumped her unceremoniously on the floor and together, impelled by the momentum of the violent assault they rolled twice before crashing into the wall some ten feet away from the big windows.

They groaned breathlessly, instinctively she attempted to struggle free.

"Stay down!"

Julian Christopher commanded, his voice given a cutting edge by the pain stabbing in his ribs.

I am getting far too old for this sort of thing!

The woman continued to struggle, powerless to break free while the whole weight of his body pinned her down and shielded her from what he *knew* was likely to happen next.

Knowing that there was absolutely nothing else he could do he waited with a sick feeling in the pit of stomach for the first explosion.

Chapter 19

Tuesday 3rd December 1963
Point Europa, Gibraltar

The man who wore the uniform of a Royal Naval Reserve Commander and presently carried identity documents in the name of William Drayton McNeill clambered out of the Land Rover onto the hard standing in the shadow of Trinity Lighthouse. A large and ever growing crowd had gathered on the southernmost point of the British Crown Colony of Gibraltar to view the drama unfolding in Algeciras Bay. His driver, a comely blond WREN Third Officer who was no more a commissioned officer in the Royal Navy than her passenger, poured herself out from behind the wheel and walked – with the upright, confident gait of a model on a Paris catwalk - around the vehicle to join the man.

Where the North Atlantic funnelled into the straits between Europe and North Africa the waves were white and angry and the air was filled with sea spume. Although wintery sunshine benignly illuminated the Rock of Gibraltar, in the south dark, dangerous clouds fell upon the seas, rolling north like some great implacable beast threatening to consume the gravely wounded ship in its path. On most days the coast of North Africa was plainly visible to the naked eye. Today the southern horizon was foreshortened by storm clouds.

The stricken ship was almost abreast of Europa Point.

HMS Albion was listing to port, slowly drifting into Algeciras Bay bleeding bunker oil from a huge underwater wound close to her bow. A mile deeper into the bay the floating debris from HMS Cassandra, the carrier's escorting destroyer now straddled the notional boundary between Gibraltarian and Spanish territorial waters. Spanish patrol boats traversed the floating debris field like gulls flocking to pick up scraps from a trawler's nets.

A thin plume of grey smoke still rose from the Albion's single tall stack; at least she still had one of her boilers lit. If she lost power for her pumps she was doomed.

"They actually did it," the blond moaned, folding her arms across her breasts. Her expression was suddenly pinched and accusative as her gaze discovered the long low silhouettes of two Spanish destroyers out in the straits. "They mined the bay!"

Her companion thought he could make out ant-like figures moving around on HMS Albion's empty flight deck and geysers of water erupting from hoses along her flanks.

Albion had fouled a mine first; then Cassandra had hit a second and blown up. It was likely that the explosion had triggered a secondary detonation of her forward magazine. The wreck of the destroyer had sunk in less than a minute. As if things could not possibly get worse there was unlimited scope for it to get much, much worse. Even now the minesweeper HMS Castleton was leading a big Admiralty tug towards the drifting carrier. From the speed at which the Castleton was surging across the relatively calm waters of Algeciras Bay it was apparent that she was not so much clearing a safe path through any remaining underwater booby traps, as breaking trail. The tug surged along in her wake, presumably damning the torpedoes to do their worst in the best traditions of the Service.

"If this sort of thing can happen here perhaps it will wake up those idiots in charge on Malta?" The blond observed to nobody in particular when her partner gave every appearance of being lost in his thoughts.

"No," he murmured. "The last thing the Italians or the Sicilians, or even those terrorists across the water in Libya want to do is block the Grand Harbour or Marsamxett. There's no profit in that for them. That's why we'll sink ships in the main channels and blow up the port installations if those idiots in England give Operation Homeward Bound the green light. We'll probably mine the South Comino Channel and Marsaxlokk Bay, too. Just for good measure. If a job's worth doing it's worth doing well," he concluded sourly.

The woman raised an eyebrow.

The crowd on Europa Point was growing fast. Small boats; fishing smacks, whalers and launches were putting out from the Naval Dockyard in a swarm.

Out in the straits the two Spanish destroyers cruised like sharks waiting for their quarry to succumb to her wounds. High above the Bay antiquated Spanish single engine World War Two vintage fighters circled like jackals gathering around the dying corpse of the British Empire.

The man's eyes flicked to seaward, to the skies, and returned to the crippled carrier.

HMS Albion had been converted into a 'Commando Carrier' before the war. By removing her steam catapults and all the other paraphernalia required to operate fixed wing aircraft, she had been transformed into floating base for two squadrons of helicopters, and a battalion of Royal Marines and all their heavy equipment. Several of Albion's helicopters had been flown off in the minutes after she struck the mine; others had had to be pushed over the side to clear the canting flight deck of fire risks. There were at least sixteen hundred men trapped on the sinking ship; nine hundred crew and over seven hundred Royal marines of 2nd Battalion 40 Commando.

"If the Spanish have mined the Bay and they've got hundreds of guns in the hills pointing at the air base," the blond woman queried, "I don't see how we can pull out of Gibraltar even if somebody in England thinks that's a good idea."

"They'll let us go if we hand everything over in pristine condition," the man replied evenly. They had been on the last transport the Spanish had allowed to land on the short, treacherous runway across the isthmus – *La Linear* - that connected the Rock of Gibraltar to the mainland. No sooner had their aircraft – a lumbering, creaking four turbo-prop Blackburn Beverley – lurched to a halt than a salvo of mortar bombs had cratered the middle of the single runway. These projectiles, lobbed fairly haphazardly across the border – the border between British and Spanish territory being the northern boundary fence of the air base – by troops positioned in trenches shielded from direct view and fire by the small village of *La Linear* had fired four salvoes of five mortars. Just to make absolutely sure that the runway was completely out of action. At least half the rounds had fallen short, some in the Spaniards' own forward lines, and several had gone long into civilian and military accommodation blocks south of the runway killing and wounding at least twenty people. The Gibraltar garrison had not returned fire. Nor had the Royal Navy but since the cruiser HMS Tiger, and four of the five destroyers of the 3rd Destroyer Squadron had departed the colony a fortnight ago, there was very little the single remaining World War Two vintage ship, HMS Cavalier, and half-a-dozen minesweepers and patrol boats could do in the face of overwhelming land based artillery. Wisely, HMS Cavalier had kept her powder dry.

Gibraltarians had viewed the arrival of HMS Albion with her helicopters and elite Royal Marine Commandos as the modern-day equivalent of the cavalry riding to the rescue. For most of the people standing on Europa Point HMS Albion's heart-wrenchingly slow-motion death represented the beginning of the end.

"The Spanish will let us go eventually."

"Eventually?" The woman asked.

"They'll want to disarm and humiliate anybody in uniform. They'll want to round up civilian men of working age to send north as slave labourers. Then they'll let their conscripts have their fun with the colony's women. After they've done that, they'll let us British go. But only *eventually*, after the bastards have had their pound of flesh."

"Would they really behave like that? I mean, in front of the whole world?"

"Franco was the last truly fascist dictator in Europe until last autumn. He came to power standing on Mussolini and Hitler's shoulders. Guernica happened because of Franco, tens of thousands of men, women and children were disappeared by the *Generalissimo* and his *Falangist* bully boys during and after the civil war. The revenge killings went on for years. Before last year's war Spain and to a lesser extent Portugal – another fascist military dictatorship by the way – were the pariahs of Western Europe, the last blood-stained relics on the proud escutcheon of the new democratic post World War Two settlement." He waved at the sky where distant aircraft circled. "The Spanish Air Force is still mostly equipped with locally manufactured copies of Messerschmitts, Dorniers and Heinkels it got from Hitler during the 1945 war!"

The woman frowned at the man. In the year she had known him she had never heard him speak so bitterly, or with such sick resignation.

"None of this is your fault. You didn't know we were going to get stuck here when you talked us onto that flight out of Malta, sweetheart."

This small show of public intimacy drew a vexed look which the woman ignored.

"Sweetheart," she persisted lowly, moving close until their shoulders were touching. "After what we've been through, I'm surprised something like this hasn't happened before. What about that time in Beirut?"

"That was hairy," he conceded with a grunt.

"Sometimes whatever you do you just get unlucky."

The man scowled. He had tried to get them on a Comet bound for RAF Brize Norton but the Redcaps at Luqa Air Base were neither as gullible or as paranoid as the Internal Security Division goons who called the shots everywhere else on Malta. It had been a transit to Gibraltar or nothing for the next week and that would have been a disaster. As if their current situation was not a disaster! He had confidently anticipated a day's delay hanging about on the Rock twiddling their thumbs while he wangled two seats on a flight back to England. He had had no idea things were so bad in Gibraltar.

In Malta Naval Intelligence had told him things were 'a bit sticky' with the Spanish, but 'when were things ever otherwise?' The general appreciation was that things were bad but that 'Franco would be mad to try anything now.' Things were falling apart and if 'he waits a year or two he'll probably be able to walk in any time he wants.

The trouble with that kind of thinking was that it assumed one was dealing with a rational enemy. Old Fascists like Franco were not *rational*. People who seize power at the point of a gun and methodically murder anybody who *might* be a threat do not usually possess thought processes which function in the same way as those of the leaders of mature democracies who – however reluctantly – actually retain some modicum of respect for the rights and the liberties of their people. Neville Chamberlain was a decent, *rational* man who devotedly yearned to prevent general blood-letting in Europe in 1938; he believed that Adolf Hitler was a statesman like him and that therefore, he did not want a war either. Chamberlain was duped by a monster in exactly the same way Stalin duped Franklin Delano Roosevelt and Harry Truman at the end of the Second World War. Good men – these things are relative but Chamberlain, FDR and Harry Truman were *not* monsters – struggle to comprehend the minds of *real* monsters like Adolf Hitler, Iosif Vissarionovich Stalin, and would be monsters like Benito Mussolini *and* Francisco Franco Bahamonde the last of the dictators of the class of the 1920s and 1930s. Before the October War the thinking in the capitals of Western Europe – rather muddied by American meddling in the Iberian Peninsula because successive administrations had had no scruples about propping up vile dictatorships if it suited their overall foreign policy objectives – was that Franco was in his cage and thus easily contained. In the fullness of time the old devil would die and then perhaps, there might be a possibility of change. In the meantime, Spain was economically, industrially and militarily enfeebled and therefore in no position to challenge British and French naval hegemony in the western Mediterranean Basin. The October War had changed all that.

What remained of France was a disparate collection of enclaves nominally loyal to the Provisional Government in Orleans. Paris, Strasbourg and Toulon were gone and with those cities the cohesion of the newly created Fifth Republic. The remnants of the French Fleet had concentrated at Brest and Lorient on the Biscay coast. There was talk of an alliance between the Italian fascists and their brothers in the Iberian Peninsula, it was only a matter of time before the Western Mediterranean became a no-go zone for the Royal Navy from the Balearic Sea to the Ligurian Sea. Given that Corsica and Sardinia were effectively rogue independent states how long could the British cling on to Cyprus, Malta and Gibraltar?

The man in the naval uniform vented a weary, somewhat disgruntled sigh.

The world was turning to chaos and in that chaos *he* ought to have known that Gibraltar would be the fulcrum around which British command of the Inland Sea would ultimately unravel. *He* ought to have known that when the collapse began it would progress with terrifying and unpredictable rapidity and that the collapse would be total. *He ought to have waited to get them onto a direct flight to England!*

He stared at the listing carrier in Algeciras Bay haemorrhaging bunker oil as her pumps fought a losing battle against the inrushing water. HMS Castleton was almost alongside her now. The big, ugly red and black liveried Admiralty tug was churning water nearby, slowly drawing beneath Albion's starboard bow. She carrier was noticeably down by the head. The first of the fishing boats was approaching the big ship. A ragged cheer made him glance to his right. HMS Cavalier was nosing out into the Bay, the merest wisp of smoke curling from her single stack. The old destroyer's decks were awash with bodies because her captain wanted as few of his men as possible below decks if he ran his ship onto another mine.

The man who had claimed to be Commander William Drayton McNeill RN in Cyprus and Malta watched the destroyer point her sharp prow at the small rescue flotilla now assembling around the dying carrier. He gazed at Cavalier for several minutes while he thought his thoughts, knowing that he had a decision to make and hating the fact that in his heart he had known what that decision was going to be all along and that *he* ought to have acted days ago.

He turned to face the woman who had been viewing him quizzically as she waited patiently for him to inform her how their mutual adventure was to proceed next.

She met his stare, thoughtful and a little distracted.

He had been pretty badly knocked about when they first met in that US Army hospital at İncirlik Air Base. He said he had been in Ankara when the world went to hell in a handbasket but she did not believe it. He had not had a building fall on him; he had been in a fight and got beaten to a pulp, even a girl could tell that. She was at İncirlik that day by accident, her overnight flight to Beirut having been forced to land by the ongoing nuclear nightmare. The Americans had failed to check her papers; they had other things on their minds and she had offered her services to the base hospital. Years ago she said she had trained to be a nurse; just until she had got a better offer. She had made a good living for herself ever since although in the year or so before the war she was beginning to ask herself how much longer rich men were going to continue to make her 'better offers'. She was not getting any younger and men were fickle animals, easily distracted, always on the look out for a younger, more nubile model. Her figure, once hour glass slim and supple had filled, become bustier – which was good because most men were actually 'breast' men whatever they claimed – but also increasingly matronly. Had it not been for the war and the slop she had been forced to live on the last year, she would have continued to bloat towards fat the way her mother had in her late thirties and early forties. Being with McNeill – she had no idea who he really was or what his real name might be – the last year had been fun and she would not have missed it for anything. However, all good things come to an end and she suspected *their* good *thing* was about to end messily. One way or another the person she had been the last thirteen months had outlived her usefulness; now more than ever she was living on borrowed time.

"I think," the man said, "the time has come to make an honest woman of you, Third Officer Porter."

"I don't need anybody to *make* me an *honest woman*!" She hissed angrily, recoiling from him.

The man held up an apologetic hand.

"An unfortunate use of words. Forgive me. I meant no offence."

"Well, you've got a funny way of showing it!"

"Let's get in the car."

Neither of them spoke until they were locked in the private cocoon of the borrowed Royal Navy Land Rover.

"There will be many Spanish agents, sympathisers, Falangist infiltrators in the Colony," he prefaced. "There's no way of knowing what their agenda is. For example, are they agent provocateurs, fifth columnists, spies or assassins, or merely stool pidgeons put in place to betray their neighbours when the Spanish move in?"

The woman stifled a moan of exasperation.

Some men were too clever for their own good!

"Either way, now that blood has been spilt we are clearly moving into a very dangerous end game. I don't want you out of my sight, Clara," he announced.

Clara always liked it when he used her 'real' name. Well, the name he thought was her *real* name. It was the thought that counted. He rarely did, of course, use *that* name.. Sometimes in bed he would get carried away, forget himself, otherwise they had got so accustomed to being in character, guarding whatever *legend* they had adopted that week or that month to stay alive that there were times when she almost forgot who she used to be. It was easier for him; he had probably lived this unreal rollercoaster shadow life his whole career.

"I can look after myself."

"Now more than ever we must guard each other's back."

"Okay, okay. Have it your way."

"We haven't got much time," he went on. "I have to speak to the Military Governor of the Colony."

Chapter 20

Tuesday 3rd December 1963
Balmoral Castle, Ballater, Aberdeenshire

Three of the four 500-pound iron bombs had exploded in the gardens and woods behind Balmoral Castle, the fourth had dropped short of the building and *skipped* headlong through the window that Vice-Admiral Julian Christopher and Margaret Thatcher had been standing at seconds before.

By some malevolent fluke the bomb, probably travelling at a speed in excess of four hundred miles an hour, had encountered neither a human body or any significant structural impediment as it exited the reception room and plunged, like an express train down into an empty dining room, through the servant's hall beyond and crashed into the castle's boiler room. There it sat in a cloud of scalding steam as water gushed from ruptured pipes and fifty-year-old electrical wiring sparked while great detonations shook the old Victorian mansion to its foundations like the approaching footsteps of an angry giant striding towards it across the Scottish landscape.

In the ear-splitting, buzzing silence that followed the bomb blasts there was an unearthly whooshing sound and suddenly the distant roaring whine of jet engines abruptly ceased.

The quietness was numbing, terrible and paralysing.

Julian Christopher could see nothing.

Nor could he move; something unbearably heavy was pressing down on his back and his legs seemed like they were in quicksand.

He tried to breath and discovered he could do no more than gasp, pant air in and out in tiny gulps. The air tasted dusty, acridly poisonous as his mind worked hard to try and understand what had just happened.

His ears were ringing, every sound he detected seemed to be far away, deadened as if his ears were full of cotton wool.

"Admiral!"

A very dazed woman's voice.

"Admiral..."

He must have passed out briefly at that juncture because the next thing he was aware off was the weight lifting off his back and strong arms gently lifting him and turning him onto his back. Then he was being carried...

Everything went black.

Somebody was dabbing at his face with a moistened cloth.

He opened his eyes.

"Ah, that's better," Margaret Thatcher declared with a housewifely relief that seemed to the old Admiral perversely bizarre.

Julian Christopher gazed at his unlikely nurse.

She was covered in grey brick dust, her hair so awry she might literally have just been dragged backwards through a hedge. The left sleeve of her blue jacket was torn and there was a blood on her blouse. The woman became aware that he was staring fixedly at the hand-sized stain which only have been dried blood approximately covering the curve of her right breast.

"You bled on me," she explained, averting her eyes in embarrassment.

Julian Christopher tried to sit up. He desisted in a wave of nausea.

"How long was I unconscious..."

"About two hours. On and off..."

"What about the others? The Queen?" He demanded, shutting his eyes and waiting for the disorientation to subside.

"The Queen and the Prime Minister are unhurt."

The deadness in her voice gave away the fact there was bad news to come.

"Alec Douglas Home is dead. There wasn't a mark on his body. They think it was the concussion, or the blast overpressure, or something...that killed him. Prince Philip was trapped under the rubble for nearly an hour. Both his legs are horribly broken. Tom Harding-Grayson was standing next to poor Alec and he seems completely unharmed. There was another attack on Birkhall, the residence of the Queen Mother. Fortunately, she was visiting Crathie at the time with the two older children, Prince Charles and Princess Anne..."

Julian Christopher realised he still had not yet heard the worst news.

"One of the two planes that attacked the castle crashed into the east wing. The Royal Nursery was completed destroyed. They're still searching for Prince Andrew's body..."

The man clasped the Angry Widow's left hand.

She tried to elude his grip but only half-heartedly.

"How could people, *our own people*, do something so wicked?" She asked on the trembling precipice of a flood of tears.

Philosophically, he knew the answer to her question.

Or at least he knew one of the answers.

To find that answer had after all been the purpose of this visit to

Balmoral.

But this was neither the time nor the place to attempt to explain as much.

"Damn," he grunted. "Help me up please."

"You have a concussion and you may have internal injuries, Admiral."

"I've had worse beatings playing rugger, madam," he retorted, wincing in pain. "I am the senior military officer in these parts and I've been shirking my duties long enough."

He was on a table in what had become a makeshift casualty clearing station in the entrance hall of the castle.

There were two bodies on the floor beneath bloody sheets a few feet to his left.

"Somebody help me to restrain Admiral Christopher!"

The Angry Widow called in voice with demanded instant obedience.

Patricia Harding-Grayson appeared out of the blurry haze.

"Admiral," the other woman said. "You had a very nasty bang on the head and several of your ribs are cracked. If you looked at yourself in the mirror you wouldn't even be thinking of getting up."

The man collapsed back onto the table.

"I promise I'll lie down if you find somebody who can tell me what's going on," he muttered unhappily, aware of the brutal pain behind his eyes for the first time.

It was like the worst black dog hangover he had ever had in his life. For a moment he thought he was going to be sick.

And then he was, violently, into a bowl Margaret Thatcher had miraculously conjured out of apparently thin air.

He retched hurtfully for what seemed like minutes but was probably only a few seconds.

Afterwards, he felt better.

Notwithstanding that his head ached like an anvil with two blacksmiths hammering at it, his vision slowly cleared.

"Can you get some water down him, ma'am," a gruff male voice asked.

"Of course."

Julian Christopher found himself being helped to sit up.

A glass was held to his lips and cool liquid dribbled from the corners of his mouth, dripping off his chin. He had been literally parched and the fluid was like nectar.

A second glass was held for him.

"You seem to have things under control, Margaret," Patricia Harding-Grayson decided. "I'll see if I can find somebody who 'knows what's going on'."

Julian Christopher wiped his face with a dust-caked sleeve.

He looked at the grubby, windblown woman who had appointed herself his personal nurse and despite the situation, grinned.

"I feel a little better," he assured her, troubled by her worried expression.

He had been wondering why his right arm felt so strange; belatedly, he discovered his uniform jacket was gone and his shirt hung raggedly off his shoulder. Most of his right arm was swaddled in thick white gauze.

"Pieces from the crashed jet fell across us," the woman shrugged apologetically as if it was her fault. "I was protected by your body but something hot landed on your arm."

As if on cue the man's forearm and elbow had started to sting.

"You saved my life," Margaret Thatcher declared almost accusingly.

Julian Christopher's ears were ringing less and the woman's words sounded as if they were nearer.

He stopped himself shaking his head knowing that would only make him retch again.

Several burly soldiers in camouflage battle dress stomped into the hall.

They took position around the bloodied and bandaged Admiral and the woman in the ruined two-piece outfit with the blasted-looking hair.

Her Majesty Elizabeth the Second, by the Grace of God of the United Kingdom of Great Britain and Northern Ireland, and of Her other Realms and Territories Queen, Head of the Commonwealth, and Defender of the Faith surveyed the battered visage of the man she was reliably informed was the 'the best fighting Admiral in the Navy' with eyes full of grief and worry and a deadly determination to carry on.

"Your Majesty..."

"Please don't try to stand up, Admiral Christopher," commanded the small, grim-faced woman wearing a camouflaged tunic at least ten sizes too large for her petite frame.

The big hard men of her close bodyguard never stopped scanning their surroundings for danger.

Each man fingered his Sten Gun secretly praying for somebody to kill.

"You sent a message that you wanted to speak to somebody who knows what is going on."

The woman who had lost her infant son in an unspeakable atrocity only two hours ago, and whose husband lay terribly injured somewhere nearby, spoke with a plummy clarity.

"That would be me, Admiral Christopher. Lieutenant Colonel McPhail, the CO of the Black Watch was killed in the attack, as were several of his senior officers. Everybody in the guard house behind Balmoral was killed or wounded by the bombs. This building was attacked by two jets. A further two aircraft attacked other residences on the estate. The aircraft which crashed here was shot down by small arms fire from the Black Watch. Its partner in crime was shot down by a Bloodhound missile as it attempted to escape. As to the other two jets," the bereaved mother's bottom lip quivered for a split second before she regained her iron control, "they may have got away. The RAF is flying something called a 'combat air patrol' over the estate and more troops are on their way to us. The fire in the east wing of the castle is now out. The Prime Minister is currently out and about organising the Black Watch against the possibility of what he calls a 'follow up ground assault'. He's been a tower of strength. He will be returning shortly. Things are therefore, under control. This being the case I am ordering you to allow the medical staff to minister to you as they see fit until such time as *they* deem you fit to resume your duties, Admiral."

Julian Christopher lay down.

He passed out within moments of his head touching the pillow.

He slept fitfully, his mind plagued with vivid, flickering dreams of the kind he had once experienced when he almost died of fever in Singapore that long-ago summer before Hitler invaded Poland.

Singapore...

Filling in time on the Staff; nothing to do but check his post in the morning, issue daily orders and go sailing in the afternoons. Around him the sweltering, stifling tropical heat of the great fortress citadel with ships coming and going, the traffic of the orient, exotic and entrancing, wrapping him in its narcotic-like arms until the reality of the old world became a chimera and he began to forget who and what he was...

Raffles Hotel, the parties under awnings on the aft decks of the big ships...

First there had been his fling with Oriane.

A delicate, pale, bird-like beauty.

The wife of a French diplomat engaged in some shady dealings with up country planters.

Of course, that might just have been a cover for the sort of routine spying that all the European powers conducted in the East, mostly to keep bored and underemployed diplomats busy and to prevent them from stirring up even more trouble.

Oriane had left Singapore after a couple of weeks on a slow boat to

Indochina. She had written to him once from Hanoi but he had never replied.

He was involved with Aysha by then.

Although, 'involved' was hardly the right word.

'Obsessed', or 'bewitched' were better words.

Aysha had consumed him heart and soul, he would have gladly died for her if she had only asked it of him. She was the mistress of one of the richer, more obviously crooked rubber planters; one of the ones who dealt contraband and kept a foot or a hand or a finger in every conceivable pot. People like him did not care who was running the show just so long as they got their cut. That was the way of Empire; people like him were the glue that held the whole edifice together. In Singapore nobody asked any questions, so long as the rubber kept flowing to the factories of the English Midlands nobody cared if the underlying fabric of the Imperium was rotten.

He had never cared.

He was too preoccupied with his career and with living the life he had always loved. He had bowed to convention and taken a well-connected wife whom he loved as best he could when he was at home in England. But what he lived for was stepping on the deck of the next grey steel warship and the thrill of the next port of call. The whole world seemed to be at his feet when he stood on the bridge of a warship.

He had become distracted between the wars, become obsessed with seizing back the America's Cup. It had not happened and eventually he had been welcomed back with open arms by the Service he had always loved.

And then Aysha had driven him past the point of madness...

Afternoons and long sultry, unbearably hot tropical nights entwined in the arms of the olive-skinned temptress of his most fevered imaginings...

It was dark in the room when he awakened, little by little, from the grip of a hallucination in which he had been on a stretcher with cold rain splashing on his face as armoured vehicles rumbled down a nearby muddy track.

He focused on a candle burning low in a bowl beside his bed.

He did not know where he was, just that he was not alone.

It was cold in the darkness and he shivered involuntarily.

The Angry Widow was holding his left hand, watching over him. He blinked stupidly, guiltily at her.

"I dreamed the Queen was giving me a SITREP?" He whispered hoarsely through cracked lips.

"You didn't dream that. That was shortly before the Prime Minister got back," the woman reported.

She had changed into clean clothes, washed her face and brushed her hair.

She was prim, proper, in control again and yet, different, as if he was viewing her though a filter that softened *everything*.

"He took charge. He insisted that Balmoral Castle be abandoned. There are soldiers everywhere. A cadre from 45 Commando was flown in by helicopter this afternoon to relieve the Black Watch. We're in a cottage about two miles from Balmoral. Patricia and Tom Harding-Grayson are downstairs. You must be thirsty?"

Gingerly, the man sat up in the bed.

The deep, luxuriant mattress creaked and sagged as he settled against the pillows the woman arranged behind him.

He hurt practically everywhere but not particularly badly anywhere in particular which he had always taken as a good sign in the past. His right arm was only lightly bandaged, itching rather than painful. He was wearing some kind of long nightshirt, and nothing else...

"Your uniform," the woman grimaced, "all our clothes actually, were ruined. They cut away most of what you were wearing to assess your injuries. Tom and Pat helped me get you into the, er, night things..."

Battered, bruised and nearer the end of his tether than he had been at any time since the world had gone insane thirteen months ago, all Julian Christopher wanted to do was hold the woman in his arms.

Chapter 21

Tuesday 3rd December 1963
Situation Room, Government Buildings, Cheltenham

Jim Callaghan picked up his cup of tea and raised it slowly to his lips, pausing to view the gathering that would have constituted - had God had an even crueller sense of humour than he had thought possible - all that was left of the United Kingdom Interim Emergency Administration if the attack on the Balmoral had gone as the conspirators had planned. *God helps us!* He thought sourly, wondering yet again if the traitorous bastards who had carried out the atrocity had had succour or encouragement from any of the men in the room.

The leader of the Labour and Co-operative Party sipped his tea, wishing he could shut out the background noise.

Ian Macleod, the Chairman of the Conservative and Unionist Party was shouting at Airey Neave, presumably because the Angry Widow's right-hand man was sitting in front of him and he thought somebody ought to be shouting at somebody. Peter Thorneycroft, Jim Callaghan's deputy at the Ministry of Defence was staring into space, still a little dazed. Across the table the three Chiefs of Staff were impersonating three brass monkeys, each horribly embarrassed by the way the politicians were deporting themselves. Several absentee Cabinet members who had suddenly emerged from the woodwork on hearing the terrible news from Scotland had demanded entrance to the meeting and been firmly excluded.

Jim Callaghan put down his cup and saucer.

"Shut up, Ian!" He snapped.

This briefly silenced the other man. However, an outraged protest was not long coming.

"How dare you speak to me like that, you..."

"Jumped up little Leftie?" The Minister of Defence and, by virtue of the agreement he had signed on behalf of his party as a non-negotiable condition of its support for Edward Heath's leadership of the UKIEA, the de facto Deputy Prime Minister, inquired coldly.

"No, I was going to say..."

"Shut up," the large, lugubrious man with angrily flaring nostrils told the red-faced Chairman of the Conservative and Unionist Party sitting to his right. "Shut up or I shall have you removed from this room." he looked slowly around the faces fixed on his. His gaze lingered on the palely stern face of the Cabinet Secretary, Sir Henry

Tomlinson, who sat at the end of the table deliberately separate from both the military and political constituents of the meeting. "This meeting of the Emergency War Cabinet is now in session," he sniffed. "Mr Neave and Mr Thorneycroft have been invited to attend by me because I believe they may have useful insights to offer. The Chairman of the Conservative Party is here by his own invitation. Since he is here, he may as well stay as an observer."

The Deputy Prime Minister viewed the three service chiefs.

Sir Charles Elworthy, Chief of the Air Staff pushed back his chair and with immense chagrined dignity stood to attention.

"Sir, with your permission I request your leave to submit my immediate resignation from my current post." The man choked on the last few words. What had happened in Scotland was tormenting him and he looked as if he was going to be physically sick with shame at any moment.

"Request denied. Please sit down, Air Marshall," Jim Callaghan said tersely. He frowned at the Army Chief, sitting uncomfortably to the airman's left. "What about you, General Hull, do you want to throw in the towel, too?"

"No, sir," the soldier replied gruffly.

Sir Charles Elworthy had collapsed back into his seat, a part of him broken perhaps beyond repair.

"Gentlemen," Jim Callaghan declared. "Immediately before I came into this room, I spoke with Her Majesty the Queen and the Prime Minister over a scrambler link to Scotland. They both made it clear to me that the Service Chiefs retain Her Majesty's, and the Prime Minister's absolute faith and confidence. There will be no talk of resignations. There will be no recriminations around this table. We are confronted with two specific crises, and one pressing strategic decision that can no longer be deferred. This meeting will be briefed on the latest developments in Scotland and in Gibraltar before we move on to a general discussion of what to do about Vice-Admiral Staveley-Pope."

Admiral David Luce's expression was blandly inscrutable at the mention of the name of the man who was Commander-in-Chief of the Mediterranean Fleet and the Military Governor of the Maltese Archipelago and those areas of Cyprus still under British control. Splitting command of the Mediterranean theatre of operations – effectively a 'Gibraltar Command Area' and a 'Mediterranean Fleet Area' had been vigorously resisted by the Navy but the Army had enjoyed a lot of sway within the rump of the Conservative Party in the weeks after the cataclysm. Moreover, the First Sea Lord was far too decent and honourable a man to remind his colleagues that 'he'd told them so' at a time like this.

"That man is an imbecile!" Ian Macleod declared

The First Sea Lord flicked a mildly exasperated look at the Chairman of the Conservative and Unionist Party.

"Michael Staveley-Pope is a man of impeccable principles and unwavering loyalty to the Service, Mr Macleod. Whatever else he is and whatever has made him take the decisions he has taken and only belatedly communicated to us here in England, he is not an imbecile and I will thank you to refrain from disparaging *any* Naval officer in my presence unless you are prepared to repeat those words to that officer's face." He spoke with a suave, smooth assurance but there was no doubt that beneath the velvet glove was a knuckleduster. He added after a long pause: "Sir!"

The politician blinked, unconsciously licked his lower lip. Like a lizard tasting the atmosphere in the room for the first time and detecting a disturbing new undercurrent of…hostility and contempt. Things were going badly wrong and the patience of the Chiefs of Staff was very nearly exhausted. Elworthy might be in a state of shock but the unquenchable light of battle shone even more brightly in the eyes of Admiral Luce and General Hull.

"I apologise for my intemperate language, Admiral Luce," Ian Macleod said soberly. Contrary to the impression many had of him he was by nature a courteous and correct man; he simply got carried away sometimes. "I'm sure Admiral Staveley-Pope is doing what he thinks is right and necessary. However…"

Jim Callaghan reasserted his chairmanship.

"Sir Richard," he growled turning to the stony-faced Chief of the General Staff of the Army, "would you be so good as to update us on the latest information from Scotland please?"

"All four aircraft from the 637 Squadron based at RAF Turnhouse near Edinburgh which attacked the Balmoral estate this morning have now been accounted for. All four aircraft were Hawker Hunters configured in a fighter bomber role and were attached to Number 27 Operational Training Unit at Turnhouse. Two of the aircraft were piloted by instructors, and two by students converting from other aircraft types. Both aircraft which attacked Balmoral Castle were destroyed, one by small arms fire or pilot error resulting in it crashing into the building, the other was accounted for by a Bloodhound surface-to-air missile strike. Both pilots were killed. The other aircraft landed at RAF Leuchars and both pilots surrendered themselves to the members of the RAF Regiment. After consultation with the other

Chiefs it was agreed that interrogators from Special Branch and the Security Services should travel to Scotland to conduct an exhaustive interrogation of both prisoners. The interrogation team has been authorised to use any or all appropriate measures to ensure the full co-operation of the prisoners. 2nd Battalion Scots Guards has invested RAF Turnhouse and all personnel within the base have been disarmed pending the outcome of the interrogation at Leuchars and any further measures which might be necessary. Elements of 45 Commando have now arrived on Deeside in battalion strength to secure the Balmoral estate. Thus far there has been no attempt by dissident elements to breach the perimeter around Balmoral Castle established by the Black Watch. I have a number of reports that groups of armed men have been intercepted in the immediate vicinity of several outlying estate buildings. The Royal Marines have given these groups short shrift."

General Sir Richard Hull's tone became grim.

"Just before I came into this meeting, I received the latest casualty reports. I can now confirm the deaths of the Lord of Home, the infant Prince Andrew, some seven other members of the Royal Household, and seventy-four officers and men of the Black Watch. His Royal Highness Prince Philip has been flown by helicopter to Edinburgh for treatment to his severe leg injuries. Vice-Admiral Christopher was initially assessed as having suffered a life-threatening head injury but it now seems that in the heat of the moment this was a somewhat pessimistic judgement. The extent of his injuries are now confirmed as being a concussion and a collection of nasty but otherwise non-life threatening cracks and abrasions. Excluding walking wounded; some twelve other members of the Royal Household and sixty-one members of the Black Watch were assessed as requiring hospitalisation. Two members of the Royal Household and three men from the Black Watch are still unaccounted for. It is likely their bodies are still buried beneath debris."

"What of the other members of the Prime Minister's party?" Peter Thorneycroft asked, venturing uncomfortably into the angry silence.

"Her Majesty the Queen and the Prime Minister were in the one part of Balmoral Castle to escape significant structural damage and mercifully, were completely unharmed. Mrs Thatcher was shaken up but uninjured. It seems Admiral Christopher threw her to the ground and shielded her with his own body just before the bomb that killed the Earl of Home and injured His Royal Highness struck the building. Tom Harding-Grayson and his wife escaped uninjured. Patricia Harding-Grayson was a tower of strength in the aftermath of the attack when it became apparent that the CO of the Black Watch and many of his senior lieutenants had been killed."

"Is it true," Peter Thorneycroft followed up, "that Her Majesty took charge of things herself in the first minutes after the attack?"

"Yes, sir. Her Majesty took control of the situation at the castle while the Prime Minister reorganised the survivors of the Black Watch to secure the immediate perimeter against the possibility of a second attack."

There were grunts of approval and nods of approbation around the table and the mood of the room lifted one chilled degree above absolute zero.

Jim Callaghan cleared his throat.

"Do you have all the resources you need to guarantee Her Majesty's safety, Sir Richard?"

"Yes, sir," the soldier retorted with grim certitude. "The head of the Security Services and I will review all arrangements subsequent to this meeting. I believe Sir Roger has already spoken to the Prime Minister."

Jim Callaghan grimaced. He had had very little to do with Sir Roger Hollis and in fact, very little use for the man or the rag tag remnants of his so-called *Security Service*. Ironically, the war had wiped out most of MI5 while leaving the beating heart of its competitor, MI6 – its offshore counterpart the Secret Intelligence Service – relatively intact. The primary reason the UKIEA was based in Cheltenham was that after the Second World War the whole apparatus of Camp X – the Bletchley Park code-breaking operation – had been transferred and expensively relocated in the town in two purpose-built centres. At the same time deep bunkers had been dug into the surrounding Cotswold and Chiltern Hills to accommodate the UKIEA in the event of a nuclear war but ironically, never used. The war was over too soon and there had been no real warning of it until the firestorm had actually erupted in the skies above London. In the last year the 'nuclear' bunkers had been utilised as heavily guarded supply depots of last resort. Cheltenham was now virtually an MI6 company town in which MI5 – the Security Service - was a barely tolerated lodger.

"Is Sir Roger on his way back from Washington yet?" He asked searching for the lugubrious equanimity that was his hallmark in the face of adversity. The Americans did not like the Director General of MI5. They believed he had had too many dubious friends in his younger days. Hollis and Sir Dick White, the head of MI6, were jointly responsible for spawning the incoherent and largely ineffectual – in intelligence gathering terms – Internal Security Department whose writ ran wild in the remaining British crown dependencies and protectorates. Hollis and White had been particularly slow to rein in the excesses of the ISD in Malta and Cyprus, and for reasons best known to them they had seen fit to allow that pernicious institution to begin operations within the Home Islands. Like 'security' institutions throughout history, ISD was more interested in building its own little empire than in actually performing its job. If MI5 could not root out treachery on such a monstrous scale as a conspiracy to bomb Balmoral Castle then what was it good for? MI6 was not much better; the situation in Algeciras Bay and the partial activation of *Operation Homeward Bound* in Malta and Cyprus had come out of the blue without so much as a by your leave from Dick White's 'Special Intelligence Service'. The man himself - the suave poster boy of British Intelligence - had flown out to the Mediterranean forty-eight hours ago to personally 'assess the situation on the ground'. The fact that the nation's two top spies were out of the country on the day traitors attempted to murder the Queen, the Spanish mined an aircraft carrier in Algeciras Bay and the pole-axing news that the C-in-C Mediterranean Fleet appeared to be having a brainstorm, was a disconcerting coincidence. James Callaghan knew he was not the only man around the table who probably felt it was exactly the sort of coincidence that would bear more than a little scrutiny in the days and weeks to come.

"Yes," General Sir Richard Hull confirmed grimly.

"Sir David," the Deputy Prime Minister asked, turning to the First Sea Lord, "what's going on at Gibraltar?"

"HMS Albion was still afloat an hour ago and I instructed my Staff to inform me immediately if she sank, so presumably she's still afloat. I'm given to believe that most of her Marines have been carried ashore, as have a large number of non-essential crewmen. The Spanish are standing off and watching. RAF Gibraltar remains inoperable and threatened by Spanish artillery. All the helicopters Albion managed to fly off are now based at Europa Point. They are safe enough there for the time being but operating them will be problematic. Fuel has to be tankered out to them, and spares, ground crews and so forth are not currently available on the Rock."

Jim Callaghan sighed. "What are our options?"

"If we lose Gibraltar, we lose the Mediterranean, sir."

"We might lose the Med anyway?"

"Yes, sir. But that's where we fall over the strategic decision you alluded to earlier."

The Deputy Prime Minister looked around the table.

"All of which will be academic if Franco's Army marches into

Gibraltar."

General Sir Richard Hull scowled: "With respect, sir," he remarked tartly, "with 3rd Battalion of the Rifle Brigade, 2nd Battalion 40 Commando, a company of garrison troops and over two hundred rounds of ammunition for every large artillery piece emplaced on the Rock, the bloody Spaniards are not about to *march* into Gibraltar."

"Nevertheless, the place is besieged, Sir Richard."

The Chief of Staff of the British Army could not deny it no matter how sorely tempted he was to argue the point.

"With respect," David Luce offered, "I suspect that Franco's preference will be to blockade and starve us out. Ark Royal or Hermes's air groups could shoot down his whole air force and the Belfast or one of the big Cats – sorry, the modern cruisers HMS Tiger and HMS Lion – could make the Spanish positions around Algeciras Bay and the coast to the north east untenable for the enemy."

The First Sea Lord's words provided a crumb of comfort to his listeners. What they did not do and what they made no attempt to do was pretend that the precarious balance of power in the Mediterranean had not just shifted at the worst possible moment. The Royal Navy was stretched near to breaking point by irreconcilable competing strategic demands. Operation Manna had stripped the Mediterranean Fleet of many of its modern ships and those that remained were fully engaged 'showing the flag' and attempting to 'maintain a visible presence' in waters over which the Royal Navy's control was at best, tenuous. The need to keep 'showing the flag' and the demands of Operation Manna had left the Navy critically weakened in Malta, virtually absent from the eastern Mediterranean and as it had turned out, horribly exposed at Gibraltar.

"I issued a turnaround command to the Lion and her screening destroyers as soon as I got word of the mining of HMS Albion and HMS Cassandra," the Admiral reported. These five ships had been tasked to make a show of force along the French Riviera, proceed into the Ligurian Sea and to pay 'courtesy calls' at Genoa and Naples, collecting intelligence as they went. The small Squadron was operating independently under the rules of 'the Christopher Protocol'; which basically meant *if in doubt open fire*. "Unfortunately, even making their best cruising speed they won't make the Straits of Gibraltar in the next seventy-two hours. Lion has sufficient fuel for a high-speed run but the destroyers will need to top off their bunkers to keep up with her. To do that the squadron will need to rendezvous with the Royal Fleet Auxiliary Cherryleaf which only cleared Malta for the original pre-arranged rendezvous position at around noon our time yesterday in company with the destroyers Scorpion and Broadsword. I have also tasked 4th Submarine Flotilla to redirect Cachalot and Sealion to the Rock at their best surface speed. Both boats were tasked to patrol the Bay of Biscay in support of Operation Manna. Theoretically, they might be off the Rock within seventy-two hours."

Jim Callaghan was sombre.

"What other ships are available within the Mediterranean theatre?"

"About half-a-dozen destroyers and frigates, and a number of smaller units at Malta. And 3rd Submarine Flotilla. HMS Sheffield arrived at the island a week ago but she's still working up and some of her equipment was removed before the war when she was placed in the Reserve Fleet. Very few of the units based at Malta are actually fully operational. Other than Sheffield, at least two of the larger ships are in dockyard hands."

Airey Neave coughed politely.

"May I make an observation, Minister?" He inquired, giving Jim Callaghan a look, which was apologetically ironic.

"Of course," the big man shrugged, turning determinedly sombre. "You are the resident *escape expert* in the room, Airey."

This drew a sullen mutter of scoffing amusement.

"That's good of you to say so, Minister," the ruddy-faced former resident of Colditz chortled, "it is just that it seems to me that although things look a bit sticky at the moment; what with the dreadful events at Balmoral, Franco flexing his muscles at Gibraltar and dear old Staveley-Pope making up grand strategy on the hoof," he held up a hand to placate a bristling First Sea Lord, "no offence intended Sir David," he said quickly and went on before he lost the floor to a second outraged complaint he could not bat away so easily, "aren't we rather forgetting something in all the excitement?"

"For goodness sake, Airey!" Ian Macleod snorted.

"Seriously, chaps," Airey Neave continued unabashed, "I'm dreadfully sorry about the Earl of Home, obviously, and the young Prince, but the Queen, the Premier and Margaret are all in one piece and this Gibraltar imbroglio notwithstanding, we're the fellows who *still* command the Mediterranean. Well, if we've *still* got the moral fibre to *command* it, that is. Yes, Operation Manna is the one thing we *must* support with all our might but that doesn't mean we *can't* act decisively elsewhere." He held up his hands to forestall the objections of the three Chiefs of Staff. "Yes, yes, I know we can't afford to expend or worse, lose, irreplaceable ships and aircraft, let alone the men in them. But we can't afford to hold our military assets back and watch our strategic position erode to such a point where all the blood and treasure in the world won't save the day either. Gentlemen, it is time we stopped worrying about our weaknesses and began to look to our strengths. I know there are a lot of things we can't do; but there are a lot of thing that we can do." He grinned puckishly, as if he was delivering a pep talk to the Colditz Escape Committee in that cold German castle in 1942. "For example, *we* still hold Malta. Always assuming we can stop dear old Staveley-Pope giving it away to the pirates, that is. Likewise, *we* hold Gibraltar and I'm probably not the only chap around this table who thinks it's high time we took the gloves off with that bastard Franco..."

Jim Callaghan sighed.

Airey Neave was only saying what they all thought, putting voice to what had been unthinkable a month, a week or even a few days ago to confront a reality that Edward Heath had travelled to Balmoral to articulate to the Sovereign.

It was all the Deputy Prime Minister could do to suppress a visible shiver of apprehension.

Chapter 22

Wednesday 4th December 1963
Rock Gun Battery, Gibraltar

They had had to walk most of the way up the mountain and then they were parked on a bench outside a checkpoint while they waited for word to be sent up – and down – the Rock. The bench had a stunning view of the entire sweep of Algeciras Bay, now polluted with the effluent from HMS Albion's breached forward bunkers and the flotsam and jetsam that still bubbled to the surface from the grave of HMS Cassandra. Off the port of Algeciras, the two Spanish destroyers that had patrolled the Straits of Gibraltar while the carrier had fought to stay afloat now lay at anchor in the middle of the Bay, watching developments beneath the beleaguered last bastion of the old world in the Iberian Peninsula. To the observers on the Rock who had witnessed the herculean struggles of the previous afternoon it seemed as if the two Spanish warships were *sulking*.

At a little after twenty-three hundred hours last night the waterlogged hulk of HMS Albion had been dragged and pushed into Dry Dock Number One, where after seven hours of counter flooding she had been stabilized sufficiently to allow the pumps to begin to drain the dock. In Gibraltar people were running up and down the streets shouting the news - every tiny development - all night long. Households had broken out their last bottles of wine, and there had been a peculiar morning after the party the night before mood in the air as the man in the uniform of a Commander in the Royal Naval Reserve and his companion, a blond shapely woman in the uniform of a WREN Third Officer had emerged from their dingy hotel off Main Street to begin their quest to find, speak to and hopefully, not get shot by the Military Governor of the Colony.

They had tried to speak to him – Major General Horace Phelps - yesterday afternoon and carried on trying to locate and secure an interview with him until they gave up for the day shortly before midnight. They missed most of the drama in the Bay that afternoon and evening; the way that HMS Cavalier had braved further mines and gone alongside the stricken carrier, adding her pumps to the fight against the rising water while she cross decked the Marines of 40 Commando onto the minesweeper HMS Castleton and a host of smaller vessels. By the early evening all the Marines and most of the carrier's crew had been carried ashore, leaving only a skeleton salvage gang on board the great ship. Earlier, around dusk a Spanish gunboat had strayed into Gibraltarian waters and been chased away by two lightly armed Air Sea Rescue launches without a shot being fired.

"You still haven't told me what you were up to in Malta," Clara, the blond woman asked the man who was currently bearing papers that 'proved' he was William Drayton McNeill, the Deputy-Director of Naval Intelligence (Middle East Command). "I don't mean the normal stuff. But what was that business with the woman Marija Calleja who was leading the protesters outside the gates of HMS Phoenicia?"

The man shrugged, stared down across Algeciras Bay.

"How high do you think we are?" He asked, idly.

"I don't know, a thousand feet. Maybe more. You didn't answer my question?"

"No, sorry."

"You knew they were about to relax the State of Emergency Laws as phase two of the preparations for implementing Operation Homeward Bound. So, what did you say to her?"

"Operation Homeward Bound isn't the only option," the man replied, dodging the question. He sighed. "I interviewed Miss Calleja under false pretences because I wanted to establish if she was biddable. For what it is worth I don't think she is. I tried *all* the standard code words on her but she didn't react."

"Oh. She doesn't know about her brother then?"

The man carried on staring out across the panoramic, breathtaking vista of Algeciras Bay. He shook his head.

"No, she's got no idea at all."

"That's families for you," the woman quirked. "It turns out that the brother of the saintly little virgin of Vittoriosa-Birgu is a Red Dawn killer."

The man frowned at her.

"What?" She asked, fluttering her eyelids.

"Marija Calleja is a good person," he shrugged. "The saddest thing is that she'd love her brother no less even if she knew *what* he was."

Clara threw him a thoughtful look, concerned by the suddenly maudlin tone of his words. "You didn't explain who this *Peter* person is that she's been writing to for years?"

"Lieutenant Peter Julian Christopher. He's an electronics expert on one of the Navy's fast air detection destroyers. HMS Talavera. A sister ship of two of the ships we saw in Sliema Creek. You know, the one's with the huge lattice masts and the big bedstead aerials."

"Oh," she muttered, not knowing whether to be disappointed by this blandly delivered response. "Oh, I see."

"No, my dear," the man said, shaking his head. "You don't see.

Lieutenant Peter Christopher is the son of Vice-Admiral Julian Christopher, the commander of the British Pacific Fleet and the man behind Operation Manna."

Suddenly, Clara understood.

The brother of the pen friend to whom the son of the famous British admiral had been corresponding for half his life was a key member of Red Dawn in the Maltese Archipelago. She had read a couple of Peter Christopher's letters to Marija Calleja, and half-a-dozen of her replies. The pair were hopelessly smitten, one with the other for all that they had never met, let alone laid a finger, platonic or carnal one upon the other. *He* was a dashing young officer on a destroyer, the son of an illustrious father, *she* the heroin of the siege of Malta; it was a fairy tale romance waiting to be publicly, cruelly poisoned. The brutal unfairness of it made her vision go a little misty. She sniffed back a tear.

"I shouldn't have asked," she said hoarsely.

Despite the sunshine it was cool on the mountainside and Clara wished she had brought a coat. She shook her head, reminding herself that she had come to Gibraltar in pretty much what she was wearing and she did not actually have a coat. Every night she rinsed her underwear – oh how she longed for lingerie – and hung her *smalls* up to dry while she slept. Some mornings her washing had to dry on her. The things she did for her country! Or, at least, the things she thought she was doing for somebody else's country...

Sleeping with a man whose real name she did not know was not one of the things she did for Queen and country, or out of any sense of patriotic duty. No, she slept with him because she liked sleeping with him and he was a man she needed to stay close to if she was to survive. Occasionally he was intense, angry, usually he was gentle and tender and so patient she had to put a hand over her mouth to stop herself screaming in delight. Last night they had lain side by side, she pressing back against him, he penetrating her slowly, nibbling her ear lobes. They had slept the sleep of the truly weary and only the bright morning sunlight falling on their naked bodies had awakened them to another, dangerous day.

"Why her? Why Marija Calleja?" She had asked him about the young woman before and he had always parried her questions. Now that he seemed prepared to open himself to her a little she wanted to know more. Whatever he claimed she suspected that *she* was the real reason they had spent so many weeks in Malta and she wanted to know *more*. She had to know *more*.

"Ah, now there's a question!" The man whistled softly. "When

Marija was five years old she was buried in a bomb shelter in Vittoriosa," he paused, corrected himself, "the Maltese call Vittoriosa *Birgu*. Practically everybody else in the shelter was killed when a direct hit collapsed the buildings above it. They did not dig her out for nearly two days and when they got her to hospital, they discovered that her left leg and her pelvis had been crushed. They took her to the Naval Hospital at Kalkara where the doctors didn't think she would survive the night. But she did, and the next night, and the next. The Hospital did its best for her but her injuries were so severe as to cripple her for life. She spent the first couple of years after the bombing lying immobilised. Basically, the doctors had set what bones they could and left her body to heal itself. Her family took her home and that would probably have been that unless a certain Surgeon Captain Reginald Stephens had not stumbled across her case papers and on an impulse, gone to visit the kid."

"Just like that? Just out of the blue?"

"No, not just like that. It seems the man was on a crusade. He'd had a pretty good war, reputation wise and so forth but he was one of those chaps who'd come out of the Second War with an itchy conscience. When he got to Malta just after VE-Day he single-handedly took it upon himself to improve the medical treatment of children on the island. Anyway, he persuaded Marija Calleja's parents to allow the kid to come back to Kalkara for tests and observation. Observation, X-rays, whatever tests doctors do in these cases. It so happened that Reginald Stephens was – on account of his war work, presumably – one of the leading orthopaedic surgeons in the Navy, and perhaps, anywhere in the world at the time and he'd been experimenting with all manner of new techniques to put 'broken' people back together. He was a real pioneer, a one-off English eccentric in some ways, but a genuine pioneer and Marija Calleja eventually became his first and greatest triumph."

Clara raised an eyebrow. While the man had been doing what he did – other than that he was a spy she only had the vaguest idea what he really got up to, she was window dressing and once or twice his getaway driver – he often gave her watching briefs, or asked her to tail, or to flirt with *persons of interest*. On Malta he had asked her to follow Marija Calleja and several times she had watched the women protesting at the gates of HMS Phoenicia, and unobtrusively ridden the bus with the young woman to Mdina-Rabat. Clara had once fallen back on her half-forgotten training as a nurse to visit the St Catherine's Hospital for Women to inquire if there were 'any vacancies for a Naval Officer's wife' like herself, who 'was fed up sitting around waiting for my husband to get back from sea'. The Director of the Hospital, Doctor Margo Seiffert had impressed Clara. The older woman was pleasantly business-like and utterly in command of her small ship. She had taken Clara on a tour of the Hospital. If Clara wished to help out at the Hospital, they would work something out; the only fly in the ointment was that as the wife of a serving officer Margo could only employ her if the Navy gave her 'a permission'.

"Marija Calleja's injuries can't have been that bad," she objected thoughtfully, picturing the slim young woman she had seen walking unaided with apparent freedom of movement, and standing holding that banner '**IS THIS THE WAY YOU TREAT YOUR FRIENDS**' for literally hours on end opposite the gates to Manoel Island.

"It took about twenty operations, several of them major, to put her back together again," the man retorted. "When the operations were over, she had had to learn to walk again. Think about that. Having to learn to walk again!"

Clara conceded the point.

He never told her who she was following or watching; unless that was, by following or watching a *target* she was placing herself in danger.

"Margo Seiffert was Reginald Stephens's principal surgical registrar at Kalkara throughout most of the period when Marija Calleja was being treated."

"Okay. Okay, I get it that Marija is some kind of local heroine..."

"Oh, more than that."

"Was that why that Redcap sergeant was sniffing around her all the time?" Clara demanded.

"No, I don't think so. Staff Sergeant Siddall is a bit of an enigma. He's still married to a woman in Southampton. Or at least he was until two or three months ago. For all I know the poor woman could have starved or died of disease since the last time anybody checked. I think it is more personal with Mister Siddall. To me his general demeanour towards Marija suggested he has appointed himself the young lady's personal guardian angel."

Clara groaned in frustration.

"Don't you ever say what you actually mean?"

"Hardly ever, no." The man smiled wanly. "Some things are best not hurried, don't you agree?"

Clara suppressed an urge; well, two urges. The first was to slap his face. The second was to kiss him. She had been fascinated and not unnaturally, horrified by the patchwork of scars, mostly superficial, on his lean torso. The newer, visible marks on his scalp when he wore is hair cropped had been fully healed when they first met so she had known he had lied about being too close to a window when the Ankara bomb went off.

"You ought to trust me by now," she complained.

"I do trust you. I trust you implicitly. I've never trusted anybody in my whole life the way I trust you, Clara. That's why I won't tell you anything that's likely to get you killed. Not until this is over."

"When will that be?"

"I don't know."

"Commander McNeill! Third Officer Porter!" Yelled a huge, red-faced, sweating Royal Marine. The man was weighed down with ammunition pouches, had a long-barrelled sniping rifle slung over one shoulder and was hefting a Sten Gun. The sub-machine gun virtually disappeared into his bear-like tanned hands.

The Marine marched the two officers through the checkpoint setting a ferocious ground devouring pace straight up the hill towards a hut built next to a broad cave opening into the citadel. Whereupon, he passed them on to another Marine, this time a slim, youthful second-lieutenant. He too carried a Sten Gun.

"Follow me please."

It was cool and very quiet inside the mountain.

The passages through which the trio walked looked hand-carved and very old. Presently the narrow tunnel – barely wide enough for two people to walk side by side – opened into progressively larger chambers lined with various types of fixed 25-pounder artillery rounds and what looked like fixed and unfixed reloads for 3.7-inch heavy anti-aircraft guns. Other passages led off deeper into the rock. The whir of generators seeped out of one opening and low voices from another, the sound of machine tools and drills reverberated further into the warren. Coming to a flight of broad wooden steps that gave the appearance of disappearing into a dark void some fifteen feet above their heads the subaltern stood aside and indicated for the man and the woman to go ahead of him. Clara went first, holding her skirt tight to herself in an exaggerated show of modesty, the men following. At the top of the stairs there was a steel superstructure supporting a walkway along one wall of another cavern. At a gesture from their escort the man and woman walked along the decking to the left and entered an airy cave which was open to the elements on one side.

They had come out another hundred or so feet higher than where they had been kept waiting at the checkpoint. The view across Algeciras Bay was growing hazy in the afternoon sun.

"The most peculiar thing happened the other day," a quiet,

sardonic voice asserted in a musical, lilting Welsh baritone out of the darkness of the inner cave. An ursine, balding man of indeterminate middle years with pink ears that seemed to extend absurdly far out from the rest of his head rumbled unhurriedly into the daylight. The man was wearing the uniform of an Army major and there were red Staff badges on the lapels of his crumpled and apparently ill-used khaki battledress tunic. He stopped directly in front of the man and the woman. Silhouetted against the light his large, protuberant ears giving him the look a character in a cartoon. "Yes indeed! There I was minding my own business wondering if that plane you were on would be the first one the Dagoes would shoot up as it landed and after all the shooting died down what's the first thing I see when I stick my head over the parapet? A sight for sore eyes, I can tell you!" The man chuckled and pulled out a packet of cigarettes. A metal lighter clicked twice, flamed. He lit his cigarette. "I won't offer you a smoke; I know neither of you indulge in the filthy habit."

Clara looked first to the man who had been her constant companion, lover, friend and protector the last year. When he gave her his blankest face and avoided her gaze she turned back to the fat man.

"You know who we are?" She asked, stupidly.

"Oh, yes," he retorted affably, pausing to take a long lazy drag on his cigarette. "You are masquerading as Third Officer Camilla Porter and your *friend*, or should I say, *fellow traveller*, is currently wearing the mask of a certain William McNeill, late of Gravesend. *Late*, as of course, are most of the residents of that particular year-old hole in the ground. *He* won't have told you his real name." The man perched his cigarette between his lips, scratched his left ear with his left hand and withdrew a silver whistle from his right-hand tunic pocked. Reluctantly removing the cigarette from his mouth, he raised the whistle and without another word blew a long, shrill ear-splitting blast.

Chapter 23

Wednesday 4th December 1963
St Catherine's Hospital for Women, Mdina-Rabat

Marija Calleja almost fainted when she walked into Margo Seiffert's ground floor office and was confronted by the tall, uniformed figure of Staff Sergeant Jim Siddall of the Royal Military Police and the smaller, stockier presence of her irresponsible, reckless little brother.

Joe Calleja grinned conspiratorially at his sister.

"Joe!" She said like an idiot. "Joe, I don't..."

Brother and sister fell into an embrace which ended with the man exuberantly spinning Marija in a circle, her feet never touching the ground.

However, sanity soon reasserted itself.

Disentangling herself from her brother Marija threw a confused, horribly conflicted look first at her friend Margo, then at the big Redcap.

The Director of the St Catherine's Hospital for Women had remained seated behind her cluttered desk when the two men had jumped to their feet to greet Marija's entrance.

"I've been ordered to release this little 'troublemaker' into your custody," the big Redcap said flatly.

"My custody?"

The man nodded.

"I don't understand, Jim?"

It was odd using the man's Christian name, somehow intimate when something inside her shrieked against even the suggestion of an intimacy that could never be.

The last time they met she had bidden him goodnight, sent him on his way as she would a friend. He would always be 'Jim Siddall' to her now, never again the enemy.

Yet she was aware how easily this tiny familiarity might be misinterpreted by others and it gnawed insidiously at her soul.

She could feel her brother's eyes narrowing, a seed of suspicion suddenly planted in his mind.

Undaunted, she asked the one question she knew would inflame his doubt.

"Is this something to do with what we spoke of the other night?"

"I don't know," the Redcap confessed as he reached into his breast pocket and retrieved a sheet of paper. "When I reported to HMS Phoenicia this morning the boys were sorting through a big stack of orders like this one." He sighed, began to read: "*Joseph Mario Calleja is hereby released into the custody of Miss Marija Elizabeth Calleja, currently registered as resident at St Catherine's Hospital for Women in the Military District of Rabat. She is to be informed that the man in her custody is forbidden to enter the Military District of Valletta and, or the Three Cities. He is further barred without exception from entering the Military Districts of Gzira and Sliema until further notice...*" He handed the single page of closely typed script to her.

It seemed that she was her brother's keeper.

His infractions would henceforth be considered as being *her* infractions and *she* would be jointly liable in the event he was found guilty of any offence – civil or criminal – or if he breached his 'movement order'.

The icing on the cake was that her brother was subject to a dusk to dawn curfew.

"Joe's release is also conditional on his finding gainful employment within seven days," said the tall Redcap.

"That's not a problem," Margo Seiffert declared. "What was your trade in the dockyard, Joe?" She inquired, fixing Marija's brother sternly in her sights.

"Er, electrician, ma'am," he replied, wilting a little under Margo's scrutiny.

The older woman had always rather intimidated him.

"And general ship fitting, low pressure plumbing, that sort of thing."

"Marija says you are good at taking things apart and fixing them?"

"Yes, and that too, ma'am."

"In that case St Catherine's Hospital for Women has a new porter and odd job man. You will also run errands. Be aware that as a mere man in what is essentially a matriarchal environment you will be right at the bottom of the pecking order. In my absence you will obey the direction of any female member of staff. Is that absolutely crystal clear, Joseph Calleja?"

Jim Siddall stifled a chuckle.

Marija's brother nodded acknowledgment with the aplomb of a man who has just been struck over the head with a cricket bat.

"Whilst on the premises," Margo concluded with maternal severity, "you will *not* flirt or in *any* way fraternize or distract *any* of *my* girls."

"No, of course not, ma'am."

"Good," the Director of the St Catherine's Hospital for Women said.

She held the young man in her vise-like stare a moment longer. Smiling a quirky, sympathetic smile she relented.

"My girls call me Margo or Doctor Seiffert, Joe. I don't mind which as long as they remember I'm the boss."

"Yes, I see... Thank you, Doctor Seiffert."

Jim Siddall slapped the younger man on the back.

"I have to go. I have other deliveries to make today," he explained dryly.

Marija walked with him out onto the cobbled plaza in front of the Cathedral.

"Thank you for being the one who *delivered* my brother to me."

The man looked to his feet. Marija stepped close to him and on tip toes brushed the side of his square jaw with a fleeting, pecking kiss.

She watched him drive away, her thoughts tumbling one over another.

Back in Margo's office the Director of the St Catherine's Hospital for Women was restating her brother's duties and emphasising – as if he had ever had any doubts on the matter - that she was the last person in the world he ever wanted to displease. In comparison to her the 'British Imperialist Pigs' were 'Teddy Bears'.

There were two rooms in the roof of the building, both partially filled with linen, bric-a-brac and odds and ends of furniture donated to the Hospital for which nobody had yet found a use. He was to clear one of the rooms and claim it as his 'cell'.

"I'm sure Marija will show you around and introduce you to everybody."

Marija noticed for the first time the brown paper bundle tied with string beside Margo's cluttered desk and realised that it must contain her brother's earthly possessions from his time in detention.

She looked anew at Joe. She was pleasantly surprised and somewhat relieved to discover that whatever else the British had done to Joe they obviously had not been starving him.

Her little brother seemed almost well fed, lacking the hungry gauntness of many of the young men she saw in the streets. He looked pale, otherwise fit although his hair was over his ears and tousled, very *Elvis Presley*.

It was a mystery to her how a would-be Marxist-Leninist dockyard agitator like her brother could be so addicted to the persona and the music of somebody that was the living embodiment of the creeping global *Americanisation* that he had professed to have so despised since he was a teenager.

Joe had been the despair of their mother, every inch the black sheep of the family.

Samuel, their elder sibling, had followed their father into the docks, become a foreman and under-manager just before the war and moved into a company house in Kalkara.

Marija had inadvertently become the saintly daughter of the family.

Poor Joe, how was he ever going to compete with his siblings?

No matter that he was their mother's favourite.

Sam had always resented that, Marija suspected although she never talked to him about such things. Sam had always been a very private person and she respected that although she still regretted how they had drifted apart after he married a plump girl – Rosa - from Valletta. Rosa was the only daughter of an old Valletta family who made it plain – in a dozen little ways that only Marija and her mother truly understood, as women from time immemorial had understood and no man could ever understand – that they only tolerated the upstart Callejas because Rosa adored Sam.

Marija had tried to be friendly with Rosa; to no avail and then the war had come and she and Sam had broken with each other over her prominent role in the Women's Protest Movement...

After that trying being friends with her sister-in-law had not seemed that important any more.

Joe Calleja coughed.

Marija blinked in embarrassment; she had got lost in her thoughts.

Margo Seiffert was smiling as she settled behind her desk.

"Off you two go. Catch up properly." To hurry them on their way she added: "Shoo!"

Marija led her brother out into the courtyard at the heart of St Catherine's Hospital for Women. In the summer the space was cool, and in the winter, it was sheltered from the south westerly wind that sometimes gusted fitfully for weeks on end. Joe had never actually been inside the Hospital and his brown eyes were wide and curious.

"I didn't expect this place to be so quiet," he confessed.

"Sergeant Siddall said they were letting a lot of people out?" She asked, moving to a stone bench and sitting down.

Things were slowly spinning around her and she needed to re-establish her equilibrium.

"*Jim*, you mean," Joe Calleja teased his sister.

"He's been very," Marija struggled to find the right word, suddenly it mattered that she found exactly the right word to describe her association – no her friendship, of a sort – with the Redcap who had been one of her brother's jailors. "Proper and thoughtful," she decided, compromising when it was impossible to find a single word to express what she was feeling.

"Jim?"

"I've only ever used his first name twice and today was the first time I have ever kissed him," Marija retorted, vexed that she felt so defensive about something so transparently innocence. "Besides, he knows all about Peter Christopher."

"The Sergeant is sweet on you, big sister."

"I think I like him, but not *that* way."

Or at least she did not think she did.

But what did she know?

She was a twenty-seven-year-old spinster who had never had an admirer, boyfriend or suitor.

She had never been held in a man's arms other than when she had hugged her father or her brother, and although sometimes she yearned – positively ached – to be *touched* by a man it had never happened and she had never invited it.

Her adult life had been that of a nun in cloisters when it came to male companionship. Every time she spoke to or met a man of her own age who in other circumstances might have been a candidate for courtship or eventual matrimony; there was the wall of her notoriety and prestige as the heroine of Vittoriosa-Birgu, the broken child from the ruins remade, the bright hopeful symbol of the post-war Malta.

After the October War she was not even that because what hope was there for a bright new future in the ruins of a whole world?

"Do you think Sergeant Siddall understand that?"

"In his head maybe but not in his heart."

Marija's brother sat beside her on the bench and they were silent together for perhaps a minute.

"What do you think will happen if the British leave?"

"I don't know."

"What does your other *special* friend say about it?"

"Peter doesn't know anything about it. Or if he does, he's never said anything. Or the censor cuts it out of his letters."

"Oh." Joe reached out and held her hand. "I thought I'd never get out of that place on Manoel Island. Either that or they'd hand me back to the Yankee animals at the Empire Stadium."

Brother and sister squeezed each other's hand.

"I sometimes think I will never see Peter," Marija confessed suddenly. "Sometimes I wonder if he really exists. I know he does, but…"

"There are other good men in the world, big sister."

"I know but I don't want *any* man's pity."

Chapter 24

Wednesday 4th December 1963
The Rock Battery, Gibraltar

Arkady Pavlovich Rykov would have felt sorry for himself if he had thought it would do him any good. If he could have got to England and recounted his story to the right person things might have been different; there might even have been a happy ending. Or if not *happy*; then at least less *painful*. He hoped they would not be too hard on Clara. She had believed all along that she was doing her patriotic duty. She had never known that she was – technically – aiding and abetting an enemy of the state in a time of war. *Was this a time of war?* That was a fascinating philosophical question – the war had only lasted a few hours, and so far as he knew nobody had actually declared it (war) on anybody else and his country, the Soviet Union did not exist anymore – but largely irrelevant to his current dilemma.

It was indeed a funny old world...

Keys rattled loudly in the lock of the rusty iron grill door that delineated his damp, cold cell from the rest of the cave complex. He did not know exactly where his cell was in the upper galleries of the Rock's defences because when Major Denzil Williams had blown his whistle every soldier in the world had jumped on him and commenced to pummel him. Beneath the hammering fists and the crushing boots he was battered into insensibility within seconds. He had regained consciousness in his vest and underpants, barefooted and bereft of his beloved American aviator's chronometer. Without a watch he had no idea how much time had elapsed. The blood had congealed on his head and face, his ribs hurt every time he took a half breath and he had been sick on himself. No matter, but for the war the KGB would have found an excuse to denounce him and treat him thus. Perversely, given the choice he would have much rather suffered this indignity at the hands of his former foes that at the hands of his old *friends*.

"Oh, God! What have they done to you?" Clara exclaimed angrily, kneeling on the floor beside the man.

He asked himself why he could not see much of the room; now he realised it was because he was lying on the floor and his left eye was completed shut. Far, far away he heard the key turning in the lock at the woman's back.

"Forgive me," he muttered through cracked and swollen lips. "I hoped they'd at least permit me to confess my sins before they..." He coughed, retched. "Then they would have known that you were innocent..."

A harsh light came on in the cell.

A single naked electric bulb over the doorway.

There was a third person in the dank dungeon.

"If you'd be so good as to support his head Miss Pullman, we'll see what we can do to tidy him up," a weary and distinctly disenchanted male baritone suggested as a shadow fell over Arkady Pavlovich Rykov.

"If you help me, I can probably sit up," the patient offered, his voice a croaking parody.

"Let me give you a look over first," the man decided brusquely.

Arkady Pavlovich Rykov was not in any condition to argue. He let the man and the woman ease him onto his back with his head resting on Clara Pullman's lap. The warm, fragrant cushion of his lover's thigh was blissful after the unyielding, hostile rock floor of the cave.

Firm, gentle hands explored his torso, applying tentative pressure and waiting for a groan or sigh from the patient. Clara stroked Arkady Pavlovich Rykov's blood-crusted brow. Then something cold and wet was wiping away the blood. The stranger's hand methodically fingered his jaw, then around his eyes.

"Nothing obviously broken," the man grunted. "Apart from his nose, of course. I wouldn't be surprised if several of his ribs are cracked. He may have internal injuries but I can't tell just by looking. You carry on cleaning him up and I'll fetch something to stitch up those gashes. Try and get him to drink a little water, too."

The man rattled the iron grill.

"Let me out of here!"

The woman started sobbing the instant they were alone.

"You bastard!" She gasped half-heartedly. Warm salty tears dropped on his face. "You used me... You bastard..."

There was clinking of metal on rock and a canteen was being held to the man's lips.

"Drink this," the woman ordered him in a small, defeated voice.

Brackish water slurped into the man's parched mouth and he swallowed greedily. The canteen was snatched away.

"You can have more in a minute if that doesn't make you sick."

"Thank you."

"I don't want your thanks!" She snapped. "For anything!"

"I am Colonel Arkady Pavlovich Rykov of the First Directorate of the *Komitet Gosudarstvennoy Bezopasnosti*. At the time of the October War I was Second Secretary at my country's embassy in Ankara." It hurt to speak so he rested a while until the pain subsided. "In the jargon of the Central Intelligence Agency," his English was suddenly heavily accented because he did not have the energy or the inclination to project the pastiche of the public school educated British naval officer he had been twenty-four hours ago, "I was the KGB's head of station in Turkey. I had been working for the Americans for over two years and my own people were watching me. Somebody in Washington betrayed me, I think. The *Committee for State Security* has many *assets* embedded in America..."

"Why are you telling me this?" Clara Pullman asked hoarsely.

"I want to go to England one last time," he muttered feeling himself being dragged into the arms of sleep, "before it is too late..."

The next time Arkady Rykov regained consciousness he was being carried on a stretcher down a gentle gradient. It was pitch black and the hobnailed boots of the men bearing the litter rang dully on the road beneath their feet. It was like a waking dream; the darkness was momentarily turned to daylight by huge flash high in the heavens. Opening his eyes again the bright light had gone and in its place a glowing falling star drifted down across Algeciras Bay.

"Fucking Dagoes!" A man nearby growled.

The man on the stretcher lapsed again in unconsciousness.

Awakening anew in a white-washed cell, his broken nose wrinkled as it was assailed by the antiseptic stench of his surroundings. Through his one partially opened eye he focused on the woman in the chair beside his low cot. Clara was dozing, her head lolling a little. Her hair was awry and she was dressed in what looked like the sort of blue dungarees worn by engine room artificers in ships the world over.

"Ah, we're back in the world of the living!"

Clara Pullman awoke with a start and stared at the third person in the small, windowless room in the bunker somewhere beneath the Rock of Gibraltar. Major Denzil Williams who had introduced himself to her – only a few hours ago but it seemed like days – as being the 'Head of SIS in these parts' had been apologetic, in a cursory way, about the 'drama' of the arrest of her 'partner in crime'. After she stopped crying and he had promised to ensure that her 'partner in crime' received medical attention, she had answered his questions. She had held nothing back – that was the advantage of having a well-constructed legend to fall back on - there seemed no point. Clara Pullman had had an eventful life! She was a little surprised the local Head of Station did not ask her more questions; it was as if he was not really interested in her life story, but just what she knew about the man he called, derisively, 'Comrade Rykov'.

"Sorry about the rough stuff," the MI6 man said, chuckling lowly. "I told the chaps you were a dangerous fellow and they took me a little too much at my word."

Arkady Rykov tried to bring the short fat man's face into focus.

"You have put on weight, Denzil..."

"These days it pays to feast when food is plentiful ahead of the coming famine. But I didn't come here to talk about me. There we were all set up to fall on you like a ton of bricks at Brize Norton! What happened in Malta, did you baulk at the jump, old man?"

"The people at Luqa asked too many questions," Clara snapped irritably.

"Ah. Comrade Rykov has obviously passed a little of his tradecraft on to you, dear lady."

"Don't you dare 'dear lady' me, you little prick!" The woman spat angrily. "We were trying to get to England to warn you!"

"Oh, yes." Denzil Williams shrugged, unimpressed. "About the darkness descending upon the Empire from the east. *Red Dawn* indeed! It all sounds rather fanciful to me." He sniffed distastefully. "Still, you'll be glad to hear that my elders and betters back in the old country want to have a chinwag with you about it all before they put you up against a wall and shoot you. I haven't worked out how I get you from here to there yet but I'm working on it. In the meantime, I'll leave you two lovebirds together."

Arkady Rykov grimaced his thanks as the woman pulled the coarse woollen blanket up to his chin as soon as they were alone. She huffed scornfully and sat on the cell's single rickety wooden chair. The man cautiously surveyed his surroundings.

"I feel such a fool!" Clara Pullman exclaimed lowly.

"Betrayal becomes a habit in my career," Arkady Rykov stated.

"I thought you loved me," she replied sadly.

"I do," he protested, raising himself onto an unsteady elbow. "Ever since Beirut. After Beirut I resolved never to put you at such risk again."

"Oh." The woman got to her feet and began to pace. Two steps one way, three shorter steps another and then back again. "But everything was a lie? Everything we've been through the last year was a lie?"

Pain shot through with red hot splinters lanced across Arkady Rykov's chest as he forced himself to sit up on the cot. His head swam as he fought to catch his breath. He thought about attempting to get to his feet; knew it would be a bad mistake.

"My name is Arkady," he groaned. "You have no idea how much I ached to hear *my* name spoken by *your* lips, Clara. No idea..."

"I don't even know you!"

"That is not true. Nobody knows me as you know me."

Clara Pullman brushed this aside.

"I don't know you!"

The man sighed raggedly. "You don't know that I was born in Kiev in 1921. You don't know that I became a member of the Party when I was sixteen, or that I was a Commissar executing soldiers who failed to stand and fight the Fascists before Moscow when I was twenty years old. You don't know that I was recruited by the NKVD – the *Narodnyy Komissariat Vnutrennikh Del* – after I returned from Stalingrad with *Nikita Sergeyevich Khrushchev*, to whom I had become a protégé during the battle. It was *Nikita Sergeyevich* who ordered me to learn to speak English 'as the English speak it', and thus I became an interpreter for *Iosif Vissarionovich* whom you know in the West as *Stalin* at Yalta and later at Potsdam..." His voice grew so hoarse he could hardly form a new word.

The woman held out a canteen and he drank deeply.

She said nothing, returning to her chair, watching and listening with a peculiarly feline intensity.

Presently, he resumed his story.

"At Yalta and Potsdam, I was ordered to fraternise – in small ways – with the British and the American interpreters, and given, by *Iosif Vissarionovich* himself, permission to 'smoke cigarettes with the *capitalists*'. He wanted to know what the British and the Americans really understood of our great motherland. Which was very little but *Iosif Vissarionovich* and his pet Lavrentiy Beria, who was soon to become my master, trusted nothing the Generals of the NKVD told them. For men like them it is always easier to believe no one than to trouble oneself with having to decide in whom one should place one's trust."

"You knew Stalin?"

"God himself could not know *Iosif Vissarionovich*. I spoke to him, that is all. Some men are beyond understanding. I imagine it was the same for the men around Adolf Hitler. It is different for men like *Nikita Sergeyevich*. He was a man whom it was possible to know had the Americans only tried. *Nikita Sergeyevich* was a hard and a brutal man but not stupid. People say he drove the Americans to war. That he caused the war; I think this is wrong. *Nikita Sergeyevich* had fought all his life to preserve the sanctity of the motherland and the future of the Union of Soviet Socialist Republics. I do not think he would have seen it swept away thus..."

He took another swig from the canteen.

His head was clearing.

"After the war I joined the First Chief Directorate of the KGB. I became an intelligence officer. At first in Berlin where I learned German. I speak, read and write seven languages; Russian, English, German, French, Italian, Spanish and Portuguese. I am fluent in several others, including most of the Scandinavian languages. After Berlin I was in London, Paris, Brussels, Bonn, Copenhagen, Rome, Washington and eventually Ankara. By then my soul was tired and I'd decided to defect. I was married once, to the daughter of a brilliant man who was too close to Beria and was shot in the back of the head one night in the basement of the Lubyanka. That was after the bastards had starved him for a week, broken every bone in his hands and knocked out all his teeth, you understand. Svetlana blamed me; I think. It wasn't much of a marriage and it too, died. She divorced me a few years back. Her and our children lived in Moscow so they are probably dead now. When the October War came, I was being tortured in the basement of a safe house outside Ankara. My 'guards' had gone outside for a smoke a couple of minutes before the bomb went off. And then I met you."

"What were *we* doing the last year?" Clara Pullman asked urgently, her emotions chaotic as she tried to pretend, she did not see through the farrago of lies and half-truths.

"*We* were trying to discover if *Red Dawn* was a figment of somebody in the Kremlin's pre-war Vodka-inflamed imagination, or a nightmare that will haunt the world for the next hundred years."

Chapter 25

Thursday 5th December 1963
Situation Room, Government Buildings, Cheltenham

Eleven of the seventeen political ministers of the United Kingdom Interim Emergency Administration, the three Service Chiefs and the Cabinet Secretary, Sir Henry Tomlinson were present when, on the stroke of one o'clock the big double doors opened. The men in the room – there were no women present – shuffled to their feet, mostly from weary habit because few were paying attention to who was actually about to enter into their presence.

"Her Majesty Queen Elizabeth!" Barked a Guardsman, presenting arms and crashing his two large booted feet together on the wooden floor boards of the old mansion.

The proclamation and the sound of other rifles clicking metallically to the 'present' in the hallway outside galvanised and, for some of the ministers, came as a horrible heart-pausing shock.

Queen Elizabeth the Second, by the Grace of God, of Great Britain, Ireland and the British Dominions beyond the Seas Queen, and Defender of the Faith walked regally into the polished, rather faded glory of the oak-panelled former grand dining hall of the dead former Fleet Street Press magnate.

The Queen's expression was forbiddingly stern and she did not make eye contact with any of the men she walked past. Only the three Service Chiefs and the Cabinet Secretary had had official pre-warning of the Sovereign's intention – or rather, *her express and indefatigable demand* – to attend this specially convened meeting of the Cabinet of the United Kingdom Interim Emergency Administration.

The Queen was dressed like the housewife she liked to think she was at home with her family, except that the knee length blue dress was obviously a pre-war Norman Hartnell creation, her hair was freshly coiffured, and her black shoes polished to a perfect, high sheen. She wore a dark jacket with a single small glittering pin in the form of a jewelled anchor above her heart.

The Prime Minister, towering protectively above his monarch escorted her to her chair and held it for her while she made herself comfortable. Behind him Margaret Thatcher, apparently unaffected by her traumatic recent experiences in Scotland escorted a stiffly limping Vice-Admiral Julian Christopher, whose bruised and battered countenance drew many fewer looks than the fact that the fighting Admiral was leaning on the Angry Widow's arm for support. Tom

Harding-Grayson closed the door after his relatively anonymous entry into the august gathering. While Julian Christopher moved painfully to flank the First Sea Lord, Margaret Thatcher went to the empty space beside Jim Callaghan, and Tom Harding-Grayson joined his old friend Henry Tomlinson.

"Everybody should sit down," the Queen declared. She waited patiently while the members of her Government did as they had been commanded. When everybody was seated and all eyes were upon her, she took a moment to review what she planned to say, collected her composure and began to speak in a quiet, determined soprano. The blistering outrage simmered just beneath the surface of her perfectly modulated calm.

In that moment the sound of a pin dropping on a carpeted floor a hundred yards away would have sounded like the crack of a rifle shot.

"The Prime Minister advised me that my presence at this *Cabinet* is in the national interest at this time of great crisis," the thirty-seven-year-old recently bereaved mother whose husband lay critically ill at a heavily guarded Edinburgh hospital fighting for his life, made eye contacts around the table as she spoke. "That was in the minutes before the assault on Balmoral. At that time, I accepted his invitation. Nothing that has happened in the interim has done anything to make me question where my duty to *my people* lies. In fact, I am convinced that my presence here, today, is all the more appropriate in the circumstances." She stopped, folded her small hands before her on her lap. "The decisions that must be taken at the conclusion of this meeting will have my unreserved support. However, it is important that everybody in this room should know before we begin that I have the utmost faith in the Prime Minister and his Deputy, Mr Callaghan."

This drew a sharp intake of breath from the Chairman of the Conservative and Unionist Party and several other members of his faction. However, Ian Macleod refrained from making a direct intervention.

"I have spoken," the Queen continued, ignoring the discomfiture of several of the men in the room with her specific recognition of the Leader of the Labour and Co-operative Party as Edward Heath's deputy, "to each of the Chiefs of Staff and assured them that they also enjoy my unqualified confidence. You will know that Sir Charles Elworthy very honourably offered his resignation following the attack on Balmoral," he looked directly at the Chief of the Air Staff, "but I cannot allow a man so capable and so loyal to my person to resign from the very post for which he is so self-evidently so admirably qualified, Sir Charles. And that is my final word on the subject. It is clear that there are divisions in our fractured and hard-hit country but no good will come of randomly denigrating good and honest men for the transgressions and failings of others."

These words were delivered like a slap in the face to the room at large.

"Frankly, there has been too much time and energy wasted in the last year," she continued, her delivery and her tone measured and level, almost unemotional, "on matters which are not critical to our national survival. Gentlemen," she hesitated, glanced in Margaret Thatcher's direction, "and lady," she corrected herself, "while so many of *my people* are living on the edge of starvation in war damaged houses without adequate sanitation or power, I will not idly stand by while my ministers and their acolytes indulge in politicking for politicking's sake. Nor will I tolerate *place holding* passengers in senior posts in *My* Government. I am informed that two members of Cabinet have elected to remain on their estates in the north, and that there are *other* absentees." She turned her disapproving stare on Ian Macleod and the Chairman of the Conservative and Unionist Party visibly flinched. "The absentees are members of your Party, Mr Macleod and I believe, one of them has very recently seen fit to entertain the American Ambassador, presumably in the style to which he is accustomed, at his country house in Scotland?"

"I believe my colleague's motivation was to promote harmonious bi-lateral relations, you Majesty."

"Yes, well," the Queen responded with a quiet snort of scorn. "Frankly, Mr Macleod I am not sympathetic to such 'motivations'. *My* realm is not yet and I sincerely hope it will never be a subservient trans-Atlantic adjunct of the Pax Americana."

She allowed herself a brief moment of reflection.

"I was quite fond of Mr MacMillan and found the company of several of his confidantes in Government entertaining and informing. However, that was before the abject ultimate failure of *his* Government's policies condemned *My* people to the trials and tribulations of the last year. Many of you around this table share no little culpability for the tragedy that has befallen us. I am bound to say that not all of those responsible seem to have come to terms with their culpability, or their *duty* to do the best for *My* people in its aftermath." The Queen sat back and nodded to Edward Heath.

The Prime Minister cleared his throat and in an unhurried, stentorian tone announced: "The following members of Cabinet will remain seated: Mr Callaghan, Mr Thorneycroft, Mr Macleod, and Mrs Thatcher. All other members of Cabinet will remove themselves from this gathering and surrender themselves to the Queen's Guard pending a decision as to your further disposition." In the horrified silence, the Prime Minister rubbed his chin and added: "those members of Cabinet who failed to attend this day have already been arrested for dereliction of duty in a time of national emergency under the provision of Section 9(b) of the War Emergency Powers Act as amended in Council on the 12th day of our Lord, February 1963."

Henry Tomlinson had risen to his feet and opened the double doors.

He beckoned two Sten Gun-armed Marines into the room.

The three Chiefs of Staff and Julian Christopher sat like statues as the drama played out. The Queen viewed the dismissal of the sacked Cabinet ministers with placid indifference. As her Premier had remarked to her the previous day 'this is a thing best done expeditiously'.

"May I say something, Prime Minister?" Ian Macleod said when it was over. His face had turned an unhealthy shade of purple-red and the veins stood out in his temples. He was trembling with rage.

"Say it and be done with it, Iain." Edward Heath had not liked conducting the affair with such brutality but he had seen no alternative. The deposed ministers were not going to be sent to die in a labour battalion or fester in a Gulag-style concentration camp; they were merely going to be fed and watered in the relative comfort of the Cheltenham complex until more pressing matters were resolved.

"Most of *those* people are our friends, Ted!"

"Neither I nor the country can afford friends who live in the past, Iain," the big man retorted bluntly. "This isn't about Party loyalties, or our class and their class, or any of that nonsense. If any of them have the guts, if *you* have the guts for the fight, you can stand against me at the next general election. You won't have long to wait. May next year. It is my duty to ensure that *our* people survive the winter and that if they do, that they have a chance of surviving the next one."

"Here! Here!" Margaret Thatcher murmured.

The Prime Minister glanced to the Queen. "With your permission, ma'am, I shall proceed with the other matters we discussed."

The small woman at the top of the table nodded.

"Today's agenda is fairly short," Edward Heath informed his much-reduced audience. "There will be new appointments to departments currently without ministers. The majority will be announced in the coming hours but I want to announce the first changes now so that the decisions we take can be acted upon immediately."

Distantly, the roar of an aircraft taking off from the nearby airfield carved out of what had previously been Cheltenham Race Course rattled the leaded windows.

"Firstly, Mrs Thatcher will become Home Secretary. The Ministry of Supply will move over to the Home Office for an interim period of not less than six months. I propose to ask Airey Neave to take on that department under Mrs Thatcher's overview. Next, Mr Callaghan, whilst retaining his portfolio for Defence will subsume all military-related research and development work related to war fighting into his remit. How he organises that will be for him to sort out and report back to Cabinet in due course. Iain," he said, fixing the Chairman of the Conservative and Unionist Party in his sights, "there is no position in my revamped *War* Cabinet for a Minister without Portfolio, or for a full time Party hack, of any political persuasion. Members of the Labour Party will be invited the fill several of the vacant posts; I have been advised as to suitable candidates by Mr Callaghan. However, if you should wish to remain in the Cabinet, I am prepared to offer you a *real* job."

Iain Macleod did not look to his Party leader, he looked to the Queen. "I am proud to serve at Her Majesty's pleasure, Prime Minister. In whatever capacity you think fit."

Edward Heath was in too much of a hurry to linger overlong on this small snub: "Very well. I want you to take over the Ministry of Information and turn it into a cross between an organ for the disseminating of essential and useful public information and the old Office for Political Warfare we had during the 1945 war."

The Prime Minister didn't wait for an acknowledgement.

"Gibraltar," he growled. "Cannot be allowed to fall." He eyed the Chiefs of Staff. "We must do whatever we have to do to hold onto it."

Sir David Luce, the First Sea Lord asked the question that even now most brave men would blanch to ask.

"In the event that I come to you with a request to activate *Arc Light* what would be your response, sir?"

Edward Heath contemplated this for several seconds.

"Negative," he replied. "At this time my response would be negative."

The Queen coughed demurely. "Arc Light?"

"The atomic first strike option, ma'am," the Prime Minister said tersely. He re-focused on the First Sea Lord. "Can we hold Gibraltar?"

Sir David Luce nodded. "Yes, sir."

"Next item," Edward Heath continued. "Vice-Admiral Staveley-Pope?"

"I can confirm that the C-in-C Mediterranean has activated the preparatory phase of *Operation Homeward Bound* on his own initiative, sir," the First Sea Lord announced. "He has been sent a direct order – by me – to immediately rescind his orders to this effect. It is my understanding that he has ignored my order on grounds that he is the man on the spot and that he knows best."

The Queen intervened again.

"Is it the view of the Chiefs of Staff that the Gibraltar crisis has been materially worsened, or perhaps, provoked by Admiral Staveley-Pope's actions?"

"Possibly, ma'am," the First Sea Lord confirmed reluctantly. "Although, the latest intelligence summaries suggest that the Spanish may have been planning their move against the Rock for some months. It may simply be that they've moved now because they think that we have taken our eye off the ball."

"Prime Minister," the Queen remarked, her tone regretful in its finality, "we have just sacked several men – all of whom honestly believed that they were, and remain good men and true – for failing to come up to scratch in the face of the cruel demands of this chaotic new world. Does not the conduct of Admiral Staveley-Pope fall into a similar category?"

"Jim?" Edward Heath asked, half-turning to face the Minister of Defence.

The Leader of the Labour Party steepled his fingers. "Staveley-Pope's *conduct* verges on treachery, ma'am." Both the First Sea Lord and Julian Christopher frowned and the latter seemed, for a moment, to be minded to protest. Jim Callaghan raised a mollifying hand.

"I am aware that you and Hugh Staveley-Pope have been personal friends for over forty years, Admiral Christopher," he half-apologised, "but the man has been behaving," he spread his hands, "eccentrically. In the last few days he's started emptying the prisons in Cyprus and Malta while at the same time cutting the daily ration of all food stuffs by half and closing all fuel depots to civilians. Cyprus is already a powder keg; Malta will be the same in a few days. Having previously prioritised civil order over virtually all other military considerations we have a very poor feel for the general situation in the central and eastern Mediterranean," he explained with ill-concealed exasperation, "which means that Operation Homeward Bound might not even be viable in the case of Cyprus, and impossible to efficiently carry through on Malta. Even if such an outcome was remotely to be desired."

Sir David Luce, First Sea Lord re-entered the fray.

"Operation Homeward Bound was conceived as a joint staff exercise to inform long-term planning in the Mediterranean theatre of operations. It was *never* envisaged as a contingency plan to be activated at the discretion of *local* commanders. If, as we suspect, Staveley-Pope has taken it upon himself to activate Operation Homeward Bound the consequences will be incalculable. Our already somewhat tenuous lines of communication with Middle East Command in the Arabian Peninsula will be severed, our remaining forces east of Suez will be cut off and forced to withdraw to Australasia..."

"I think we all get the picture, Sir David," Edward Heath interjected impatiently. "Somebody is going to have to remove *that* man from command in the Mediterranean." He looked Julian Christopher in the eye. "How soon can you fly to Malta and take over as C-in-C, Admiral Christopher?"

Julian Christopher's one visible reaction was the barely perceptible elevation of his left eyebrow. "As soon as transport can be arranged, Prime Minister," he replied. "However, I have two caveats."

If Edward Heath cavilled at the invitation to discuss terms it was not apparent to the witnesses to the exchange.

"Two caveats?"

"Gibraltar and the Western Med must be reintegrated into a unified Mediterranean Command."

The Prime Minister nodded. He had never understood why the two commands had been separated in the first place. When the Spanish had begun to re-apply pressure to Gibraltar, he had kicked himself for not having attended to the matter sooner.

"Yes, I agree."

"Thank you, sir." Julian Christopher quirked a half-smile at Edward Heath in acknowledgment. "In voicing a second caveat I apologise in advance for my *presumption*," he looked to the Queen. "Ma'am, Hugh Staveley-Pope is a man possessed of immense personal honour. The one thing I can be absolutely sure of is that whatever he is doing, he *believes* that he is doing it for the best possible reasons and in *your* loyal service. Respectfully, may I request you to write Hugh a personal letter?"

The Queen thought about this.

"If the Chiefs of Staff have no objection to my communicating with a serving officer *over their heads*," she decided, "I will write to Admiral Staveley-Pope commending him on his loyal service to my person and regretfully relieving him of his command."

This concluded the business of the shortest Cabinet meeting in the short history of Edward Heath's United Kingdom Interim Emergency Administration.

Chapter 26

Thursday 5th December 1963
The Embassy of the United States of America to the Court of Balmoral,
UKIEA Compound Number 2, Cheltenham

Captain Walter Brenckmann (United States Navy Reserve) hesitated a moment before he signed. Then, with a sigh not so much of relief as of sad despair he pushed his chair back from the desk and stared out of the window. The Embassy was a quarter of a mile from the end of the runway of RAF Cheltenham. As if on cue a big turbo-prop transport – a Britannia – swooped overhead and landed in a puff of spray on the great, broad swath of tarmac that cut the old race course in half. The former grandstand still served as the reception terminus. Signs like 'Members Only' and boards giving directions to 'The Royal Box' had yet to be removed.

The previous evening, he had formally protested to the British about 'the Dreadnought incident'. He had previously advised the Ambassador that it was a bad mistake to protest about an 'incident' which had demonstrated a critical shortcoming in US Navy's tactical anti-submarine doctrine. HMS Dreadnought had shown, conclusively, that the Navy's newest, biggest carrier was virtually defenceless against a single well-handled nuclear attack boat. While the *Big E's* air group had been playing stupid and dangerous 'war games' against the Ark Royal's screening destroyers the Enterprise herself had been squarely in the periscope sights of the Dreadnought.

The CO of the USS Scorpion had handled things nicely and the sensible thing to do now was *nothing.* Unfortunately, the Pentagon did not see things that way. *Sanity* had never been a *given* in *that* place.

He had protested; the First Sea Lord's Secretary, Captain Thomas Pakenham, had accepted the protest with grace and tact even though he must have been laughing inside. Afterwards, Tom Pakenham had offered him a drink and informally slipped him the chilling intelligence that 'over a number of days Dreadnought had achieved as many as seventeen firing solutions on the Enterprise'. He'd added: 'I do hope your chaps understand that if the situation had been reversed and Dreadnought had found one of your boats in the vicinity of, say, Ark Royal or Hermes, she'd have opened fire?'

Before writing his letter of resignation Walter Brenckmann had gone for a walk in the cold, crisp frosty evening twilight. He strolled to the air base perimeter fence in time to see a Comet 4 land while high in the grey wintery skies the four silhouettes of jet interceptors circled. A little later he had watched a convoy of staff cars headed by a Ferret armoured vehicle drive at speed across the airfield and cluster around another, waiting Comet 4. He had wondered what was going on. Presidential type cavalcades were hardly the Brits' normal style so *something* had to have been going on and true to form the Ambassador, Loudon Baines Westheimer II, was not at Cheltenham to see it.

The Ambassador had flown off to a conference in, of all places, Dublin. The State Department had started building a compound south west of the Irish capital in the summer. Walter Brenckmann assumed the 'compound' was probably a CIA project, a combined 'listening post' to replace the facilities destroyed in Germany and the Low Countries during the war, and the now wholly British Government Communications HQ at nearby Cheltenham. He had doubted the new Irish 'compound' was solely an eavesdropping asset and the Ambassador's summons confirmed his suspicions.

The Irish Republic had been neutral during Hitler's War and played no part in the October War, other than as a helpless, terrified witness to the madness. In recent years the Republic had been developing economic ties with the United Kingdom and relations between the two countries had been if not cordial, then slowly thawing somewhat. Unable or unwilling to offer significant assistant to the partially devastated isles across the Irish Sea and worried by the looming civil war in Ulster which threatened to spill over onto its soil, the Irish Republic's economy had crashed in the last year and there were rumours that famine again stalked that beleaguered land. It was hardly surprising that the Irish Government should turn to America for succour, and whereas, aiding the United Kingdom was an expensive and potentially open-ended commitment, materially aiding the Irish – whose population was a tiny fraction of that which survived in the UK – was a relatively cheap option which played well with exactly the constituencies John Fitzgerald Kennedy needed to keep happy if he was going to get re-elected next year. The argument went something like; if the United Kingdom did not want to be America's bridgehead in Europe then Ireland was an acceptable second best. The Irish Republic lacked the ports, road and rail infrastructure and the military would have to bring in *all* its own logistical support, airfield, docks and new roads would need to be built, but that was all doable. Washington was looking for a new 'special' trans-Atlantic relationship in which its 'special' client knew its place. It was only a matter of time before American GIs were on the ground 'keeping the peace' along the fractious border with the six counties of Ulster.

The phone on Walter Brenckmann's desk rang jarringly.

"It is the Ambassador for you, Captain," the woman on the exchange said flatly.

The United States Naval Attaché waited while the caller was put through.

"What the fuck is going on over there?"

Walter Brenckmann was not entirely sure why the Ambassador was asking his Naval Attaché this question when he had a retinue of supposedly competent professional State Department first, second and third secretaries at his beck and call twenty-four hours a day.

"In what respect, Ambassador?"

"The fucking coup!"

This genuinely baffled the sailor.

"I'm sorry, Ambassador. There's been a deal of coming and going around here in the last twenty-four hours but everything seems calm. I know nothing of a coup?"

"The Royal Air Force bombed Balmoral Castle, god-dammit!"

Walter Brenckmann was stunned into silence.

"And that arrogant little prick Franco mined the Straits of Gibraltar and damned nearly sunk a fucking Brit carrier!"

Walter thought it highly unlikely the two events were linked but the timing explained the increase in take offs and landings at RAF Cheltenham and the general non-availability of many of his British contacts since yesterday morning.

"There's been nothing on the BBC, sir," he reported lamely.

"The *new* Foreign Secretary rang me just now and..." Loudon Baines Westheimer II choked on what he wanted to say. He spluttered and hyperventilated for some moments. "The bastard gave *me* a fucking ultimatum!"

"The new Foreign Secretary, Ambassador?"

"That Douglas-Home guy was killed up at Balmoral. So was one of the Queen's kids, the youngest one, I can never remember all the kids' names..."

"Prince Andrew, Ambassador. He was three years old."

"Yeah, that's the one..."

Only in America, Walter Brenckmann mused, could a red-neck with a mind like a colander be appointed Ambassador to his nation's most important – and by any standard only *irreplaceable* – ally.

"Who is the new British Foreign Secretary?"

"That little shit Harding-Grayson!"

The Lord of Home was dead, the British Royal Family, the nation's most sacred and most inviolable symbol of unity had been desecrated, a British carrier had been mined off Gibraltar, and *finally*, the man with indisputably the finest mind in Government had been appointed Foreign Secretary. And Loudon Baines Westheimer II, Washington's man in England, did not get it.

"An ultimatum?"

"The Brits think we put Franco up to it and they claim to have intercept and radio signal triangulation evidence that at least one of the fighters that hit Balmoral was in contact with a control station in Ireland. It's fucking unbelievable. If our guys were involved there's no way, they could be so fucking stupid!"

Walter Brenckmann wanted to put his head in his hands.

Loudon Baines Westheimer II, the American Ambassador to the Court of Balmoral might not *get it*, but he did. He was *getting it* so loud and clear it was very nearly making his ears bleed.

The Spanish would never have mined the waters around Gibraltar without at least a tacit go ahead from Washington. And if the CIA had had anything to do with the attack on the Royal Family...

The ramifications did not bear thinking about.

Loudon Baines Westheimer II was ranting but the rant went over Walter Brenckmann's head unheard, lost in translation. The Ambassador's words were just so much white noise. Like the ramblings of some ignorant, uncultured spoilt child baying at the Moon.

"Fools," the naval officer heard himself say. "Fools. You are all fools and history will dam you for all eternity. Or at least I hope it does."

Loudon Baines Westheimer II fell silent.

"What, I..." He spluttered eventually.

"I'm through with all of you. I am about to hang up now. When you return to Cheltenham you will find my resignation on your desk. I have taken the liberty of transmitting its contents to the Navy Department. As of midnight, this day I cease to be a commissioned officer in the Reserve. Good day to you, Ambassador."

The last act of Walter Brenckmann's naval career was to gently replace the receiver on the old-fashioned Bakelite black phone.

Chapter 27

Friday 6th December 1963
HMS Talavera, 9 Miles North of Cabo de Lata, Northern Spain

The manoeuvring bell rang twice, the destroyer heeled into the turn and steadied onto an easterly heading more or less parallel with the indistinct low grey blur of the coast of Northern Spain. One thousand yards astern of Talavera, HMS Aisne her sister ship, and the new County Class destroyer Devonshire another thousand yards astern of the Aisne, steered to maintain station on their leader.

"Point Alpha!" Leading Electronic Warfare Rating Jack Griffin reported with an underlying wolfish hunger.

Lieutenant-Commander Peter Christopher eyed the plot and touched the stud of his new throat microphone. He had 'requisitioned' a batch of the new devices from stores in Gosport several months ago. The kit was similar to the intercom equipment the RAF had been using since the 1945 war but as always, the Navy had been unbelievably slow getting its hands on it.

"CIC to Bridge. Point Alpha! Repeat Point Alpha!"

"Very good, EWO," returned the Captain's relaxed drawl. Captain David Penberthy's position when the ship was closed up at actions stations was a somewhat moveable feast. The Navy had not yet got used to the new science and technologies of war and individual commanders tended to be reluctant to bury themselves in the sterility of their ship's Combat Information Centres when nothing specifically prohibited them from fighting their ship from the bridge. Today the Old Man was on his bridge while his Electronics Warfare Office – twenty-seven-year-old Lieutenant-Commander Peter Julian Christopher – to all intents, controlled and managed the battlefield around HMS Talavera and her two consorts.

Operation Albion was going to be a long-range gunnery engagement. The battle plan assumed – a calculated risk – that even this close to the enemy shore the largely antiquated Spanish air force was unlikely to pose a threat to the three destroyers of Task Force 1.2. HMS Ark Royal, steaming seventy miles off shore was flying a four Sea Vixen CAP over the target and in the unlikely event any attacking aircraft got past the CAP the three destroyers' GWS 21 Sea Cats and 20-millimetre cannons would be more than capable of dealing with World War Two vintage Dorniers and Heinkels.

Peter Christopher saw the other destroyers forming up astern of Talavera on the tactical plot. Ark Royal's Sea Vixens were circling over the port of Santander at thirty-three thousand feet. Otherwise, the plot was empty.

'Spanish forces have invested Gibraltar and cratered the only available runway capable of operating fixed wing aircraft. Two days ago, HMS Albion struck a submerged mine entering Algeciras Bay in Gibraltarian territorial waters. Shortly thereafter HMS Cassandra was mined and destroyed by a secondary magazine explosion with heavy loss of life. Some twelve hours after her mining HMS Albion was towed into a dry dock. Nearly two hundred naval personnel are dead or missing and many others were injured.'

The Captain's voice had rung with righteous anger as he addressed the crew in the minutes before the ship closed up for battle.

'A state of war now exists between the United Kingdom and the Fascist Republic of Spain!'

There had been no jeers, only resignation in the faces of the men in Talavera's gloomy CIC.

'If the last year has taught us anything it is that actions speak louder than words. The Spanish probably expect there will be diplomatic overtures. They might even anticipate that we will meekly surrender Gibraltar to their tender mercies. If that is what they expect they are going to get a very nasty surprise in the next few hours!'

Resignation had become grim determination on the faces of the men around Peter Christopher. The die was cast.

'While Talavera, Aisne and Devonshire are shelling Santander, Task Force 1.1, made up of elements of Hermes's screen will be administering the same medicine off Cadiz. While that is going on four of Hermes's Buccaneer's will attack shipping in Cadiz Roads. I have also been notified that Bomber Command V-Bombers will conduct precision attacks with conventional munitions on several military targets in the Spanish hinterland and in the Madrid area at around the time we will be going into action.'

Peter Christopher had never been of an overly bloodthirsty disposition. He had not joined the Navy to get himself killed or to kill anybody else. He had joined up because it was expected of him and because the Navy promised to allow him to play with all manner of new and exhilarating toys. When he first come on board Talavera his cup had run over; the ship was a veritable smorgasbord of brand new and experimental radars, communications and electronic warfare counter measures devices. He had discovered technologies on board the reconstructed and modernised destroyer that he had previously only read about in science fiction comics. Some days when he was sitting in CIC – if he actually had a minute or so of spare time to think – he felt like *Dan Dare*. However, even Talavera's easy going, unwarlike EWO's blood was up today. There had been an unprovoked, murderous attack on two Royal Navy warships entering harbour; and that could not be allowed to go unpunished.

"Point Bravo!" Jack Griffin, once the destroyer's talismanic bad apple but now its beating heart announced.

"Time to run?" Peter Christopher asked, checking the timings on the plot.

"Six-zero seconds, sir."

The Bridge speaker confirmed the clock was running down.

The three destroyers would open fire as one.

Thereafter, they would fire broadsides at will across the isthmus upon which the city of Santander perched, into its port and onto any shipping sheltering within that the Sea Vixens identified.

Each destroyer had a broadside of four 4.5-inch Mark III and IV 45 Calibre guns in two twin turrets mounted forward of their bridge superstructures. Theoretically, the 4.5 inch Mark III or IV gun had a rate of fire of between 12 and 15 rounds per minute but in the current seas and to accommodate corrections fed back into Talavera's CIC by the high-flying Sea Vixens, effectively the rate of fire was going to be as low as ten rounds per gun per minute.

In an action timed to last no more than ten minutes this still meant that around twelve hundred rounds – each weighing 55-pounds with an eleven-pound high explosive bursting charge - would fall within the city and port.

In a former age Peter Christopher and many – possibly the majority – of those on board HMS Talavera would have baulked at attacking a civilian target, which just happened to be an enemy naval base, without warning. However, his personal well of pity and the last of his pre-war moral scruples about such things had gone out of the window when he heard what had happened to HMS Albion and HMS Cassandra in Algeciras Bay.

"Thirty seconds!"

Talavera's main battery was slaved to the CIC.

Peter Christopher watched radar ranges constantly updating the firing solution, noted the periodic modification of the elevation and traverse of the guns in the twin turrets. It would have seemed so bloodless, so straightforward to an impartial bystander; it was anything but. If he fed the wrong assumptions, the wrong targeting co-ordinates into the system Talavera's fire would land hopelessly short or long and potentially, kill entirely the wrong people…

Thou shalt not kill…

He was about to kill people he had never known, never met and who had never done anything to personally hurt to him or his. At some level he was reconciled to that. That after all was the nature of war. However, surrounded by the marvellous multi-faceted technologies of making war, of *killing*, he knew himself to be viscerally disconnected from the nightmare of the reality he was about to orchestrate in the streets of city he had never visited, never seen and that would never be the same again.

"Twenty seconds to run!"

"Check range to nearest coastline?"

"Eight point seven nautical miles, sir."

Peter Christopher studied the plot.

"Eight point seven miles, aye," he repeated. "CIC to Bridge. The board is green for a full calibre shoot!"

"Ten seconds!"

"Main battery pointers match!"

The report was superfluous; so much was automated.

"Five seconds!"

Four…three…two…one…

"SHOOT!"

The ship shuddered as the four guns of Talavera's main battery spat fire towards the distant lee shore.

Chapter 28

Friday 6th December 1963
RAF Cheltenham

Vice-Admiral Sir Julian Christopher - the Queen had ennobled him yesterday afternoon for 'making Operation Manna a reality' - walked stiffly into the high security transit lounge beneath the Grandstand of the old race course. He had been patched up, and his medal ribbons transferred onto the breast of his brand-new uniform for the benefit of the photographers. Oddly, he felt a little uncomfortable wearing Sir David Luce's ceremonial sword. His own was still in a locker on board Ark Royal with practically all his other personal effects.

Margaret Thatcher with her two-Marine bodyguard – the Prime Minister had mandated that no member of the newly remodelled *War Cabinet* was ever to be without 'adequate security' outside the Government compound – arrived some ten minutes after the C-in-C Designate of the Mediterranean Fleet and the newly reconfigured Joint Combined Mediterranean and Middle East Command, had settled to wait until his aircraft had finished ground checking and refuelling for the four hour flight to Malta. The woman found him thumbing through a sheaf of briefing papers.

The man struggled to his feet.

"Margaret," he smiled, "I hoped to see you before I jetted off but I realised how busy you must be right now."

Margaret Thatcher waved her Marines away and shook Julian Christopher's hand. She had been so eager to get to the airfield in time to wave him off that she not given any thought to what she was going to say or do in the last few minutes they had together.

"It was the least I could do," she asserted, her voice betraying how trite she realised it sounded. She viewed the man with concern. She noted that he had washed off the stage make up Iain Macleod's people had smeared all over his face to conceal the worst of the bruising and the stitches from the eyes of the cameras. Having seen the welts and bone deep bruises all over his lean torso, the burns to his arm, now heavily bandaged under his pristine uniform she was astonished by how well he looked. "I only wish you'd had a few more days to," she shrugged helplessly, "recover your strength."

"Never fear," the man grimaced, "there's life in this old sea dog yet!"

"I shall miss you," she said simply.

"And I shall miss you, Margaret."

For a moment, Julian Christopher's emotions completely distracted him from his aches and pains and the brutally hard decisions he was going to have to start making the moment he stepped off the plane in Malta. Hugh Staveley-Pope had been his first brother in arms at Dartmouth all those years ago when they had been snotty-nosed cadets. They had sailed together on the old Warspite, joining the great battleship in Scapa Flow a month before the end of what they then called the Great War. Well, the *war to end all wars* had signally failed. After that war they had steamed out to take the surrender of the Kaiser's High Seas Fleet, a seemingly endless row of rusty, weather beaten, unkempt walls of steel meekly steaming into captivity. Hugh Staveley-Pope had stood beside him at the lee rail in the shelter of Warspite's mighty X-turret as they stared in wonder and perversely, shame, as the Grosser Kurfurst, Derfflinger, Seydlitz and the Markgraf and a dozen other massive dreadnoughts and battlecruisers slowly, ignominiously passed under the guns of the Grand Fleet. So many memories, so many mistakes repeated. It had been Hugh Staveley-Pope – on all his ships his men had nicknamed him 'the Pope' for his bookish demeanour, his high forehead and his religious devotion to maintaining the traditions of the service – who had introduced him to his wife...

"Forgive me, Margaret," he said eventually, breaking the shackles of remembrance. "You and I were strangers a week ago. But a lot has happened in the few days of our," he struggled because he did not begin to know how to describe the bond which had spontaneously formed between them, "acquaintance," he said feebly, cursing his ineptitude. "No. Our *friendship*," he corrected himself instantly. "Believe me when I say that you will be much in my thoughts in the coming days and weeks."

"And you will be in mine." The Angry Widow straightened, snapped out of her threatened slide towards the dreaminess she so deeply mistrusted, and regarded in others as an inexcusable weakness. The fighting admiral had come into her life in the hours that her political career had leapt ahead, propelling her into a position of power and influence unimagined before the October War. She had no particular hunger for high office just for the sake of holding *high office* but she had always thirsted to be of service, to *get things done* and now she had a golden opportunity to be of great service and to achieve great things and in the very core of her being, she *knew* that with *this* man at her side the sky was the limit. She liked and trusted Airey Neave - the man everybody suspected pulled her strings like some well-meaning opportunistic puppeteer - but Airey was only her adviser, a faithful lieutenant whom she had been meticulous careful to keep at arm's length both emotionally and intellectually. Julian Christopher would never settle for being just that and if she had believed, for a moment, that he would have she would have walked through fire to douse the troubling, possibly debilitating feelings that his mere proximity stirred in the wellspring of her very being.

"I know that you won't," she prefaced, a little tight-lipped, "take care, Julian. I don't think that is in your nature. However, at those times when you conspicuously determine not to *take care* please spare a thought for those of us back in England in whose thoughts you will always be foremost."

Julian Christopher read volumes into the convoluted sentiments expressed so painfully and thought: *What a remarkable woman!*

"I promise I will bear that in mind, Margaret."

"Thank you. When we meet again, I am sure we will have a lot to discuss." She took a deep breath, composed herself. "I must return to my duties," she announced.

The man considered asking permission; in the event he damned the consequences and acted. He bent his face to the woman's and kissed her. His lips brushed her cheek and lay, momentarily on her lips.

And to his astonishment she kissed him back likewise.

The old admiral watched the newly appointed Home Secretary marching across the concourse, her heels clicking on the newly laid concrete pan, flanked by her Sten Gun toting Royal Marine bodyguards. She did not look back, or wave. She had swept into his life and now she was sweeping out of it. For how long neither of them could tell...

"They're ready for us on the tarmac, sir," squeaked his ludicrously young-looking Flag Lieutenant, Sub-Lieutenant Alan Hannay. Sir David Luce, the First Sea Lord, had recommended the boy, who had served on his staff since the summer.

'If the young man is not to your liking send him back to me at your convenience, Julian," Christopher's old friend had suggested as they had mulled over the problems awaiting the new C-in-C Mediterranean and Middle East Command, after breaking into the First Sea Lord's last bottle of Laphroaig Single Malt Whiskey. 'Hannay's not quite as young as he looks, he's as keen as mustard and he's got a talent for tactfully dealing with people who have inflated opinions as to their own importance. That comes in handy around here, so, as I say, I shall miss him and welcome him back if it comes to it.'

"Mrs Thatcher is a lovely lady, isn't she, sir," Julian Christopher's new Flag Lieutenant remarked innocently – or at least, with a convincing air of innocence – as he followed his master's gaze. "Now that she's been promoted, I'm sure she'll really shake things up!"

The Admiral gave his Flag Lieutenant a paternally severe look.

It seemed he was not the only sea dog in Cheltenham to have fallen under the Angry Widow's thrall.

"The Flight Line Supervisor apologises for the delay, sir. There was a problem of some kind loading the Marines' heavy equipment into the hold.

Julian Christopher had not felt it necessary to take his own security detachment with him; the Prime Minister had put his foot down. B Platoon, 3rd Battalion, 43 Commando equipped with enough guns and ammunition to re-enact a World War Two night time hit and run raid on Hitler's Atlantic Wall would be accompanying him to Malta.

He reached down to collect the battered attaché case containing his orders, the Queens's graciously sympathetic and unambiguous hand-written letter to Hugh Staveley-Pope recalling him to England, and a sheaf of briefing papers.

Lieutenant Alan Hannay got there before him and clutched the case.

"Let me, sir." The younger man hesitated, then launched on: "Will you be all right getting up the steps to the aircraft, sir? It is very wet and windy out there?"

Julian Christopher struggled to hold down a guffaw of genuine amusement.

"Lieutenant," he murmured quietly, "I've raced an America's Cup yacht in a force ten storm, I survived scores of the old Prince of Wales's parties in the twenties, I survived having my ship torpedoed under me in the Second War, the Yanks couldn't get me sacked when I was in the Pacific, and a few days ago a castle fell on me. I think I'll live through walking up a few steps in the rain," he fixed the younger man with a mildly admonishing severity, "don't you?"

"Oh, yes, rather, sir," the youngster hastily agreed.

Chapter 29

Friday 6th December 1963
St Bernard's Royal Military Hospital, Gibraltar

Major Denzil Williams, head of Station of SIS on the Rock wore the dark frown of a man whose pet parrot had just escaped from the aviary.

He glared at the two lovers sitting side by side on the hospital cot in the white-washed underground room. Women were strange creatures.

He had never – not in a million years – expected Clara Pullman to forgive Arkady Pavlovich Rykov.

The man had lied to her about *everything* and spent most of the last year trying to get her killed.

She had been angry, upset, wounded but somehow, he did not begin to understand had *forgiven* the duplicitous, scheming and lethally dangerous KGB Colonel.

Now the pair of them sat together like two peas out of a pod although since he had arrived, they had stopped holding hands.

That was a small mercy, at least.

Arkady Pavlovich Rykov, formerly of the First Chief Directorate of the *Komitet Gosudarstvennoy Bezopasnosti*, looked a mess. X-rays had identified undisplaced fractures to his swollen lower left jaw, three ribs and to bones in his right hand. One of his eyes was still virtually closed by swelling and bruising and beneath the hospital gown his torso and abdomen were half covered in purple-black contusions and livid, bone deep welts.

The SIS Station Chief still regretted calling off the beating so soon. But Clara Pullman had been beside herself and he hated seeing a comely woman crying, so he had reluctantly blown the whistle a second time and the boys had, eventually, stopped what they were doing.

He was getting soft in his old age!

If he had learned anything in his career in SIS it was that some people were simply better off dead.

Especially, people like Arkady Pavlovich Rykov.

Never mind, what was done was done.

The chaps with the over-sized brains in Cheltenham had spoken and bad things happened to people who did not obey orders.

Dammit!

If he had let the boys go about their work another few seconds, he would not have to be eating humble pie now. He was sorely tempted to drag things out, make a meal of carrying out his new orders but that would have been churlish.

Major Denzil Williams was many things; churlish was not one of them.

Notwithstanding, that was, his hatred of Arkady Pavlovich Rykov was real, visceral and was not about to go away any time soon. The man was responsible for the death of too many good men and the news – if it was true - that he had been in the Americans' pockets for several years before the October War rubbed salt into old and very painful wounds.

But orders were orders.

Denzil Williams's mood was not enhanced by the nagging certainty that it was only a matter of time before some trigger-happy Falangist decided to start lobbing artillery rounds into the tightly packed streets of the colony. The BBC had reported that large fires were still burning in Santander, Cadiz and on the outskirts of Madrid, where it was believed an airfield, a supply depot and several road and rail bridges had been attacked. Spanish radio was playing patriotic music and a period of seven days national mourning had been declared.

When he heard about an airfield near Madrid being hit, Denzil Williams had paused for thought. The only airfield anywhere near the Spanish capital was Madrid Airport, which made him wonder what else the RAF had targeted within the Iberian hinterland.

"Something has happened?"

Arkady Rykov observed.

"The Navy shelled Cadiz and Santander. We think a Spanish destroyer was sunk in Cadiz Roads. At the same time the bombardment was going on the RAF was 'demonstrating' over Madrid. Right now, we're waiting for the Dagoes to retaliate."

"Oh, I see."

The former KGB Colonel's English was lightly accented with hints of his Slavic mother tongue. He found it pleasurable not to be having to mind – literally speaking – his Ps and Qs; although he would have preferred to have reached this juncture without being beaten to a pulp in the process.

"Your attack on the fascists was without warning?"

Denzil Williams nodded.

"The bully has had his fingers burned and a sharp kick administered to his hind quarters," the man on the bed went on.

He had never really been a citizen of the Soviet Union in his head. He always remained a *Russian*, perversely proud of his Muscovite routes, having been born in Tulskaya near the banks of the Moskva River. As a child he had been able to make out the spires of the Kremlin from the window of his family's fourth floor apartment.

His childhood had been as miserable as any of his peers, years of hunger and fear punctuated with savagely cold winters that killed the old and the weak and sick even more effectively than the NKVD's death squads. He had become an apparatchik to survive and discovered a brutal, cynical world in which he had eventually become the hunter rather than prey until finally, his Achilles heel had tripped him up.

The one thing a man in his position could not afford was a conscience.

"Before Generalissimo Franco *retaliates,* he will do what all dictators of his kind do," he decided. "He will blame his subordinates for not warning him of the consequences of his actions. He will punish the innocent, rage a while, and probably wet himself in his panic. All this he will be doing from the deepest underground bunker in Spain. Also," he grinned crookedly, an act that sent a splinter of red-hot pain across his face, "*we* might have wounded him more deeply than we know."

The Head of Station of SIS in Gibraltar grunted.

"Perhaps. Anyway, the people in England want to 'debrief' you."

The Russian said nothing.

"And Miss Pullman."

"Oh."

"They probably want to hear what you've got to say about *Red Dawn* before they hang you."

Denzil Williams held up a hand.

"No, they won't hang you, Miss Pullman. Just Comrade Rykov."

"*Red Dawn* is no figment of my imagination," Arkady Rykov said wearily.

"Don't waste your breath trying to convert me."

"How on earth are we ever going to get back to England?" The woman demanded angrily.

"Arrangements are in hand, dear lady." Denzil Williams would have elaborated had he not been distracted by the noise of running feet in the corridor.

A nurse with her cheeks flushed with excitement stuck her head around the door.

"There are Fleet Air Arm jet fighters overflying the Bay and there are two of *our* destroyers out in the Straits!"

"Comrade Rykov," Denzil Williams inquired, not hiding his disdain, "are you able to walk?"

"I think so."

"In that case I suggest you and *Clara* follow me."

Progress through the corridors and up two flights of steps was slow and painful. It was some minutes before the trio emerged into the late afternoon windblown winter sunshine.

By then Arkady Rykov was virtually being carried between the man and the woman.

The whistling whine of jet engines roared across Algeciras Bay, reverberating off the Rock.

A Bentley in drab Army green was idling outside the service exit. Arkady Rykov and Clara Pullman were gestured to get into the back seats and Denzil Williams dropped beside the driver a hatchet-faced Redcap who seemed to know where to go.

Arkady Rykov thought he was going to be sick when the car lurched forward.

The Bentley rumbled across Main Street down towards the docks. In the fading light the slab-sided bulk of HMS Albion nestled in the safety of her dry dock. Moored just inside the sea wall the dark silhouette of HMS Cavalier lurked, her hull partially masked from view of watchers on the other side of Algeciras Bay, her guns elevated to fire over the wall.

Every door they passed seemed to be heavily sandbagged and most of the side roads were barricaded or obstructed with checkpoints.

"Where are we going?" The prisoner asked.

"England, eventually."

"Oh..." The man felt Clara's hand squeeze his.

"First you get to go on a little helicopter trip out to the Hermes. Assuming you don't get shot down by the Dagoes – their copies of the old Messerschmitt 109 are just about up to shooting down a chopper – it'll be up to the Navy to get you back to Blighty. Probably, in its own sweet time knowing the Navy."

HMS Albion's surviving helicopters were parked with their rotors folded back on every available piece of hard standing on Europa Point.

A landing pad had been cleared on a grassy area near the eastern shoreline and on it sat a Westland Wessex with its rotors milling slowly.

Denzil Williams clambered out of the car with the agility of a fur seal hauling itself up onto dry land and half-jogged, half-waddled over to two Royal Marines carrying L1A1 SLRs. They pointed him towards a figure emerging from the cabin of the Wessex. He and the SIS man and he fell into conversation for some seconds. Hands were shaken.

"They're ready to go as soon as the current combat air patrol is relieved," Denzil Williams explained cheerfully when he got back to the Bentley. "The chaps up above right now are running low on fuel so they'd be in a bit of a jam if the Dagoes got cheeky. You two love birds better get on board sharpish. When the chaps get the word to go, they won't be hanging around."

Arkady Rykov had to be lifted into the cabin of the helicopter.

The crewman who dragged him into the aircraft – as carefully as was possible in the circumstances – frowned worriedly at him.

"Jesus, shouldn't you be on a stretcher, mate?"

The man was even more taken aback to discovered that the injured man's companion was a shapely blond attired in what looked like a Royal Navy engine room artificer's boiler suit.

"No luggage?"

"No," Clara Pullman replied, sparing the man a harassed smile. She had got to the stage where she was becoming totally disorientated by events.

Both passengers were strapped into jump seats on the port side of the fuselage opposite the big hatch through which they had entered the machine.

Suddenly, the engine noise became a whining, deafening roar and the whole world began to thrum and shake.

A few seconds later the Wessex rolled forward and then, as if by magic it was rising into the air.

"It's about a thirty-minute run back to the *Happy H*!" Shouted the crewman who was obviously the helicopter's load master.

"The 'Happy H'?" Clara yelled in confusion. She was beyond confused, baffled, bewildered; she was about to start giggling hysterically.

"HMS Hermes, ma'am!"

"Clara?" Arkady Rykov asked anxiously, his smashed face contorted into a mask of worry as he clasped her arm.

The woman heard somebody yelling to her through the infernal din of the engine above their heads and the thrashing of the great rotor blades; she heard herself sobbing, and felt her whole body convulsing with...relief.

Utter, uncontrolled, insane *relief*.

They had survived.

She did not understand how they had survived a week, or a month let alone a whole year, running, hiding just hours, or minutes or seconds ahead of their pursuers, never knowing what awaited them around the next corner or if their next encounter would be with a friend or a mortal enemy.

But they had survived.

In a few minutes they would be on board one of the Royal Navy's biggest and most powerful warships.

They had survived and at last they were homeward bound.

Or rather, *she* was homeward bound.

She had wanted so badly to go home with *him*, whoever *he* was.

But *he* could never go home and that was so achingly, heartbreakingly unfair…

Chapter 30

Friday 6th December 1963
Government Building, Cheltenham

Tom Harding-Grayson picked up his phone and spoke clearly, crisply with the voice of a man on a mission: "If you would show the American Ambassador in now please."

He had kept Loudon Baines Westheimer II cooling his heels for forty-one minutes during which time he made three calls. One to his wife promising to be home 'at a sensible hour for dinner', a second courtesy call to the Angry Widow asking if 'the Admiral's flight' had taken off on time and wishing her good luck and his sincere solicitations on her elevation to the post of Home Secretary, and thirdly, he had briefly, succinctly rehearsed what he planned to say to Loudon Baines Westheimer II with his old friend Henry Tomlinson.

As the door to his room opened, he closed the folder on his desk.

The two surviving pilots who had participated in the attacks on the Balmoral Estate - now unfortunately barely surviving but he had no sympathy for the plight of either traitor - had been bled, in every sense, of what little information they possessed about the people and the forces who had actually been behind the attempted assassination of the Royal Family.

What little had been beaten out of the two pilots confirmed the veracity of the preliminary intercept and signals triangulation plots the RAF had been able to reconstruct, and the provisional inferences drawn from radio traffic analysis by the cipher and communications experts at GCHQ here in Cheltenham. The intelligence at Tom Harding-Grayson's disposal would not necessarily have convinced a High Court Judge, or a jury *beyond reasonable proof* of the guilt of the men and or of the foreign organs of state implicated in the atrocity but right now, nobody in the United Kingdom Interim Emergency Administration or in the higher echelons of its military and intelligence communities was worrying overmuch about the legal and diplomatic niceties of the *atrocity*.

"Good afternoon, Ambassador," the Foreign Secretary smiled, stepping around his desk and risking his sinewy pale right hand to the bear like grasp of the American's large fleshy paw. He need not have been concerned for the safety of his hand because the lumbering bear like man who stormed into his office with a face like thunder completely ignored it.

Loudon Baines Westheimer II poked a thick sausage shaped,

nicotine stained finger in the shorter man's face.

"What the fuck are you Brits playing at?"

Tom Harding-Grayson had resolved to remain calm and statesmanlike in the manner of his predecessor the Earl of Home, whom for all his old-world mannerisms and occasional disconnection from reality, he had rather admired and moreover, personally liked and respected as a man.

The Englishman met the blazing stare without flinching.

He waved to a chair in front of his desk.

"Please take a seat, Ambassador."

Without waiting for an acknowledgement, he moved behind his desk and sat down, waiting for his visitor to get used to the idea that throwing his weight around like a small child in the throes of a temper tantrum was not going to cut any ice.

Loudon Baines Westheimer II fumed, his fists balled. He leaned forward, unwrapping his fists so he could rest the palms of his hands on the edge of the desk. He loomed over the Foreign Secretary.

"I don't give a shit about what you did to those Spanish civilians!" He spat breathlessly. "But when you kill Americans..."

To Harding-Grayson remained impassive.

"You hit three NATO bases..."

"Ambassador!" The man seated behind the desk rasped softly with the threat of a Cobra flashing its hood at its next target.

The big man pushed himself away from the table.

"Ambassador," Tom Harding-Grayson repeated, coolly. "There is no such thing as NATO. *You* stood by while the North Atlantic Treaty Organisation was destroyed. *You* decided to make war at a time and under circumstances of your own choosing with no reference to or thought of the survival of your *NATO allies*. There is no NATO. There are only friends and enemies in the world that *you* have remade."

Loudon Baines Westheimer II turned away, took a pace to his left and wheeled around to renew his attack.

Tom Harding-Grayson held up his right hand, palm forward.

"We would have cratered the runways of Torrejón, Zaragoza and Morón Air Bases," he explained coldly, didactically, "regardless of the intelligence emerging from GCHQ and the RAF's ongoing investigations into radio intercept and radar plot triangulation analysis of the missions flown by the four fighter aircraft which attacked the Balmoral Estate earlier this week."

The American Ambassador opened his mouth to speak but said nothing. He stood there for a moment gaping at the slight figure of the newly appointed Foreign Secretary. He had not noticed the icy resolve in the smaller man's dark eyes until then and it gave him pause. He grunted, shut his mouth and began to form a fresh complaint...

"We believe," Tom Harding-Grayson continued evenly, "that the attack on Balmoral was co-ordinated, controlled and directed from a facility located in the Irish Republic or by a vessel in the Irish Sea or the North Channel. It is my duty to inform you that at such time as we conclude our ongoing analyses of the available technical and operational data associated with the Balmoral *atrocity,* we reserve the right of retaliation at a place and a time of *our* choosing." His voice was a flat, bland monotone that reflected none of his inner outrage. "Please sit down before I get a crick in my neck, Ambassador."

Reluctantly Loudon Baines Westheimer II dumped his bulk into the nearest high-backed chair. His girth flapped unsupported on each side of the averagely proportioned seat.

He opened his mouth to speak but was again forestalled by the British Foreign Secretary's raised hand.

"You requested this meeting, Ambassador. I acquiesced to it only because my Government wishes me to communicate verbally to you the contents of a note that our man in Washington will shortly be delivering to your State Department. We've found in the course of our routine communications with that somewhat sclerotic organ of your Government, that it invariable ignores such notes for a week or so and then claims to have lost them 'in the post' when we follow up." He smiled ruefully. "When one's friends befriend one's enemies – General Franco among others – and base several Wings of A-bomb capable B-47s on their territory a little over ninety minutes flying time from where we presently sit, it is bad enough. When one's friends set up a telecommunications and spying facility and start building airfields and military docks on the territory of an avowedly neutral neighbour – the Irish Republic – whose leaders have been tacitly fomenting civil war in the six northern counties of that troubled land, 'bad enough' becomes *pretty well intolerable.* I could complain about the United States Navy's posturing in the Western Approaches to these islands. I could complain about all the broken promises to provide aid and fuel. I won't recite the full list of our grievances at this interview, but rest assured that our many grievances are fully detailed in the note which will soon be in the hands of your State Department. Furthermore, I could complain about the quality and the competence of the person our erstwhile *allies* sent to England to represent their interests. However, over on this side of 'the pond' my colleagues and I assumed that you owed your appointment to your current post to some bizarre aberration in your system of government. No matter. The United

States of America has succeeded – in a little over a year – in turning its staunchest friend in the world into a *former ally*. Personally, even after the October War, I wouldn't have thought it was possible. But you chaps have managed it, so hat's off to you all!"

Loudon Baines Westheimer II's brow was furrowed so deeply that he could have stowed half-a-dozen of the Lucky Strikes he normally chain smoked in the folds of pale flesh and nobody would have noticed.

"You've made your play," he growled. "What do you want?"

"What do we want?" Now Tom Harding-Grayson's brow furrowed.

"You've had you grouch. What do you want from me? From us?"

The Foreign Secretary of the United Kingdom Interim Emergency Administration was tempted to demand the surrender of General Curtis LeMay to a tribunal authorised to try him for crimes against humanity and genocide. Unfortunately, that was no more likely to happen than John Fitzgerald Kennedy surrendering himself to the same tribunal charged with conspiracy to wage aggressive war and war against peace.

"What we want is one thing," Tom Harding-Grayson retorted. "What we are actually doing is to take immediate steps to alter the basis upon which the United Kingdom, its allies, Dominions and friends in the Commonwealth will do business with the United States of America in future."

"Business?" Loudon Baines Westheimer II could not conceive of a context in which the word 'business' meant something broader than commerce, industry or graft. He began to smile, his thoughts – such as they were – turning to writing off the Brits' bad attitude to some kind of passing phase they were going through. A storm in a tea cup. "The sooner we get back to business as normal the better," he declared, mistakenly imagining that he was being in some way emollient.

"The particulars of the note our man in Washington will deliver to your State Department make that impossible in the foreseeable future," the small man seated behind the big desk said grimly.

Suddenly the gravity of his misunderstanding hit Loudon Baines Westheimer II like a baseball between the eyes.

"What are we talking about?"

"Firstly, there will be a unilateral cessation of all military co-operation."

Shit! That doesn't sound good!

Tom Harding-Grayson did not need to be a mind reader to realise that Loudon Baines Westheimer II had finally got the message.

"Secondly," he went on, "as of midnight tonight any American military assets in, around or above United Kingdom or Dominion territory or airspace will be liable to seizure."

Loudon Baines Westheimer II was now physically incapable of speech.

"Thirdly," the Foreign Secretary bored on remorselessly, "United Kingdom airspace is now closed to non-UK aircraft. Aircraft approaching UK airspace without the appropriate permissions will be challenged and in extremis, shot down."

Tom Harding-Grayson let this sink in for a count of five seconds before he moved on to the next and probably most inflammatory clause in the UKIEA's ultimatum to its former ally.

"Fourthly, the UKIEA forbids any foreign naval power to carry out exercises or manoeuvres within five hundred nautical miles of its shores. Any foreign naval units found within this exclusion zone will be liable to arrest or attack without warning."

Loudon Baines Westheimer II stuttered as his brain began to posthumously catch up with what his ears were hearing.

"The *Big E's* Battle Group is operating in international waters," he blurted angrily.

Tom Harding-Grayson pursed his lips and steepled his hands as he fixed the American Ambassador with a sphinx-like scrutiny.

"The aforementioned exclusion zone will come into effect in seven days' time," he said blankly after a silence which had lasted some fifteen seconds. He re-gathered his wits. "Fifthly, given that a state of war now exists between my country and the Fascist Republic of Spain I strongly advise you to remove all American personnel, both military and civilian, and all military assets from the Iberian Peninsula. The rule that will apply to this and all future combat operations conducted by British armed forces will be that my enemy's friend is my enemy."

Loudon Baines Westheimer II was breathing in short, shallow seething breaths. "Washington won't stand for this!"

"We shall see. We shall see."

The American Ambassador heaved himself to his feet.

"One last thing, Mr Westheimer," Tom Harding-Grayson announced, "we shall be withdrawing our embassy from Washington as soon as transportation can be arranged. As of midnight, this day you and all accredited representatives of the Unites States of America are deemed persona non grata. Her Majesty's Government would, therefore, be obliged if you would pack up your bags and go home at your earliest convenience."

Chapter 31

Friday 6th December 1963
Glebe Cottage, Government Compound, Cheltenham

Patricia Harding-Grayson brushed a strand of straw grey hair out of her face and slowly, carefully lowered her stiff and aching body onto the threadbare sofa by the fire in the front room of the small cottage she shared with her husband, Her Majesty's newly appointed Foreign and Commonwealth Secretary.

Three days ago – it seemed like a lifetime – she had found herself thrown to the floor by the blast of the first bomb in the grounds behind Balmoral Castle. Although she escaped serious injury she had been battered and bruised, and subsequently exhausted beyond measure setting up the makeshift casualty clearing station in the hallway of the partially demolished Castle.

"Oh God," she sighed, accepting the glass of whiskey and water her husband pressed into her hands, "is it really true that the Americans may have been behind what happened in Scotland?"

Sir Henry Tomlinson, the Cabinet Secretary and Tom Harding-Grayson's oldest friend who was sitting in an arm chair by the low fire in the hearth, nodded sadly.

"*Some* Americans," he qualified dubiously. "Not perhaps JFK or a member of his immediate circle but we're pretty certain the fellows over in Ireland at that big CIA compound near Dublin had something to do with it."

Tom Harding-Grayson patted his wife's knee fondly: "The Bay of Pigs fiasco and practically everything else that went wrong in US policy towards Cuba in the years before the October War was the handiwork of the Central Intelligence Agency," he told her morosely.

"Is it wise thumbing our noses at the Kennedy Administration so, so," she was too tired to think of the right word.

"Gratuitously?" Her husband suggested.

"Yes. No, I mean so *finally*? Haven't we burnt our boats with the Kennedy people for all time?"

"Kennedy's people want to put a man on the Moon," Henry Tomlinson remarked, sourly, "the rest of us can go to Hell in a hand cart for all they care. We're better off alone."

Tom Harding-Grayson was nodding.

"The Americans have moved to dominate the countries of the Pacific rim and abdicated their responsibilities to Europe. As far as Washington is concerned what's left of the old world can tear itself to pieces. In a few years they'll fly back in and pick up the pieces."

"Should a British Foreign Secretary be so dreadfully cynical, darling?" Patricia Harding-Grayson teased her husband.

"There's not a lot to be cheerful about," he re-joined mildly.

"I thought the Queen was awfully brave," his wife said, changing the subject.

"She is the Queen," Henry Tomlinson guffawed gently.

"She and Margaret were real bricks just after the bombing, you know. The Prime Minister went off organising the Black Watch in case there was a second attack and the Queen and Margaret just, well, took over..."

Tom Harding-Grayson eyed his wife mischievously for a moment.

"Since when did the Angry Widow become 'Margaret'?" He queried.

"Since I saw the other side of her, darling," she explained patiently.

Her husband had told her that Edward Heath had offered Margaret Thatcher the Foreign Secretary's job but that she had recused herself on grounds that at some stage in the future, the post might require 'somebody of a naturally less confrontational temperament that I'.

"She does seem to have taken quite a shine to the 'fighting admiral'," Henry Tomlinson observed, his humour improving with every sip of his Scotch.

Patricia Harding-Grayson could not stop a ghost of smile flitting across her face.

Later that evening the two men talked in low tones so as not to disturb her as she dozed with her head on her husband's shoulder.

"We have burnt our boats," Henry Tomlinson ruminated. He knew he ought to get some sleep, for tomorrow and every other day of whatever remained of his life was surely going to be a great trial.

"Is it true that the Prime Minister dreams of some kind of a European rebirth?"

"I'm sure he dreams of it, yes. I doubt if he'd put it so grandly, but yes, I think he honestly believes we have a responsibility to hold the line and to begin the process of rebuilding. He's right, too. Otherwise, what do we say to our people out there in the post-cataclysm world. That surviving is the only thing that matters? What sort of a message is that? No, I think he's right to believe that just surviving isn't enough. Our people have to have hope, Tom. Our people must feel that that are worthy of surviving."

"My goodness, old man," Tom Harding-Grayson exclaimed lowly, "all these years I've known you and I never realised you were a closet philosopher."

"That's as may be but you know I'm right."

His host nodded.

He opened his mouth to speak; there was a staccato knocking at the front door of the cottage.

Patricia Harding-Grayson blinked awake, yawned and made as if to rise.

"I'll get it, my dear," he insisted, waving her to stay where she was.

The Foreign Secretary rose to his feet and walked leadenly to the door.

Outside in the frigid darkness where snowflakes curled and floated - mercifully only in ones and twos without settling on the ground - stood a grey-haired, calm-eyed man in a United States Navy braided cap and greatcoat.

The officer seemed familiar; the Foreign Secretary had seen him before; could not put his face to a name.

"I apologise for disturbing you, sir," the visitor said with uncomplicated sincerity. "I'm Walter Brenckmann. Until a few hours ago I was the Naval Attaché at the Embassy. May I come in and have a few minutes of your time, sir?"

Tom Harding-Grayson ushered the American in and shut the door.

"Captain Brenckmann, isn't it?"

Henry Tomlinson checked as hands were shaken and the newcomer unbuttoned his greatcoat.

"Yes, sir."

If the newcomer was surprised to find the Head of the British Home Civil Service sipping whiskey in the parlour, he hid it superbly.

The Foreign Secretary introduced his wife. She appraised the American officer with veiled suspicion.

Everybody had got to their feet and nobody sat down.

"The Ambassador doesn't know that I'm here, sir," Walter Brenckmann said tersely.

Tom Harding-Grayson groaned inwardly. Today had been just the latest of several very long and enervating days and he was very tired.

"Oh, I see."

"My Government has taken its eye off the ball, sir. The people in Washington are preoccupied with domestic issues and with the consolidation of a post-war sphere of influence in the Pacific and Latin America. European questions have been neglected. In my opinion this is a national disgrace but that doesn't change the fact that my country's policy towards Europe, the Mediterranean and Middle Eastern theatres has been left in the hands of a bunch of people I personally wouldn't trust to find their own arses in a darkened room."

Walter Brenckmann quirked an apologetic grimace towards

Patricia Harding-Grayson.

"Begging your pardon, ma'am."

Henry Tomlinson eyed the visitor gravely.

"What are you saying, Captain?"

"I want you to know that whatever is going on in Spain, the presence of a powerful US Navy Battle Group off your coast and the CIA forward base outside Dublin *are not* all part of some great White House initiated plot to undermine the United Kingdom. Frankly, sir, I don't want our countries to get into a shooting war because we've finally become separated by our common language."

Tom Harding-Grayson almost smiled.

"Very pithy, Captain Brenckmann."

He realised the American was attempting to play the role of honest broker without knowing all of the facts of the matter.

"Tell me, if British Intelligence had set up a clandestine base in Newfoundland and vectored American aircraft with turncoat pilots on bombing runs targeting the White House while the President and Congressional leaders were in conference in the Oval Office," he put to his visitor, "how would you expect the United States Government to react?"

Walter Brenckmann felt the blood draining from his face. Simultaneously icy fingers clutched his soul.

The British Foreign Secretary viewed him with a strange sympathy.

"I am aware that your Government does not speak with one voice. In fact, it is my professional opinion that no US Administration in history has been capable of speaking with a single voice. Allies of the United States have long been aware that a promise made by one person in authority in Washington can be un-promised at any time, without warning, by a member of another faction on Capitol Hill. We could live with that before the October War because, on balance, it was in our interests to so do despite the constant sniping at, and undermining of the United Kingdom's ongoing administration of its colonies. But that was then and this is now, Captain."

Walter Brenckmann knew that the other man was going to tell him something he did not know. Something his own people had kept from him.

"We suspected some months ago that American aid and *technical* support which would otherwise have been available to alleviate the worst of the United Kingdom's privations was being freely traded to buy – albeit on the cheap - the, shall we say, coalescence of the Governments of the Irish Republic, Spain, Portugal and Italy. Presumably, the object of this military, economic and intelligence penetration of these new client states along the Atlantic seaboard of Europe and in the Central Mediterranean was designed to undermine British interests and eventually to render untenable, our position in the Mediterranean. The UKIEA wasn't happy about these developments but our preoccupation with Operation Manna – unlike *your* people in North America *our* people will starve this winter if Operation Manna fails - dissuaded us from confronting the White House. "

Walter Brenckmann knew he was wasting his time.

"We are not fools," Henry Tomlinson said lowly. "Your countrymen delight in castigating us *Brits* for our colonial *excesses* and *mores*. How strange it is to contrast our post-1945 de-colonization with the ongoing imperial machinations of the 'Land of the Free'?"

"I'm not sure that's fair, sir."

"No? Spain, Portugal, Italy, Eire? The first three are military dictatorships. Their governments no better than the Nazis. As for the Republic of Ireland," Henry Tomlinson shrugged, "an agrarian backwater dominated by the dead hand of the Catholic Church. The country has no industry to speak of, no natural resources and no national purpose other than to wrest back the six counties of Ulster from perfidious Albion. Are these *fine* bastions of democracy and reason fit partners in the new world order for the 'Land of the Free'?"

Walter Brenckmann was silent.

"I don't think we're telling you anything you haven't already worked out for yourself, Captain."

This Tom Harding-Grayson said, placing a comforting hand on the naval officer's elbow.

"Because of their nature the regimes in those countries were understandably receptive to your overtures. Their territories are relatively untouched and uncontaminated by the October War, notwithstanding that we all now breathe the same fission-enriched air. How the mighty are fallen, what? Twenty years ago, you fellows were our partners in the great crusade against Fascism; now here you are propping it up in Spain and Portugal, especially Spain, as in fact you've been doing in Latin America ever since that war."

"What will happen next?"

The American asked dully.

"God only knows, Captain."

Chapter 32

Friday 6th December 1963
HMS Talavera,
42 miles NW of Ferrol, Northern Spain

Lieutenant-Commander Peter Christopher clung to the rail as the spray lashed back from the bow across the open flying bridge. HMS Talavera and the big, cruiser-sized newly commissioned HMS Devonshire had been racing west at twenty-seven knots for the last eight hours.

They had received the order to detach from the Ark Royal's air defence screen while running north to re-join the flagship.

HMS Aisne, her fuel bunkers two-thirds empty had signalled 'GOOD HUNTING' and reluctantly parted company with the other ships shortly before noon.

"Devonshire is signalling, sir!"

Peter Christopher swung around to focus on the long, elegant grey ship just discernible in the fading light effortlessly pacing her smaller Leader slightly abaft and to starboard at a range of about two thousand yards.

The signal lamp on the County Class destroyer blinked frenetically.

Peter did not wait for the speaker to call out the message.

"NO MAJOR MECHANICAL DEFECTS STOP NO AIR OR SURFACE CONTACTS ON MY PLOT MESSAGE ENDS"

"Acknowledge signal," he called. Behind him he listened to Talavera's lamp clattering.

The destroyer carved deep into a green grey wall of water and surged forward.

Running at high speed in a wild sea was like no other roller coaster ride on earth.

To be on the bridge of a three-thousand-ton ship charging into the teeth of an Atlantic gale was what every red-blooded sailor lived for and longed to experience.

And to be the officer of the watch and in command of that ship was the culmination of a dream.

No matter that everything that could be lashed down was lashed down thrice, life below decks when the ship was racing harum-scarum towards the distant – hundreds of miles distant at the bottom of the Iberian Peninsula in this case – sound of gunfire was a thing Peter Christopher had never really believed would ever happen to him in his lifetime.

He had joined a peace time navy, a *peace keeping* force that occasionally involved itself in old-fashioned gunboat diplomacy but was never, ever going to get into a real shooting war again.

Notwithstanding the October War, this still felt *bizarre*.

Perhaps, it was because they had spent so much time in harbour in the last year. So much time messing around with and tweaking the ship's expensive and fiendishly complicated systems.

Or perhaps, it was because he – and most of his shipmates – had come to the conclusion that their leaders simply did not have the stomach for the fight any more.

Either way, the events of the last few weeks had come as a rude shock and he very much doubted he was the only one who was still struggling to adjust to it.

HMS Talavera was at war.

Everybody was still buzzing with the tense excitement of the early morning action off Santander.

Peter Christopher had watched the radar traces of the destroyers' broadsides flying over nine miles to their target. Talavera had been the first ship to cease fire having emptied her magazines of contact-fused high explosive rounds.

She had fired 387 shells of which approximately a dozen had fallen short and forty-four had been fired long – speculatively – into an area of Santander Bay where a number of vessels were reported at anchor by Ark Royal's high-flying Sea Vixens.

HMS Aisne had taken another ninety seconds to exhaust her HE rounds, and the Devonshire, firing slower than the two Battles, a further three minutes.

Then the small task force had turned away and headed north at twenty-eight knots.

"How is our big friend doing?"

Yelled Commander Hugo Montgommery, Talavera's executive officer joining Peter Christopher at the rail without the younger man noticing.

"Riding a little better than us, I think, sir!"

The two men laughed into the teeth of the wind.

"God! This is the life!"

Talavera's second-in-command chuckled.

"Just so long as we don't shake the old girl to pieces before we get to where we're going!"

Where *they* were going was to join the gun line plugging the Straits of Gibraltar in general and the approaches to Cadiz Roads and Algeciras Bay in particular.

Peter Christopher and the Talavera's Executive Officer had both been advanced in rank half a ring in anticipation of Talavera operating as a Destroyer Leader, commanding and administering her own squadron but until today that role had not materialised.

First the ship had been assigned to the Ark Royal's air defence screen, then assigned to lead the Santander raid, now she was rushing to join yet another hastily formed flotilla off Gibraltar.

War was chaos; and chaos was war.

That was something Peter's father, the Admiral, had told him the last time they – purely accidentally – encountered each other at a Navy Day in Portsmouth two-and-a-half years ago.

Having studied electrical engineering and physics at University Peter suspected that what the old timers called 'chaos' was actually *entropy*. Simply a case of all the most likely outcomes playing out in a volatile medium.

Good luck, bad luck when all was said and done, was just *luck*.

War and conflict stressed people, systems, faith to the limit and the October War had ripped asunder the fabric of the old world.

None of the *old* rules counted now.

Given that the average temperature of the universe was around two degrees above absolute zero; a rational mind could only conclude that in such a universe the well of pity was empty most of the time...

Peter Christopher realised he had allowed his spirits to darken.

The freezing spray whipping into his face brought him out of his introspection with a rude slap.

"Putting the helm over in this sea will be a thing!"

Hugo Montgommery shouted above the roar of the wind, clapping the younger man on the back.

"Make sure you ring the collision bell first!"

Peter Christopher waved as the executive officer departed for the dry warmth of the conning bridge one level below his feet. Then he went back to watching the seas, trying to predict the angle of the confused, storm flecked swells building in the south-south-west.

Odd that, he would have expected most Atlantic gales to blow more from the west than the south but half the world had gone up in flames a little over a year ago.

It stood to reason that it had to have had some effect on the weather?

People talked about the last winter in the northern hemisphere being a 'nuclear winter'. The early onset of the present winter seemed to lend credence to the theories about the smoke, ash and dust from the great firestorms blotting out the light of the Sun like the eruption of a great volcano like Tambora in Indonesia in 1816. In Europe the following year – of 1817 - had been remembered as the 'year without summer'.

Somebody would work out what was going on one day.

Until that day came, he would stick to doing what he was being paid to do; he would watch the pattern and the height of the waves, attempt to calculate how close to due south Talavera could steam without having to reduce speed or risking putting the ship on her beam ends.

All things considered it was much better, he decided, to focus on the things one understood and over which one had a modicum of control.

"CIC to Bridge."

"What is it CIC?" He called, snatching up the nearest comms handset.

"The plot is painting unidentified aircraft. Eight targets at level one four and climbing at five-zero-zero feet per minute bearing one-zero-five, range six-five miles. Closing speed five zero knots, sir."

Peter Christopher frowned.

The climb and closing speeds seemed positively pedestrian.

"Very good. Label the contacts as hostiles and keep me informed."

Next, he hit the button to put him through to the Captain's day cabin.

"We have unusual air activity over the Spanish mainland, sir."

Captain David Penberthy didn't hesitate: "Ask Mr Montgommery to take the bridge watch and get yourself into the hot seat in CIC. Then tell me what we're looking at."

Hugo Montgommery stepped onto the flying bridge before the younger officer could summon him.

"I have the watch!"

He smiled piratically.

Like many members of the wardroom he had begun to cultivate 'a set' – a beard - and this gave his facial expressions a new aspect of humour or menace, depending upon his mood.

Peter Christopher handed off his wet-weather gear to a willing pair of hands as he entered the Combat Information Centre. He scowled at the developing plot.

"Prop aircraft?"

He asked, thinking aloud.

Then: "Are we picking up any other radar signatures."

"Negative, sir."

The Spanish might be painting the two destroyers passively;

tracking Talavera and Devonshire's electronic emissions but he did not think the enemy had kit sophisticated enough to do that. Unless somebody had given them state of the art former NATO equipment.

"CIC to Bridge."

He waited.

Hugo Montgommery joined the circuit.

"What do we have, Peter?"

"It looks like we can expect to be visited by a gaggle of 1945-war vintage aircraft. With the ship working the way she is in these seas we're having trouble updating the plot but I'd say what we've got is half-a-dozen bombers and about twice as many fighters. Unless the fighters have got drop tanks, they'll be getting their feet wet by the time the bombers reach us."

There was a touch on Peter Christopher's arm.

"Several of the bogeys have begun squawking unidentified IFF codes, sir."

"The enemy seem to be tracking us by our electronic emissions, sir," Talavera's Electronic Warfare Officer reported. "They may be homing onto us using some kind of antiquated cat and mouse targeting system. Several of them seem to be inadvertently squawking IFF."

The Executive Officer didn't wait to hear any more.

"Tell off Devonshire to come to Action Stations."

Something odd was happening and that was never good news.

The klaxon sounded above decks and the sharp, jarring of the ringing of the alarm bell filled the spaces below.

Positions began to report in so quickly that many of them must have been fully manned ahead of the call to Battle Stations.

Hardly anybody could sleep or rest properly with the ship smashing her way through the storm swells, and often a man's ready post was as comfortable as anywhere in such conditions.

Peter Christopher watched the amber system status lights blink green on the GWS 21 Seat Cat board.

More men piled into the CIC and dropped into empty seats, senior men replacing their juniors and apprentices.

"Main battery reports ready!"

The two 20-millimetres cannon mounts showed green moments later.

"The Royal Marines report four heavy MGs lashed to the amidships deckhouse and ready for action!"

HMS Talavera's EWO grinned.

The destroyer had taken on board six Royal Marines, a Sergeant, a

Corporal and four tough looking troopers on the same day the infamous 'defaulters draft' came up the gangway at Portsmouth.

That was less than a fortnight ago but might have been months.

The Marines had been pestering Guns, Lieutenant Weiss the ship's Gunnery Officer, for an appropriate action station ever since. Now they were topsides, each trooper manhandling a big general-purpose machine gun with several 'defaulters' primed to feed ammunition and fetch more if the need arose.

"TWO HOSTILES!"

"LOW!"

"RANGE TWO-THREE MILES!"

"BEARING ZERO-SIX-EIGHT. CBC!"

Constant bearing and course...

Collision course...

"Paint them as bogey one and two for the Sea Cat launcher," Peter ordered without a pause for conscious thought.

"They're coming in hot," somebody observed dispassionately.

"SPEED FOUR-TWO-ZERO!"

Two fast jets skimming the top of the waves.

They had been invisible, lost in the chaos of returns from the rocky coast. The old piston engine bombers and fighters climbing slowly over Ferrol had probably been a deliberate diversion but it would not have worked if the jets had not been so low.

"TWO MORE BOGEYS BEARING ZERO-SEVEN-EIGHT!"

"RANGE ONE-NINE MILES!"

Peter Christopher touched the microphone stud at his throat.

"CIC to Bridge. I recommend we show the bogeys out stern to increase the odds of achieving a Sea Cat firing solution."

Captain David Penberthy's voice acknowledged this calmly.

"Very good," the destroyer was already heeling hard to port as the manoeuvring bell clanged repeatedly. "Devonshire has been flashed to manoeuvre independently." He commanded: "Flush the Sea Cats whether you get a firing solution or not."

"Aye, aye, sir."

Peter Christopher did not think the Sea Cats had a snow flake's chance in Hell of achieving a target lock on any of the four aircraft barrelling across the wave tops at over four hundred miles an hour.

Not in these seas, not against four wildly manoeuvring small fast targets.

He was suddenly icily calm.

It never occurred to him – not for a nanosecond – that this was anything but a deadly, carefully planned and professionally executed attack against two targets with absolutely no air cover.

The range closed with terrifying speed.

"Bastards!"

Grunted the man on the ranging table as the sweeping bedsteads pf the Type 965 resolved the nearest bogeys into symbols they had grown familiar with in pre-war NATO war games.

"Bogeys Three and Four are A-4s!

US Navy Douglas A-4 Skyhawks.

Peter Christopher's mind seemed to slow as he mulled the options at a thousand miles an hour.

First, a low-level strafing attack with cannon and, or ground attack missiles.

Second, if the Skyhawks were carrying iron bombs; they would climb and lob their weapons from as far away as a mile.

A tricky evolution, rather hit and miss.

Ideally, the attacking jets would prefer to climb to at least ten thousand feet and dive bomb the two destroyers but if they tried that they almost certainly risk being locked up by the Sea Cats before they had a chance to drop their bombs.

"NO LOCK! NO MISSILE LOCK!"

Peter Christopher decided it was time to gamble.

He was the man in the CIC hot seat; he was the man controlling and fighting the ship's state of the art systems.

The ship shuddered as the main battery opened fire.

"Devonshire has launched her Sea Cats!"

They had run out of time.

"Flush ALL Sea Cats!" He barked.

Chapter 33

Friday 6th December 1963
Gzira Waterfront, Sliema Creek, Malta

There was a peculiar party atmosphere that Friday evening when Marija met her father and mother at the taverna where, before the October War, the whole family had often congregated on a Saturday afternoon. It seemed odd that neither Marija's younger brother, Joe, or her elder sibling, Samuel were present but then the one was forbidden to set foot in Gzira, and the other was estranged from her and to a degree, her mother.

Marija had inherited her willowy, sparsely formed frame from her father whom today, looked ten years too old and too grey and worn to be only fifty-two years of age.

Peter Calleja nursed a murky cup of coffee – not the real thing; that had not been available for months – and viewed with wry amusement his daughter's discomfiture.

"I have told you many times that Staff Sergeant Siddall is a good man. That he is not like so many of the others," she hissed this lowly, her face flushed with colour, "but he is a friend and no more I tell you!"

Her idiot little brother had given her a long letter to hand to her parents and she was regretting not having torn open the envelope and – if necessary – censored whatever he had written that had so greatly *amused* and *entertained* her mother and father.

She was a good Maltese daughter who dearly loved and respected her parents; notwithstanding that sometimes they drove her to distraction.

Like now, for example.

"Jim," she went on, caught herself instantly after she had inadvertently used the big Redcap's Christian name, "Staff Sergeant Siddall may well feel things for me that I do not feel for him. That is not my fault. Why are you always trying to marry me off?"

Peter Calleja sighed and put down his cup.

He had forgotten how much he enjoyed these slow, early evening family *occasions*, especially at this time of year when the weather tended to be balmy some nights despite the advancing season.

He planned to visit Mdina-Rabat sometime in the coming week, to take his wife to be reunited with her miscreant *bambino*. Joe would always be the baby of the family if he lived to be a hundred; that was the way of things. He wished his first born, Samuel, was sitting at the table beside him but some things were not destined to be so he happily settled for every small mercy that the loving God who had thus far preserved his little family from serious harm deigned to grant him.

He and his wife had lived through Hitler's War.

In that terrible war they had nearly lost the jewel in his life, Marija, but with God's will she too had been saved. Looking at the vivacious - unfortunately angry at present - young woman sitting with her back to the sea front Peter Calleja complacently counted his blessings.

Marija belatedly realised that her father had been teasing her.

She huffed once or twice and forgave him.

"Do you think the British will leave Malta?" She asked.

Her father avoided her eye, shrugged in that perversely Gallic way of his that he cultivated to deflect the many vicissitudes of his life.

"Will they?" His daughter pressed.

Her father's gaze took in the broad sweep of Sliema Creek.

This evening there were only two big ships, destroyers, swinging around their mooring buoys.

Both were moored on the Manoel Island side of the anchorage. Several patrol boats were tied up alongside the jetty where the inner Creek narrowed and was eventually closed to navigation to even the smallest of boats by the low brick bridge from the Gzira waterfront onto the island.

He was afraid in his soul that the British had already left Malta.

Given up hope.

Their aircraft, their soldiers and a few of their ships remained but, in their hearts, the British had already packed their kit bags and decided to go home.

He saw it in the faces of many of the officers he dealt with on the Senglea Docks; and among the rank and file of the occupiers there was a strange end of term euphoria.

"One hears so many rumours one doesn't know what to think," he obfuscated, making a throwaway gesture with his right hand. "It is so good to see so many young people out and about on the waterfront," he added.

Although far from everybody had come out to celebrate the ongoing prisoner releases, a large number of people had and many of them were promenading along the front in memory of older, better times.

"The detainees are being set free, you should be happy for them," Marija's mother declared.

Marija wondered sometimes what world her mother was living in, although she loved her none the less for her wilful blindness.

Around them the rickety tables were occupied by other family groups, some celebrating, others communing together, hoping or fearing for the future.

Before the October War the taverna would have been a constant riot of buzzing, burbling, laughing voices. Tonight, the mood was sombre, cautious because everybody understood that this might be the lull before the storm.

"It is for the best that Joe is under your wing," Peter Calleja told his daughter. "This isn't the time for thumbing one's nose at the British."

Marija relented.

"Margo has Joe under her thumb already," she giggled. The formidable Director of the St Catherine's Hospital for Women had promised 'not to let the little Bolshevik' out of her sight while Marija went home for the weekend.

"Ah, Dottoressa Seiffert," Marija's mother beamed as if her daughter had mentioned the name of a guardian saint. "Such a woman!"

Marija looked at her feet until her muddled emotions washed over and away, like a wave breaking on a nearby beach. Her mother had an unrivalled knack of making her feel guilty, proud, happy, melancholic and utterly *mothered* that caught her unawares. It must be like this for daughters everywhere in every epoch, she reflected, briefly submerged in her thoughts and as she often was in the throes of this and similar passing moods, she suddenly thought about Peter. She picked up her gaze and half-turned to look over her shoulder down the sun dappled length of Sliema Creek; at the big grey warships, the grey blue water lapping at their cold steel hulls as overhead occasional gulls wheeled above the tall black silhouettes of the destroyers' great latticed masts. One of the destroyers, HMS Agincourt – her pennant number, D96, painted in letters several feet high on her almost square transom – was making steam, a hot, hazy, wispy column of almost invisible smoke rising from her single funnel and being swept away the moment it rose out of the lee of her forward superstructure. Occasionally, the taint of acrid burning bunker oil wafted across the Gzira waterfront but it was a familiar, vaguely comforting taint that reminded the majority of the promenaders of happier times when Great British had been Malta's friend, protector and ally and not her jailer.

Marija sighed; Peter Christopher could be anywhere.

Most likely his ship was still swinging around its anchors in 'Fareham Creek', which he had confided, more than once, was nowhere near as scenic or picturesque as it sounded and did not in any way rival what he had heard about *any* of the 'sun-kissed safe harbours of sunny Malta'. He had applied for a transfer to the Mediterranean Fleet but even if that now happened there was this dreadful talk about the British leaving. The sudden ache welled from deep within her psyche like a physical pain until she forced her thoughts to move on, to step away from potential despair. Peter had said he would come to her. If God was willing; one day Peter Christopher's ship would sail into Sliema Creek and tie up alongside one of her sisters. Perhaps, HMS Talavera would slowly churn to a halt and moor to the buoys next to HMS Agincourt. She continued to stare at the destroyer, her graceful, fighting lines somewhat marred by her great masts and – she noticed for the first time – the slowly revolving huge metal bedstead radars at its peak.

Her brow furrowed a little as she saw that men were moving, running on the destroyer's deck and as she watched the destroyer blew her steam whistle. A banshee shriek of angst seared across the anchorage as an outpouring of grey black smoke billowed from her single stack. With a sensation of unreality Marija stared at the slowly traversing forward turrets of the anchored destroyer, the long guns rising towards the heavens. It was then that she noticed that on the stern deck house men were tearing at the protective shrouds around the missile launcher mount and the big anti-aircraft cannons.

HMS Agincourt blew her horn a second time.

"We must take cover!" Peter Calleja ordered. His chair crashed to the floor as he reached to grasp his wife's arm. "Marija!"

His daughter turned and blinked at him.

And in that instant the flash of the first explosion reflected in his eyes.

Chapter 34

Saturday 7th December 1963
HMS Talavera, 27 miles ENE of Ferrol, Northern Spain

The destroyer was alone in a pitch black, wind-maddened sea as the full force of the winter storm tried to drive her back onto the rocky shores of Northern Spain. The pungent stench of burnt insulation – and much worse – filled the Combat Information Centre and the shipboard public address relayed a constant stream of new and updated damage control reports. HMS Talavera was holding her own but only just and nobody knew how long her luck would last. If she lost steam on her remaining boiler, a pump failed or the five-hundred-pound unexploded general-purpose bomb lodged in the flooded bilge abaft the forward main battery magazine went off it was likely that every man on board would die.

The two Douglas A4 Skyhawks had lobbed four big iron bombs at Talavera. One had crashed through the deck between the bridge and the back of B turret and come to rest in the bilge. Another had exploded at the base of the main mast. Fortuitously, blast coefficients being viciously capricious and fickle things, apart from bringing down the mast – which had gone over the side and in fouling the starboard propeller had comprehensively wrecked the shaft's reduction gear – caused few casualties. Unfortunately, the bomb that detonated in the water on the port side of the after deck house had killed virtually everybody on deck and left the stern a burning splintered charnel house. Commander Hugo Montgommery was among the thirty or more dead, cut to pieces as ran to his battle station in the auxiliary conning post when the warheads and propellants of two unfired GWS 21 Sea Cat surface to air missiles exploded ten feet above his head. Nobody had any idea what had happened to the fourth bomb, although a stem to stern search of the destroyer had confirmed that it had not lodged anywhere onboard.

After the bomb run the Skyhawks had circled and returned.

They had made two strafing runs. Opposed by only a pair of Royal Marine manned heavy machine guns lashed to the amidships deckhouse rail they had raked the burning destroyer virtually from end to end. That was when CIC had been hit. Peter Christopher had observed the world around him become a smoky, spark-filled bad dream before he lost consciousness. He had awakened on a stretcher on the wardroom floor. Somebody had been screaming; mercifully the screaming had stopped after a few seconds. He had wondered if he was the man screaming then strong, gentle hands had helped him into a sitting position and Leading Electrical Artificer Jack Griffin's bare-headed and bearded filthy, blood-stained visage had been grinning at him.

"What?" Peter had muttered. His ears were ringing and his head hurt. He was bloody but had no idea if the blood was his.

"You hit you head, sir!" The other man shouted.

"I don't..."

"When I jumped on you, sir! If you'd carried on sitting in the CIC high chair a second longer you'd have been mincemeat!"

Peter Christopher blinked down at himself.

His right trouser leg was shredded below the knee. His jacket was torn and singed. That explained the smell of burning. His face was caked...with blood. His left shoulder felt like somebody had hit it with a hammer.

Jack Griffin pressed a tin mug to his lips.

"Drink this!"

HMS Talavera's dazed Electronic Warfare Officer did as he was told.

He gagged on the heavily rum-laced chocolate.

"You going to throw up, sir?"

"No," Peter Christopher decided after several long moments.

"The Old Man says for me to get you back in CIC. We're blind. No radar, no comms..."

That was hours ago.

Peter Christopher did not know how many hours ago except that when he had been half-carried back into the smouldering chaos of CIC there were still body parts on the floor and it was still daylight outside.

Nobody knew what had happened to HMS Devonshire.

The big County Class destroyer had been dead in the water and on fire several miles downwind as night fell. They had seen the fires flickering in the north east for about an hour after darkness, and then nothing...

Talavera had not gone to her consort's aid because she was too busy trying to save herself. It was all the crippled destroyer could do simply to keep her relatively undamaged bow pointing into the teeth of the storm.

Peter Christopher brooded.

They had been taken almost completely by surprise and it was his fault.

Only God knew how many fine men had died today because of his failure to grasp the tactical situation. It was no comfort for the Old

Man to tell him that Command knew the risks when they dispatched Talavera and Devonshire on a route so close to the Spanish coast. It had seemed a calculated enough risk at the time. The Gibraltar gun line needed every barrel the Navy could beg, borrow or steal and it needed those barrels *now*. Terrible things happen in war and today's debacle was nobody's fault.

Surgeon's mates had appeared and attempted to clean him up a couple of times. Blood still oozed from his scalp and his left arm was in a sling. They guessed his collar bone might be cracked or broken. A shot of morphine had deadened the worst of the pain.

"We've got the Type 293 back on line, sir!" Somebody reported, breaking though Peter Christopher's drowsy ruminations. They had restored radio communications about an hour ago.

"Anything on the plot?" He asked, afraid of the answer he was likely to get.

There was a long, horrible hesitation.

"Negative, sir. No surface or air contacts. The way we're bouncing about in these seas we'd lose anything inshore in the ground clutter, sir."

Peter Christopher groaned inwardly.

They had *lost* four fast, low flying jets in that clutter but a five-thousand-ton cruiser-sized destroyer ought to stand out like a sore thumb. HMS Devonshire was gone. In seas like these most of her crew of around four hundred and seventy men would have little or no chance of rescue or of reaching the storm lashed shores of Spain.

After the strike both destroyers had been burning, defenceless hulks.

A second strike would have sunk them then and there.

"Messenger please."

It was Jack Griffin who stepped up.

While isolated CIC systems had been restored to some minimal level of operation all intercom links to the bridge remained severed. The only way Peter Christopher could report to the Captain was by messenger.

"Find the Captain. Report the 293 set is nominal but only in basic search mode." He swallowed hard. "Report that we have no major surface targets in range at this time. That is all."

The other man nodded and hurried away.

The ship had a sickening, waterlogged motion as she pitched into each long angry Atlantic swell and slid like a sodden log down the other side.

Peter Christopher became aware of the presence of Talavera's

Master at Arms, Chief Petty Officer Spider McCann. The wiry, teak hard little man spared the young officer a weathered, rueful grin.

"It'll be light in a couple of hours, sir," the older man observed. "Things will seem better in daylight."

"If you say so, Master."

Spider McCann chuckled.

"Trust me, sir. Things always seem better in daylight."

The two men were in the middle of a ruined compartment in which four men had died and five had been seriously wounded. Everybody else had survived as walking wounded as cannon shells had ripped through the thin skin of the destroyer as if it was wet paper. The majority of the hits – presumably with armour piercing rounds - had gone straight through the ship without exploding, only those whose progress had been impeded or obstructed by a piece of kit, a human body or had landed short of the ship and ricocheted into their target had actually detonated.

The senior non-commissioned officer on the ship had disappeared the next time Peter Christopher looked around. He made a concerted effort to pull himself together.

"Status report on the 293 set," he demanded.

"Still nominal, sir. The forward mast has a lot of fragmentation damage around the cable ducts. I think we're getting water in the system somewhere. That or the stabilizer isn't functioning..." The man cursed in the darkness. "Sorry, sir. The repeater dropped out again. Everything to the 965 must be cut. For all I know the aerial might actually be fully functional, but..."

Peter Christopher acknowledged this without comment.

The four-ton double bedstead type 965 air defence radar fifty feet above his head had not done Talavera much good against low flying targets approaching out of the loom of the land.

HMS Devonshire had been sunk.

Half of Talavera's crew were dead or wounded and the ship was in a sinking condition in the middle of a North Atlantic winter gale.

Hundreds of men were dead because he had not reacted fast enough; he had made a mistake and people had died...

Chapter 35

Saturday 7th December 1963
Gzira, Sliema Creek, Malta

Joe Calleja and Margo Seiffert stood on the Gzira waterfront and stared. The fire blackened stern of the British destroyer rested barely awash on the shore of Manoel Island; her bow sunk in the deeper water in the middle of the Sliema Creek anchorage. Her great lattice foremast leaned forward at an unnatural angle of about thirty degrees towards Gzira.

"Which ship is that?" The woman asked, unable to drag her eyes off the surreal sight of the oily, wreckage strewn harbour. The stink of the fires that still smouldered in Fort Phoenicia and behind the gutted shell of what once had been the Royal Marines' Headquarters. The atmosphere was hazy, the acrid air caught at the back of the throat. Fires still burned in Valletta to the south and smoke cloaked Luqa airfield west of the Three Cities. "D96," she added redundantly, squinting at the scorched numerals on the destroyer's splinter-riddled stern.

"Agincourt," the young man by her side reported numbly. He did not really believe he was seeing what he was seeing. They had heard the raging of jet engines and the distant rolling drumbeat of huge explosions, run to the top of the citadel walls of the ancient city of Mdina; and watched the rising flames and the mushrooms of dirty black and brown smoke rising into the clear balmy Mediterranean evening with horror and mounting incredulity.

Even from several miles away it was apparent that the targets were the ships moored in Sliema Creek and Marsamxett on the northern side of Valletta, the British Headquarters on Manoel Island and the big air base at Luqa. Valletta itself had disappeared beneath a pall of smoke. The attacking aircraft had been tiny silver slivers in the distance and the sky had pocked with clouds of bursting shells interlaced with a vicious tracery of gunfire and the far away whooshing of missiles reaching for the heavens. Several of the attacking aircraft had been shot down; or the attackers might have shot down the RAF fighters that attempted to get off the ground. Nobody knew. Parachutes had been seen floating down over Hal Far and the Three Cities. The nightmare had flared for ten, perhaps fifteen minutes and ended as if a curtain had fallen on proceedings, not so much with a whimper but with sudden, crushing finality. The guns fell silent, no more missiles criss-crossed the azure canopy of the sky between the high clouds; there was only the crackle and boom of exploding munitions, the oil fires, the columns of smoke rising from the sea and the ground like pillars of salt over Gomorrah. On the ground there was the rushing of troops, the clang and rattle of fire engines and ambulances, the urgent, angry tramping of booted feet, the screams, the shouts and a kind of awful, dreadful, shameless panic.

All night the fires had raged as a frightened curfew had fallen over Malta. Joe Calleja had wanted to walk through the night to his Sliema home. Margo had not forbidden it she had simply taken hold of his arm and told him that he could not help his family if he got himself shot. If he waited until the morning, she would come with him. She was a doctor after all and if he was with her, he might actually survive the journey. Incidentally, they might actually be of some small service to people who desperately needed their help. They had set off from St Catherine's Hospital for Women – Joe carrying a heavy, bulging rucksack stuffed with medical supplies, dressings, antiseptics, sutures and needles - in the pre-dawn twilight and had been walking ever since.

At every checkpoint Margo had declared: "I am an orthopaedic surgeon and this young man is my son. Let me through or I'll report you to the Military Governor!"

The soldiers on the roads were twitchy, trigger happy and in a funny way, reassured to be confronted with somebody in authority who was trying to *do something*.

Margo and her companion were dust caked, footsore and hoarse from arguing with soldiers and talking to everybody they met. Nobody seemed to know what was going on. Or rather, anybody who did know what was going on was not talking about it. One thing was palpable, shock.

There were bodies bobbing brokenly in the oil-fouled waters of Sliema Creek. Tarpaulins covered bodies along the waterfront. In places there were large, dark, congealed puddles of what could only have been blood on the roads and pavements. Houses had been shattered, there were bullet holes in walls here and there and as the couple picked their way east along Triq Ix Xatt towards the landing stage for the ferry across to Valletta the road was cratered and impassable other than on foot.

"Doctor Seiffert!" A man shouted from behind the couple.

The woman grabbed Joe Calleja's arm

"Don't even think about running," she hissed, pulling the young man close. No British soldier was going to shoot the kid and risk shooting a woman. Or at least she hoped not. This morning she was a little afraid the old rules no longer applied.

"Doctor Seiffert!"

Margo Seiffert frowned, recognising the voice. She turned, retaining her steely hold on Joe Calleja's sleeve.

Staff Sergeant Jim Siddall jogged towards the pair. He was as dusty as everybody else and his face was streaked with perspiration even in the cool morning air. He viewed Marija's younger brother grimly. "*You* shouldn't be anywhere near here!"

"My family..." The younger man began to protest but broke off when Margo Seiffert kicked his left shin so hard, he reeled away hopping with pain.

"I'm looking for *your* family!" The big Redcap roared in exasperation. "What are you doing here?" This he demanded of the woman, making a concerted effort to rein in his angst.

"The same as you, Sergeant Siddall!" Margo rasped back angrily. The soldier raised his arms in mock surrender, pausing to gather his breath and his wits. Several other soldiers, each fingering long black L1A1 SLRs were approaching the small group.

Jim Siddall waved them to halt nearby.

"We're trying to find everybody on the Emergency List," he explained. "Key administrators and managers, doctors like yourself, and so on. After the attack we were afraid there'd be a repeat of the murders and assassinations after the October War. We don't think that's happening this time but we still need to find everybody on the list. Basically, so we can start to sort out the mess." The Redcap looked around at the craters in the street, the demolished houses and down the length of Sliema Creek. "God, what a mess!"

"What happened, Sergeant?" Joe Calleja asked, gingerly testing his painful leg.

"Pearl Harbour in reverse," the big man grunted, sourly.

"What do you mean?"

"What happened?" Jim Siddall mused aloud while stealing a lingering look in the direction of the wreck of HMS Agincourt. "*What happened is that the bloody Yanks bombed us!*"

[THE END]

Author's Endnote

In case you were wondering *'Love is Strange'* is a play on the title of the Stanley Kubrick film of 1964 entitled *'Dr Strangelove or: How I Learned to Stop Worrying and Love the Bomb'*.

'Love is Strange' is the second instalment of a history of the World after the Cuban Missiles War of late October 1962. I use the word 'instalment' very deliberately in the context of how this alternative history will develop in subsequent 'instalments'; and I make no apology for leaving my readers contemplating the cliff hanger denouements at the close of *'Love is Strange'*. There will be more cliff hangers and the ride is going to be, at times, a very bumpy one.

The story of our lovers, their friends and their enemies and the perils that will confront them all in the coming years continues in the third verse of the Timeline 10/27/62 Series *'The Pillars of Hercules'* in which the story picks up the day after the traumatic events which concluded *'Love is Strange'*.

Without giving away the challenges facing our heroes and heroines in the *'The Pillars of Hercules'*, the third instalment of the Timeline 10/27/62 Series, suffice it to say that things are about to get a lot worse for the survivors of the October War. And then, just when they pause to draw breath, things get really bad.

To the reader: firstly, thank you for reading this book; and secondly, please remember that this is a work of fiction. I made it up in my own head. None of the characters described in *'Love is Strange: Book 2 of the Timeline 10/27/62 Series'* – are based on real people I know of, or have ever met. Nor do the specific events described in *'Love is Strange: Book 2 of the Timeline 10/27/62 Series'* have, to my knowledge, any basis in real events I know to have taken place. Any resemblance to real life people or events is, therefore, unintended and entirely coincidental. However, *'Love is Strange: Book 2 of the Timeline 10/27/62 Series'* is an alternative history of the modern world and because of this, real historical characters are referenced and in some cases their words and actions form a significant part of the narrative. I have no way of knowing for sure if these real, historical figures, would have spoken thus, or acted in the ways I depict them acting. Any word

I place in the mouth of a real historical figure, and any action which I attribute to them after 27th October 1962 **never actually happened.** As I always say in my note to my readers, *I made it up in my own head.*

A brief note on ships and ship names

HMS Talavera (*Yard no. 617*) was a later Battle Class destroyer laid down at John Brown and Company's Yard on the Clyde on 29th August 1944 and launched, on 27th August 1945 to clear the slip. The hull was sold to the West of Scotland Shipbreaking Company Limited of Troon, in South Ayrshire, where it was beached on 26th January 1946. Breaking up commenced on 5th February 1946 and was completed on 27th March 1946.

Four of Talavera's sisters - Agincourt, Aisne, Barossa and Corunna – were actually converted to Fast Air Detection Escorts and all served, at one time or another, with the Mediterranean Fleet and were once based at Malta. Their conversions were interim, stop gap measures which were almost immediately overtaken by events. First, Harold Wilson's Labour Government cancelled the new big fleet carriers they were supposed to be escorting, and secondly, new technology and new ships soon rendered them obsolete. All four Fast Air Detection Battles were decommissioned before the end of the 1960s in a universe in which HMS Talavera never steamed.

HMS Dreadnought was the United Kingdom's first nuclear powered hunter killer submarine. On 27th October 1962, Dreadnought was fitting out at Barrow-in-Furness.

As with real historical characters, real historical ships are treated in a documentary –where they were and as they were deployed – fashion up to and including 27th October 1962. Thereafter, all bets are off because in this post cataclysm timeline, *everything changes.*

As a rule, I let my books speak for themselves. I hope it does not sound fuddy-duddy or old-fashioned, but broadly speaking I tend towards the view that a book *should* speak for itself.

However, with your indulgence I would like briefly – well, as briefly as is possible without being overly terse – to share a few personal thoughts with you, the reader about the *Timeline 10/27/62 World*.

I was not yet seven-and-a-half years old in October 1962 when I realised my parents were paying an awful lot of attention to the radio, devouring every line of print in their daily newspaper and were not quite themselves, a little distracted in fact, now that I think about it. I heard the word 'Cuba' bandied about but did not know until much later that the most dangerous moment of my life had come and gone without my ever, as a child, knowing it.

I was not yet eight-and-a-half years old when one day in November 1963 the World around me came, momentarily, to a juddering halt. I had heard the name of John Fitzgerald Kennedy, and I even knew that he was the President of something called the United States of America. I did not know then that he was a womanising, drug dependent and deeply conflicted man who had lied to the American people about his chronic, periodically disabling illness which in any rational age ought to have disqualified him from the Presidency; *but I did know that he was a charismatic, talismanic figure in whom even I, as a child more interested in soccer, model trains and riding my new bicycle, had invested a nameless hope for the future.* And then one day he was gone and I shared my parents' shock and horror. It was not as if a mortal man had been murdered; JFK had become a mythic figure long before then. It was as if the modern-day analogue of King Menelaus of Sparta - hero of the Trojan Wars and the husband of Helen, she of the legendary face that launched a thousand ships - had been gunned down that day in Dallas.

The Cuban Missiles Crisis and the death of a President taught a young boy in England in 1962 and 1963 that the World is a very dangerous place.

Many years later we learned how close we all came to the abyss in late October 1962. Often, we look back on how deeply Jack Kennedy's death scarred hearts and minds in the years after his assassination.

There is no certainty, no one profound insight into what 'might have happened' had the Cold War turned *Hot* in the fall of 1962, or if JFK had survived that day in Dallas. History is not a systematic, explicable march from one event to another that inevitably reaches some readily predictable outcome. History only works that way in hindsight; very little is *obvious* either to the major or the minor players *at the time* history is actually being made. Nor does one have to be a fully paid up chaos theoretician to know that apparently inconsequential events can have massive unforeseen and unforeseeable impacts in subsequent historical developments.

I do not pretend to *know* what would have happened if the USA and the USSR had gone to war over Cuba in October 1962. One imagines this scenario has been the object of countless staff college war games in America and elsewhere in the intervening fifty-three years; I suspect – with a high level of confidence - that few of those war games would have played out the way the participants expected, and that no two *games* would have resolved themselves in exactly the same way as any other. That is the beauty and the fascination of historical counterfactuals, or as those of us who make no pretence at being emeritus professors of history say, *alternative history*.

Nobody can claim 'this is the way it would have been' after the Cuban Missiles Crisis 'went wrong'. This author only *speculates* that the Timeline 10/27/62 Series reflects one of the many ways 'things might have gone' in the aftermath of Armageddon.

The only thing one can be reasonably confident about is that if the Cuban Missiles Crisis had turned into a shooting war the World in which we live today would, *probably*, not be the one with which we are familiar.

A work of fiction is a journey of imagination. I hope it does not sound corny but I am genuinely a little humbled by the number of people who have already bought into what I am trying to do with *Timeline 10/27/62*.

Like any author, this author would prefer everybody to enjoy his books – if I disappoint, I am truly sorry – but either way, thank you for reading and helping to keep the printed word alive. I really do believe that civilization depends on people like *you*.

Other Books by James Philip

New England Series

Book 1: Empire Day
Book 2: Two Hundred Lost Years
Book 3: Travels Through the Wind
Book 4: Remember Brave Achilles

Coming in 2020

Book 5: George Washington's Ghost
Book 6: The Imperial Crisis

The River Hall Chronicles

Book 1: Things Can Only Get Better
Book 2: Consenting Adults
Book 3: All Swing Together

Coming in 2020

Book 4: The Honourable Member

The Guy Winter Mysteries

Prologue: Winter's Pearl
Book 1: Winter's War
Book 2: Winter's Revenge
Book 3: Winter's Exile
Book 4: Winter's Return
Book 5: Winter's Spy
Book 6: Winter's Nemesis

The Bomber War Series

Book 1: Until the Night
Book 2: The Painter
Book 3: The Cloud Walkers

Until the Night Series

Part 1: Main Force Country – September 1943
Part 2: The Road to Berlin – October 1943
Part 3: The Big City – November 1943
Part 4: When Winter Comes – December 1943
Part 5: After Midnight – January 1944

The Harry Waters Series

Book 1: Islands of No Return
Book 2: Heroes
Book 3: Brothers in Arms

The Frankie Ransom Series

Book 1: A Ransom for Two Roses
Book 2: The Plains of Waterloo
Book 3: The Nantucket Sleighride

The Strangers Bureau Series

Book 1: Interlopers
Book 2: Pictures of Lily

James Philip's Cricket Books

F.S. Jackson
Lord Hawke

Audio Books of the following Titles are available (or are in production) now

Aftermath
After Midnight
A Ransom for Two Roses
Brothers in Arms
California Dreaming
Empire Day
Heroes
Islands of No Return
Love is Strange
Main Force Country
Operation Anadyr
Red Dawn
The Big City
The Cloud Walkers
The Nantucket Sleighride
The Painter
The Pillars of Hercules
The Plains of Waterloo
The Road to Berlin
Travels Through the Wind
Two Hundred Lost Years
Until the Night
When Winter Comes
Winter's Exile
Winter's Pearl
Winter's Return
Winter's Revenge
Winter's Spy
Winter's War

Cricket Books edited by James Philip

The James D. Coldham Series
[Edited by James Philip]

Books
Northamptonshire Cricket: A History [1741-1958]
Lord Harris

Anthologies
Volume 1: Notes & Articles
Volume 2: Monographs No. 1 to 8

Monographs
No. 1 - William Brockwell
No. 2 - German Cricket
No. 3 - Devon Cricket
No. 4 - R.S. Holmes
No. 5 - Collectors & Collecting
No. 6 - Early Cricket Reporters
No. 7 – Northamptonshire
No. 8 - Cricket & Authors

Details of all James Philip's published books and forthcoming publications can be found on his website
www.jamesphilip.co.uk

Cover artwork concepts by James Philip
Graphic Design by
Beastleigh Web Design

Made in the USA
Columbia, SC
29 April 2022